I0788169

Cassandra Featherstone

Little Tailfeather Publishing

SECRETS OF
STATE U

BLOOD ON THE ICE

CASSANDRA HEATHERSTONE

content information

This is a *paranormal whychoose romance with poly elements*—our FMC, Morgana, will not have to choose between love interests.

There are many situations included that are intended for <u>mature audiences (18+)</u>.

In these books, there may be instances/references (be they small or lengthy) that could trigger some individuals such as:

- discussion of mental illness
- gargoyles
- attacks on the FMC/MMCs (no on or off page non-con)
- within series: MM, MF, MMMMMF, and more
- bullying (medium from MMC)
- abused woman
- alphahole/possessive MCs
- cinnamon roll MC
- forced proximity
- damaged grumpy MC
- big,sweet guy MC
- unhealthy coping mechanisms

- spoiled rich supes
- extremely aggressive boundaries
- age gap (FMC is 300 to youngest MMC in 20s)
- dead ex whose legacy persists
- mean girl adults
- bodyguard and royal
- BDSM discussed (D/s relationship)
- horns, tails, scales, magic, stone, claws, and forked tongues
- some asshole parents, some decent parents
- adopted FMC
- alcohol use and abuse
- threats of bodily harm
- death
- body modifications
- MMC accused of murder
- treacherous authority figures
- bullying (in person)
- PTSD
- blood
- emotional abuse by ex-partners
- body dysmorphia
- adult language
- pop culture references
- literary references
- emotional manipulation
- power play
- adorable nicknames
- physical intimidation
- emotionally abusive/manipulative parents (MCs)
- markings/tattoos
- Easter egg character cameos from other series in the universe
- family dysfunction
- absolute disrespect for shitty parents
- brief mentions of non-body positive dieting culture
- very liberal re-imagining of history
- ancient secret society who only cares about bigger picture

- official corruption
- discussion of arranged marriages
- poisoning
- rituals
- inappropriate professors
- lawyers (ugh)
- name calling
- occasional misogyny
- really cool Nana
- discussion of parental physical abuse
- mention of parents doing drugs
- elitism
- bribery
- corpses
- drama
- physical threats to FMC and others
- speciesism

No practices in this book should be taken as safe or appropriate for real life application.

Content information is important and I don't ever want to harm a reader with inaccurate information.

stalk cassandra featherstone in the dark corners of the web

JOIN MY FACEBOOK GROUP AND FOLLOW ME EVERYWHERE!

WANT MORE?

SIGN UP FOR MY BI-WEEKLY MANIFESTO FOR A FREE SERIES SAMPLER:

Join my Ream as a FREE follower or exclusive subscriber to get access to cover reveals, WIPs, Serial Stories, and personal chats from me!

CASSANDRA FEATHERSTONE

reader's note

A FEW THINGS YOU SHOULD KNOW...

I am so excited to bring this series from Vella to book format.

Blood on the Ice is book **one** of the *Secrets of State U* series. There are five books planned and they will start on Vella/Ream, then come to print/KU after they are re-edited and formatted. This is a multi-book series, so *everything will not be revealed at once*. Some plot lines will continue throughout the series in a larger arc and not get resolved in the first or even the third book.

I write lengthy books with intricate world building, strong character development, and *lots* of tiny threads that stretch throughout a series that may not always seem important at first glance. However, I promise nothing I put to paper and leave in the book is unimportant; it may simply become *more* important later on. There is no 'throw-away' detail in my worlds, so every scene will mean something eventually.

I promise it will all get tied up and have a HEA; don't worry!

Blood on the Ice is a why choose/poly romance, which means our FMC will not have to choose.

I would consider it a ***medium*** burn, but I know some may not agree. It will get spicier in the following books. If you're looking for porn with little to no plot, no judgment, but this isn't the series for you. It won't be closed door or FTB, so I believe the spice will be worth the wait. I realize spice scales are subjective and everyone has different opinions on it, so forgive me if mine and yours aren't totally aligned.

There are some characters and creatures that speak in other languages. I made the *translations clickable end of chapter notes* to help.

There are some words that are slang, jargon, or foreign that may seem to be spelled wrong—*please email the author or find her on social media rather than report to Amazon* if you think something is wrong. This has been proofed and edited *many* times since release; if you believe you found errors, you may not be correct. It could be a stylistic choice or a dialect choice. Please do not assume the two ARC teams, betas, alphas, and several proofers missed everything you believe is incorrect. Contact me if you find things; I want to make sure it doesn't get taken down so everyone can read!

If you see this book *anywhere besides Kindle Unlimited or Kindle Vella in ebook format,* please reach out to me via social media or email. Pirating kills my ability to write full time and I am so grateful for your help.

Contact Cass for issues or to report piracy: teamcassandra@cassandrafeatherstone.com

author ramblings

Readers,

I cannot overstate how amazing this year has been in terms of finding my groove, getting my writing and my worlds out, and gathering such a baller community of readers.

Between Vella, Ream, FB, and all the other places you see and pick up my books or hang with me, it's been absolutely life-changing... so I thank you.

Morgana is in this really interesting place for an FMC: she's not young, but she has lived within a quietly abusive relationship with someone who was supposed to love her. It's not physically violent—or wasn't until she took her vengeance for his treachery—but it made her pause her life in place to keep him happy. If you've ever had a partner, co-worker, friend, or relative who starts your day off with a volley of nastiness every day, no matter how far away they are, you know that even the strongest of us can fall prey to this kind of self-centered abuser.

She's smart, accomplished, strong, educated, and has amazing powers —but she was demeaned, demoralized, and locked away as her partner made a fool of her behind her back for years before she broke free.

Now she's serving her penance for that necessary, but frowned upon act of salvation—at the very place he humiliated her over and over. Yes, Morgana was left to clean up the mess he made on her own and like a cosmic middle finger that many of the abused receive, she has to live among all the people who resent her for taking back her life. It's a sad fact of life, but never fear, my lovelies.

Like the phoenix but hissier, Morgana is going to rise from the ashes of her shitty punishment and the judgment from those who have never deigned to get her side of the story. She's going to be successful and find love in this hellscape of dirty looks and untrustworthy people.

And you're going to adore her when she's able to spread her wings.

Again, thank you to everyone who has read and recommended on Facebook, Instagram, TikTok, on Goodreads, and on Amazon. Your recs in groups and continued support help me get closer to my indie muppet dream of going full time.

In a world where there are hidden pitfalls and people that smile to your face and slide the knife in your back when you aren't looking, I want to thank my author besties who support me every day, my alpha/ARC team, and all the others who chat and help me every day.

Finding true support that doesn't require me to give up part of myself has been a goddess blessed event. I feel more and more like the confidence I had when I first entered this genre has returned and the abuse that caused me to falter is fading.

For that, I can never repay you.

However, I never give up and I never back down, so I'm going to be here with silly puns and smart FMCs who aren't afraid to show how big their hearts, libidos, *and* brains are.

Enjoy the newest series in the *Legends of the Ouroboros* universe, and fall for the adorable men like our girl will... eventually.

Blood and guts,

a note to my loving family members and their friends...

THANK YOU FOR SUPPORTING ME BY BUYING THIS BOOK!

WHOOPS. YOU CAN'T READ THIS ONE—SUCKERED YOU LAST TIME, RIGHT?

THEMS THE BREAKS.

THIS ONE HAS ALL SORTS OF MAGICAL DICK AND STEEL AND WINGS AND STUFF I REFUSE TO EXPLAIN TO YOU.

NO, I DON'T CARE IF YOU READ THAT ONE FAIRY BOOK EVERYONE IS TALKING ABOUT—IT'S NOT THE SAME.

CAVEAT: IF YOU CHOOSE TO KEEP READING, KNOW THAT AT NO TIME WILL I EXPLAIN TERMS, POSITIONS, THEMES, TROPES, OR ANY OTHER PART OF THIS NOVEL AT FAMILY EVENTS, IN GROUP CHATS, OR ON SOCIAL MEDIA.

DON'T ASK.

blood on the ice playlist

CHAPTER TITLE SONGS

Blood on the Ice Chapter Playlist

BONUS PLAYLIST

Morgana's Revenge Playlist

Karma is a bitch?
Oh, no, honey.
Karma is a wise and classy elder
who will calmly sit down and
serve you tea you later realize
was laced with the same poison
you served others for years.

~Anonymous

State University

state university directory

Characters, Pets, & Creations

Morgana LeCiel (mor-GAN-uh lih CEE-el) hybrid gargoyle/gorgon shifter; adopted by gargoyle and witch parents; educated and previously employed at Swallowtail Academy; killed her dragon fiancé, Magnus; stood trial before Society and sentenced to clean up State U; has one unruly gorgon snake in her hair called Des.

Nicknames: babe, Salaadir, M, Lass, Lady M, *Macushla*

Channing Oswald (chan-NIN-g oz-wall-d) PR team member at State U; impresses Morgana and becomes her personal assistant; becomes assistant to legal team as well. Ice elemental.

Nicknames: Chan, sweet cheeks, Channie, Chan-o-rama

Slade Finn (slay-duh fihn) siren grad student who works at the campus coffeehouse; meets Morgana and invites her to dinner with his pined for roommate Ignatius Briarton; son of crime lord family in Bay City.

Nicknames: Pretty Boy

Ignatius Briarton (ig-NAY-shus bry-er-TON) professor and head of Witchcraft & Wizardry department; mage; womanizer; lived with Slade since they met when he was an undergrad; snobby elitist; rich old family.

Nicknames: Iggy, Professor, Prof, Magic Man

Lucas Wolfberg (loo-CUSS Wolf-berg) grandson of Wolfenberg dynasty; polar bear shifter; star hockey player for State U Bonecrushers; accused of murdering rival team member at State U rink; mates with Morgana on accident; gets poisoned; has shitty playboy/girl parents.

Nicknames: Papa Bear, cub, babe, big guy

Prince Liam Spéirgheal (Lee-UM Spur-jill) one of the Princes of the Daybreak Court; attending grad school for interspecies diplomacy Masters; lives in staff housing close to Morgana.

Nicknames: Prince, Li, Your Highness

Kaspar (cass-par) storm dragon; security detail for Liam; been with family since a kid; grumpy and suspicious.

Nicknames: Kas

Magnus Corona (mag-NUSS core-own-uh) Morgana's cheating, crooked, thieving ex; former Dean of State U. Dragon.

Pierre LaMount (pee-air LAH-mont) rival team player murdered at rink; Lucas accused of killing him.

Duchess Gretchen Madeline von Wolfenberg (gret-chen mad-uh-lin vaughn wolf-en-berg) Lucas's grandmother; member of German Council; Society maven. Grizzly bear.

Nicknames: Nana

Braden (bray-den) kidnapped little brother of Liam; happened when they were kids. Daybreak Fae.

Knaves (nay-vz) Daybreak Court spies; masked; only accountable to King.

Rhoda (Roh-duh) science building robot

Antares Simone (anTAR-ees sim-own) executive assistant to science department head

Professor Zuzanne Shadwell (zoo-zan shahdwell) B.S. in B&B from Stanford, Masters in Shifter Sciences from Yale, Ph.D. in Shifter Zoonotics and Shifter Psychology from State University. The professor has been head of the Shifter Physiology and Sociology department since 1999.

Nicknames: Zuz; Z

Beatrice (bee-uh-triss) undergrad work study assistant on Shadwell's floor/

Coach Driftwood (drift-wud) Yeti shifter hockey coach.

Skye (sky) girl Iggy and Slade knew who was killed.

Professor Kimiko Nakamura (kim-eeko nah-kuh-mur-uh) is in charge of the greenhouse; head of Botany department; herbologist; wronged by Ignatius when he cheated on her; dryad/earth elemental hybrid.

Nicknames: Kimmi

Lailani Bergstrom (lay-lahn-ee berg-strom) is one of Magnus' floozies; reported him missing in Egypt; confronts Morgana in Wally World.

Detective Kowalski (koh-WALL-ski) walrus shifter, detective on the LaMount murder case.

Nicknames: Detective Kaiser Roll

Jackson Thorne (jack-son Thor-n) Lucas's lawyer; ties to the Hollow and Jolene; has a team he's bringing for the defense; lion shifter.

Nicknames: The Shark, Jax

Eli Lindstrom (ee-lie lin-strum) Jackson Thorne's hacker boyfriend, tech mage.

Rainier Milan (rain-ear mill-on) member of Jackson Thorne's team; Ex-CIA; griffin shifter.

Nicknames: Rain

Foley McNamara (foe-lee MACK nuh mair uh) member of Jackson Thorne's team; jury consultant; clurichaun from Faerie.

Nicknames: Leprechaun

Kendrick Noctem (ken-drik Nock-tehm) member of Jackson Thorne's team; mysterious last member with unknown talents and species.

Nicknames: Shadow Daddy

King Alwyn Spéirgheal (al-wynn spearghal) King of Daybreak Court; Liam's father.

Queen Iola Spéirgheal (ee-oll-uh spear-ghal) Queen of Daybreak Court; Liam's mother.

Chief Ponylakitu (cheef poh-ny-lah-kit-oo) police chief in the precinct Kowalski works out of

Veronica Valencia (ver-on-ick-uh vall-en-see-uh) ADA for that district

Tracer Finn (tray-sur fih-nn) is one of the heirs apparant to the *Sons of the Seven Seas* gang; kraken; Slade's brother.

Coral Finn (core-uhl fihn) Slade's triplet sister; part siren, part mermaid

Isla Finn (iz-luh fihn) Slades' triplet sister; part kraken and part shark

Roxy Finn (rocks-ee fihn) Slade's triplet sister; part selkie, part mermaid

Beck and Duke Finn (behk and dook fihn) Slade's hammerhead brothers

Axel Finn (ah-xul fihn) Leader of the *Sons of the Seven Seas* gang; runs with iron fist; Slade's dad.

Azul Finn (ah-zuhl fihn) mother to Beck, Tracer, Duke, and Slade for sure; Old Lady of *Seven Sons;* Axel's wife.

Locations/Groups

State U- college where it all takes place

Morgana's house- previously Magnus' filled with his gross shit

Swallowtail Academy- secondary academy in a hybrid enclave in England; where European lost ones are sent; Morgana's alma mater.

The Beanery- campus coffeehouse where Slade works

Beauregard Fine Arts Building- Arts building dedicated to the Beauregard family

Miyako Academy- Asian secondary academy for lost ones in Asian enclave

Von Lichtenstein Science & Medical Center- Science and medical school building and med center on campus

Chancellor Row- where staff housing is located on campus

Wally World- megastore in the city

Belle's- Southern restaurant run by supes in the city

Whistler's Hollow- hybrid enclave an hour away; many residents come to State U

Wolfberg Winter Sports Arena- rink where LaMount died

City Police Station- where Lucas is taken

Daybreak Court- Liam's home

Faerie- also called the Veil; where Liam and Kaspar are from

Bay City- supe city on West Coast where Slade's Family lives

Hand of Morrigan- Fae rebellion group

 Sons of the Seven Seas - gang in Bay City run by Slade's family

Thorne Enterprises- Jackson Thorne's family business

Mapleleaf University- LaMount's school

killer queen

Looking around the campus with a critical eye, it isn't hard to notice the differences between the campus of Swallowtail and State U. The major difference is age, of course, but even secondary schools overseas are unlike the blatant marketing machines that are American universities. State U doesn't resemble the colleges I've seen in American movies or on TV, though much of that is the Society's doing.

However, banners, statues, plaques, signs, and even architecture are emblazoned with the school's motto—*Honoris. Veritas. Potentia*—as if constant reminders will enforce the virtues it extols. *That* differs from the places in Europe I attended or worked in.

"Getting used to the sales aspect of education here won't be your biggest challenge and you know it," I mutter to myself.

When the outcome of my trial led to a guilty sentence, I didn't expect the punishment they handed down. Instead of being jailed for the murder of my ex, they decreed I would replace him as the Dean at State U. I wasn't the only one who disagreed with my purgatory—the vote on the High Council was split down the middle until a mysterious figure cast a vote in favor of my exile. They summarily dismissed me from Swallowtail Academy and sent me home to pack my shit for a journey overseas to the nest of corruption created by the man I thought I would marry.

Not only am I the youngest Dean to ever hold the title, but I'm the only hybrid to head one of the Society's schools.

Placing me at the helm of the crown jewel of their American institutions made their unorthodox punishment even more bizarre, but I've never believed the group that guides our kind to be infallible. The irony of replacing the being responsible for all the university's current issues with the fiancee who killed him hasn't eluded me. It's like my penance for not blowing the whistle on him instead of taking my vengeance in blood.

They did not impress hard line elders with the eventual outcome, but that had to be expected. Some supernaturals don't believe in the young being given positions of power, especially when that young candidate is also a woman and a hybrid. Given that I believe Magnus had cronies at various levels of government he was paying off, some of them must be worried I'll expose them to prove I was right to remove him from this world. Either way, the assholes who are screaming I'll ruin their precious programs and reputation haven't shut up since I left the trial chamber.

Let them whine about their outdated, elitist standards. I'll show them.

I turn away from the greenery of the campus, leaving the balcony to take a seat at the enormous desk in my overly plush office. Knowing the way parents and donors behave in this country, I assume every inch of this space has been purchased not by the college, but by donors who had 'one little request' for my ex. Magnus Corona was well-known in academic circles for milking the wealthy Americans until they ran dry, but his lack of ethics couldn't go on forever. My greedy, dragon lover went on the lam after a series of scandals involving kickbacks, illegal sponsorships, sports, and sexual harassment. The last one is why I hunted him down and eventually watched the last breaths he took on this planet with vengeful glee.

I'll start looking for a decorator immediately. If it's not in the budget, my trust fund will cover it.

Like most lost ones, they left me on the doorstep of a very talented witch and her gargoyle mate. I never found my 'real' parents, but growing up on Swallowtail's campus was not a burden. It was different when my adoptive parents were professors there—three hundred years brings a lot of changes. When I graduated, I attended Oxford and came back to work there in administration because I missed the old buildings and libraries.

That's the gargoyle in me, I know.

My adoptive mother is blind—except for the gift of future sight. Being a beautiful, blind witch couldn't have been easy when she was teaching, but she met my father in college and they've been together ever since. When they graduated, they came back to Swallowtail to teach. Eventually, she became the head of the Witchcraft & Wizardry department at the Finishing School and my father was the chair of the Physical Education & Training program. Over the years, my mother's gifts made their investments and ventures fruitful enough to retire while they could still enjoy it. They live on a small island in the Mediterranean where supes of their caliber like to soak up the good life.

Once I get settled here, I might invite them to come tour the campus. My father would particularly enjoy the Gothic structure of the buildings; they were constructed to evoke the feeling of Oxford and he loves those old buildings. I give the picture of them on my cherry wood desk a half smile and sigh when I realize it's going to be awhile before I can extend that invitation.

First, I have to figure out how to get this ship back on course. Loyalty divides the staff; the students are due to arrive in two weeks, and I have a lot of house cleaning to do within these hallowed walls. It's going to ruffle feathers to do the things that are necessary to keep our supernatural accreditation *and* our human sports certification. I'll have to let some staff go, shuffle departments and assignments, and bring in new people to monitor certain aspects of the college's accounting to satisfy all the requirements we need to meet by the end of the semester.

State U has never been forced to toe the line quite as closely as we must now, and that is all because of Magnus Corona's lack of scruples and inability to think without his dick.

Not that any of his adoring fans will believe it for a second—and that is the rock I'll have to push up the hill for the foreseeable future.

"They'll have to get on board or get the fuck out," I say as I compare the list of coaches, trainers, and support staff for the football team. "I don't have a choice and neither do they."

WHEN I FINALLY FINISH GOING OVER THE MASSIVE BUDGET for the major boys' teams, my brain is damn near fried. I cannot fathom how colleges here justify the expenditures of these programs compared to the paltry sums I saw on the balance sheets for academic programs. Americans truly have lost their focus on education, and it doesn't surprise me at all that Magnus could manipulate this to his advantage. There's so many discretionary funds and black holes in the books that I'll have to find someone much more numerically inclined than myself to help me wade through this shit.

It's almost like it left room for loopholes and nefarious deeds.

Pushing to my feet, I rise from the high-backed leather chair and slip my shoes back on. I've been at this for hours and because I don't have office staff, no one was there to remind me I should eat or take a break. I had to fire everyone who worked in Magnus' immediate circle—both out of principle and necessity. I can't prove they knew what he was doing, nor that any of them would try to harm me as retribution, but I'm also not stupid enough to let someone with loyalty to my ex pour my goddamn coffee.

Coffee.

The word makes my blood hum and I know it's time to find sustenance—particularly caffeine. I locate my phone on the massive desk and slip it into the pocket of my suit pants. My appearance has been a topic of gossip on campus since I arrived—social media is a terrible curse when you're in the spotlight, even if it's for the right reasons. I've seen staff and alumni commenting on the 'uptight murdering bitch' strutting around campus dressed like someone from the *Addams Family* as if their vitriol isn't public when they post on Facebook.

My lips curve as I look down at the bespoke Tom Ford suit, Zegna tie, and Louboutin heels. Dressing the part has always been a theme of mine, but Magnus preferred the 'rumpled academic' look. He allowed the staff to run around looking like grad students and that will soon end. If they hate me for looking sharp compared to my frumpy ex, they're going to hate the new dress code when it rolls out in a week. I will not go as far as the Society schools did at home or in other countries, but I refuse to have the press haunting our grounds while taking pictures of grubby looking professors and coaches for their rags.

If this is the crown jewel, it needs more polishing than the Council realizes.

Before I go out, I shake my purple and black curls out of the messy bun, letting my hair settle over my shoulders. A quick check with the selfie mode on my phone tells me my makeup doesn't need to be freshened—thank hell—so I close the camera and put on my sunglasses to keep my sensitive eyes from the waning sun.

I'll need the State U app to find a place that's out of the way. I open it and cringe—the damn thing is hideous in form and function. I make a mental note to interview app designers and web developers; the website has to be as poorly maintained as this bullshit. Yet again, I marvel at the level of incompetence men can show without consequence. It finally loads the map and I scroll around until I find a coffee shop on the edge of campus. I don't want to go to a break room or the food court—there will be far too many eyes on me and I'd like to relax.

Noting the landmarks around the shop, I walk out onto the balcony and touch the amulet at my neck. My wings spring free, sprouting through the suit without a single tear, and I leap into the air. Catching a wind shear, I glide to the far end of the commons, then bank to the right towards the arts building. They nestled the little beanery I identified between the theater and the gallery, so I pull my wings back to descend slowly as I approach.

When I land, the magic of my mother's amulet helps me slip my appendages back in gracefully and walk towards the door without missing a beat. I open the door, take off my sunglasses, and stride in with confidence. I'm not here to throw my weight around, but I can't let anyone see me sweat, either. I look at the menu board before I lower my gaze to see the barista behind the counter.

Holy. Mother. Forking. Shit.

The guy behind the counter is beautiful, and I don't say that lightly. His long blond hair is pulled back in a ponytail, but somehow, it doesn't look douchey. Paired with his patrician features and thin silver framed lenses, he projects the air of a student, but not a new one. My guess is a grad or doctoral student and this is his side hustle. The muscled forearms and powerful hands tell me he's not just a bookworm, so I ponder what discipline this lithe, gorgeous supe is studying. When I finally drag my eyes back to his, the aqua color of his is mesmerizing.

"Can I take your order, ma'am?"

Yikes. That destroyed my brief fantasy.

"Um, yes, sorry. It's been a long day. I'd like a triple espresso and a club sandwich, please." I feel my cheeks heating not because I was staring—he's got to be used to it—but because I got caught checking out one of the students.

It's not forbidden at State U, but I am the murdering bitch with ice in her veins that's here to destroy everything the university stands for. Or, so the article in the *State U Review* said last night. There's no way this gorgeous coffee-serving man doesn't recognize me and I'm sure I'll get an earful about my evil ways once he's done making my order. In fact, I should continue watching to make sure he doesn't mess with my food for revenge.

Yeah, that's why I want to watch him.

"I don't blame you for coming here. It's not one of the campus hot spots. Mostly we get professors, arts kids, and the occasional normie who wants to hide from the masses."

I blink, realizing he's nailed my reason for choosing this shop without even trying. "I think it's rather cozy."

"You don't have to pretend, Dean LeCiel." His pretty eyes meet mine again and I feel that heat creeping up my spine. "I'm aware of how contentious your appointment was. It doesn't bother me, honestly. I've been a student through much of your ex's reign and since the music department was of little concern to him, I don't have any allegiance to the former administration."

Definitely a doctoral candidate. His thesis is probably massive.

Covering my mouth as the unintended double meaning of my words occurs to me, I wait until the urge to giggle like a teenager fades. It would be extremely unprofessional of me to comment on his... attributes... especially since that kind of bullshit helped bring Magnus down. Of course, that doesn't mean I'm not wondering now...

"Dean? Hello?" The hot barista is waving his hand as he looks at me curiously.

"I'm sorry to be so rude. I didn't catch your name?"

There we go. That sounded totally normal.

"I'm Slade," he replies with a slow smile.

That doesn't surprise me in the slightest, and I wonder if he might be part Fae. Not giving me his real name is part and parcel with them, and so is the ethereal beauty. "You may call me Morgana when I am here. I think titles are dreadfully stuffy, but..."

"Set boundaries early because you have mutinies to deal with."

Frowning, I tilt my head. "You aren't reading me with magic, are you, Slade? Even during my ex's time, that kind of invasion of privacy wasn't allowed."

"No, no!" He stops making the sandwich and gives me a sheepish look. "I inferred it. I mean, I don't run with the undergrads or the popular crowds, but I hear things. It wasn't hard to figure out that you're at the hole in the wall shop so you don't have to be on stage while you eat or that you're going to make big changes because of all the charges against the former dean."

I nod, observing him. "I believe you, though I probably shouldn't. Betrayal hides in obvious places; I'm living proof of that."

His features look sharper as he smirks. "There are those of us who don't believe what you did was unjustified, Morgana. Living here at State U will provide you with plenty of evidence to give the Council that will mitigate your actions."

"That's both my desire and my deepest fear, Slade. There's only so much bad PR this place can take before the Council shuts it down and moves on."

A coffee cup and a plate with my sandwich slide across the counter as he murmurs, "You'll have to decide if that's what you want when the time comes."

"I know."

who are you, really

I don't know why I said so much to the eerily tall woman who now runs our university. Normally, I barely speak to customers unless they're regulars because I don't want to fight the urges. Ignatius says I have excellent control, but I've never been able to believe that. All the incidents in my childhood tell a different story, and it's why I pursued music as a career. I can feel the delicious chords and notes race through me with an instrument and it lessens my need for the song.

That's what I tell myself, at least.

Morgana took her order with a sad smile, and I could feel the emotions pulsing around her, begging me to lure her in so I could taste them. I expected her to be icy and unforgiving—that's how she's been portrayed in the media. Given she hunted her fiancée down and killed him, that's not a shock, but the descriptions of her made the new dean seem like a monster. After meeting her, I don't think any of the profiles are doing her justice.

She's definitely larger than life and dressed to kill, but there's something about her that makes me think the story she told at the highly publicized trial isn't entirely true. As a siren, I frequently hear, see, and taste the emotions of others; it helps my people know what to sing to lure our prey. But what I got from Morgana wasn't a calculating killer or a psychotic ex-girlfriend—I felt the weight of an immense burden and a blinding rage that has yet to be quenched. That's why I hinted she should look for secrets and evidence that the former dean was into more than the Council knew.

I want to help her let go of that burden.

Shaking my head, I turn back to the cleaning sink to wash the items I used to make her food. I have to be out of my mind to think a woman like that has any need for an introverted music nerd like me. I've been in school most of my life and I'm likely to eventually work here when I finally finish my thesis. The crusty old bat who runs the music department now needed to retire half a century ago, and when one of the other professors ascends to her throne, there will be a permanent spot on staff I can apply for. Lifelong academic is going to be my fate.

The buzz of my phone vibrating on the counter makes me jump a little and I grab the towel, drying my hands so I can pick it up. Walking into the back room so I don't disturb the dean as she eats and zones out, I swipe to answer. "Hello, Iggy. Need me to prep your usual?"

Ignatius Briarton, head of the illustrious State U Witchcraft & Wizardry program, snorts at me through the line. "I have you so well trained, Slade."

"I'm not a dog, Iggy. Don't be a dick. I was trying to be nice. What the hell do you want?"

I'm not mad at him; I'm frustrated with his inscrutable flirtations that never seem to come to fruition. Iggy and I have been thick as thieves since he was my TA my freshman year. He's only a decade older than me, but his family has connections and his rise to the top of the magic studies department was almost a foregone conclusion.

"Intel, my musical mate. The word is that you have our infamous boss in your humble shop."

Ignoring the whole 'mate' thing, I look around the room with narrowed eyes. Morgana is the only person here, and the shop is on the opposite side of campus from Iggy's office. While I don't doubt people are watching the new dean, gossip didn't spread that far this fast. He's got some sort of scrying object hidden in here, and I'm going to find it and shove it up his ass. His incessant need to keep tabs on me is borderline obsessive for someone who claims to only be my 'roommate.'

"You'll never find it," he sings into the speaker when I don't respond.

"I'm going to murder you." Seething, I walk out behind the counter and start searching the cafe.

"Your new friend can advise you, I'm sure. Now tell me about the woman who holds our future in her talons." The note of concern in his voice almost makes me laugh. He was never part of Corona's inner circle because Iggy actually has a moral code, but who knows what the rest of his family might have been up to. Even his promotion to department head could fall into question, and he's desperate to get a bead on Morgana.

Walking back into the prep area, I whisper, "Morgana seems a little aloof, but she also seems sad. I don't think she's anything like the news is reporting."

"Morgana? You're calling her by her name? Did you sing or something? Spill it, Slade!"

"Iggy, she's not deaf and I have no idea how good her supe hearing is. I'm not having this conversation while the woman is twenty feet away, sipping a triple espresso."

His sigh is filled with irritation, but he finally relents. "Okay, okay. But don't sit behind the counter like a wallflower. Chat her up or something—I need to know if she's planning to gut the entire staff and start new. Our apartment doesn't pay for itself, you know, and the stain of even being at this place during the scandal will make finding another job a nightmare."

No pressure or anything.

"I'll do what I can, Iggy. But turn this spy bullshit off. I know you just like to see what's going on, but it creeps me the hell out."

"If I must," he grumbles. "But don't blame me if you lose control and I don't know to come running."

"Bye, Iggy."

Hanging up the phone, I lean against the fridge and close my eyes. I shouldn't be upset that he cares enough to watch over me, but his mixed signals are driving me up the wall. Paired with his newfound paranoia about the Dean, it makes my anxiety ramp into oblivion. That's the *last* thing I need with Morgana perched at one of my tables.

Thanks, buddy.

BY THE TIME I GET OFF SHIFT AND HEAD HOME, I'M BEAT. Morgana was in the coffeehouse for another hour and, as promised, I attempted to talk with her as she drank a few more espressos. I got a little out of her, but then, I'm not a fucking interrogation expert.

I push open the gate in front of our townhouse and latch it behind me carefully. Iggy isn't worried about intruders because he's confident in his abilities, but I grew up in a part of Bay City that wasn't nearly as nice as the State U campus. Old habits die hard and being the heir to the leader of the Sons of the Seven Seas—gang that runs the docks in Bay City—taught me to keep a close eye on my surroundings. My parents always had enemies looking for a way into our community, and they weren't hoping to join the HOA.

"Slade, is that you? Get in here and spill your guts! I have Thai food and ice cream."

As much as Iggy pisses me off, this is the shit that makes it worthwhile. I could afford anything I want without him, but he acts like my lack of gilded family heritage makes me his responsibility. He's always making sure I don't forget to eat or finding reasons to check in on me during the day. Rarely does a month go by when I don't come home to some random purchase he made online that he knew I couldn't live without.

Like I said... mixed. fucking. signals.

"I'm coming," I mutter as I trudge into the living room. "You wouldn't believe how crazy it got in there after the theater program auditions let out. I was up to my ass in freshman reciting lines and belting *Les Mis*."

Iggy grins at me from his usual spot on the couch. His dark hair is tousled, and he's shirtless, clothed only in a low slung pair of jogging pants as he reclines against the fat cushions. "I don't know why you even work in that hellhole. You don't need to."

"You know exactly why, Briarton." I huff as I drop my messenger bag and flop down on my spot to kick off my shoes. "Part of my requirements for work study are hours in one of the campus businesses and I prefer slinging bean juice to shelving books or picking up sweaty gym towels."

His full lips pout at me and his brow furrows. "Come on, Slade. I could convince that harpy in the office to waive your req and you know it. Besides, you don't even *need* work-study money."

I know that, but I like to make my way.

"My family paid for undergraduate school and I decided to do the rest on my own. It keeps me from owing Axel more than I want to repay."

Iggy frowns petulantly, but he doesn't understand why I want to keep as much of my life here as separate from my crime syndicate relatives at home. The more of their 'help' I accept, the more likely I am to get a phone call demanding a favor someday. I don't want to use my gifts for their bullshit, so I try to limit how much exposure to my life here I grant them. My mother isn't as bad as my father and uncles, but she's no pushover, either.

"What did you get out of the mysterious murderess?"

Grateful for the change of topic, I loll my head over to look at him. "She seems nice, Ig. A little distant, but I think she's earned that in the past year since…"

"Since she killed our former boss after hunting him down like a dog?"

"I guess. I mean, I'm sure she has sharp edges, but the woman in my shop today was sad and alone. She definitely would have preferred prison to being sent here." I pull my glasses off, sitting them on the coffee table and pick up the glass of wine he had waiting for me.

"Do you think she's going to clean house or what?" His expression is more unsure than I've ever seen before, and I realize he truly is scared.

"Not entirely, I don't think. If I were to guess, I'd say she'll ferret out Magnus' loyal minions first. She can't do any of the shit the auditors want if she has crooked assholes working behind her back."

My enigmatic friend nods, considering my words as he grabs the containers of food and a pair of chopsticks. Opening the first one, he grins as he picks up a small dumpling and holds it up for me. "Sounds like you got a good read on her, even if you didn't get solid answers."

I lean in and catch the proffered food with my teeth. If I don't, Iggy will get pouty and fuck knows I don't have the spoons left to deal with that after today. "I did what I could without being obvious I was grilling her, man."

"Is she pretty? The pictures always make her look big and angry," he says as he scratches his chin with his free hand.

"Gorgeous," I mumble around the pot sticker. "Tall as hell, but the gothic CEO look is very hot."

He blinks and gives me a slow, knowing smirk. "You like her! Oh, Slade, that's precious. The stony Domme look has your motor running."

"Shut up, Iggy."

"We could try the sharing thing again; we're a lock when we work together. The chicks dig our brainy nerd sandwich." He bobs his brows and I roll my eyes.

"I am not committing to seducing our new boss, who murdered her former fiancée for being an unfaithful crook, with my roommate. Don't be ridiculous."

"Ah, but that's not a 'no'. It's more of a 'it's a bad idea' and *that* I can work with."

Poseidon save me from ambiguous best friends who have no boundaries.

in my head

The Dean's house still reeks of Magnus, and I *hate* it.

My stuff is coming, but it won't arrive for at least three more weeks. After the human virus bullshit for the past few years, shipping is a goddamned nightmare, even with supernatural moving companies. I'd planned to pare down my belongings before I moved to the US when my ex and I got married, but that was over a year away. When the Council handed down their edict, I was left scrambling to pack every damned thing I owned in short order and get my ass on a plane to start here.

I could have flown trans-Atlantic, but it would have taken longer, and they refused to set my stupid monitor to allow for it.

Growling in frustration, I look down at the amulet my mother gave me when I graduated from Swallowtail in my teens. It's why I can shift without destroying my clothes, so I never take it off, but now that it's part of my sentence, I resent its presence. The hex added to ensure I didn't run out on my prison time keeps track of me and makes it impossible to remove the pendant until they deem my sentence served.

Here I am, stuck in a house filled with the ghost of my ex, imprisoned in a job I didn't want, and locked down like a rabid werewolf. My life has become one huge cosmic joke, and it makes me want to go on a vengeful rampage through this idyllic countryside. I could entomb half the males in the dorm before anyone even realized I'd gone rogue, then break the chain around my neck and fly free. But that would mean living on the run for the rest of my lengthy lifespan and I'm not cut out for hiding in caves and abandoned churches.

Rubbing my hand over my face, I head to the kitchen in search of a nice bottle of Cabernet. If I'm going to live with the rustic, Ernest Hemingway-esque decor my dipshit ex picked, I'll need to get very drunk. It's Friday, anyway, so it's not like I have anything else to do besides plow through books so complex I'm going to need a forensic accountant to make heads or tails of them.

"I wonder if Jackson Thorne has one of those on staff," I murmur as I rummage for the corkscrew. He lives nearby and stood out as one of the rare agents at the trial who didn't seem eager to condemn me.

That thought brings a wave of fury and shame. Memories of being shackled by magic and glared at by an enormous gathering of high-powered supes flood my mind, making my shoulders sag. I'll never outlive the humiliation of that scene, and *that* is the ultimate indignity Magnus left me with. Without proof of the things he told me before I struck the final blow, no one would believe the evil that lurked under a skin that pretended to be merely shady. So I didn't use any of his vile admissions as evidence in my trial; I merely had my lawyer use the laws of both my people to justify my actions based on publicly known crimes.

"They'd be shocked down to their expensive jockey shorts if they knew what kind of filth he'd been up to." Muttering to myself has become a bit of a habit, but I don't have any friends left to vent to about the unfairness of my life.

Fuck, I'm a sad sack of a supernatural.

I grab the glass and bottle, heading into the living room. I splayed all the folders and printouts I could gather out on the huge couch, so I can see the bigger picture. I probably need to buy some kind of big wheeled cork board so I can track this shit, but that's a task for tomorrow. That and a hundred other things, including gutting this damn man cave to make it livable. I know that's *definitely* not in the budget, but I can not spend the rest of my tenure here with this macho adventurer shit.

Propping myself up, I run through numbers line by line, marking lines in the P&L I have issues with as I go. I finish the first glass of my well-aged Cab and pour another, wishing I'd paid more attention to sports when I was younger. Some of this shit sounds made up, but how the fuck would I know if the hockey team really needs forty new graphite sticks? They could purposely bloat these purchase orders for many reasons and none of them legitimate. And this is a less daunting task than tackling the football team's folders—I could bludgeon someone with their goddamned budget, but the art department is begging for enough supplies to get through the semester.

I am so *the wrong person for this job.*

Again, the unfairness of my pseudo-punishment hits me. My job at Swallowtail didn't involve accounting, nor did it have deadlines as serious as the ones I face here. I'm certainly smart enough to figure this out, but given that Magnus and his cronies had *years* to warp things here, I'm behind the eight ball with the cue at my back. People expect me to fail—truthfully, they probably want me to—and I can't allow my reputation to take another body shot because my two-faced dickwad ex was a goddamned criminal.

I pinch the bridge of my nose, feeling overwhelmed and ready to cry, when a shrill tone from my phone makes me jump. As a general rule, I don't keep ringers on and haven't for over a decade, but this is the sound I programmed for the 'hell has broken loose' Dean calls. I set the office phone to forward to my cell and made certain a call to this 'Batphone' would always wake me. That's a choice I'm regretting as I look at the red wine that sloshed on my pajamas, but that's a complaint for another day.

Grabbing the phone, I click the screen open with an irritated, "What?!"

The babbling admin on the other end isn't really making sense, but I caught 'accident', 'hockey rink', and 'police.' I'm pretty sure that means I'm needed immediately. Closing my eyes to collect myself, I bark into the speaker. "Stop. I'm on my way. No one speaks to law enforcement until I arrive. *No one*. Do you understand?"

That said, I strip the stained shirt off and stomp upstairs to find another. I don't have time to get appropriately dressed, but I'll be damned if I'm going to show up soaked in wine like a fucking hobo. Pulling an old Grateful Dead tee out of the overflowing trunk on my bedroom floor, I vow to prepare an emergency clothes pile for shit like this in the future. I shed my soft yoga pants and wiggle into a pair of holey jeans, then shove my feet into combat boots. I don't even bother lacing them; I have to get outside and take flight before some moron talks to the cops or worse, the press.

Shoving the French doors open, I step onto my small balcony. Magnus probably built this so he could do the same thing I'm doing now, and that's one thing I'm grateful for. His dragon status is the sole valuable aspect of that worthless bag of bones. Touching my amulet, I let my wings stretch and bend, then push off the stone railing with my legs. I catch the night breeze easily and start scouting for the ice rink. I should have looked at the damn map before I left, but I was too angry and wine soaked to think straight.

If this isn't a genuine emergency, whoever called me is definitely fired.

I LAND BEHIND THE ARENA, AVOIDING THE CORDONED OFF parking lot in the front. Luckily, the cloudy night made for suitable cover and I'm able to fold in my wings before I stride towards the back door. There's a campus security officer at the door and he gives me a suspicious glare as I walk past him. He's not wearing a name badge or number on his uniform, so I add that to my list of new regulations to add or enforce. Thinking about what armed, uniformed guards with no way to be identified could get away with at a university full of kids makes me shudder.

I refuse to allow this kind of dangerous nonsense to go on at State U during my tenure.

The back hallways are full of offices and equipment rooms, so I keep walking until I can feel the chill of the ice. Stepping into the arena, I immediately evaluate the scene. Spectators are still in their seats looking uncomfortable and irritated, cops and security are standing around jabbering, and at the front entrance, there's a nervous-looking shifter with blond hair. She's fiddling with the tight bun, shuffling her feet as she tries to peer out a crack to see outside, letting no one in. This must be who called me because she's alternating between looking out that sliver and looking at her phone.

"Interesting. She looks worried, but not hostile. That works for me," I murmur to myself as I slip through the crowd. Being dressed down keeps people from paying attention to me, and I tuck that information away for later. To avoid attention, I must blend in with the students on campus. It may also help me get information on bad actors without putting people in a hot seat, so that's a plus, too.

When I get to the doorway, I'm ashamed to say the local cops and our security have paid no mind to me. I could be anyone and I could get to the exit easily—one that's only being watched by a five foot two woman who looks like I could blow her over with a feather. Her scent says ice elemental, so perhaps she has some powers, but I doubt she has the gumption to use them. Since I have no idea what the emergency is, their lack of professionalism is shocking.

"Excuse me. I believe you're waiting for me," I say as I tap her on the shoulder. The sound she makes as she jumps is nothing short of adorable, and I wait for her to gather herself before I speak again. "I'm Dean LeCiel."

"Oh, boogers!" The woman exclaims as she adjusts her thick black glasses. "I was sure you'd come through the front. I meant to greet you and fill in you before anyone else got to you and now I've made a mess of everything!"

Her flustered babble makes me smile a little, so I take it easy on her. "I didn't want the press to see me. My... infamy... precedes me and it might distract from whatever situation we have here. I quietly slipped in unnoticed."

"Well, of course not! You're usually so well put together and snazzy; tonight, you look like one of us normal people." Her eyes widen as she realizes what that sounds like and she rushes to add, "Not that you're not normal. Or that not normal is bad. I mean, life is full of rainbows and everyone of us fits in somewhere and—"

I hold my hand up to cut off the flow. "I get it. You weren't being judgmental. Forgive me for asking, but who are you? I don't believe we've met yet."

"Dumb, dumb, dumb, Channing!" She smacks her head several times and I finally reach over to stop her. Once she feels my grip, she looks up with a bright red face. "I'm sorry to be so high-strung. Crisis management is usually my forte, but since you arrived, there's been a lot of upheaval in the support staff. So I'm stretched a little thin and when I feel overwhelmed, my anxiety goes haywire."

"I can tell," I reply as I give her an amused look. "Let's take this step-by-step, shall we? You're Channing, and you work in what office? We can talk about that support staff comment once we have this situation under control."

"Okay. Got it. Uh, I'm Channing Oswald and I work in the PR department." She takes a deep breath and smooths her hand over her hair. "They promoted me to VP yesterday because most of the department quit when you arrived—which, forgive me for being blunt, is stupid as fuck."

I like people who don't mince words.

"Channing, I agree with you. Unless they're all as crooked as my rotting ex, quitting was a major mistake on their part. But I'll see to that later." I look around, feeling the unrest mounting among the locked up people. "Now, tell me what's happening here. We don't need a riot because we held these folks too long."

She nods, giving me a serious look. "It's bad, Dean. Like, terrible. Follow me."

I nod, waiting for her to lead the way. Eyes track me as the two of us walk back the way I came and I know that means they've figured out who I am. No one stops us or says anything, but I know the minute we're out of sight, the tongues will start wagging. "Where are we going?"

"To the home team locker room," Channing replies. She looks over her shoulder, her dainty features pinched with concern. "We've kept it contained, but we won't be able to hold the police off much longer."

"Why would we need to keep them held ba—" The words die in my throat when she pushes the door open and I see a blond hockey god sitting on a bench with his face in his hands—in front of a dead body with blood pooling around it. "Holy fuckwhistle."

"You don't say." The guy lifts his face out of his hands to reveal Viking features and a sexy scruff that makes my stomach do backflips.

"Dean, this is Lucas Wolfberg. He's a freshman recruited to be the new star goalie for the *Bonecrushers*."

Squinting, I look over at Channing curiously. "Our hockey team... is called... the *Bonecrushers*?"

"Rumor has it," Lucas drawls as he looks me over, head to toe. "Though rumors can be quite unreliable. They said you'd come here dressed like a mafia don, but you look like you watched *Reality Bites* too many times in the 90s."

My gaze meets his and icy blues clash with my dark gray orbs. "You're awfully snarky for someone who's about to be arrested for murder, Lucas."

His lips curve, and he smirks. "I'm no science geek, but I watch enough TV to know they won't have enough evidence to hold me. I'm here because I got sin binned too many times, so Coach sent me to cool off, so to speak. Dude was here when I arrived, and I called for help without touching him. No CSI bullshit for me."

Touching two fingers to my temple, I rub it lightly. The prevalence of crime drama in the media leads people to believe they know what they're talking about and though I'm not sure Lucas killed whoever this is, I believe he could be in big trouble. Losing an important sports star, finding a dead body, and not protecting a student won't be a good start to my inauspicious career here.

"Channing. I need you to call Lucas's parents and have them send their lawyer immediately." She salutes me and scurries off quickly, yet again earning my internal praise. "Lucas, I can see this will be difficult for you. I need you to shut the fuck up until your mouthpiece gets here."

His grin is sinful, and I have to fight off a shiver. "A lady who enjoys giving orders—nice."

"I'm not joking, you idiot. You're in a closed room with a dead body that appears to have its throat slit. You're wearing *knives on your feet*. It doesn't take Poirot to figure out who the police are going to focus on. Do you know the identity of this corpse?" I frown, realizing I hadn't even considered asking that until now.

My people's longevity dampens death or murder's horror—you lose perspective.

"Pierre LaMount." He runs his hand through his hair and sighs. "He's the goalie for Mapleleaf University. I took the spot on this team he wanted."

Fuck me right in the ass. That's means, motive, and opportunity in one fell swoop.

"Son of a bitch," I mutter. "You definitely need to keep your big yap shut until a suit gets here. For your sake, the university's sake, and for my sake, *do not say a word*. If those yokels get any of this out of you, you're headed for the state pen before you can whistle 'Dixie,' buddy."

"I figured that. You're the only person I've spoken to since I got the coaches in here. Probably not the best plan since you have to throw me to the wolves if it benefits the university, but…"

I arch a brow. "But what?"

"Killing old Magnus for his sins took guts and character. You're not the kind of woman who sells her soul to others, even when it would have benefitted you to do so. I'm gambling on you extending that courtesy to me."

"You act awfully mature for a freshman, Lucas." I give him an assessing look, trying to figure out if he's one of the species that has long life spans and stunted life phases.

"Polar bear shifter. But my parents held me back from school for three years as a kid to make me bigger for sports. They do that here," he says with a shrug. "So I am an older freshman, but you should see some of the football dicks. Some of them look like they're in mid-life crisis range."

They hold kids back from school to make them bigger for... sports? What backwards shit...

Lucas snorts. "Don't think about it too hard. That's the shit that goes on in the South."

"Seems like I've got a lot to learn about living here," I murmur.

He stands, moving around the blood and towards me. "That you do, ma'am."

ice in my veins

The new dean is *smoking* hot even in her band tee and ripped jeans. She's not afraid to be blunt, and she's got an air of dominance that's sassy enough to mean she'd be a fighter in the sack. I'm not worried about why she killed that crooked old lizard, nor that she's older than me by several centuries. After this ends, I'll find a way to get closer to her.

Chicks always dig the hot guy in sweaty sports gear, so it shouldn't be too hard.

I stalk closer to her, grinning as I invade her space. To her credit, the dean doesn't back down—she lets me walk right into her until we're mere centimeters apart with a defiant look on her face. She's taller than me, which never happens, but not by much. That puts her at about six foot six in heels and I enjoy having her almost at eye level in flat shoes. She doesn't look breakable, like most of the girls I've dated in the past. Instead, she's tall, broad shouldered, and solidly built. It's refreshing, truthfully.

"Lucas, what the actual fuck are you doing? They'll return shortly. Don't be stupid," Dean LeCiel snorts harshly.

Brushing a stray hair off her forehead gently, I arch a brow as I turn on the flirting. "What's wrong, Morgana? Are you worried they'll see how much you like me?"

"Oh, please. I am *not* a freshman ingenue and those cheesy lines won't work on me." Her eyes narrow and she looks like she's struggling to decide if she should push me away or pull me closer. "And you do not have permission to call me by my given name."

"But we're going to be so close—I can *feel* it." She rolls her eyes and lifts a hand as if to push my shoulder, but I catch it and press my lips to her palm.

The shocked look on her face makes me grin against her skin and she tries to yank it away. "Lucas, this is highly inappropriate! Let go of me."

Shrugging, I nip the base of her thumb lightly. "I live for inappropriate, Morgana. How do you think I ended up in the penalty box so many times tonight? I play for keeps."

"Dean, I have the—oh!" The PR woman comes stomping in and gasps when she sees us.

Goddamn it, of course, that frazzled, pint-sized elemental would walk in right now.

Morgana pulls away, giving me a sharp look of displeasure. "No worries, Channing. I was just explaining the college honor code and policies on sexual harassment when you came in. Clearly, he's got a lot to learn about the phrase 'no means no' before he's suitable for public appearances."

Giving her an amused look, I step back and cross my arms over my chest. "I've never had to resort to questionable consent to get my bed warmed. I'll be fine without the lecture, Dean."

Her expression says she doesn't like that, and it makes my inner bear preen a bit. I'm not sure if she's going to need to be chased to give in, but the thought of it gets my motor running. I'm all in for a little primal hunting, especially if the media is right about her being part winged shifter. The chase is sweeter when they can match my pace.

"Bring the authorities in now, Channing. Lucas knows what he's supposed to do and not do. He'll *behave*."

Oooh—or maybe I won't, just to see what she'll do.

As if she can sense my defiance, the dean turns her head and gives me another stern look. I simply smile and walk over to a bank of lockers away from the mess on the floor, leaning casually as we wait. When the bushy faced detective comes in with a group of squirrely looking science geeks that must be crime scene techs, I watch quietly. He eyes me up and down, frowning under the thick, bushy mustache that is woefully out of style or means he's a walrus shifter.

"Are you the one who 'discovered' the body?" he barks as he approaches.

Backing up to keep the space between us, I nod. "I am. Coach sent me to the locker room to chill when I got my last penalty of the game."

Morgana glares at me again—she expected me to say something to the tune of 'lawyer' and nothing else.

"A hothead, huh?" he murmurs as he scribbles something in a notepad. "Good to know. You came back alone and found this young man on the floor, but did not provide help?"

"I didn't say that."

"There are no signs he was turned to clear an airway or anyone tried to resuscitate him. The blood pool isn't smeared!" The detective's face reddens a little as he points to the victim.

"I'm not sure giving someone CPR would be prudent when their throat is hanging open like a sliced ham," I reply coolly.

"Detective, I'm sure Lucas called for help as soon as he saw the situation. We can't expect him to react like a medical or law enforcement professional, can we?" Morgana steps closer to the sweaty man, looking every bit as regal as she would wearing one of the trademark suits everyone talks about.

He whirls on her, getting in her face as he snarls, "I'll thank you not to meddle in police affairs, Dean LeCiel. We're all aware of your shortcomings surrounding murder."

Nope. That's not gonna work for me.

With the speed of my bear, I slide in between them, looking the pastrami-eating fool right in the eyes. "It's downright rude to speak to a lady that way, especially when you're spitting your deli dinner in her face. Apologize to the Dean and show her the respect her office commands—I won't ask again."

"Lucas, it's fine. I—"

"No, it's not. This bearded clown is not only addressing the Council appointed Dean of State U, but a full-blooded Wolfberg as if we're the crumbs on his jacket. It will horrify my grandmother to hear of this." I look at him with a sly smirk as I continue, "Perhaps you've heard of Nana? Duchess Gretchen Madeline von Wolfenberg of the German Council is not someone I suggest trifling with."

The detective turns white as a sheet and he backs away quickly, barking orders at the crime techs before he looks back at me. "The Dean will escort you to the precinct for further questioning. Do not be late."

Morgana waits until he leaves to hiss at me, "Are fucking kidding me? Burying the lede that you're related to the matriarch of the European bear clans is dirty, you little shit."

"Morgana, if you find that dirty, I have a lot of work ahead of me."

The ride to the station was quiet, though I could tell Morgana wanted to ask questions. Her gaze roamed over the interior of my 2014 Morgan Plus 8 Speedster curiously, but she didn't comment. It was a gift from my Nana and I love it more than most people love their significant others. I'm only thirteen years older than this car, but the 1940s feel of it makes me happy. I've got a serious adoration of the Rat Pack, Vegas during the mob times, and hockey—not always in that order. I love riding around in a car that evokes the feel of jazz clubs and smoky bars rather than some tiny dick show-off Italian bullshit.

But I don't tell her that; I let her wonder.

When we arrive downtown, I insist on pulling into a lot to escort her inside rather than drop her off, which she grouses about half-heartedly. I feel she's spent a lot of time taking care of herself because of the unorthodox engagement she and Magnus had, and now she can't relax enough to allow anyone to help. I don't know if I'm game to work on changing that or looking for a quick, albeit hot AF, hop between the sheets. It's too soon to say if I'm considering my ban on relationships that last past breakfast or if I'm just juicing on the instalust.

"Lucas, *please* do not run your mouth until your lawyer gets here. I'm sure you're used to the spotlight and I don't doubt you can handle yourself, but I don't aspire to be the reason your grandmother goes on a rampage. I have enough problems with the Society and the Councils; don't add to it because you're being ornery," Morgana says as she takes my hand to get out.

My lips quirk. Her plea is authentic and personal, so I might agree. "We'll see. I assume the text I sent to my parents activated some legal eagle they have on retainer locally. It'd surprise me if whoever it is doesn't actually beat me to the crusty detective's desk."

By the time we get to the entrance, I see my assumption was correct because a blond surfer looking dude in a Balenciaga suit is waiting for us outside. His teeth sparkle white in the lamplight and I hear Morgana suck in a breath behind me. She knows this guy and I can't tell if it's a good or bad thing, so I block her halfway, just in case.

"Jackson Thorne! Of course, the Duchess would have Thorne Enterprises on their payroll in these parts." Morgana pushes past me and sticks her hand out to shake.

The lawyer takes her hand, shaking it first, then turning it to lift to his lips and I swear to Odin, a fucking growl pops out of my lips. His head whips around and he gives me a knowing look. "It is my blessing and curse to be available to beautiful women who collect adorable young men with an inability to stay out of trouble. In fact, I was awake speaking to another such client who is currently overseas with her cadre of drooling boys."

"Lucas is *not* someone I've collected, Jackson. He's a student in trouble with very influential relatives who I'm ensuring gets appropriate representation, so they do not hold the school liable. You of all people should know I'm not out cherry picking lovers." The dean bristles, striding up the stairs and leaving the two of us in her wake.

I turn to the well-known supe with an irritated expression. "So far, you suck at your job, dude."

"Oh, I suck *very well*, but it's not part of my job, young Wolfberg. Neither is helping you figure out how to crack that stony exterior, so let's get inside and dispense with the nonsense of the local police. This may be a bigger city, but the law enforcement is no more competent than the yokels further out. They will try to blame you out of convenience and laziness. Let's not give them the chance by standing out here bickering, eh?"

I don't want to like this guy because he pissed off Morgana, but I kind of do.

"Understood."

"I'm sure you've been told, but when I say it, I mean it. *Keep. Your. Mouth. Shut.* I will answer every question or allow you to give me answers privately before we address the issue. I will assert your right to remain silent and provide information at other times. Follow my lead and you can chase that lovely hybrid home instead of sleeping on a dirty cot tonight. *Capiche?*"

"I'm not stupid," I retort. I *have* visited a police station in the past.

"Not surprising, hot shot. Now button it until you're given permission to speak."

He turns, heading into the precinct with the air of someone who knows exactly what they're doing and expects to accomplish it without a hitch. Grumbling under my breath, I follow him, hoping his confidence isn't misplaced.

I didn't kill that fucker, Pierre, but I'm not sad someone else did.

"Hopefully, that isn't obvious," I mumble to myself as we head into the lion's den.

Thorne turns around and pins me with his gaze. "What isn't obvious?"

I smile, batting my lashes as I make a motion, mimicking zipping my lips. He rolls his eyes and mutters something under his breath as we catch up to Morgana. Her features are creased with concern as she looks at the lack of bodies working at this hour other than Detective Kaiser Roll and a small weasley looking fellow in the corner. This is nothing like I'd expect for a city of this size, but that virus hit everything in the human world hard. Unfortunately for me, unless the crime violates a Council or Society law, I'm stuck with the unevolved for the duration of this mess.

Hell, I'm lucky they even have a shifter detective on staff here.

Usually they don't allow our kind to take these jobs, but with State U nearby, I suppose they needed someone to keep all the secrets. College kids aren't known for good judgment and campus security can't wrangle anyone who leaves the University to party in the clubs or bars. I doubt they thought this big goombah would tackle a murder case when they pushed him up the ladder, though, and that doesn't bode well for me. Morgana and Thorne are right; this dude will close the book on this in a red hot minute if it means he gets to go back to taking a nap at his desk.

"Mr. Wolfberg," the lout yells. "Follow me to interrogation."

Jackson steps in front of me, giving the cop a blank expression. "I thought this was a non-custodial interview, Detective. Was I misinformed?"

The big guy runs his hand over his whisker and snorts. "It is. But I'd be more comfortable if your client gave his statement on camera. For the record, you see."

"Ah. I see." Jackson gives him a dark glare. "However, I'm unconcerned with your comfort. My client will speak with you at your desk, with the two of us present as witnesses, and only when I permit him to. You will not record or video the interview and if a written statement is required, I will prepare it with him and have it delivered to you tomorrow morning."

Holy shit, this guy is good.

"Well, I, uh, you see, my Captain..."

Thorne pulls out his cell phone, scrolling through the contacts with a smile. "Which Captain? I have all of their personal numbers and the Council's. Whom shall I call to approve my terms?"

I look over at Morgana, and she gives me a tiny smile. It appears she knew this guy was a superstar, and that's why she didn't stick around for his lecture before we came in.

I don't think there's a damn thing wrong with her judgment or her methods—she's smart as a whip.

snakes

My instincts about Jackson Thorne from the trial don't appear to be incorrect. He's taken control of the situation in a truly admirable fashion, even to the point of getting that stubborn bear to shut his big yap. I'm grateful for his intervention, because I know Lucas was flirting when Channing walked in. Given the testosterone-filled youth of our star hockey player, I believe he would have continued to dig his heels in because it might impress me. It definitely would *not*, but I've had centuries to mature while he's only early twenties. The folly of false bravado is something you grow out of as you age, especially when you're a supe with an extremely long life-span like me.

That doesn't mean his brash overconfidence and ballsy overtures were lost on me.

My eyes dart to the student in question, roaming over his relaxed form as he leans back in the chair next to the detective's desk. He's slouched with his long legs sticking out and his hand behind his head like he doesn't have a care in the world. No matter, they're questioning him about a murder in which any rational person would consider him the prime suspect; no, Lucas Wolfberg is as cool as a cucumber as Thorne navigates the questions being spit at them. Being part of a family as distinguished as his probably had him learning this kind of shit the minute he could talk.

His gaze skates to meet mine as if he can hear my thoughts and I feel the heat flare under my skin. I don't have to worry about my mother's lineage because of the special contacts they invented for my kind in the 90s, but the other side... Let's just say the gargoyle I get from my father is a lot more aggressive than defensive. It helps me scent the pheromones coming off the lean, muscled male staring at me—and it likes what it smells. To regain focus, I have to glance at my phone and pretend to scroll. A message pops up from Channing, and I sigh in relief.

Thank fuck. I need a distraction or I may have an incident I can't cover up.

"Feeling the need to let something loose, Dean?" Lucas's question has a teasing tone, but when I raise my eyes to meet his across the room, I can tell he knows exactly what he's saying.

Fucking shifters can smell everything; it's annoying as hell.

Pursing my lips, I give him a stony glare. "No, Lucas. I'm doing well, thank you. You should focus on your own issues."

His grin is lazy and knowing as he scratches his stomach, pulling his henley up over taut, defined abs. The display is on purpose and I sniff, going back to my phone without giving him the reaction he's looking for. I refuse to play games with someone suspected of murder on my campus and besides, I have no idea how to handle such an arrogant alpha display. I'm usually the aggressor with sexual partners and I've always been in charge in that arena.

Magnus shifted that paradigm slightly because he was haughtily overbearing with damn near everything, but he wasn't the one who pursued me in the beginning. After I learned what kind of person he really was, I realized his easygoing attitude and shower of affection when we started dating were simply a method of luring me in so he could isolate and dominate me behind the scenes. Once he had me in his web, the slimy dragon hoarded me like some ancient vase he'd found on an expedition. When we were together, he trotted me out when it was convenient and I made him look good, but the second I disagreed with anything he said or did, I was blasted with his fiery temper.

I don't know how to feel about this much younger, sexy ass hockey player stalking me like I'm a flank steak and he's been starving for a month. Ethical concerns aside, I can't imagine he has a good track record for sticking around and though I'd enjoy a one night only performance, I think it would reinforce some rumors being spread across campus about my morals. If I wasn't the Dean, I wouldn't give a rat's ass, but I have a reputation to repair and they expect me to represent the school.

My phone beeps and I look down, smiling a bit. Channing is turning out to be a lot more likable than my first impression. Since I gave her permission to handle the gamut of issues at the arena while I accompanied Lucas to the station, it seems she's got the crowd dispersed, the players and fans out, and is waiting for the CSIs and coroner to clear the area before she locks everything up. Her last-minute promotion may have uncovered a hidden gem in the PR department, and I may have a conversation with her about further opportunities once this shit is settled.

I could use a personal assistant that is loyal to me and not the prior administration; I feel Channing may be just the person for the job.

"What's the good news?"

Rolling my eyes, I look at Lucas again. He's not paying attention to a damn thing Jackson and the grumpy detective are talking about. He's only focused on me, it seems, and while it may be a little flattering, it's not smart. Keeping his mouth shut about finding Pierre unless told to speak is good; sitting there staring at me like a fucking stalker is not. I have to dissuade him from setting his sights on me further—I'm a bucket full of crazy without a lid since the trial. No one deserves to be part of cleaning up such an enormous mess left by a scumbag like Magnus.

"None of your business, Lucas. Concentrate on your own problems," I snap.

His rumbling laugh feels like it's vibrating over my body despite being across the room. "My family is paying someone to do that for me, Morgana. I have plenty of free brain space to focus on you."

Well, that's just ducky.

"If you must know, Channing is getting the crisis at the rink taken care of efficiently and I'm pleased." The beep of another message gets my attention and I look down again, sighing in relief. "It seems like the team working the scene is done and she'll have everything buttoned up soon."

"Ah, that's excellent. She could be a valuable ally for you. I got the sense she's been overworked and underappreciated for a long time. You need as many friends as possible."

My expression tightens and I nod sharply, uncomfortable with his insight being so spot on. I'll have to be careful with this one; he sees way more than he should and he's clearly determined to make me a notch on his bedpost. Worming his way into my good graces won't work the way he's hoping, though. I'm no longer a naïve academic from a nouveau riche family who isn't familiar with how the rich play their games. My ex made certain I got an unforgettable lesson in keeping myself closed off. It's the best way to avoid being hurt again or ending up in a secret jail in Argentina.

"I don't need staffing suggestions from a freshman sports star. Thank you for your opinion, but I can handle myself," I reply as I lift my phone up and scroll through the mountain of emails accumulated since earlier in the evening.

The incident at the game triggered a deluge of donor, staff, board, and angry parent communications I'll be sifting through until sometime tomorrow. I already have enough work without dealing with this damn school's nonsense. That's going to come out of budgets from the goddamned hockey team—we'll see how this smarty pants likes when his coach has to cut some corners.

I think I'll tell the little shit on the ride home. It might distract him from hitting on me.

The scenery flies by as Lucas speeds along the highway away from downtown. He's definitely annoyed with my blunt statement about team budgets, but he hasn't said anything. The tick in his jaw makes my gut curl in satisfaction. I wanted this reaction, and I played my cards exactly right to get it.

"My grandmother will pay to clean up our locker room."

I frown. "What do you mean 'our' locker room?"

Arching a brow, he gives me a sexy smirk that's full of pride. "We paid to build the thing when they broke ground a century ago and we've paid to upgrade it every time the university has requested it to keep up with other programs. It's basically ours. So I'll call her tomorrow and she'll send in a team of elves to deal with it. No worries; that fee is what she spends on tea cups for her collection monthly."

"Thirty grand?" I snort before I can stop the words from exiting my mouth.

"I take it back. She spends that on hats. Her tea cups are far more expensive," he says as he swerves into another lane, racing around a slow-moving car.

Rich people are a pain in my round, tight ass.

"Fine. But she'll need to speak with me before she sends her people on campus. Everything is locked down for the moment because the board is convinced that if you *didn't* kill Pierre, whoever did is hiding there." I shake my head as I stare out the window. I don't agree and despite several passionate emails back and forth while Lucas was being questioned, I was overruled.

"Hmm," he mumbles. "That's interesting. I doubt it's true; anyone leaving that messy a scene without drawing suspicion seems too thorough to get caught snoozing in an empty dorm or crouching in a broom closet."

Looking over, I don't hide the surprise on my face. "That's what I think, too."

"Obviously, you also like crime shows and mysteries. Dame Agatha or Sir Conan wouldn't make the solution so obvious and likely, neither would someone with that skill set. The way they set me up spoke to this being planned—they knew it would be believable because I have a rivalry with that lunkhead. But they also had to be watching; no one could predict me getting fouled out that soon into the game."

Sweet baby Zeus, is this guy for real?

"Lucas, you're not the detective in this case. If Jackson gets you cleared, you need to stay way the hell away from their investigation. You'll end up looking guilty again if you meddle or gossip about it." I look down to see my hand on his and yank it back, scolding myself internally for initiating the touch, even innocently.

"I won't bite," he says with a wolfish grin. "That is, unless you ask nicely."

This time it's my turn to arch a brow and smirk. "I don't ask for things like that, Lucas. I command. Despite whatever rumors may be going around the community, Magnus was *not* the ruler of my world before his well-deserved death. And he certainly isn't running my life now."

"You're locked in this region until your sentence is complete, Morgana. He may not be in charge of you, but his ghost is haunting you." His expression turns sympathetic as he glances over at me. "Sorry. I hear all the good stuff from my family, so I know you have a tag that lets the Society know where you are. Kinda shitty of them to tie it to the thing that helps you keep your shifting under control when your emotions are strong, though."

How in the motherfucking hell did his family get all of that info? Some of it was sealed at the trial!

"My privacy has been invaded enough as it is. I'd appreciate it if you'd stop making it worse." I pause, considering whether I want to correct him or not. Finally, I decide it's better to be honest than to hide shit if rumors are circulating. "My amulet doesn't suppress shifts. I can do that on my own; I *am* three hundred years old. It helps me keep my clothes intact when I shift to either form, so I'm not running around naked afterward."

The sound he makes when I say 'naked' is sinful. "As much as I'd appreciate getting to see that, the convenience of it makes sense. The gargoyle or the Gorgon form would definitely tear your lovely designer suits to pieces."

A tiny hiss echoes in the car, and I reach back to the back of my head. That's Desdemona, the one snake I cannot control about ninety percent of the time. All of them have names, of course, because I have to talk to them when they are being unreasonable, but Des is the absolute worst one with acting out. "Goddamn it, Des," I mutter under my breath.

"You *name* them?!" Lucas's voice is full of wonder as I reach back and pinch the unruly shit to hopefully force her to go away.

Inhaling deeply, I glance at the car's roof, praying I can leave soon. "Yes, I name them. How else am I supposed to talk to my hair when I need individual strands with minds of their own? If I didn't, I couldn't scold the ones who misbehave—like Des."

"That's possibly the coolest thing I've heard in a while. They all have, like...sentience?"

Unfortunately, like djinns and other rare supes, both gargoyles and gorgons are insular groups whose numbers are dwindling for various reasons. Neither are commonplace and most supes won't meet one of either of my descendants in their entire lifespan. That's another reason Magnus loved showing me off, and it rankles a little to find out Lucas knows. It makes me believe I'm definitely a checkbox in his macho diary; he wants to tick off another rare supe on his long list of conquests he can brag about.

"Yes. But I prefer not to discuss it and I'd rather you not tell people. I'm not a sideshow, nor am I a circus freak for people to gawk at. The trial made me infamous for my crimes and that already puts me under a microscope."

"I get that. People treat me differently once they hear about my Nana, too. I hated it as a kid because I could never trust if someone was my friend or if a girl liked me for me. Still can't half the time, to be honest," he replies as he pulls into the parking lot in front of the rink.

I tuck my phone into my purse before opening the car door. "Thank you for the ride, Lucas. Please remember what I've told you. I'd hate to see your career end before it begins because of something you didn't do."

"Where's your car?" he asks, ignoring my statement completely.

Stepping out, I touch my amulet with a grin and my wings unfurl, stretching out behind me. "I didn't drive here. Goodnight, Mr. Wolfberg."

As I push off the ground, his wide eyes follow me as I take off.

That will quiet him for a bit. At least, I hope so.

fire under my feet

The next morning is, as predicted, utter bullshit. My email crashes every couple of hours because I'm receiving so many missives from parents, alumni, staff, and, of course, the authorities. If I had a fucking assistant, I'd fob some of the less pertinent shit off, but after my placement here, much of Magnus' ex-biddies quit. I wasn't shocked or upset by that development until now. I'm buried by this incident, and I have more than enough on my plate. When my computer reboots itself—*again*—at noon, I avoid throwing the damn thing across the room by pushing to my feet and walking away from the desk.

I need to address this situation now before I lose my composure.

A touch of my amulet allows my wings to burst free, and I step onto the balcony again. Looking at the poorly designed app, I find the public relations office tucked in a side building close to my coffee shop. That makes me smile and I swipe to the text screen quickly.

> Morgana LeCiel: Channing, I need to speak with you about something of utmost importance. Are you able to meet me at The Beanery in five?

> Channing:...

> Channing: Yes, I believe so. Let me move a few things around and I can meet you there, Dean. May I ask what this is regarding?

> Morgana LeCiel: No. I'd prefer to speak in person. I'll see you there.

Smiling to myself, I realize the nervous elemental is probably convinced I'm firing her for something she did the other night. That wasn't my intent in refusing to give her info over text, though. I have no idea what kind of snooping shit the board had the IT department install on the university phones and though I'm using one of my own with plenty of protection against intrusion; she is not. I don't want anyone getting a whiff of what I'm planning before I set the wheels in motion. Keeping my council is the only way I'm going to achieve the lofty ass goals they set for me without interference.

I tuck my phone in the inside pocket of my suit coat and jump onto the stone railing. With a leap, I catch a slight current and glide upward into a slipstream. The campus looks idyllic from above; I'll give them that. The well-kept grounds, fully restored buildings, and shiny new facilities at the edges make it seem like the perfect place to send your young shifter or magic user, especially if you want them to learn to fit into an elite society mold. Unfortunately, I'm assigned to uncover the source of evil at State U, buried deep within. I'm going to peel all the layers of gentility, politeness, and polish away so I can figure out what Magnus buried under the surface.

That's going to piss more than a few people off and might even put a bigger target on my back than killing the sleazy lizard did.

When the Beauregard Fine Arts building comes into view, I angle my wings back to descend to the ground at a gentle speed. My feet touch the ground and I steady myself as my wings disappear into my back. I'd prefer not to answer questions about my supe sides if possible and hiding the wings is a good way to discourage the conversation.

Walking to the cafe, I pull open the door and notice that Slade is here again. I assume he's doing this as part of a work study, but I suddenly feel compelled to check into that when I get back to my office. I'm not sure why, but I want to know more about the pretty barista. He turns and gives me a brilliant smile, the expression gentle and sweet in opposition to the naughty arrogance of Lucas.

Why am I thinking about him? I need to get laid, that's why.

By the time Magnus' treachery was revealed, an ocean had separated us for months. His visits grew sparse once I accepted his proposal—the excuse was always working, and I was stupid enough to believe him. Of course, I had lots of nightstand options for gratification, but I missed the warmth of a live person. Those weren't available while I awaited trial after I hunted him down and I didn't have the privacy to help myself.

That can easily change now that I'm imprisoned in Dixieland. I'll dig out all of my toys. Maybe it will help me keep my mind off lithe, lovely music students and muscled hockey gods with wicked smirks. I bite my lower lip, grinning as I promise myself mentally to indulge in self-care tonight. I deserve it, after all.

"What's making you look so giddy?"

Slade's voice brings me out of my mental smutfest and I feel the color rise in my cheeks as I find my tongue. "Coffee always makes me look happy. I'm a caffeine junkie."

His brow arches disbelievingly, but he humors me. "Luckily, I've got plenty of that. Snack or sandwich, your choice?"

I'm pondering that when the bell on the door chimes and Channing comes bustling in. She looks much less harried today, and I'm pleased to see she brought a laptop with her. I enjoy knowing she came prepared to either be fired or put to work. It makes me think I've made an excellent decision to contact her to meet.

"Dean LeCiel, I'm sorry I ran a little behind," she says as she joins me at the counter. "Hello, Slade. How are you?"

The adorable grad student nods and pours a mug of black coffee, I assume is for her. "Afternoon, Channing. I just asked Morgana if she'd like pastry or food this afternoon. Do you want your usual?"

They both look at me expectantly, and I fold. "Okay, fine. I should eat. Load me up with a club sandwich and one of those big cookies, Slade."

Channing beams. "Fruit salad and a chicken salad croissant for me."

Once we have our coffee, we head to the table by the window while Slade works on our order. I settle in with my back to the wall—I'm not fond of having people behind me since the Council hunters used that to corner me. Channing sips her brew with a happy sigh before she sits her laptop on the table.

"May I ask why now, ma'am?"

I take pity on her, though my instinct is to wait until the food is done. "Yes. First, I wanted to thank you for your efficient and thorough work at the rink. You made it easy for me to accompany one of our students and deal with a potential PR mess without worrying that another one would be waiting when I returned."

Her face turns bright red, and she fiddles with her chignon, not meeting my eyes. "Oh! Well, I appreciate that. I tried to make sure I covered all the bases so you wouldn't have more work."

"Considering your grace under pressure, I have a proposal for you," I continue as Slade walks up and sits the plates down. "I'd like to transfer you."

Channing blinks, looking worried. "T-Transfer? I mean, I just got promoted and I don't think the department head is leaving, so..."

"Not within your department." I shake my head, grinning. "I would like to offer you the position of Executive Assistant to the Dean."

Her jaw drops, and she blinks at me wordlessly.

"Before you tell me that doesn't sound like a promotion, I assure you, it is. Since my ex's departure, the admin pool in the office is thin. You would report directly to me, oversee the few staff we have currently, and if we need to allocate more resources, you would hire them."

Channing still doesn't speak.

However, our bean slinging friend looks at her with excitement. "I bet it comes with a raise, Chan! And you hate the people in PR."

"Thanks for ruining my bargaining leverage, Slade," she snaps. Her features soften immediately and she gives him a fond expression. "Slade and I were here as undergrads. I went to work, and he stayed in school forever like an over-educated Peter Pan."

Were they...?

Before I can ask, he cuts in. "Channing liked to hang out with my roommate and I—we had a standing board game night with a few other students."

"Oh," I say, not sure why it makes me happy to hear they weren't involved. The roommate bit was a little dodgy, though, and I'm not sure if he's being discreet or not. "That sounds fun. I'm more of a card player myself, but I enjoy strategy."

The bell dings again and we all turn to see a handsome bearded man in an expensive suit walk in. His eyes dance as he looks at Slade and I squint, trying to remember where I might have seen this dude before. He seems very familiar and certainly older than a student—he must be a staff member. Channing catches my gaze as I turn back, her eyes sliding to the man in warning.

Interesting...

"We should organize a group game then, Slade," the stranger says as he approaches. "I'd love to host the Dean in our humble abode."

"Iggy, I don't think that's..."

"Maybe that's not a good..."

Channing and Slade speak almost simultaneously and if that wasn't a signal to be cautious, I don't know what is. They both know the professor who joined us and they don't dislike him, but they must suspect his motives. It's excellent information to have because I doubt they'd be this friendly if he was one of Magnus' acolytes, but demurring tells me they know he's got a less-than-generous reason for his offer. When I glance at Slade, his cheeks have flushed and a delicate sniff tells me he's very much attracted to this man. I need more information on this situation and though I can pump Channing later, I also want to observe the potential enemy in a less formal setting.

"I think it's a marvelous idea." I smile coolly at all of them, making certain my true intent isn't reflected in my expression or my eyes. "I'm growing weary of spending my nights working alone. A small gathering would be most welcome, Prof...?"

"Ignatius Briarton, but my friends called me Iggy. You probably haven't gotten to the Wizardry & Witchcraft department in your research yet. The sports programs are in the most peril and resolving that will take intense focus, so you'll get familiar with the other staff once you're free to dig into their programs," he replies with practiced nonchalance.

He's pretending it didn't bother him that I didn't know him, so I know his ego will be a substantial source of power over him. Either courting it or popping it will make it easy to get what I want from Iggy and I'll start by showing him that his charming exterior isn't phasing me. "That is very true, Ignatius. I am eager to expand my knowledge about State U and perhaps the three of you can give me your perspectives when we meet for the game night."

"I'm sure we can." His brows furrow when I don't call him Iggy and I know my gambit worked. "Channing, if you're going to take over our Dean's schedule, get started as soon as possible so you can book our little party."

Channing rolls her eyes, completely unbothered by his knowledge of a conversation that occurred before he was in the building. "Iggy, you'll hear from me when I've settled and reviewed the current commitments. Now, both of you, shoo. The Dean and I have private matters to discuss. Turn off any objects and go away."

My grin widens as she stands up to the guys and their reactions tell me she doesn't normally do so. Perhaps my influence or the power of working for me gave her strength, but I like it. "She's right. I appreciate the invite and the service, Slade. But we do need privacy."

"Okay, Morgana. Just wave if you need a refill," Slade says as he grabs Iggy's arm and tugs him back towards the counter.

It's not a date, but that was definitely headway in finding people who might not rat me out for the price of a tea bag.

ONLY AN HOUR WAS NEEDED TO FINALIZE THE DETAILS with Channing.

I wasn't surprised that she balked at first, but as soon as Professor Ignatius zeroed in on me, my new assistant jumped in with both feet. She's going back to her office to pack up and I'm headed back to mine to make lists. Channing suggested I send the emails necessary to transfer her and then create lists of the things I want her to focus on based on how soon they need to be accomplished. I'm not sure that thirty-sixty-ninety-one hundred eighty day lists will make the things we need to do *less* intimidating as she proclaimed, but rather than sift through all this shit myself? I'll try whatever organization method she wants.

Landing on the balcony of my office, I step into my office and head for my desk. I kick off my heels and curl up in the big executive chair, clicking away at the keyboard. It's imperative that I get all the paperwork done before four, so I'll have Channing here tomorrow morning to dig through this backlog of parent emails about the murder. I had to answer the board and law enforcement this morning, so I didn't make even a small dent in the less critical, but no less angry, communications from people who couldn't fire or arrest me.

"Morgana?"

Sucking in a sharp breath, I look around the room in surprise. I'm not usually this careless, but I am running on very little sleep. "Where the hell are you? Better yet, *who* the hell are you?"

With a smirk, Lucas emerges from the fireplace at the opposite end of the room. "I'm hurt. After all the sleepless nights..."

My eyes narrow as I take in the amount of shit I just learned in this three second encounter. One, my goddamned office has a not-so-secret passage in it. Two, I need to get it sealed or install security, plus cameras and a safe for my secure documents. Three, the light of day has *not* discouraged the sexy sports star from pursuing me. None of that is helpful; in fact, I'm certain every bit is downright disastrous.

"Lucas, what made you think sneaking into my office in a secret tunnel would make me happy?"

His grin widens as he stalks across the room like a feline, not a bear shifter. "The part where I'm going to take you to dinner tonight to thank you for protecting me."

For the love of Hera's screeching peacocks...

"Unnecessary. Besides, I had lunch with Channing recently and I won't be hungry until much later. I'm going to make myself something simple when I get home. My workload is too heavy for frequent breaks."

The hockey player shakes his head and comes to a stop inches from me. With my heels off, I'm still not much shorter than him. His eyes are warm as he looks down at me in amusement. "I can cook, you know. My Nana taught me. Nothing fancy, of course, but it'll taste good and I assure you I can bribe someone to get into your house before you arrive home. You might as well consent now and we'll save a lot of time."

I rub my fingers between my brows, then pinch the bridge of my nose. He's basically telling me he won't take 'no' for an answer and if I get this over with, he might get over his mini obsession with me. "Even if I don't get home until like nine or ten? You won't mind then?"

"Scout's honor," he says, holding up two fingers in a salute. "Any allergies? Dietary concerns? Plain dislikes?"

"Pushy ass young dudes who won't listen," I mutter as I step back, needing to put distance between me and the heat emanating from his frame.

His hand catches my wrist and he tsks. "Oh, I *know* that isn't true, Morgana. Now be serious. I'd hate to ruin the evening by making you hurl on my shoes."

Rolling my eyes, I sigh. "Fine. Shellfish and pistachios are no-nos and I prefer red meat to pork or chicken. Is that good enough?"

Leaning in, he brushes his lips against mine so lightly I think I imagine it until he whispers, "That'll do me."

The temptation is too great, and I rest my palms on his chest before pushing him away. "I appreciate your offering to compromise. However, I must return to work."

Lucas pouts, but his eyes betray his actual feelings. "If you say so, ma'am. But when you get home to my amazing meal, that's when work ends. Understood?"

I blink, tilting my head as I consider my answer. 'Normal' Morgana wants to tell him to get fucked, but 'weirdly attracted to a bratty alpha cub' Morgana doesn't want that at all. I feel split in two and not in a good way. So I settle for neutral. "I'll do my best. I can't predict emergencies, but I won't actively get distracted if possible."

"Good girl," he says as he kisses my cheek.

A snort escapes before I can stop it. "Oh, you're barking up the wrong tree with that."

Shrugging, he winks at me. "We'll see."

"What if I don't think *you've* been a good boy?"

He turns and heads for the door, looking over his shoulder before he reaches for the knob. "I'd expect you to do something about it—depending on who wins, of course."

My face turns bright red and I'm *very* glad when he gives me his back again. "Who wins what?"

"The struggle for power, of course. Unclear at the moment, but sounds like a helluva good time." He opens the door and then pauses again. "And lock that damn passage. It's not safe to leave yourself exposed like that."

No shit, Sherlock—I would have done that if I'd known it existed.

Now I get to wonder what other hiding places Magnus had installed in this office, or worse, the house I'm living in.

Great. There goes the idea of sleep for the next week.

whatta man

Getting a maintenance person to let me 'borrow' a key to Morgana's place was both a piece of cake *and* a bargain. I wasn't worried it'd be an issue, but since I crowed about it beforehand, I didn't want to look like an idiot. Thankfully, she didn't level the playing field by putting some sort of memo out to deter me. Honestly, I don't blame her for holding back—finding me in her house hours later will confirm her fears about her safety here.

I'm glad I got it, but not happy when I think about it that way.

Shaking off the odd sensation of worry, I step inside the old house and look around. The decor screams the influence of the previous owner and that has to suck. Morgana's stuff is likely being shipped from overseas and she can't very well spend vast amounts on upgrading the house she's staying in without looking like Magnus' version two-point-oh. That means she's stuck in this weird *Indiana Jones* nightmare the former dean called his own. It's stiflingly old world masculine and even I feel the misogyny leaking from the walls.

"Gross," I mutter to myself as I explore the front hallway and adjacent rooms. "This guy has his own fucking award room masquerading as a formal living room. Hell, even I don't display every award someone has ever handed me like this."

Turning away from the 'tiny dick' area, I walk through the dining room to find a gorgeous kitchen. The setup here is far nicer than one would assume an educator would have in their university accommodations. SubZeros, professional ranges and ovens, and marble with polished chrome make this room the least objectionable I've seen so far. At least it doesn't feel like a good old boys smoking room—this feels like a setup that had a paid staffer working and cleaning it. Fuck, that dragon bilked the shit out of this place. Morgana will struggle to fix the accumulated errors in her audit.

Which means she'll have to deal with living in this nightmare, whether she likes it or not.

I'm not fond of that idea. In fact, I sort of hate it and I don't know why. Frowning as I open the fridge to find leftover takeout containers, condiments, and very little else, I sigh. The only time I find empty food storage like this is when I select high-powered women who don't have the funds for staffers to make sure this doesn't happen. I'm not knocking a driven career gal; I find the clash of dominance hot. But they seem to run everything in the world like a well-oiled machine and treat themselves like shit. I don't know if society ingrains that in chicks or not, but I'd be surprised if it didn't.

I need help, as this plan won't suffice. Deciding to figure out what else needs done to make this night what I envisioned, I walk into the living room and note that the huge couch is made up with linens and pillows. She's sleeping here rather than the goddamned bedroom, for fuck's sake. Those assholes on the board must not have even cleared out the private spaces in this museum to Magnus' massive ego.

Fuck this. I'm calling in the big guns.

I open my phone and click a contact as I take the stairs two at a time. The need to verify the abusive behavior of the people who sentenced Morgana to her exile here thrums in me as I listen for the voice to answer. When the line opens, I'm stepping into a bedroom that is massive and has the scent of... things I don't want to imagine. As a shifter, I'm well acquainted with powerful scents, even long after the people are gone. I don't know how sensitive gargoyles or gorgons' noses are, but if she can smell *any* of this, I know why she's not living in this damn room.

"Nana!" I cut her off as she fires questions about the murder and how Thorne handled himself. "That's all fine for the moment. There's something important I need to talk to you about."

The silence on the other end isn't unusual, so I let it sit as she recalibrates her thought process. "If that changes, I expect to be notified, Lucas. Your mother and father aren't concerned with how their actions affect our family name, but you have always been more flexible."

I snort. My mother and father could give a red, randy fuck what I do or what she wants—that's why they aren't the heirs apparent of the Wolfenberg fortune. "Yes, Nana. But I have a situation here and I doubt you'd be pleased to hear about it. In fact, despite the notoriety of the person, you'd still be horrified to know what those morons have done."

"Does it reflect poorly on us, Lucas?" Her tone is flinty, and I can see the look in her eyes without actually seeing her.

"I believe so. You can judge for yourself." I take a breath and steel myself for her reaction. "The Dean's house is filled to the brim with Magnus' old belongings. It's mostly clean, but has not been deep cleaned, and the bedrooms stink of his affairs. Whether or not Morgana broke the law, the board left her to wallow in his filth and betrayal. They haven't provided adequate housing, food service, or staff to clean. This place is disgusting and you wouldn't even take your gloves off if you walked in, Nana."

Again, the line goes quiet. Finally, she asks, "Why are you in the Dean's home, Lucas?"

I expected it to be a problem. I'll have to carefully dodge her radar.

"She refused my generous offer to take her to dinner for her help last night because she needed to work. I countered with another option—cooking for her at her house so she could work on her tasks. However, once I got someone to let me in, I was aghast. This is not the image we would want portrayed should someone slip pictures to the media, Nana. I knew I had to call you."

Hopefully, that was obsequious enough. I don't want her knowing that I'm interested in Morgana, or she'll shut me down immediately. The possibility of scandal would make her send someone to spy on me or the dean without batting a lash. I need her to believe I'm concerned about our image in the press and she'll move mountains. Luckily, I'm skilled at getting Nana to buy what I sell because I'm the one who follows her rules—mostly.

"Hmmmph. I find that unacceptable as well. If some paparazzo broke in, they'd slaughter us in the press." I hear fingernails tapping as she thinks. "Plan to fix this, Lucas—get it done immediately, no matter what it costs. Please supervise the necessary account charges. Spare no expense."

Whew. She didn't figure me out.

"I'll handle it, Nana. Thank you for putting your faith in me."

"Mmmm," she says. Another pause and then the ice creeps into her tone. "Lucas, I am well aware Morgana LeCiel is an exquisite woman. You'd do well to keep this professional, but I know you have a mind of your own with chasing skirts. Don't do anything to embarrass me and keep me apprised of any information I should know. Do you understand?"

I swallow hard, fighting the urge to protest. Besides being uncomfortable talking about my sex life with my fucking grandmother, I'm a little disturbed by her willingness to put a stamp of approval on me sleeping with Morgana if it provides insider knowledge. Growing up in old families is more ridiculous than outsiders could ever fathom and if they knew the weird shit we get thrown at us from the time we can be leveraged, it would shock the shoes off most supes.

"Understood, ma'am. I'll make sure I am keeping you updated on anything I learn while I oversee the renovations of the house."

"Excellent. Now, I must go. I have a conference call with Zurich in thirty minutes, and I'd like to gather my thoughts before Hans pops up on the screen. *Auf Wiedersehen*, Lucas."

She hangs up without another word, and I blink. It never fails to surprise me when Nana peaces out before I can respond. The woman doesn't waste a second, no matter who it's with.

Now I have to contact people to start this process or she'll skin me alive.

I CHECK MY WATCH IMPATIENTLY AS I STIR THE SAUCE. It didn't take long to get in touch with my grandmother's assistant, and she could send me contact details for personal shoppers in the area. Once I found one willing to make emergency runs to several locations and drop things off as they were purchased, I built a list of necessary kitchen and personal items that I felt would be the most urgent needs. I could have had food delivered, I suppose, but I promised to cook for her and not doing it myself felt a bit like cheating.

It's entirely unlike me to care what a woman thinks of my integrity, especially one I haven't so much as laid a finger on yet. This is an odd experience for me, but something about Morgana makes me want to impress her, and now that I've wormed my way in, I don't want to fuck it up.

Of course, cooking her dinner isn't really 'in', but it's close enough to give a shit.

The shopper delivered the food first, as requested, and I loaded up the fridge while I was making the caprese salad. Once that was chilling, I prepped the bolognese so it could simmer. My au pair was Italian, and I spent much of my younger years watching her cook when my parents were off doing whatever the hell they were doing at that point. A nice bolognese, pasta, and bread will be filling and the tiramisu I made afterward is just showing off, honestly. I could have gone much simpler or even more complex, but I have extremely mixed feelings about how I want Morgana to perceive me.

In the front hallway, there are boxes with linens, cleaning supplies, and other things I left alone because the service I contracted will show up tomorrow afternoon to disinfect this entire place. I didn't want to piss Morgana off by having it done while she wasn't here—I have the feeling there's only so much alpha asshole stuff I can get away with and changing her space without permission might be over the line. Despite the infamy the trial granted her, I feel she's intensely private. Invading what little autonomy she has here wouldn't win me any points.

Looking at my watch again, I resist the urge to call the office and see if she's on her way. The anxiousness I'm feeling is so unusual that it's making me hyper; I just don't get attached to women like this. Is it because she's so much older or because of something else I haven't put my finger on yet? From the minute I saw her at the arena, there was a magnetic pull and I haven't been able to back away since. If she wasn't such a dicey prospect in terms of publicity, I'd ask Nana if she knows why I feel like this. She's always been my source of information about my powers and abilities—my parents were never around. But I can't mention it because Morgana is off-limits in more ways than one.

I wish I gave a fuck about friends—maybe that'd help.

Hangers-on and sycophants follow my family around, though, so I've never let anyone in. I'm tight with the guys on whichever team I'm on at the moment—up to a point. I can party with them, grieve losses with them, and even travel with them, but I don't give them access to the real me. Mistakes in my childhood that lead to disaster taught me that having a famous name with a huge inheritance rarely gains you loyal companions. People who want to absorb your light surround you, use your name, or benefit from your ability to pay for things, but when you need someone, they're a ghost.

So I don't have a single soul to call and ask if they know why I'm so damned mixed up about a woman I met yesterday. All I can do is watch my bolognese and grit my teeth as I wait for her to walk through the front door.

That blows goats in a big way.

As if by magic, that door opens and I hear a muttered 'what the fuck' that makes me grin. I reduce the sauce heat and proceed to the hallway. Morgana looks at me with wide eyes, taking in the apron and spoon in my hand in surprise. I wink at her playfully, hoping it will deflect her grumpy reaction to the boxes. "Told you I could get in. Hopefully, you don't mind, but I sort of had to take over your kitchen."

Her eyes narrow. "This pile of shit isn't all for the kitchen. What is this?"

I wait until she takes off the towering heels, placing them next to others in a row by the door. Next, she places her leather messenger bag on the side table, along with her keys, and tugs the hair tie out of her hair. Watching her shake the long locks out with a sigh makes my cock throb, but I ignore it for the moment. There's plenty of time for that later. "Imagine my shock at discovering this house wasn't properly cleaned and packed up prior to your arrival. I pulled a few strings and had a few delivered tonight, but tomorrow the cleaning service will get this place ship-shape while you're at the office."

"I didn't ask for that, Lucas!"

Giving her a firm expression, I shrug. "I know, but you should have. It's disgraceful to shove you in this house full of Magnus' shit and fuck knows what else. That was a purposeful slight by people who should have better decorum and you not complaining stinks of punishing yourself for ending up here. Since I neither believe you need to be punished further nor wish to get petty revenge, I took care of it. Your pride will survive, Morgana."

That seems to stymie her. She opens her mouth, closes it, then opens it again before she actually speaks. "I... I never thought of it that way."

"Well, I did. The minute I explored, I figured out why you're sleeping in the living room and it's not just waiting for your things to be shipped from England." I shake my head and gesture for her to follow me. "It wasn't hard to arrange, and I was happy to do it. Come back and help plate the food so we can eat. You look exhausted."

"Gee, thanks," she mutters as she pulls off the suit coat and hangs it on the bannister.

I was right; she's absolutely smoking hot under those fancy duds.

Letting my eyes roam over her curves, I realize she's not only older and more put together than my typical woman, but also completely opposite in body type. Her height is a major factor; however, her sturdy frame and soft curves are reminiscent of that chick in the human show. She's built like the warrior woman—broad, but feminine. I suppose it's the gargoyle in her; she'd have to support the wings. Those are hot as hell from what I saw when she left yesterday, but I'm curious about her other supernatural attributes. What happens with the stone shit? And I can't wait to see the snakes again... that almost has me giddy.

"Don't be sour. I promise to ogle you the entire time if you lighten up a little."

She rolls her eyes and then pauses, giving me a sincere look. "Your ego doesn't need stroking anymore, but I am grateful for this. It's one of the nicest things anyone has done since I arrived, and I shouldn't let my tired, cranky bullshit prevent me from thanking you—even if I suspect your motives are less than pure."

"Gotta stick a fork in me, don't you, babe?" I tease. She grins a little and nods, so I turn on my heel. "Let's go fill your belly and we can discuss that later."

As long as I can keep that smile on her face, I might actually have a chance.

"So your grandmother basically raised you?" I say as I wipe the remnants of the delicious sauce off of my chin.

Lucas's eyes dance as he watches me. "Yep. My folks are... exactly what one would imagine for trust fund kids who got married. Nana took over, so I wasn't being parented only by nannies and au pairs."

I think about how lonely that would be, especially if he was automatically suspicious of all his peers because of the Wolfenberg family fortune. My brow furrows and I tilt my head. "Why is your name Wolfberg and your grandmother's is Wolfenberg?"

"She's the matriarchal grandmother. And yes, a lot of the families are intertwined from a bunch of inter-marriages centuries ago. It's sort of like two dudes named Travis getting married and having the same name." His grin is playful as he bobs his brows. "I've never been worried about what will happen with that because I told Nana I'm not continuing that bullshit. I'll date or mate or marry with whomever I want and we'll negotiate that when I make my choice."

My face flushes bright red when I realize he's being very purposeful with that information. Obviously, I didn't mean for my curious question to lead *there*, but I'm sure some women fish in that pond early on to test their chances. "I guess I'm lucky my parents were never concerned with family lineage because their money is 'new money.' They never liked Magnus, though, and boy, does my mom love to remind me how right she was."

Lucas reaches over and picks up the chianti bottle, pouring me another glass before he replies. "So she has excellent instincts—that's good to know. How are your parents dealing with the whole... trial and punishment thing?"

Looking down at my plate, I shrug. I've done my best to keep them out of my mess and it's been convenient that they live in that chic retirement community with gates and security. Paparazzi and lookie-loos can't get in and they don't get constantly hounded; it's something I'm incredibly grateful for. "My dad supports me entirely; my mother thinks I should have made better choices. However, they're not disowning me or withdrawing support. Mom is just tired of people quizzing her all the time—gossip and such in their neighborhood. It disrupts her *joie de vivre*, as she calls it."

"Interesting. I wondered why they weren't at the trial—hearing they disagree on their support makes that understandable," he says as he leans back in his chair.

"No!" I shake my head. "I asked them to stay away. Magnus made poor decisions, and I did what I had to. No one besides the two of us should suffer the consequences of those actions."

"Ah, but *you* are the only one suffering, Morgana. He's dead, and you faced all the censure, plus they have sentenced you to cleaning up his fucking mess. How is that fair?" His features tighten and I realize he means it—he doesn't think they should punish me this way.

How odd. No one reacts this way.

I let my gaze move to his hands, then up his arms, and finally to his chest before looking him in the eye. "It's not fair, but neither is life. There's always a price to pay for vengeance; my mother is a witch, and she's been preaching that my whole life. You can have your justice, but you can't run from the blowback."

He rubs his hand over his face and then shakes his head, looking frustrated. "I don't believe you killed the creepy ass fucker just because he cheated on you. I know there's more—which means you're doing penance you don't deserve. It doesn't sit well with me, Morgana."

This fucking guy—it's like he can read me, but he's a shifter, not a mind bender.

"Why do you say that?" I ask as I twirl the stem of my wine glass nonchalantly.

Pushing to his feet, Lucas stands and holds a hand out. I try to ignore the urge to do as he wants, but my body has a mind of its own. When I'm standing in front of him, mere inches from his frame, the polar bear shifter brushes the hair away from my face as he looks down at me. The heat from our bodies is making me tingle and I have to actively work to keep my eyes open. It's been so long since... everything. I haven't been this close to a man since well before the trial.

"Because something about you clicks for me, Morgana. I don't know why, but the minute you walked into the locker room, it slid into place. It was damn near impossible to focus on the dead body and the goddamned police station for all those hours." His hands land on my waist, tugging me forward until I'm pressed against him in a way that makes it impossible to misconstrue how he feels.

"Lucas," I say as I put my palms on his chest. "Maybe it's the thrill of something forbidden. You're young, and based on how you behave, I doubt you've really had many serious—"

A hungry kiss cuts off the flow of my protests and my arms slide up behind his neck of their own volition. Our tongues tangle and teeth clash as the pent-up tension between us is finally unleashed. Large hands slip from my waist over my ass to my thighs and he lifts me up without the slightest bit of effort. My brain screams 'bad idea,' but my thighs wrap around his hips and squeeze. I can feel his erection through my thin suit pants and even though I know better, I rock against him as we kiss until we're breathless.

I've never been good at listening to my logical inner voice—it's what landed me here.

When our lips break for air, my eyes meet his and something in his gaze entrances me. The creatures inside of me practically purr with approval—and neither of them is the purring type. Blood and gore, yes, but kitten-ish satisfaction? That's a new one for me. I lick my swollen bottom lip, our harsh pants the only noise in the room as we continue looking at one another as if hypnotized. The stand-off finally ends when I whisper, "What is happening to us?"

His laugh is part humor and part growl as he bears semi-elongated canines at me. "Fuck if I know, Morgana. This shit doesn't happen to me. I don't lose control."

"I lose it all the time," I reply as my fingertips brush over the hairs at the back of his neck. "But... this isn't that."

"No shit." He rests his forehead on mine with a rumble in his chest. "I want to devour you. But that's not all."

I tilt my head, trying to ignore the crawling under my skin that indicates one of my supe sides wants me to shift. "Then what, Lucas? What else do you want?"

The smile that curves his lips up is sinful. "Other than to strip you naked on the island and make you scream? Hell if I know, Morgana.

I'm a one night carnival and the rides don't close; that's as much as I can promise you. But at least I'm honest."

It's sad that's a step up from anything I've had recently.

"And if I want to climb on the Tilt-A-Whirl tonight? What then?" I look at him through my lashes, my expression unsure. "You plaster it all over the internet to draw attention away from the impending murder charge?"

He snorts, backing me into the counter he just mentioned and pinning me there. "No. What we would do here is no one else's business and we enjoy every second until it's over."

Closing my eyes, I savor the feel of a hard body and equally firm cock pressing against me. It's been so very long and I don't allow myself the luxury of taking what I need very often. Except for my vengeance, I haven't given myself permission to enjoy anything since I discovered Magnus' treachery.

Aren't I owed just a little pleasure in this never ending punishment I'm living?

"Okay," I breathe as I lean back on my hands, bracing on the marble countertop. "You win, Lucas."

A purely masculine laugh escapes his lips as his hands grasp my thighs and lift me onto the cold island with ease. "Oh, no, Morgana. Trust me when I say *you win.*"

His hands knead my legs through the suit pants before he uses his palms to push my shoulders until I'm reclining on my elbows, looking up at him. Dipping his head, he nuzzles my breasts through my shirt and uses his hips to bump my legs apart. Teeth tug at my nipple through the thin button down and I let my head fall back on my shoulders as his mouth wets the fabric while he plays. A low throb builds in my pussy as he works his way down my body until he drops to his knees and yanks my hips forward to the edge of the counter.

"Lucas..."

"Shh." His fingers work the buttons of my slacks and he lifts me a little to tug them over my ass to drop them on the floor. "I'm busy."

I'd argue, but since his teeth are tugging my lacy thong down while he holds me up, I can't say he's mistaken. My ass hits the cool stone when he lowers me and warm hands spread me open so he can blow lightly over my bare mound. The juxtaposition of the temperatures makes me shiver, and he turns his head, sinking his teeth firmly into my inner thigh.

How he knew I'm a sucker for teeth, I have no idea.

"Baby likes to be marked. Good to know," he murmurs before nipping and suckling at the tender skin leading up to the juncture of my thighs eagerly.

"Uh-huh."

When his mouth hits me, I know I'm damn near dripping. Lucas might be young, but he's got skills. His tongue traces along the seam of my pussy, then further back to my entrance, drawing a low, dark moan out of me. My core clenches when he finally flicks the tip of his tongue over my clit and he growls softly in response. His tongue traces circles around the aching nerves, teasing me in a way I've never experienced before. At least, not without the help of a toy. I've dated a handful of men over the centuries and I haven't met one yet who seems to enjoy this activity like the hungry bear in front of me.

But I can't tell him that; it would be far too pathetic to admit.

"You taste like spicy peaches," he mutters. I open my mouth to scoff, but that falls out of my mind completely when he thrusts two thick fingers inside of me as he continues torturing my clit with patterns and licks that make my thighs tremble.

My back arches off the counter and I can't help but rock into him, letting the jolts of pleasure rocket through me. Between teeth, tongue, and fingers, the sensations assault me and melt every protest and worry from my brain. It doesn't take long before I realize I'm going to come—and hard—all over his face and hand. Wiggling a little, I try to push him off so he can fuck me, but he holds firm. There are definitely going to be bruises on my hips from his firm grip because he will not let go until I...

The orgasm that slams into me takes me by surprise and I let out a strangled scream, grasping at air with hands that have shifted into dark, charcoal claws unbidden. I know my skin color is changing and I vaguely hear the low hiss of the girls emerging, but my body is shaking with the intensity of the climax Lucas pulled from him. He laps up the juices slowly, as if savoring me, and then places an oddly gentle kiss at my apex before he lifts his head to snarl.

"By Odin's beard, Morgana... you're..."

I flush, knowing that the dark gray color of my skin as it partially shifted paired with my hair writhing under me is weird and unattractive. That's what I've always been told, especially by Magnus, and I want to wrap my arms around myself to hide it all in shame. "I know; I'm sorry. I lost control and I can't..."

"Oh, no. Baby, don't you *dare* cover an inch of yourself. You're fucking stunning."

What?

"I..."

A loud growl echoes out of his chest and before I can find the words, his clothes drop to the floor and he's yanked me against him in a way that tells me he's not lying. His cock is pressing against my entrance and I have to strain not to rock until it fills me. "Clean? Pill?"

Swallowing hard, I nod. "Yes."

His grin is feral as his hips slam forward, and our bodies are joined. I'm more full than I've ever been and for a moment, I wonder exactly how big my one and done shifter is. My questions float away when he leans down and bites the juncture of my shoulder hard, causing me to whine in pleasure. He likes that and his hips withdraw, swirling the tip of his cock around briefly before he thrusts into me again, hard. I shudder, enjoying the opposing sensations as he repeats the motion over and over. He doesn't let go of the bite, even when the snakes hiss and snap above him.

Motherfucker, this boy is goddamned perfection.

My hands lift and claws rake down his back as we pant, and our hips slap together wildly. I dig in harder and he lets out a dark growl that says his own beast is close to the surface. I have no idea what that would look like, but if he keeps fucking me like this, I don't care. Every time his hips piston and he buries his cock in me, it feels like it's going deeper. When my walls flutter around him, I let my head fall back on my shoulders again and bury one hand in his shaggy hair.

"Lucas, I'm gonna come," I breathe, squeezing my hips on the outside of his thighs hard as the tremors zing through me like electricity.

His answer is another primal sound, and he stays right where he is, holding on as I drop over the edge and his cock swells inside of me. The waves of pleasure make my gut tighten and he finally lets go of the bite to throw his head back with a roar that vibrates over my skin. His body pins me in place as sweat rolls down my spine and my breathing hitches. Something about the way our bodies are connected, and he's buried inside of me, keeps me still as the colors behind my eyes slowly fade.

The room is silent for a few moments and I hear him mutter under his breath in a weird, gravelly voice. "Mine."

My lips curve and I decide not to correct him—after all, he did just rock my world off of its axis.

His head dips and he pins me with darkened pupils, his large bear canines poking out of his normal mouth oddly. "We're in deep trouble."

working bitch

Lucas and I spent the next couple of hours cleaning up the kitchen mess, and by the time we finished, it was less awkward. He was quiet and despite my penchant for frankness, I couldn't bring myself to ask what the hell he'd meant by 'we're in trouble.' It was obvious the situation rattled him, but Magnus and his antics left my self-esteem in tatters. My fear mightily outweighed the need to know if I'd done something wrong—after all, what the fuck did I know about polar bears or their sexual habits?

I'm not inexperienced, but I didn't spend three hundred years getting dipped by every species out there, either.

When everything was righted, he walked over, pressed a kiss to my forehead and told me he'd see me later. Not the worst brush off ever, but also not the kindest 'thanks for the good time' I've received. I gathered my clothes up and headed to the first floor bathroom for a shower. That lasted far longer than it should have because I kept drifting off into space and the only thing that pulled me out of the trance was the water turning cold. I dried off and headed for the nest on the couch, tucking myself in with numb limbs and a heavy heart.

Getting up this morning wasn't easy, but I packed up my breakfast, snacks, and a huge tumbler of coffee so I'd be able to stay in my office as much as possible. Since I had no idea if my indiscretion was all over the campus, I wanted to make certain I could hide out. Plus, that plan had a bonus of preventing me from running into my one night fuck-up. Staying busy with work and putting Lucas Wolfberg in my rear-view mirror is for the best.

That decided, I finished getting dressed in my sharpest black pinstripe Zegna suit, a killer pair of heels, and a high ponytail that said 'all busi-ness' before I left for the comfort of my cloistered office.

Hopefully, Channing beat me here, and she's already cleaning up the mess that is my fucking calendar.

I WAS RIGHT TO ASSUME MY NEW ASSISTANT WOULD HAVE things well underway when I arrived. Coming in at nine is late for me, but when I saw the progress made in the office, I knew Channing had arrived hours earlier. She cleaned out the desk of Magnus' old gatekeeper, reorganized the waiting area, and had neatly stacked papers waiting on my desk. I peeked at them for a moment before looking for the efficient elemental in the copy room next to her office. She was humming under her breath as she made collated copies of what looked to be various forms, stacking them cross-wise as they spit out of the heavy duty machine.

"Channing?"

Jumping a foot in the air, she turned and pushed her glasses up with a surprised expression. "Oh! Dean! I didn't hear you come in over this thing. Good morning."

Smiling to myself, I lean against the door frame, nodding at the papers. "What are those?"

"The assistant previous to me didn't have a recognizable filing system. As I went through her files, it appeared protocols for most things weren't being followed and I'm sure that contributed to the situation they sent you here to address. I'm setting up the system so that going forward, we do everything legitimately." She pauses for a moment and tilts her head. "Is that okay?"

"Of course it is! I'm grateful that you are familiar with the correct procedure, to be honest. Having someone who can execute and monitor the paper trail is significant going forward. Fixing the mess left by those who didn't, intentionally or unknowingly, will be a nightmare for me. Speaking of which, what are the stacks on my desk?"

Channing presses a button on the machine, stopping its progress. She turns on her heel, gesturing for me to follow, and we head into my office. Picking up the stack on my desk, she lays them out one by one as she explains. "These are expenditures already approved for review, these are additional requests, these are parental communications I will respond to after you make notes, and the last one is personnel files for the remaining admin staff in this office. Once you review their information and give your opinion, I'll decide who stays and who goes. That will allow me to build a new team."

I blink as she fires off the different paperwork. This isn't even a dent in what she has for me, I'll bet, but it's what she wants me to look at first. "Okay. I'll settle in and focus on these tasks until lunch. If you need me, just pop in and I'll pause. Does that work?"

"Of course! That's *exactly* how it should work, in fact." She looks at me for a moment, squinting. "Are you okay this morning? Something seems... off. Did you sleep poorly? Shall I order more coffee?"

"I'll always accept coffee, Channing. However, you're right—my night was fitful and I'm still debugging my hard drive, so to speak. Don't worry; I'll be okay once I get enough caffeine in me."

"I'll go order a delivery and make sure it's strong." She gives me a mock salute, and I chuckle as she heads out quickly.

Well, at least one decision I've made since I arrived isn't a disaster.

Dropping into my desk chair with a heavy sigh, I kick my shoes off under the desk and fold myself into a pretzel in the chair. Thinking about last night makes my head and my body throb—for different reasons. I still don't know what happened with Lucas or why everything came to an abrupt halt. At times like this, I wish I'd dated around more than I did. I was always so focused on my career and rising in the ranks at Swallowtail that I looked at sex more as a physical need than an emotional one. Before Magnus, I only dated seriously a handful of times and most of them were more towards the magical or mythical end of the species spectrum—not the more animalistic shifters—so I'm lost.

It would be easier if every damn supe type didn't have their own weird sexual habits and behaviors, but I guess that's not realistic, is it?

I pick up the first pile of papers, hoping to distract my wandering mind with the approved expenditures. I'm sure the things that were approved before I arrived will anger me and maybe it will keep me from thinking about the affair that was *supposed* to be a fling. Squinting at the first page, I see an outrageous amount of money allocated to new football uniforms. I'm not stupid enough to even consider messing with *that* budget yet; it's a hornet's nest of alumni, coaches, and very involved families that have been around since this place was founded.

That means this page just gets a checkmark in the top right corner and I move on. Gradually, I tackle the pile of invoices, occasionally frowning at a few. Most of it makes sense and though I believe they could save money by exploring different vendors, I can justify a good number of the various expenses. However, a few literally scream 'something is wrong here,' and *those* I set aside to submit to the forensic accountant the board gave me access to. Either the amounts or descriptions tweaked my suspicions, and by the time I read through the details, I knew there was a problem. However, I need experts to verify this before using it against anyone.

I won't make many friends here by the time I'm done cleaning house.

My brows furrow and I put the papers down, opening the laptop on my desk. Everything about my life now is depressing—I can't even get laid without it becoming a giant mess. That brings me back to Lucas and the weird behavior and I drop my head to my desk, banging it on the wood in frustration. I am *not* a clingy, easily attached woman; this has to be a function of the damage my asshole ex did. Never in my life have I been this obsessed with a random person I banged and I can *not* figure out why it's happening now. The timing is shit and I have to get myself together.

But how? I'm sure as hell not contacting him first.

With a low growl, I open the browser, ducking under the VPN I installed so I can browse with no trace. Perhaps some research will ease my worries.

THE TIME FLIES BY AS I SCROLL THROUGH THE VARIOUS sites looking for information on various supes and their proclivities. I have to pick through the listings so I'm not hitting accidental porn, but it's a lot to take in even without moaning people on the screen. I suddenly feel sheltered and naïve, considering my age. My relationships in the past were with a dragon, a warlock, a vampire coven, and twin demi-gods. Nothing they did seemed out of the ordinary for the sex ed I received in school and their kinks were pretty standard.

According to the internet, I've been missing out. Animal shifters have widely varied behaviors even before you throw in shifting. Fae are a smorgasbord of species related shit. All that is before I even get to the more rare mythical creatures like sirens, oracles, hounds, or phoenixes. Putting my face in my hands, I feel color rushing to my cheeks as I try to process exactly how stupid I feel at the moment. Worst of all, I'm no closer to finding out why Lucas got wigged out.

Morgana LeCiel, accept there are things you aren't an expert in and deal with it.

My inner voice of reason is right, but that doesn't mean I like it. Intelligence was highly valued in the world I grew up in and I feel like the class dunce at the moment. It's sitting like a stone in my gut and I don't know what to do with that. My usual method won't work here. On the surface, it sounds like a fun challenge, but I know it would bring more trouble to my doorstep.

Plus, it wouldn't change whatever happened last night, even if it helped me understand. I rub my temples as anxiety plagues me, hoping to calm my nerves. My life is in such shambles since the truth about Magnus came out and nothing I do balances it out. It's like I'm damned if I do and damned if I don't. I hate it and I want off this fucking merry-go-round of bullshit.

I need space, and I need it now.

I push the button on the intercom, hoping it's set up the way it should be. I've not used it yet, so hell if I know. "Channing?"

"Yes, Dean?"

"First, call me Morgana. Second, I'm stepping out for a bit. I need some air, but I'll be back. The stack of reviewed, approved expenses is sitting on the left corner of my desk. The ones next to it are the ones I need to look into."

"Got it. Have a pleasant break, Morgana."

I shake my head at her chipper tone and slip my shoes back on. Heading out onto the balcony, I touch my amulet and take off as soon as my wings escape.

The sky is my safety, and that's where I'm headed for a while.

do my own thing

"Kaspar, is that what I think it is?"

My bodyguard narrows his eyes and looks up to see what I'm pointing at. The shadow gliding through the air in the clouds continues on its way, but my old friend grunts in his typically grumpy fashion. "Yes. It appears to be the new Dean, Prince Liam."

I roll my eyes at his insistence on formality in public. It's annoying as hell and I can't get him to budge, even when I try ordering him not to act like he has a stick up his ass. "She has an impressive wingspan. I've met gargoyles of all sizes and shapes, but seeing one backlit against the afternoon sun makes her form a little awe-inspiring."

"She's not that big." Kas shrugs as he looks around. "I'm not worried."

I wasn't saying he should be worried; even if the woman murdered her ex-fiance, I don't think she'd risk execution for harming a prince from the Daybreak Court.

"You assume everything is a threat, old friend. Sometimes, it's nice to simply enjoy the scenery."

The storm dragon snorts, shaking his head. "That's not my job, Prince."

"Kas, you're only five years older than me. Your brother and I went to Miyako together. Stop acting like some hotshot bodyguard and be *normal,*" I chide. This time he rolls his eyes at me and I walk towards the Humanities building again. "You know, my parents chose State U for the safety it offered. A Masters in Poli Sci would be much more meaningful from Harvard or Yale, but SU has both the best supe politics professors and a mostly non-human student population. We *should* be okay on campus."

"Yeah, well, tell that to Pierre LaMount," the dragon says with a pointed look. "A murder happened on the first day, Liam. Your father was mistaken about this place. Something in the air makes my circuits crawl."

His infamous 'circuits' are Kaspar's way of saying the electricity around him feels disturbed. No one really knows how storm dragons can sense things by the change in currents, but it's akin to a seasoned police officer's gut. Unfortunately, my protector and childhood friend is rarely wrong. If he believes there is something going on at State U, it's very unlikely that he's incorrect.

That doesn't mean I'm going to let him snitch to my father, though.

"The death of that hockey player was a shock, but I refuse to allow some insignificant sports rivalry gone bad to derail my education. They gave us clearance to move into the house my parents purchased and that's exactly what we're going to do, Kas." I tilt my head as we approach the classical architecture of the building labeled 'Beauregard Fine Arts.' There's an enormous fountain with a Sphinx sculpture in the middle, and I frown. "It's a bit much, don't you think?"

"Everything here is a bit much, Prince. The supes on this side of the Veil often do things that make me wonder who they're trying to impress."

He's not wrong.

"You realize few dragons refer to Faerie as their side of the Veil, right? You're spoiled, Kaspar." I enjoy teasing him, to be honest. Kas used to be a lot more fun, but that was before he accepted my father's offer to become my royal guard. Now he walks around like he has a stick lodged firmly in his ass and it drives me crazy. We're too young to only care about Court stuff.

"That's the chamber pot calling the toilet a shitter," he retorts. "You're one of the most spoiled dicks I've ever met."

I laugh, gesturing for him to follow as I head up the steps of the building. "Truer words, my friend. I won't bother denying it. Let's get this meeting with my advisor over and we'll head back to the house until dinner. That new Pokemon game is calling my name from afar."

"As you wish, Prince."

"Stop it, asshole."

"Fine. As you wish, Prince Dickface."

I guess it could be worse.

"Were they testing to find out what's being said about the new administration?"

Kaspar nods gravely. "I did. I don't know what the Society was thinking putting that poor woman here, but she's landed in a nest of snakes, for sure. It's best if we keep our distance from it."

Shrugging, I grin a little. "All they accomplished was to make me curious. Everything I've read on social media seems to indicate old Magnus made his bed and shit all over it. Perhaps his death was warranted. Both of our people have blood debts, so we're in a suitable position to understand better than other species."

He snorts and shakes his head. "There are ways to reconcile those in our clan as there are in your courts, Liam. Vigilante justice isn't even accepted in the human world, much less the supernatural."

"Some people deserve what they get, no matter how the retribution lands at their doorstep." My thoughts drift to the Unseelie traffickers who kidnapped my little brother when he was young. It was a scandal, and they never found him. He'd be in his late teens now and my parents' detectives have never gotten close to finding a trail to follow. It damn near destroyed them, but it's been over fifteen years since we lost him. Hope was gone a long time ago. I just wish they'd found his body so my mother could find peace.

"Braden was a different story, Prince. I would slay his kidnappers in a blink if we could find them."

I nod, my expression tight as I look at my old friend. "I know, Kas. I'd help if I thought it would give my mother the closure she desperately needs."

The reminder of a painful past quiets us as we walk across campus. My eyes skate over the landmarks, making miniature map points in my mind as we head towards the back of the main green. The designers of this university wisely included green spaces full of lush foliage for the species who are connected deeply to nature. That bodes well for me as I go about my days here because I cannot stand to be stuck in concrete jungles where the life force that helps feed my powers is not present. That kind of set-up nixed quite a few choices on my list for grad schools, and the bucolic look of State U definitely added to my desire to be here.

"I can't believe they allowed your father to purchase one of the staff housing units. He really is silver tongued," Kas says as we approach the lane leading to the houses.

My lips curve up. "Yes, my father is quite the persuasive old coot when he wants to be. It doesn't hurt that he doesn't look a day over forty despite being well over a millennia old."

The dragon chuckles, giving me a wry grin. "You assume the seller was a woman."

"I do not. I know for a fact the person he dealt with was that idiot Magnus. But I'm sure they offered some sort of payment for 'brokering' and my father has already gone to great lengths to cover up his participation in the ex-Dean's corruption. That's what is so funny about this whole situation—none of the species leaders or royals are innocent of influencing the crooked fool, but they damn sure jumped on the train to indict him."

"Are you worried it will be tied back to you?"

"Not even a little. You know how the King is, Kas. He wouldn't have made the deal if it wasn't completely sealed and covered. The new Dean won't even catch a whiff of Daybreak Court involvement in any schemes. The Knaves leave nothing to chance."

"I hate those fuckers." Kaspar huffs, smoke blowing out of his nose at the mention of my father's secret guards. "Accountable to no one and masked. I don't trust people who won't show their true faces."

This is not the first time we've had this conversation, nor will it be the last.

"I'm not a fan, either. But I have no say in the Knaves' existence until I take the throne," I remind him. "My father loves his troupe of concealed criminals and no one can talk him out of them—not even my mother."

"Your dad is a douche."

"I'm well aware."

I turn to look at him, and we burst into laughter. These are the moments I wish were more frequent. Kaspar is far too serious now and I love when he lets go. It feels normal and when there aren't a bunch of gaping onlookers, there's no reason for him to not drop the act and be my friend. Out of nowhere, he socks my arm, jerking his head at the house we're walking past.

"Dean's quarters," he explains.

So this is where the enigmatic Morgana lives... interesting.

"Who are those people coming and going?" I frown, wondering if this is a scheme by the less-than-friendly staff.

"Looks like decorators? Makes sense. I wouldn't want to live in the cheating, thieving ex I killed's house, either."

I roll my eyes at him as I watch the elves in coveralls hustling in and out. "I guess we won't stop by to say hello today, then. She'll have her hands full when she comes home to this nonsense."

"Liam, we're not stopping by to say hello *ever*. Why do you insist on courting trouble, man? The last thing you need is to have some ridiculous paparazzi sneak on campus and catch you leaving the house of a convicted criminal."

"Don't be such a drag." I pick up my pace as we head down the street, eager to get home where I can let go of my glamor. "Danger is fun and boredom is a mind killer. Besides, we *just* admitted she was likely justified."

"But she went about it the wrong way and you need to stay away from scandal for the next three years, Prince. Your family has enough issues without you bringing negative attention to it." Kas looks exasperated, but I will not let him guilt me into not living my life.

"No press is bad press, dude. Besides, anything to distract the folks from my long gone brother or party-going sisters is probably more of a blessing than a curse. Even my inappropriate behavior is better than anyone else's. My mother said so herself." I stop as we reach our doorstep, batting my lashes at him playfully.

"Mab, save me from spoiled, rotten *brats* with no common sense," he grumbles as he walks up the stairs to clear the house before I enter.

Ignoring him, I look around, making a list in my head of what modifications I want Kaspar to schedule for the front and back yard to accommodate my nature fix. I'll need a lot more vegetation to wander in and I don't give a single fuck if the other people on this street are put off by the impending 'Fae upgrades' I'll be making.

When he finally comes back out, he arches a brow. "It's clear."

"Oh, good. I was worried some evil villain was camped out in the linen closet."

"Liam, shut up and get inside before I shock the shit out of you and haul you in over my shoulder."

I ponder that for a moment. I'm not adverse, but I don't think he's ready to hear *that* yet.

Fae are incredibly flexible with finding pleasure, you see.

i need help

As I glide over the campus, my mind is racing. I'm not sure what the information I found on all the different species means, especially since I've been trying to apply it to my former lovers and coming up short. None of them ever did the things I know their people for around me—a fact that only highlights our relationship defects. Apparently, I wasn't intended for any of them, despite it feeling real. I'm not denying my feelings or those of my exes —well, except the dead fucker—but simple biology seems to say that I've never found my genuine family.

It's both depressing and enlightening, that's for certain.

I still don't know what happened to Lucas. Certain species, including mine, are rare and secretive, resulting in insufficient documentation or verification of their habits. My information quest didn't shed more light on what I should watch for regarding myself, nor polar bears. The latter seemed odd, but since those shifters are tied to an ancient, very influential family tree, it's possible the details are well-guarded. I can't imagine Fraü Wolfenberg or her ancestors wanted people to fake mating behaviors with their family members. It would facilitate several issues with marriages and media, even in the time before the Internet.

My only option now is to seek expert advice. I bank right on the next updraft, squinting at the buildings I'm above. The *Von Lichtenstein Science & Medical Center* looms like a shiny, boxy eyesore at the farthest edge of the northeast portion of the campus. I assume they placed the new building there for ready access to the main roads, allowing transport to the city hospital with ease. What I read about the ugliest structure at State U told me it houses labs, lecture halls, the health center, a morgue, and various fancy-ass facilities in one huge mirrored sub-campus that extends seven levels underground and fifteen floors into the sky.

I hate it already.

It's probably the gargoyle in me, but all the lovely architecture of the rest of the university makes me feel at home and this monstrosity reminds me of L.A. or Singapore. Everything is cold—made of glass, steel, and a soulless design that does nothing for your heart when you look at it. Plus, there's zero places to perch outside of a rooftop and that's a tragedy. At a college with various species of winged creatures and animals, there should *always* be places for us to rest on high. The person who designed this place was a major asshole, if you ask me.

With another grumble of disgust, I pin my wings back and descend. My feet hit the ground a few feet short of the statue in front of the entrance. The post-modern sculpture is some kind of abstract of a DNA molecule in colorful metals and polymers—yet another abomination in construction masquerading as art. I have a distinct feeling this place will be one of my least favorite on campus after the sports stadiums and arenas. As long as nothing shady is going on, I won't mess with their budgets out of bias, but there's no way this high-tech nightmare is operating within its constraints. They will put my face on dartboards in the offices here.

"Good afternoon, Dean LeCiel! Welcome to the *Von Lichtenstein Science & Medical Center*. How may I direct you?"

My eyes widen as a sunny woman beams at me from the screen of an iPad on some sort of Johnny-Five robot contraption. *What in the name of Zeus is this?!* It takes a moment to compose myself and thankfully, the remote assistant chick allows me to do so without interjecting. "Hello. Have we met before?"

"No, ma'am! The *Von Lichtenstein Science & Medical Center* is a state-of-the-art facility. Facial recognition notified us of your entry immediately and Rhoda was dispatched so I could greet you. Since this is your first visit, would it be presumptuous to assume you'd like a tour?"

Facial recog... is she shitting me? How is that even legal?

"Uh, no. I didn't come for an official tour, Rhoda. I'm here to speak with a professor." I tilt my head and paste an imperious glare at the screen. "I'd be interested to know how your software is being used without violating Fourth Amendment rights, though."

The woman blinks and laughs softly. "Rhoda is the robot, Dean. My name is Antares Simone and I'm an executive assistant to the Head of the Science and Mathematics department. All the EAs in this building can access Rhoda when non-program students, staff, or visitors enter the VLSMC. They include disclaimers about the use of the recognition software in legal disclosures when admitted, hired, or entering campus—most people simply do not read the fine print."

That's not sketchy at all. I'll have to review that shit.

"Thank you, Antares. I appreciate your help. Can you direct me to the Shifter Biology professor? I need their expertise." Forcing a smile, I wait. I'm not revealing *why* I want to visit with that educator; this fucking building already has more information than I'd prefer logged in its servers.

Antares nods, clicking on a computer keyboard before turning back to her camera. "Yes, ma'am. Professor Shadwell is in sector two, floor ten, in office number four hundred eighty-two. Her credentials are: B.S. in B&B from Stanford, Masters in Shifter Sciences from Yale, and Ph.D. s in Shifter Zoonotics and Shifter Psychology from State University. The professor has been head of the Shifter Physiology and Sociology department since 1999. Please knock before entering."

I blink. "Thank you?"

"Have a lovely day!"

Rhoda the robot spins in place like a damned Battle Bot and heads back in the direction she came from. I have to physically force myself to walk to the bank of elevators and push the button; that's how astonished I am. When the doors open, I step inside and yet again, I marvel at this damn place. The LED touchscreen on the wall lists the sectors and once I punch in two, it changes to a screen asking which floor. A disembodied voice comes over the speakers, confirming my choices, then advises me to step away from the doors and hold on to the handrails.

What in the Willy Wonka bullshit is this place?

I don't even have time to ask before the elevator takes off like a shot and I'm on my way.

My hands grip the rails as the metal coffin I'm in zips at an impossible speed horizontally, then diagonally, then vertically. The chocolate factory reference was accurate. I marvel at the board's ability to keep this tech a secret. There has to be some kind of goddamned NDA woven into admission and hiring papers just like the damn surveillance release is. I didn't have a choice but to simply sign whatever the Society put in front of me after the trial, but I'd bet my bottom dollar most of the people on this cursed campus don't have a clue they signed away their lives to be here.

What other horrors are in that paperwork?

Resolving to get Channing to dig into it once we get my schedule somewhat normalized, I suck in a breath as the speed increases as we climb up the floors until the screen says 'ten'. The disembodied voice announces our location, gives directions to the office I need, and wishes me a good day before the doors open. When I step out, I have to pause as my equilibrium settles. That fucking thing was like a theme park ride and while I enjoy the hell out of a good rollercoaster, I prefer being prepared for the twists and turns. I didn't know I was riding a death trap, so I'm stunned in place.

Once the world stops spinning, I look at the waiting area. It's fairly normal, though the furniture looks new and comfy. I can't imagine who is left here to wait for appointments, but it must be frequent, because I notice long power strips with various USB and power hubs, along with lap desks resting against a table. Students often come here for quiet or to meet with advisors. Before I go left down the hallway, someone's head pops up from the counter near the closed door.

"Welcome, Dean LeCiel! We have notified Professor Shadwell of your arrival and she will see you at once."

I blink at the tiny shifter in front of me. She looks like a student and I wonder if this is a work study assignment. I haven't seen many possum shifters, but from her scent, I can tell she's not a hybrid. "Thank you. Are you working full time, or is this a work study arrangement?"

Her laugh is adorable, and she appears to climb up on something to make herself taller. "I'm an undergrad in costuming. Most of the work studies on campus place people in the complete opposite area from their specialty because it encourages us to broaden our horizons. Plus, it keeps us honest—or so they say. My name is Beatrice."

"Nice to meet you, Beatrice. I appreciate you explaining that, but I'm afraid I'm still learning all the ins and outs of State U. It's overwhelming to step into a culture where everyone simply *knows* things."

She titters again and nods. "Oh, SU is *definitely* like that. When I started two years ago, I came from further down in the state and man, is it a hard transition. But I love it! Professor Shadwell is amazing. Whatever you need, I know she'll be able to help."

"Thanks, Beatrice." I smile and tilt my head at the hallway. "I don't want to keep her waiting."

"Have a lovely day!"

Is that overly cheerful shit required of everyone who works in this building, or is it just because of who I am?

Sighing as my paranoia gets the best of me yet again, I stride down to the end of the hall where a placard on the door reads, 'Dr. Zuzanne Shadwell, B.S, M.S, Ph.D-Head of Shifter Physiology and Psychology, Professor Emeritus.' I stand there, staring for a moment at the intimidating name plate as I ponder.

Whoa.

Either this woman is going to be a great ally or a really powerful enemy—no one has that much alphabet soup without gathering influence. I raise my hand to knock, but the door swings open quickly and I see a plump woman with smile lines crinkling the corners of her eyes. Her grin is genuine and when she shakes my hand vigorously, I wince. I'm not usually out-squeezed by people, but this lady has meat hooks for hands. I study her for a second, trying to suss out her heritage before I go any further.

"Oh, bother. I did it again, didn't I?" She lets out a bellowing laugh and I look at her with wide eyes. "Sorry! I can't always gauge how strong a shifter is by their species; I should know that, but I can't help trying to guess. It must be the giantess in me—she's a playful sort."

Ah-ha! She's a hybrid.

"Don't worry, Dr. Shadwell. I won't break," I reply as I give her an understanding expression.

"Please! Zuzanne is fine. Come in, come in. I admit to being curious about your visit. You have so many things to do since that blasted group of hoity-toity asskissers sentenced you. I didn't expect to see you in this building for months."

I don't know how to respond. Having someone who dislikes the Society and the Council as much as I do would be nice, but experience has taught me not to trust what I can't verify. I can't verify her allegiance until I do some background searches and though her scent isn't giving off a liar vibe, I'm not putting myself at risk. "I agree. There's *a* lot on my plate. But honestly, I have some questions to ask that landed squarely in your area of expertise. I'll try to be as brief as possible, but I'm helping a student who has questions I'm not able to answer."

"Look at you, adopting stray students already! I can't say I ever saw your predecessor do that unless he could leverage them somehow. I suppose you know that now, though I'm being rude again by mentioning it. Fie on my cursed mouth!" She smacks her fist on the desk and it rattles like it's going to fall apart. "Damn. If I break another one, Facilities is going to grind *my* bones."

This woman is fascinating and I think I might actually like her.

"Well, I'm not offended, Zuzanne. I find bluntness refreshing." Moving to the big chairs in front of her desk, I take a seat and cross my legs. "Let me explain what I need to know before the janitorial staff goes on strike."

Her smile is bright and eager. "Tell me. I am eager to be of help, Dean. You seem like good people."

Looks can deceive, I suppose.

the fear

Practice was so subdued, it might as well have been a book club instead of a hockey team. Frustration at the cancellation of the game and the lack of access to the rink for two days simmered in the air. Coach was terse as he barked orders and watched us scrimmage against our second and third string players. Not-so-subtle looks of suspicion pinged between the guys and me, making my already rankled disposition even more edgy.

I might be new this year, but I've been nothing but a good team member and a hardworking player. They all know I hit the gym daily before dawn and go for long runs that half of them wouldn't be able to keep up on if they joined me. My shifter animal is bulky and large, making my human form larger, but I keep myself in top condition. Playing professionally in leagues that take shifters is a completely different ball game than college level sports, even at a top tier school like State U. Getting soft because I can is not an option, nor is it in my nature.

Nana Wolfenberg doesn't raise lazy assholes—well, except my father, I suppose.

"Wolfberg! Get over here! The rest of you hit the showers!"

The irritated shout comes from Coach as I skate towards the exit, and I roll my eyes. If he tells me I'm suspended until this bullshit is resolved, Nana will go ballistic. He'll be lucky if she doesn't send Thorne and a cadre of lawyers so expensive that one meeting would be equivalent to purchasing a car. On one hand, it would keep me from being benched, but on the other, the pressure on Coach to do what he's told is likely to make my first year miserable.

So I turn, skating over with a quizzical look on my face, hoping that lack of aggression will make him calmer. "What's up, Coach?"

"What was that shit out there? You were holding back, Wolfberg."

Despite my height, I have to look up at the angry Yeti shifter glaring at me. Coach isn't the biggest shifter I've ever met, but he still has a half-foot on my seven-and-a-half feet. "You know why, Coach. With the shit that happened the other night, I didn't want the guys to—"

"Bullshit! You were brought here because of your talent and skill. Downplaying that because of some ridiculous small town dick's accusations doesn't help the team. What helps the team is you playing to your capabilities *without* excessive violence so they realize you're not guilty. They have to trust you for who you are, not some watered down horseshit." Scratching his snow-white beard, Coach Driftwood's icy blue eyes look like cold fire as he stares at me.

Well, I'll be a son of a siren. He's not kicking me off.

Dipping my chin, I nod. "Yes, Coach. I understand."

"Good. If I catch you holding back again, *then* I will bench you. Are we copacetic?" He crosses his arms over his chest and I look at the muscles the size of Yule hams on display. Hopefully, he doesn't intend to use that bulk on any of us if we step out of line. That guy is ridiculously enormous.

"We are, Coach." I conjure up a small smile, hoping it looks sincere.

He can't know that I'm a tumultuous mess inside at the moment. It's not about the stupid Detective—I'm confident the brash Thorne will handle that. The problem leaving me unsettled is what happened last night with Morgana. I haven't been able to wrap my head around it yet and it's making my bear stay just beneath the surface of my skin. The night was full of surprises, but the last part will cause problems.

I have to figure out how I feel, and talk to Morgana before this gets out of hand.

To do that, I need to find someone to talk to about it. Obviously, it can't be Nana and my parents are useless. They'd sell me out to her for the price of a new Rolex, so Dad is out. I don't want rumors to fly around the locker room more than they already are because of LaMount's death, which means my team members aren't able to help. No, the only option I have is to find a third party—someone with no skin in the game who can talk to me about this shit without bias.

Once I get dressed, I'm heading to the Science Building. Is there a professor available for me to ask a hypothetical question to? That would be convenient.

If someone can help me confirm what my animal is telling me, I'll know what to do next.

THIS BUILDING IS AN EYESORE.

Helmut Von Lichtenstein's family has been friends with Nana's since forever, of course, but they've always been a little... showy. They aren't what people in the South would call 'new money,' but they're not ancient wealth like many of the Society board members' lines. That's likely why this place has been upgraded to appear as a hub of future technology and research. Unfortunately, it just looks tacky and soulless instead of fancy.

I open the doors only to be greeted by a weird robot with a tablet mounted on it. My eyes widen when the screen flashes and a woman with horn-rimmed glasses appears. She glances to the side, then turns back to me with a bright smile.

"Hello, Lucas Wolfberg! This is Rhoda, our virtual greeter. How may I direct you today?"

What. The. Actual. Fuck.

Shaking my head at the ridiculousness of using this rather than an assistant at a welcome desk, I give the woman an irritated glare. "I need to see someone in shifter biology—preferably an expert. It's urgent."

The woman behind Rhoda the robot frowns a little as she glances at her screen again. "Oh, dear. It looks like the professor is still at her current meeting. I can send you to her floor to wait."

My patience is stretched thin already, but I nod. "Fine. Who should I see and where should I go?"

"Professor Shadwell is in sector two, floor ten, in office number four hundred eighty-two. Her credentials are: B.S. in B&B from Stanford, Masters in Shifter Sciences from Yale, and Ph.D.s in Shifter Zoonotics and Shifter Psychology from State University. The professor has been head of the Shifter Physiology and Sociology department since 1999. Please wait until you are called."

With another pasted-on smile, the assistant points toward the elevators before the screen goes dark and the robot trundles off. I rub my temples with my hand, annoyed as hell that I'm dealing with some sort of robot instead of a person and I have to wait for the answers I desperately want. Each delay today means less time to apologize to Morgana for my sudden shutdown. Normally, I wouldn't give a shit about peacing out on a one-night stand, but this was definitely *not* that. I didn't understand why I felt so drawn to her until we fucked and that finale cemented the instincts I'd been ignoring—I think. I need to know for certain before I see her again. She'll be furious if I find her and give her a supposition. That is, if she doesn't run for the hills when I broach the subject at all.

This is the worst possible timing.

Stalking over to the elevators, I find the one that says it goes to my destination and hop in. A sign above the buttons tells me to hold on, so I do, and when the damn thing shoots off like a rocket, I almost piss myself. *Hermes on skates. This thing is like a damn space shuttle!* My eyes narrow, irritated that the Rhoda-thing chose not to warn someone who doesn't belong in this building about the damn blast-off. I'd bet my left fang the security people spend their days laughing their asses off at people losing it. This fucking thing is a health hazard.

When it zips across, then up, then diagonal, I'm thankful I haven't eaten in a few hours. I get motion sick at these speeds and the staff in this place is lucky I haven't yakked. The elevator finally jerks to a stop and I stumble out, groaning a little as I drop into one of the big chairs in the waiting room. Suddenly, I'm grateful the professor is occupied —I'd hate to go in there green at the gills and ready to puke my guts up.

It's undignified.

Leaning my head against the back of the couch, I close my eyes and try to get control of my roiling guts. This day has been one disaster after another, including the weird behavior of my team at practice. It's almost like I've got some sort of curse plaguing me, but I know that can't be true. I left Morgana's last night, went straight to my apartment, and then to the rink immediately afterward. I haven't had contact with shit out of the ordinary, so that's impossible. Besides, a bad day doesn't equal magical punishment.

"You look awful!"

I blink, looking around for the source of the sound in confusion. When I don't see it right away, I hold my stomach while I continue squinting at the waiting area. "Who said that?"

A tiny girl comes out from behind the empty desk, her dark eyes wide as she assesses me. "I did. You look very sick. I should call for someone to look at you!"

It takes everything in me, but I shake my head. "No, no. I'll be fine. It's probably just motion sickness from that death trap. Don't call anyone."

"Oh, dear," the shifter frets as she scurries behind her desk and reappears with a bottle of water. She sniffs the air as she comes closer and frowns. "Maybe, but I doubt it. I can smell... something. I really need to get the professor."

Just fucking great. I probably gave Morgana some ridiculous stomach virus, and she's cursing my name as she barfs at her place.

Taking the water, I sip it slowly, looking at her as she twiddles her small hands. She's clearly upset and I don't know what to do with that. I'm not sure why she's so certain, but I may have to humor her before she has a nervous breakdown. I close my eyes and let my head fall back. "Okay. Call whoever."

"Thank fuck," she mutters as I hear her skitter across the floor and climb something. A beep sounds as she uses the intercom, and I vaguely hear her speaking to someone who sounds jolly and exuberant. When she's done, the diminutive girl walks back over to stand near. "Professor Shadwell and her appointment are both coming. They're concerned, too. My kind can smell when there's something off with chemistry and we have some resistance to poison in our bloodstream. That's why they're taking me seriously, if you're wondering."

I wasn't, but good to know.

The sound of footsteps rushing over the carpet fills the air and before I can even open my eyes, a familiar voice gasps, "Lucas!"

Well, now I'm truly fucked—I didn't want to see her until I got answers.

dirty little secret

"Help me get him to my office, if you will, Dean." Zuzanne walks over and puts one arm under the pale hockey player. "Beatrice, if you will call Ignatius and light a fire under him in case this is magical, it would help immensely."

I walk over and give Lucas my arm, biting my tongue when a jolt of energy crawls up my arm when our skin touches. His eyes fly to mine, but he says nothing. I don't know why he's here, but suddenly, I'm very glad whatever is happening to him has picked the perfect location to manifest. He leans heavily on the two of us as we work to get the big bear shifter to the office. I'm glad Zuzanne is at least as strong as I am, because I'm not sure we would have made it otherwise. Once we get there, we dump him on the small couch under her windows and he sprawls out on his back.

"His breathing is heavy," I whisper. My hand comes to my chest and I rub it unconsciously as fear slices through me. Lucas seems to be getting rapidly worse and I have absolutely no idea what to do. Not only is he a student damn near collapse, he's also the grandchild of a Society member and a guy I let get too close the other night. All of those worries are flying around in my head as I stare at the prone form in front of me.

How much worse can I screw up this job before they toss me in jail instead?

Of course, that's not the reason I'm panicking, even if I want to pretend that it is. In reality, I'd come to this building to have a serious conversation with Professor Shadwell about my encounter with Lucas last night, even if I didn't tell her my questions applied directly to me. What she told me was concerning enough, but now I have the subject of my research laying on a couch looking like death warmed over. As if he can hear my thoughts, Lucas opens his eyes and gives me a sheepish expression. His posture is so haggard that I can't stop myself from grabbing a chair and dragging it over next to him.

"Morgana, if you could ask him a few questions about his day while I grab some supplies from the closet?" Zuzanne's request pulls me away from blue eyes, and I nod. She bustles out the door, leaving us alone for the first time since our tryst.

Lifting my hand, I push sweaty strands of hair off of his face gently. "So... tell me where you've been today. It's important, I guess."

His eyes close as he murmurs, "I shouldn't have left."

Not the time, my guy.

"Lucas, we can get into that later. Zuzanne wants to know your whereabouts and activities. You appear unwell. Let's address one issue at a time. I promise we will talk once you're well."

That seems to help him focus, and he coughs, then nods. "Okay. I got up and had breakfast at my house. Then I went to practice. Coach talked to me for a bit afterward and then I came here. I haven't done much, honestly."

"Why did Coach Driftwood need to talk to you?" I ask curiously.

"The team is not gelling due to the incident in the locker room. Typical 'be a leader' shit," he mumbles before a shiver runs over him. "Damn. I never get cold."

I can't help it; I snort. Of course he doesn't; he's a fucking polar bear! "Well, you seem very ill, and it might be related to that. If you ate at home and didn't go anywhere but the rink, I don't think it's something slipped in your food."

"Where was your water bottle, boy? Left unattended on the sidelines?" Zuzanne returns with a disapproving expression. "If so, it could have been dosed anytime. Now, *why* is it a bit more complex, hmm?"

My mouth drops open and I look up at her as she brings over a bunch of medical equipment. "You think someone *poisoned* him?"

"Perhaps. It could be some sort of hex or enchantment as well, but I'm not taking any chances with Fraü Wolfenberg's favorite grandson." Her expression is fierce and I wonder if she knows Lucas's grandmother or is just aware of who he is. "So we're going to assume it could be and act accordingly. That's why I had Beatrice call Iggy."

Iggy? Like Slade's Iggy? Fuck me.

"Lucas, why would someone target you in this way?" My brow furrows as I consider it, and I can feel him squeezing my hand. I don't want to admit how good it feels, so I keep my reaction to myself.

He shrugs the other shoulder. "Take your pick, Dean. LaMount's murder, my spot on the team, something to do with Nana, some bullshit my parents pulled, or maybe even... something to do with my personal life."

Horror washes over me as I realize he means someone might know about our night together and took it out on him. Many on campus hate me; they could punish me for moving on from Magnus. It wouldn't matter that he's dead—by my hand—if it was one of his secret lovers that is lurking around this place like land mines.

"Oh, shit," I whisper to myself. "It's my fault."

"Don't be ridiculous!" Zuzanne booms as she takes a band and ties off the top of his arm so she can find a vein. "You can't be everywhere, Morgana. Luckily, the boy was nearby and I can help avert the crisis. His numerous enemies could be to blame. After patching him up, we'll find the fool responsible."

"We?"

She laughs as he winces when she slides the needle in and starts drawing blood. "Well, not *you*, boy. The Dean, campus security, myself, and likely Iggy. Whether it's magic or science, we'll have to keep this in-house or your grandmother will yank you out of here so fast your head will spin. I assume you don't want that, right?"

"Uh, no, ma'am," he mumbles and his hand grips mine tighter. "That's not what I want."

"But we'll have to tell that Detective," I start and she shakes her head.

"Absolutely not! I highly doubt they have anyone skilled enough to do what Iggy and I can once we have the right ingredients. Plus, he'll definitely rat this boy out to his lawyer and his Nana." Her grin is smug, but I can feel the determination wafting off of her.

Professor Zuzanne Shadwell is a force of nature. I'm glad she's on my side right now.

BY THE TIME ZUZANNE FINISHED TAKING SAMPLES FROM Lucas, he looked exhausted. It was hard to watch him shrink from the larger than life, brash alpha to a pale, weak shifter sweating it up on this tiny couch. It definitely wasn't made for a guy with his size and bulk, but he hasn't complained once. In fact, all he's doing is answering questions in a gravelly voice and holding onto my hand like it's a lifeline. That scares me, but I keep my fears to myself until we have more information.

Could it be that someone knows about us? Or is Occam's Razor more likely—the simplest explanation is usually the right one.

"You said the guys were standoffish at practice?"

He nods a little. "Everyone was on edge, but no one was rougher than normal. It's not like I felt like any of them were gunning for me. I doubt its jealousy."

His admission doesn't help me because it solidifies his illness was less likely a nasty prank and more likely a targeted attempt to harm him. I don't know if that's because of me, his family, or the fucking dead player, but that's because Professor Ignatius hasn't trucked his ass here yet. At least if we can eliminate magic, it might shed some light on what's going on. But apparently, an urgent call from Beatrice didn't clarify that he was needed post haste.

I'll discuss his lack of professionalism with him later and he won't enjoy the conversation.

The man in question enters hurriedly with an old doctor's bag. He gives me a charming smile, then nods at Zuzanne. "Well, well. What do we have here?"

My gaze swivels to the mischievous look on his face, and anger fills me.

"We have an incapacitated student and a professor who clearly didn't feel an urgent request was worth complying with."

Putting his hand to his chest, Iggy sighs. "You wound me, Morgana. I actually rushed, but I had to stop by my place to pick up a few things in order to test for various causes. Unlike you, my dear, I cannot take to the skies to get places faster."

"Hate… magic… assholes…" Lucas grunts, and I snort.

We agree on that.

"Despite your feelings, man, you'll have to allow me to check you out. I'm sure Zuzanne would like to take her samples to the lab while I do so?"

Zuzanne also snorts, looking at Iggy as if she'd like to nut punch him. She gathers her stuff and walks over to the door, addressing him directly. "You can portal jump, Ignatius. I hope you packed better excuses than that in your bag for when the Dean tears you a new one."

"Portal?" I feel Des move underneath the cover of my normal hair, and I know my temper just rocketed into the stratosphere. I'm going to lose control of the girls if Iggy doesn't quit acting like a douchebag. "You could have arrived here in seconds."

Lucas tugs on my hand and gives me a small wink. I tilt my head and he darts his tongue out to lick his lips quickly. I'm not sure if that means he's figured out I have a hissing problem or if he's thirsty. One eyebrow quirks, and I turn away so I can smile. Now I know—he either heard or sensed my snakes and is trying to calm me down.

That's also never happened before. Magnus never, ever saw my snakes or my fangs coming.

"Relax, Morgana. He'll be okay." Ignatius clicks his tongue as he pulls things out of his bag and I watch him suspiciously.

Arrogance normally makes me want to smash things, but here I am trapped in between two men who have the market cornered on self-confidence and I'm indulging both of them. *Oh, how the gargoyle has turned...* I quiet my obnoxious inner voice, knowing I'm only allowing Iggy to behave this way because I'm so damned concerned about Lucas. Of course, I'm letting Lucas behave like this because... well, we're not going to think about what Zuzanne told me before the polar bear almost passed out in the waiting area. That's just more bullshit than I can process right now.

"I'm not sure why you expect me to believe that when neither you nor Zuzanne have any proof it's true yet."

"Because sometimes you have to have faith, that's why," he mutters as he lays a bunch of magical crap on the table. "You should know about that—isn't your mother a witch?"

"Yes, my adoptive mother is a witch. No, I didn't inherit any of it, and she never taught me much of anything. I'm hopeless with it and since my dad and I share a species, I focused on that." I pause and study him for a moment. "Not that I owe you an explanation or the courtesy of using my given name."

Iggy laughs, and the sound rumbles over me like a caress. "I'd heard you were sassy, and I can't say I'm disappointed. Is that what *you* see in her, young shifter?"

Lucas's eyes pop open and he glares at the professor as if he might just rip his arm off and beat him with it. "Who said I have any opinion on the Dean? I'm just lucky she was here."

"Oh, yes. I forgot the lovely Morgana flits about campus, holding the hand of every student in need like a teenager. Please forgive my assumption." He fiddles with his instruments, obviously trying not to laugh at us as he puts together something in a bottle that smells oddly tasty.

My cheeks flush and I grit my teeth, tilting my neck until it cracks loudly. I don't enjoy being condescended to even if I deserve it and this little shit is going to find that out. Always the troublemaker, Des shoots out from under my raven locks and hisses loud enough to startle the wizard. Lucas covers a laugh with his other hand, turning his head away so he's not looking at us. The errant snake darts her tongue out and bobs back and forth for a moment before hissing again and I sigh.

"Your sarcasm isn't helpful, Ignatius. I don't know what research you've done on me, but it must have included my notorious and now felonious temper. Don't push me—everyone knows I have very little to lose at this point."

Instead of looking angry, he looks absolutely delighted, and I have no idea why. "It's been years since I've encountered a gorgon. This will be so much fun. And so very helpful if Zuzanne finds different things than I do."

What? Lucas is already cursed or poisoned—he certainly doesn't need me to make it worse.

"Start talking, dickhead," Lucas murmurs, and I nod.

"What he said."

i put a spell on you

Non-magical supes are irritating.

Despite what they may have been taught in schools or at home, they always seem to think I can wave a wand like that kid in the human movies and whatever they need will appear. That's simply not how it works and the time I spend explaining magic has a process is exhausting. However, I'm quite interested in the new dean, even if it is for selfish reasons, and I'll indulge her rather than the snooty beefcake she's clinging to. So I smile and nod at their demands, if only to make peace.

"There are several possibilities that might explain this sudden onset. One is some sort of poison, be it organic or man-made. If the needle went unnoticed, it could have been inhaled, ingested, or injected. That's what Zuzanne is busy running tests for." When they nod in understanding, I almost sigh in relief. It would be much harder if either of them was too stupid to understand that basic breakdown. "If it's not a compound identifiable by science, it may be from a magical source. Unfortunately, that would make it much more difficult to pinpoint quickly."

"But you can, yes? Zuzanne seemed to think you were the person to call, Professor Ignatius."

I like the way my name rolls off her tongue and, for a second, I get distracted. Slade told me she was enchanting, but I didn't see it as clearly as I do in this proximity. "I can, but time is a factor. I'll need to scry for hexes, curses, spells, potions, and magical poisons in order to determine the source. Then we need to figure out what form of enchantment it is and what it entails. I'm very good; Zuzanne is right. However, this is one of those times where you can do it well or do it fast."

A low growl comes from the big shifter, and I look at him with an arched brow. He tries to hide that he's squeezing Morgana's hand, and I smile to myself. The big, burly hockey player is scared, and he doesn't want me to know. I'll play his game for now because I think pushing on him too hard will make my true target angry. Something is happening between them, unsure if it's just Mrs. Robinson or more. It's interesting, that's for sure.

I'll have to talk to Slade and see if he can pump Channing for information.

"Don't worry, big guy." I smile brightly as I pull an athame, a talisman, and several other necessary tools from my bag. "But I hope you're up to one more poke. I'll need to have a few drops in my little travel chalice here and one on the talisman."

Morgana frowns. "Are you sure it's necessary?"

I blink, tilting my head. "Of course I am. Why do you ask?"

Something that looks like fear crosses her face and she shrugs. "I avoid allowing magic users access to pieces of me for... very good reasons. I don't wish to give you pieces of Lucas if it isn't absolutely required."

Smart, but unexpected. I wonder why she's worried about it.

"It's fine, Morgana," Lucas says softly. "Nana will have the family mage do whatever the hell she has them do, and I'm sure it will negate whatever this dude does."

"You have a *family mage*?" I blurt incredulously. Being employed to work only for one family line is an incredibly lucrative yet dangerous occupation for one of my kind. You have a lifelong patron, but you also risk being terminated with ruthless efficiency if you don't do your job well—and I don't mean fired.

Lucas nods, closing his eyes as he puts his arm up on Morgana's lap. "Mmm hmm. The Wolfenbergs have had them in several countries since forever. Cyrus is the one in the States; it'll probably be him dropping by to check me unless he's stuck trailing my parents again."

"I think you need to cut and get on with this," Morgana says in a worried tone. "I'm not sure he's supposed to be blabbing all this stuff. Whatever it is may be affecting his inhibitions, and I know neither of us wants Fraü Wolfenberg to think we took advantage of his condition to get gossip."

"Quite so," I reply as I lean in and make a surface cut to his forearm. Lucas doesn't flinch, so I hold the chalice under his arm with one hand and squeeze his limb to get the blood dripping with the other. "Now we wait for a few moments and then I'll dip the talisman."

Morgana's face softens, and she looks down at the prone man, using her free hand to brush strands of hair off of his face. "Not too much longer, Lucas. Once we figure out what this is, I'm sure Zuzanne or Iggy can fix you right up."

When I have enough blood, I dip the end of the talisman into it and set them both aside. My hand leaves his arm and I wait for the shifter healing to kick in. It takes longer than it should and I frown. *That's odd.* I watch until it seals up, then turn to my materials. Pulling an old scrying scroll out of the bag, I spread it out on the other end of the table Morgana is perched on and start murmuring the words to activate it. It glows once and I pick up the chain of the talisman, swinging it over the paper back and forth as I chant the spell. The most dangerous possibility combines science and magic, but I don't want to claim that just yet. If some nut decided to get back at the old goat in charge of one of the most powerful Society families through her heir apparent, they could easily have mixed old and new to keep us from saving him in time.

That's the scheming that starts wars and we haven't had a full-on supe war since the 40s.

There have been small skirmishes, of course, and the humans always think it's their history, but that's exactly what they formed the Society to do—protect all the people by preventing the dominant species on the planet from annihilating everything not like them.

Too bad the asshole deities who are part of the Councils didn't consider that before they created the fucking humans.

"Ignatius!"

I glance up as Zuzanne appears in the doorway with a troubled expression. The scrying is being difficult and I haven't ruled out magic yet, but she clearly has something to say. My eyes cut to the Dean and Lucas, who were speaking in low tones as I worked. "Yes?"

"I need to speak with you." She crosses her arms over her chest and I can see the tension in her frame, so I dispense with my usual snark. Clearly, she wants to keep it a secret, which is concerning.

Rising to my feet, I place the scrying stone on the map carefully and let her shepherd me a few steps away from the doorway. "What is it, Zuzanne?"

"My findings were concerning. The levels of wolfsbane in young Lucas's system were alarming and even worse, he had a build-up of digitoxin that can only be from small, repeated doses or it would have killed him. In fact, if he weren't a shifter with healing gifts, it definitely would have."

I frown, mentally adding that to my list of suspicious thoughts I've been having. "Zuzanne, I'm having a difficult time ruling out magic. However, finding oleander and wolfsbane in your bloodwork means the culprit is banking on the effects of science or magic to not only harm this young man, but kill him eventually. They're used as ingredients in a variety of hexes and curses—particularly ones that are aimed at shifters."

"No shit, Ignatius! If he'd been a wolf shifter or hybrid, he'd be in the ground already," she scoffs. "We have to speak with Morgana privately before we tell him. My serum is in progress for the medical aspect. Discover the enchantment type and the responsible person."

"The university's relationship with his grandmother is not my concern," I reply with a glare. "This is a police matter and you know it."

I don't even see her fist before I feel the punch in my arm that nearly knocks me off my feet. "Fuck, Z!"

Grinning smugly, she tilts her head. "A pox on you for thinking that was what I cared about, Ignatius. I'm worried someone tried to kill this student and when it didn't work fast enough, they attempted to frame him for murder. I don't know why, of course, but we have no idea who's involved and if they have eyes in law enforcement. Telling the idiotic campus security or the hapless moron in charge of magical incidents in the police will only put him at further risk."

I didn't consider that and I'm disappointed in myself—I'm a globally ranked chess player and I usually think five steps ahead.

"That's an excellent point, Zuzanne. I should have thought of it." Scratching my chin, I sigh. "We need to go in and finish my scrying. Once I have a better idea of what we're dealing with, we'll speak with both. Based on what I've seen, Morgana will not allow us to leave Lucas out of the discussion. There's something going on with them and he'll convince her in seconds."

Her eyes widen, and she slaps her forehead. "Buggering hell, Iggy. I know why."

"Why?" I ask curiously.

"Because the conversation we were having before he arrived was a bit too hypothetical for my taste, but I indulged it because Morgana is the Dean." She rolls her eyes to the ceiling and mutters something before looking at me with a resigned expression. "I think Morgana and the star hockey player accidentally mated last night."

Holy. Fucking. Hephaestus'. Fiery. Balls.

Hissing curses under my breath, I scrub my hand down my face. "That explains a lot. Is this intrigue related to her? The last thing I want to do is get on the bad side of some groupie still in love with dear old dead Magnus."

"No. Lucas's poison levels go back at least three weeks, if not more. The person trying to hurt him has been doing it since he arrived on campus for hockey orientation and Morgana hasn't been here that long. She's just gotten caught in the crossfire of another high-level PR nightmare." Zuzanne cocks her head at the room. "Let's go talk to them and we'll all develop a plan from there."

Something tickles my brain and I remember how wired this building is. I've always hated coming here because of the invisible tech and I can't imagine whoever installed all of this isn't monitoring it. I made certain our conversation was shielded when I stepped up to Zuzanne, but I don't have enough materials to extend my personal shields to all four of us. We cannot have that conversation anywhere in this place; if we don't know who's involved, it would put all of us in danger.

"No. It's not safe." I roll my eyes around the hallway, then stare at her for a moment until she gets the idea. "Morgana was supposed to meet Slade, Channing, and I for a game night. You go back to the lab and finish your serum. Hopefully, that will help the kid long enough to get him out of here. He can go back to Morgana's with her and we will meet at my place to have a more serious discussion. It's warded so tightly that Merlin wouldn't be able to get in."

Zuzanne laughs and shakes her head. "Your ego will be the death of you, Iggy. But I see your point. Go figure out the witchy woo things. I'll handle getting Lucas up and moving."

She turns on her heel and marches off, making me chuckle. An alliance with someone as rooted in the provable world as her is unexpected, but that kind of networking will be even more valuable than saving Fraü Wolfenberg's grandson. I grin to myself as I walk back into the room with a fake smile.

"Zuzanne has something cooking that might help while we're figuring this out. I'm going to finish my scrying and once she gives Lucas the serum, you should be able to take him home. Then we'll research some more and she's going to meet us at my place tonight. It will add seriousness to game night, but it's a good gathering place."

Morgana studies me and the single snake she called a troublemaker darts out to lick the air. It hisses low and I'm pretty certain by the change in her expression that she knows I'm not telling the truth. I didn't know that a gorgon's snakes could do that, and it makes me a little giddy to add it to my mental encyclopedia. She stays quiet, though, as I look around the room, hoping to let her know why I'm being cautious. When she nods, I almost sigh in relief.

"Okay." The Dean's shoulders square and she uses her free hand to brush sweaty strands off of the polar bear's forehead. "That sounds good, right, Lucas? You can come to my place and you can tell me about the other contractors coming next week."

Contractors? He hired people to renovate her house? Slade and I are so screwed.

The hockey player opens his eyes, looking exhausted but happy. "I can come to your place? Can I feel the new sheets?"

Morgana's laugh is rich and smoky as she nods. I watch her go from worried to soft care as she nods. "I suppose I could put the new bedclothes on that you had sent. I'm too old to be sleeping on the couch and living out of suitcases, anyway. I don't think I told you how much I appreciated you doing that. Living in Magnus' shadow was eating away at me more than I wanted to admit."

Suddenly, the talisman stops on a familiar building and my gaze narrows. The greenhouse near the Natural Sciences building would be a perfect place to gather the physical ingredients needed for this type of poison and magic. It doesn't tell me who is doing this nonsense, but it definitely gives me a place to look.

"Did you find something?"

I look up and see both of them staring at me hopefully. "A start, perhaps. However, more work is still needed to fix it."

Zuzanne shows up with a flask of red liquid right at that moment, holding it up with a triumphant smile. "First, we help him stand up. Then, we read."

Hopefully, whatever this is gives us enough time to find the source and take it out or I have a feeling the Fraü won't be our only problem.

truth hurts

I *t's a damn good thing I'm strong as an ox.*

Otherwise, hefting the tall, muscled hockey player from across campus at the science building to my house would have been unsuccessful. We all agreed that as long as I could make it, we wouldn't bring anyone else into this mess. Including Beatrice and the lab techs working on her 'secret project,' there were already too many people involved.

What did that human say? 'Two can keep a secret if one of them is dead?'

This is where we stand currently. Iggy and Zuzanne are working their angles and I'm carefully toting the weakened Lucas up my stairs. I honestly couldn't tell you how many people saw us on the trek, but I'm hoping that paying no mind to the lookie-loos discouraged them from filing the image in their head for later. Sometimes, simply pretending what you're doing isn't weird makes everyone else accept that as reality.

"Just a few more steps, big guy," I grunt, as I help him up the final few stairs on my porch.

He's still pale and all the effort has exerted the hell out of the sick shifter. "You didn't have to do this, Morgana. I could have found someone to—"

"Shut up and get inside." I give him a crooked grin. "I know your big, manly self can't stand that I half-carried you across campus, but I'm not a wilting flower. Gargoyles are incredibly strong. Get used to it."

"I have to get used to it?" Lucas asks, his face looking heartbreakingly hopeful.

Son of a goat swilling deity, how am I supposed to say 'no' to that face?

Pressing my lips together, I give him a stern expression. "We need to talk, but not until we're inside."

"Okay." His steps are slow as he shuffles into the house. I watch him look at the stairs to my bedroom and shake his head. "Nope. I want to go, but I'm exhausted."

Thank fuck.

I nod, guiding him to my nest in the back living area. "Good choice. I think it'll be easier if we need to get you to the bathroom."

His eyes widen. "Hell, no. I can do that myself if necessary."

"Lucas, it's not like I haven't seen you—"

"No way." His voice is a low growl, and it makes my body light up like a candle.

Rolling my eyes, I finally maneuver him to the couch where I've been sleeping, and he drops onto it with a groan of relief. That, too, makes my lady bits sing and I bite my lip. Should Zuzanne's information be accurate, the situation will deteriorate. Our issue is even more significant, but his survival is crucial. "Fine, but you're not walking there on your own."

"Yes, ma'am," he says with a weak salute.

I sigh as I look at him, sprawled in my only personal space in this entire museum, to my douchebag ex. Honestly, I'm shocked. I acquiesced to Zuzanne and Iggy's suggestion for him to come back here. I'm already a popular gossip topic and so is he—people finding out he's staying here wouldn't be good. Frowning, I pull out my phone and quickly text Professor Shadwell about the 'meeting' we're all supposed to attend this evening. Carting Lucas back and forth isn't the smartest plan, and we may have to change the venue to my place. Luckily, the back porch here is massive and has a nice built-in firepit, so if the temperature changes, we won't freeze.

Also, I'd prefer all those people not to realize what a ridiculous mess I'm being forced to live in.

"What are you doing?"

Walking around the end of the couch, I smile at the handsome man. "I'm asking Zuzanne to get our co-conspirators to meet here tonight, rather than trying to sneak you to Slade and Iggy's place. I think we're better off with fewer witnesses, don't you?"

He lets out a slow breath, closing his eyes. "Probably. However, I understand your reluctance to have others present."

I shrug. "We'll meet in the back. Don't worry about it, Lucas."

"But I do!" His vehemence shocks me and I meet his gaze in confusion. "There's this thing in the pit of my gut—not the sickness, but a feeling that I *have* to protect you. It's making my bear lose his damn mind. All my thoughts during practice revolved around finding you and removing that expression from your face after last night."

A shiver runs down my spine and heat floods my veins. Des pops out, bobbing her head back and forth as she slips from under my hair, and I can feel my wings burning at my back. The emotions his words are evoking have completely shattered my long perfected control. If I doubted what Zuzanne told me earlier, this would have convinced me immediately. Her assessment of what happened between Lucas and me was spot on—but how do I tell him?

He's far too young and we're both in complicated situations.

"You know why I came to that building?" Lucas whispers. "I wanted to see the prof, too. My bear is telling me things I wanted to ask her about, and then there you were. Is that because you know?"

"Lucas, I—"

"Don't think, Morgana. Just tell me what you feel."

Whirling around, I give him my back as I try to plan the right words. I know what he means, but it makes everything *so* much harder. It's not in my nature to force people into paying for my mistakes and if he's tied to me by the fucking Fates, he's definitely going to have a target on his back. Nothing about this is fair—not to either of us. We missed the chance to explore and make deliberate choices.

By the decree of the Universe, Lucas Wolfberg and I are mated.

"I know what happened, Lucas. Zuzanne and I spoke about it. But... it can't be." Turning around to face him, I look at him pleadingly. "I have so many enemies because of my choices. You have a bright future both in hockey and because of who you are. Having people know you're attached to me will be like a giant stone around your neck."

His smile is bright for the first time since he arrived at the office. "Fuck those haters. I've got enough money and good looks to charm anyone I please. Plus, I can promise once Nana wraps her head around this, she'll slit throats if people come for either of us—literally and figuratively."

Frowning, I shake my head. "Your grandmother will *not* want you mated to a convicted criminal."

"I bet you a shiny hundred that she says it's better than a bubble headed bimbo like my father." He snorts and shakes his head. "Nana's tough, but she's always had my back despite my parents constantly fucking off to Hades knows where."

Scrubbing my hand over my face, I give in and drop on the couch to sit next to his legs. "I don't know. There will be a scandal if I'm suddenly tied down to one person again. The trial wasn't that long ago and people have already vilified me."

He shrugs and grins broadly as he stacks his hands behind his head. This conversation seems to distract him from the poison, and I'm glad about that. "So date the stuffy magic dude and his roomie. No way they aren't interested in you if they invited you over to their house."

I blink at him. "What?"

"I'm not shy, nor do I have self-esteem issues, Morgana." Lucas shifts as he meets my eyes with a serious expression. "Poly families are pretty common where I'm from and if you think we need to keep our mating a secret until the heat dies down, I'm fine with you dating them."

"But what about... you?"

"Uh, no fucking thanks. I hit the lottery. I'm not interested in jumping back into the shallow end of the pool." He pauses and thinks for a minute. "Though I could be convinced to experiment. I like new experiences."

My eyes go wide as *that* movie plays in my head and I slap my hand over my mouth.

"At least you're not denying that you might be a smidge interested in the arrogant wand waver. That makes it easy. As long as I get to be with you and we're bonded, I'm surprisingly okay with whatever you need." His brow furrows and he shakes his head with a laugh. "I've never felt like this in my entire life. It's so fucking weird."

You're telling me, buddy.

"Maybe we should take a beat and think about this? You're sick and who knows? You might even be delirious," I say carefully. I prefer not to form attachments that can be abruptly taken away, like Magnus. Both gargoyles and dragons live in communities similar to what Lucas described, but Magnus dangled the carrot until he had me locked down—then he tore it away with fury.

"Naw. If they fix me tonight, I'll even show you," the blond says as the corner of his lips quirk up. "Scout's honor."

I have no idea what he means, but since I don't think this is going to be solved by this evening, I just nod. "Okay. For now, let's prioritize water and the threat to your safety."

He pouts, making me groan internally. I wait and he finally nods. "Fine. I'll sit here and be good while you change into something less formal than an Armani if we can sit together."

When did this become a negotiation?

"Sweet baby Hermes, Lucas. You're a spoiled brat."

"That's true, but I'm a cuddly, adorable one." Winking, he waves his hands at me. "Scoot. Go change, and I promise to be an obedient patient from now on."

It won't do any good to argue with him; that much is clear. Besides, I don't want to wrinkle up my suit sitting around the house just to spite him. So I nod and rise to my feet before I say, "Behave and I'll be back in a moment."

Leaving the prone polar bear in my living room, I stride through the hall to the stairs. When I get to my room, I kick off my heels and pad to the closet. I grab a comfortable shirt and lounge pants, then take off my work clothes. I'm not going back to the office and I'll need to make sure Channing brings my stuff from there when she joins us tonight. After I dress, I text her quickly and walk back into the room.

I didn't get the chance to use all the lovely things Lucas had delivered yesterday, but I'd like to set it up when I have time to pack up the rest of Magnus' bullshit simultaneously. It'll need to wait a few more days. I surely don't have time now and though I'd love to sleep in a proper bed, I don't want the taint of my ex touching what's going on now.

I have an actual mate—one who wants me however he can get me.

The entire situation is almost laughable—that's how far-fetched it feels. I'd committed to Magnus because I loved him and thought he loved me, but I knew we weren't mates. Frankly, I figured I didn't have any because I've lived such a long time without once feeling the slightest twinge that would make me think one existed.

Reaching up to smooth a hand over my hair reflexively, I realize Des has receded and the others are staying quiet. *Did accepting Lucas do that?* I have no idea, and I definitely don't have anyone to ask. Gorgons are rare and secretive, as Iggy mentioned. There aren't a lot of records of the true shifters, only human myths.

Who can I ask to find one who might know more about that side of me and mating?

It comes to me in a burst of brilliance: playboy lawyer to the rich, Jackson Thorne.

Getting him to answer me is the trick.

finesse

Iggy's been in a snit since he came home.

He canceled his afternoon lectures to work on the scrying keys he found in Shadwell's office, but he's had a devil of a time getting his efforts to produce leads. Being an overachiever and a Type A personality with a healthy ego, he can't admit defeat—ever. His hair is a mess from raking his hands through it, and there are books on every surface of our living room. I'd offer to help, but I haven't been able to get more than growls out of him since he showed up with a floating box of supplies and a wild story earlier.

Ignatius Briarton is stubborn as a lame mule and ten times as likely to kick out your teeth when frustrated.

As long as I've known him, my roommate has boasted his prowess in magic and his rise to the head of the department at State U proved he wasn't simply bragging. But he rarely encounters a puzzle he can't solve and his inability to narrow the focus of a simple scrying spell beyond a particular building is making him lose it.

"Iggy, I'm sure they will understand if you can't resolve this before tonight. Zuzanne said she'd have something with her to counteract some of the chemical effects. That should buy us some time," I cajole him as I walk up and rub his shoulders gently.

Throwing my hands off, he looks up with a countenance more concerned than I've seen in a long time. "If I can't triumph over a basic spell to help Morgana's pet hockey player, how will I convince her to fund the department so I can elevate its program? She'll be angry and it will only hurt the current and future students, not me. They set my position for life through the endowment, so she can't ax me. However, she can make me irrelevant when I have no new, promising students enrolling because we can't keep up."

I give him a pointed glare. "Also, the bear might die, and that seems like a bad outcome."

"Yes, yes. The idiot sportsman might die, which I normally would shrug at, but given his lineage..."

The smirk that crawls over my face is unstoppable. "Given his lineage, you'd also have some serious 'splainin' to do, and the woman listening is known for *eating* her rivals."

Shuddering, he nods. "Yes. Fräu Wolfenberg isn't the *last* person I'd want to piss off, but she's up there. Being a Kodiak bear whose departed husband was an alpha she fought, killed, and consumed in a sanctioned clan battle makes her fearsome. Her personal net worth being higher than most undeveloped countries gives her power. But her ruthlessness in wielding her seat on the Society's highest Council? That gives her absolute immunity from normal laws."

"Yet she's still a grandmother protecting her cub," I murmur. "Word has it she sent The Shark to defend him."

Iggy raises his head at that. "The Shark? She sent Thorne to deal with an obviously trumped up charge made by a lazy ass detective?"

Plopping down on the couch behind him, I go back to rubbing his tense shoulders now that he's distracted by the conversation. "Yep. I heard he showed up at the station, worked things out for now, and seemed to be familiar with our lovely dean."

"That makes sense," he mutters. "Probably the high-rollers at the trial. His family business opens more doors than a butler."

I dig my fingers into the tight muscles and make a soft sound of agreement. Times like these are hard; I know it affects the two of us differently—a fact that is entirely *my* problem, not Iggy's. But I worry when he goes off the rails like this and I don't want his frustration and desperation to cause him to take unnecessary risks. The time he dabbled in the dark to save his sister during our student years was a close enough call for me. I'll never allow my friend to get so out of control again.

"I realize there's a lot at stake here, but you can't push yourself too far. We both know what happens if you do." I lean down, getting into his space so he has to look at me and listen. "When Skye was sick—"

His eyes narrow. "Stop, Slade. I remember what happened."

"And it was for naught in the end." I arch a brow at him, not allowing him to silence the truth because he isn't fond of hearing it. "The magic was too strong and no one—not you or the Councils—could fight it off."

Rising to his feet, he stands close enough for me to feel the anger vibrating from him. "They sent Skye into a volatile situation with bad intel. It's their fault she was injured."

Shaking my head, I stand as well. Iggy is a hair's breadth from me and, though it tortures me, I don't allow him to intimidate me. "It was unforeseeable. She was protecting her charge—or trying to. She wouldn't enjoy knowing you almost killed yourself in a half-assed attempt to save her anymore than I did."

Iggy huffs for a moment, then waves his hand at me, turning back to his books. "So you've said many times. It doesn't change that I'm once more presented with a rogue magical dilemma with a finite time limit. Especially since I can't seem to get this one under control, either."

"Perhaps it's time to allow me to help? You aren't the only one with magic, even if mine is geared more keenly towards the arts ." I arch a brow at him, a smile quirking at the corners of my mouth.

"Fine," he sighs. "If it will keep you from nagging me, I yield. You can bleed for the stone as well, and perhaps the combination of our essence will force it to give me a more accurate location for the spell source."

"Did that hurt so badly?" Grabbing his athame, I slice a fingertip and squeeze a few droplets onto the object before sucking my finger into my mouth. Iggy rolls his eyes at me, then we both turn to watch the chain as it moves over the maps he has laid out on the table.

This has to work; there is no other option.

"WELL, IT'S MORE ACCURATE THAN THE NATURAL SCIENCES area," I say with a sigh.

Iggy pinches the bridge of his nose, looking like he wants to shoot himself. "Yes. You *know* who runs that *greenhouse*!"

Point of fact, I do.

"You might have to end this childish feud with Kimiko and ask for her help. It will probably be painful to admit you were a horse's ass," I grin broadly as I think about it, "but it will be worth saving Lucas and winning the favor of the mighty Nana."

My mirth doesn't help his temperament, because he stands up and makes a beeline for the bar. Very little bothers Ignatius more than having to admit his foibles and the way he ended the casual relationship with Professor Kimiko Nakamura was a total cock-up. He made an unrepentant enemy of her because he refused to simply apologize for taking her for granted and using her access to that very greenhouse for... let's say, untoward aims.

You really shouldn't ever cheat on a dryad/earth elemental hybrid in their own greenhouse with a supe whose power is aligned with fire—so many things can and will go wrong.

"I didn't *mean* to burn down her other greenhouse! It was an accident. How would I have known that pretty little firebird didn't have control of her shift?" Iggy throws his hands in the air, his hackles up at the suggestion he could have thought with his big head and not the little one with someone he liked and their beloved babies.

"Kimiko nurtured all those plants like her children, Ignatius. You might as well have killed someone's familiar. She almost cracked afterward, and all you did was give her excuses. Since you've grown up since grad school, you might try burying the hatchet; it's been almost a damn decade now."

"She's the one still holding a grudge!" He slams two fingers worth of whiskey down, then pours another. "How am I going to even approach her? Every time I come within a thousand feet of the greenhouse, I get attacked by pixies and sprites."

That's true. Kimmi definitely has the nature supes after him.

"Maybe I'll go with you? She's never been angry with me because I didn't know what stupidity you were up to. I'm water based, but she knows I wouldn't want her precious plants destroyed again."

My offer mollifies him a little, and he sips the dark liquid again. "Fine. But we can't go today. We have a meeting with everyone at Morgana's, and I'm not missing that to play games with my psycho ex."

"Kimmi isn't psycho, Iggy. You fucked up, hurt her, destroyed something she loved, and shrugged. I know you were younger and a *much* bigger douchebag then because of your father, but you've owed her a genuine apology for a long time. Making you give her one may be the Universe's way of teaching you a lesson about hubris," I reply softly. "Pride goeth, the humans say."

"Oh, fuck off, Slade." His words are grumbled, but I can feel the lilt in his voice.

It's dirty pool to use my powers to determine people's verity or emotions, but sometimes, I can't help it. Our enchantment extends beyond just our voices; sirens possess numerous capabilities with sound and music. Tonality, pitch, vibration, rhythm—all of it is part of our musical inclinations and it applies to any sound we hear. People are unaware that our hearing is comparable to dogs. I suppose my people have never corrected it, either, because it suits us.

"Now, now." I walk over and bump his shoulder with my own. "Don't take your frustration with your wicked deeds catching up to you out on me. I've done nothing but work to reform you, jackass."

His lips quirk at the corner, and he gives me a knowing look. "You have, at that."

This is the shit that throws me off and I swear to Apollo, I have no idea what to do about it.

"Should I throw together something to eat or will we be eating at the meeting?" I ask as I clear my clogged throat.

"Dinner there, I think, though I'd bet Morgana hasn't considered it while taking care of the polar cub." He scratches the scruff on his chin, tilting his head. "Think we should order something from Belle's and have it delivered? That would be neighborly, right?"

Sometimes, I forget that despite Ignatius growing up in a rich, generationally wealthy family with high expectations, he wasn't taught to deal with normal people as well as I was growing up with gangsters. His manners are excellent if you're attending a fancy dinner or glad-handing at a fundraiser, but put him with regular supes doing regular shit and he acts like Jane Goodall with the gorillas.

"Yes, it would be a considerate thing to do. Don't say neighborly unless we transport back to Mayberry in the 1950s, though." I shake my head as I locate a menu from Belle's in the kitchen junk drawer. At least his desire to impress the new Dean and the Wolfenberg matron have distracted him from the ugly task we'll have tomorrow when he has to fix shit with Kimiko.

Iggy takes the bottle and his glass over to the table where he was scrying, sitting in front of it with a frown. "The thing that puzzles me, though, Slade... This greenhouse surely has poisonous plants and herbs that would heal, but that's the science part. Who is casting spells in Kimiko's sanctuary? And how has she not noticed and kicked their ass?"

I have to admit: it's a fair question. If he had attempted to locate the poison's origin, it would be different. But his incantation was keyed to finding the source of the magical component, so this result means there's a person casting there. I can't see why Kimiko would try to kill the young heir, nor discredit the dean. She might hate Ignatius, but that venom is reserved for him because of his actions. This kid didn't do anything to her and since she wasn't a Magnus supporter, neither has Morgana.

The whole thing is hinky, my dad would say.

"I don't know, Iggy. I agree it's suspicious, and we should be very careful tomorrow. But we also have to share these thoughts and theories with the others tonight. Maybe another viewpoint will shake loose a clue?"

His expression is grim. "It has to or we're going to fail at saving that kid. That will mean hell to pay—for all of us."

a little help from my friends

"**O**h, this tea is *hot and spicy* like a good masala chai and I *love* it!"

It's hard not to chuckle as Jackson and the disembodied voice he introduced as his boyfriend, Eli, chatter about my current problem. "I don't have much time. He's not stupid; he'll know I'm not taking this long to change, Jackson."

"How 'bout this, sweet cheeks? I'll have Eli do some surreptitious digging—he's got a lot to do for a bold, brassy supe woman at the moment—and we'll confirm everything you and the hottie hockey boy toy discussed. If your nerds are telling the truth, then you can make better decisions."

That eases my worry a little, and I stop chewing on my thumbnail. "Okay. Can he investigate potential threats against Lucas? I can't find the first mate that called me in three hundred years and let some dipshit, half-assed assassin take him out on my watch."

The higher pitch voice of his lover echoes as he calls, "Oh, oh! But if you need a better one, I know one. Expensive as hell and based in Europe at the moment, but I can help broker it."

Alrighty then. Chaotic good Jackson's boyfriend is neutral evil—good to know.

"Thanks... I think," I say to Eli as I shake my head. "I don't need to hire a killer. If you guys can continue working on that for Lucas and add my minor dilemma to the plate, it'd be amazing."

"Aces, Morgana. We're on it." Jackson pauses and I almost hear the hesitation in his voice. "You've been around a long time, right? It seems odd you'd never felt the whole 'mating' thing in all your exploits. You aren't feeling that pull to anyone else, right? I'm testing a theory."

I blink. *How did he know?* "No, I hadn't felt it, even with Magnus. I'd given up, truthfully. Dad always said it arrived young. Three hundred isn't old for us, but it felt like time to be realistic."

"She didn't say yes or no," Eli sings in the background. "You got another one of *those*, Jax."

"Another what?" I demand. I don't even know this kid; what the hell is he talking about?

Jackson chuckles. "He means I'm working for another shifter gal who's still picking her team. The other woman I mentioned is doing the same, though she's working on a starting line for football, it feels like. I don't know about you yet because you're only giving up the chilly bear."

"Yeah, well, I wasn't even looking for one, and I'm not trying to build a clash, Jackson. Keep your starry-eyed romantic on a leash."

Of course, there's no need to say anything about Slade or Iggy; I have done nothing with them and I'm not going to.

"Gotcha, Boss Lady," Eli calls over the line. "One delusional gargoyle task list in progress."

Jackson sighs heavily and I realize he's so fond of this playful hacker that he's not even worried about him pissing off his clients. That also tells me just how good they are—people put up with their eccentricity because the results are worth the annoyance. I'd probably enjoy meeting this other chick they keep referring to; I bet we'd get along.

"I'll call you if we have anything to add."

"No, no," Jackson interrupts. "Eli will send you links to an encrypted website where you can pass information unless it's benign. He monitors our phones for all the bad stuff, but until I can shake loose and have him go through your office and home, we shouldn't discuss this over the air anymore."

Merciful Aine. He really believes one of us is being hunted by a paid killer, not a random psycho.

"Okay. Do we need to take precautions tonight when I have visitors?" I ask, suddenly concerned.

"Yes. Go outside, put music on in the background, and have your magic user cast a silence circle. Don't take any chances, Morgana. We don't know what we're dealing with."

My chest tightens and I feel both of my inner beasts stirring, angry and protective over the people they consider mine—even Channing. "Understood. I'll talk to you later."

"Don't do anything I wouldn't do!"

I think we're covered there, buddy.

Once I hang up, I pad downstairs to find Lucas still sprawled out on the couch but looking a lot less like he's going to burst. He gives me a brilliant smile and my heart thumps in my chest like it's going to escape if I'm not careful. I walk over and sit on the edge of the couch, brushing a lock of blond hair off his forehead.

"Do you think I'll need to intervene with the Coach? I don't know if everything will be fixed tonight, and I bet you have practice tomorrow."

His eyes soften, and he shakes his head. "We do, but I can text him. I haven't had an attendance problem and with the need to talk to the team without me, he might welcome one skipped practice."

Nodding, I think about that. If what he told me about having issues with the other players at the morning practice is true, then the coach definitely needs to have a conversation with the team. Lucas shouldn't be there, either, because he needs to get those guys to understand that they should support their team member until there is a reason not to. I'll shoot him an email if Lucas ends up not being able to go. A word from me reminding him of how generous a donor the Wolfenberg matriarch is might grease the wheels, too.

Not that I'm going to tell Lucas that, of course.

His eyes flutter and I can tell he's tired. We should definitely get some rest before the crowd arrives. Whatever this is, it's draining the hell out of the big guy and he refuses to admit it. "Hey. How about we leave some of this until later? We'll watch a movie and if we take a nap, well, then it happens."

"I highly doubt a woman like you naps, especially during the day," he grumbles.

I shrug and give him a bright smile. "There's a first time for everything, Lucas, and you seem eager to claim some of them."

"I like the sound of that."

L ucas was mistaken… I *definitely* fell asleep.

I look around, squinting at the waning light in the living room as I take in my surroundings. My phone is on the table in front of the couch, buzzing with some notification. I pause, waiting to see if it's followed up by a phone call and when it's not, I close my eyes and soak in the warmth. Lucas, warmer than expected, wraps around me from behind. I'm worried about him—hell, even my beasts are worried. They're seldom of the same mind as me, but I haven't lived this long without learning control.

However, Des has popped out from under my curls to put her head near his ear, and that's never happened before.

If I hadn't accepted Zuzanne's theory before, waking up with my most cantankerous snake snuggling this man tells me everything I need to know. She hated Magnus, and her feelings about past lovers ranged from dislike to indifference. There's no going back from the swirling magic of mating, it seems, even if you didn't intentionally allow it to happen. At least Lucas is sweet, smart, and has a biteable booty—it could be so much worse, I suppose.

"I can feel you overthinking from here," the polar grumbles under his breath. His arms tighten on me and he shifts his hips, rubbing against me in a way that gives me *very* inappropriate thoughts as someone taking care of a poisoned person.

Turning my head a little, I look across the arm I'm pillowed on. "Stop that. You are definitely *not* well enough for anything that vigorous, buddy."

His lips form an adorable pout, and I laugh. That only gets him to bat his lashes like an ingenue as he sticks his lip out. "But I'm being a good boy. I took a nap and everything."

Oh, that revved my engine. I enjoy a very good boy and it's been a long ass time since I've been able to play with one.

I give him a stern look, leaning back a little to help neutralize the lip I want to bite. "Seems more like you're being a brat to me. You know you're too weak to play this game."

Lucas huffs, still looking put out. "*Fine.* But I'm owed spankings if I wait this bullshit out. I get the feeling you *really* enjoy the thought of being in charge."

"How do you know that?" I frown as I finally give in, dragging my teeth over the delectable lower lip, then tugging on it before I let go.

His eyes dance, and he lifts his free hand, tapping his nose with a smirk. "You smell delicious. It's impossible to ignore."

My face reddens despite my lack of shame. I have no problem admitting I'm a very sexual being and taking what I need is normal for me. But something about him lying here, being so damned cute and soft, is making my body act like an idiot. I haven't felt this ridiculously girly since I was a teenager—and people rode in carriages back then, for fuck's sake.

"I suppose that can be part of your punishment for being saucy, then. Ignatius isn't a shifter and I don't know about Slade, but I don't get shifter from him. Only you'll know and you can suffer because you can't do anything about it." My lips curve up in an evil grin as I look at the pale bear. "That will teach you a lesson, I think."

"Mmmmm," he replies, leaning in to nuzzle the shell of my ear. "I suppose it will."

That was too easy.

I give him a suspicious look, but he just smiles innocently. Finally, I tilt my cheek into his face, enjoying the casual intimacy. "Why do you look so happy to get a punishment? Am I wrong about Slade?"

"Nope. He's a siren or something, I think. I heard someone talking about the grad student who lives with a professor and plays so beauti-fully it will make you bawl."

I'm not focused on departments other than sports right now, so I hadn't heard that.

"I'd like to hear it. I've always enjoyed music and London was full of amazing experiences in that arena, both human and supernatural. There was always somewhere to find musicians and singers making melodies that even calmed the beasts inside me." I frown, turning my head away for a moment as I mutter. "I had to go alone, though. I've never been able to share that love with anyone."

He raises his hand and pulls my face towards him. "I'll go with you. Musicals, symphonies, ballet, jazz bands... anything you want. I grew up attending everything from state dinners to private celebrity concerts. The arts may not be my gift, but I love them. Though, you'll have to help me with visual art—unless it's well known, recognizable shit, I don't always catch the meaning."

My heart damn near stops as I gaze into his eyes, gauging the sincerity of his words. He's not lying; he really will go to any damn artsy fartsy thing I want without a word of complaint. *Holy shit.* Ducking my head, I whisper, "Thank you. Maybe you can... show me why you love hockey? I'm not very sporty, but I can learn. And I'd want to see you play, of course."

Lucas beams. "Sure. I'll teach you if you'd like. Hell, you might even enjoy some of it. It gets rough and you're a scrapper, I can tell."

"I killed a dragon, Lucas. I can hold my own if need be."

Shit. Why did you bring that up, Morgana?

The silence hangs in the air for a moment, then he shrugs. "You must have had a good reason, and I hope someday you'll tell me. I sense it's more than what has made it out of the trial transcripts and maybe even more than you told them. I don't think you'd kill without a reason; it doesn't feel like you."

"You just met me," I point out, not meeting his eyes.

He snorts. "Yeah. But I watched you take in that body at the rink. You weren't studying it like it was a *thing*; your face was sad because it was a person. Stone cold killers can't mimic empathy, Morgana."

Frowning, I shrug. "Everyone has a dark side, Lucas. We're all capable of very bad things when pushed and sometimes, it's easier to hide what you're feeling than allow others to use your emotions against you."

I can't go any farther until I'm ready to talk about Magnus and the past. He might not feel as kindly towards me when he hears the actual story.

But that's for another time.

black magic woman

I had to cut off Iggy's coffee and whiskey at one point. He's oddly nervous about this meeting and, for the first time, I can't tell if it's because we don't have all the answers or because of the woman we're visiting. I've known him for so long it feels like I can barely remember a time when he wasn't a major part of my life, but this is a side of him I've never seen.

Ignatius Briarton might actually like *this woman.*

Chuckling to myself as I drive back from Belle's with the feast we ordered, I swing into the drive of our townhouse and park Iggy's Bentley. I'm not overly fond of tooling around in a car that costs more than most people's yearly income, but when you live with a Briarton, you have to get used to that kind of shit. Iggy has ties that could pay someone's rent for a month, and I'm still terrified to ask how much his damn pocket watch is worth. It's clearly pre-Witch Trials, inscribed in Aramaic, and looks as though it belongs in a museum under twenty-four-hour guard. But Iggy swears it's been passed down to the heir apparent of every generation forever and doesn't seem to be bothered because it's worth so fucking much.

I grin and shake my head. *Fucking rich people.* Pulling out my phone, I text my roommate impatiently.

> MusicMan: Iggy, time to go. Please tell me you didn't drink more while I was gone.

> MagicMan: No! I'm sober as a judge. Okay, maybe as an American Idol judge, but I can certainly walk.

> MusicMan: Fucking hell, Iggy.

> MagicMan: I'm coming; I'm coming. Keep your pants on.

If only...

Of course, Iggy has no clue I wish he'd look at me that way. I've always kept that little crush to myself because I value his friendship so much. I never want to destroy that relationship by broaching something I'm not sure he's even into. Although, sometimes, I swear he's either taunting me or daring me—I've never been able to figure out which. I'm too much of a coward to take the bait.

The tease in question walks out with a tipsy grin, his magic kit in hand and every inch of him looking casually hot. Iggy has the sexy professor look down to a science and, though students fawn over him like he's a rock star, he typically does his playboy act amongst staff and graduate level women. It wouldn't be against the rules to date an underclassman, but I think he knows those girls simply haven't seen enough of the world to be with someone who has no intention of putting a ring on their fingers. Not to mention all the damn rich parents who'd be knocking his door down trying to sell their darlings for a chance at being part of the Briarton legacy.

I've always played wingman and gatekeeper for that kind of shit when he's...inebriated in some form. It doesn't make me a lot of friends, but it keeps my friend safe and free from scandals. I'm much less concerned about being popular; hell, if I flouted my connections from home, I'd have hangers-on and wanna-bes draped all over our front door. Nothing like 'connected' bad boys to get chicks' motors running—trust me. It's why my father hasn't stayed faithful to my mother for a day in his entire marriage.

"Slade, you look like someone pinched you very hard," Iggy says as he opens the door. "I suggest you clear whatever thoughts you're having about your dad out of your head before we get to Morgana's."

How does he always *know?*

"It's spooky how you do that, man."

He grins and shrugs. "You have a specific expression that gives it away. Whenever you think about home, you look like a crab climbed in your ass and started pinching you. It's a cross between pain and anger that is a dead giveaway."

"You waited this long to tell me that? What the hell, man?" I grumble as I pull out of the driveway.

Iggy shrugs, the look on his face telling me everything I need to know. "I enjoy you believing I'm more powerful than I am. Reading micro-expressions is far less impressive than looking like a mind reader."

"As if you're not impressive enough without being psychic," I retort, turning off of our street and onto the main drag of the campus. "Your ego does not need more fluffing."

"Everyone needs to be fluffed every once in a while."

This. This is what I fucking mean!

"Do we need to pick up Zuzanne?" I change the subject as I grumble internally at his erratic flirting. It has to be a reflex; Ignatius Briarton has never been shy about sex. He rather enjoys detailing his various adventures, so I doubt he'd be shy if he was really interested in me that way.

"No. She's going to work in her lab and call us if she finds anything pertinent. You know how she gets when she finds a mystery," Iggy chuckles. "The woman would *live* in that lab if she could."

"Okay, so it's going to be Channing, Lucas, Morgana, and us?"

He looks over at me with a rueful look. "You know, I seem to have forgotten to invite Channing. Do you think she'll mind?"

Ignatius never *forgets.*

"Uh-huh. Well, we're going to have to remember her invitation because Morgana left her office without any of her things when Lucas got sick. At least, that's what you told me. All her necessities are there, and she'll want them. Give Channing a call while we're making our way through the dinner crowds in the square."

With so many dorms on campus, dinnertime is a flood of students coming from facilities, classes, and other areas of the green to either their dorms or to cars to leave campus. The admin housing is opposite us, so we must navigate through the middle mess to reach Morgana's house. Usually, we'd avoid going anywhere at this time that required traveling across the quad, but with rush hour traffic outside of campus, we can't cut around it, either.

"Fine. I'll call her." Iggy rolls his eyes and pulls out his phone, dialing my favorite icewoman. "Channing, love! How are you this evening?"

My lips quirk as he lays on the charm. He deserves to have to make excuses; he's the one who tried to exclude her.

The real question is... why?

Before today, I've never cared to find out what the houses in the elite staff housing block looked like. The arts program isn't one that garnered a lot of attention for the school—at least not to the level sports or high-profile research does. No invites for parties at the Dean's house or high teas at other homes here.

Honestly, I have no idea who the hell lives in the other three houses on Chancellor Row.

"Who else lives back here?" I whisper to Iggy as we unload the car. "I thought only the Dean had special quarters."

My roommate chuckles, his eyes dancing as he points at the houses. "Private Royal Residence, Visiting Society Member Lodging, and housing for visiting families of high-profile sports recruits. Mostly, they sit empty."

That irritates the hell out of me because they're larger homes, kept in pristine condition with no one even living in them to keep watch. So many scholarship students would readily accept a work study in one of these and make certain they stay clean even after visitors. With the opportunity to stay in the houses, I can think of twenty grad students who would be thrilled to have that offer. Instead, they sit wastefully empty as shrines to the wealthy.

Fucking bullshit.

"Slade, stop obsessing about unfair housing practices and pay attention." Iggy pokes me in the arm, handing me two more shopping bags. "We have to help cure this beefcake—he's important to Morgana, and his grandmother has immense power and sway. There is no room to fuck this up."

I narrow my eyes at him, unsurprised by his singular focus, but disapproving of his callousness. "Iggy, we also don't want this shifter to die. That's kind of important, too."

He finishes getting the rest of the food out and nods. "That's true. Lucas seems like an okay kid and he might not even be as dumb as most jocks. Plus, I'm curious how Morgana is going to deal with accidentally mating with the Wolfenberg heir."

Something about that makes my chest tighten, and I shake my head. "She will face considerable negative publicity when the truth emerges, especially given the incident at the rink."

"I don't want the board to give her the boot. She's beautiful, but beyond that, I think she may be good for the university. Morgana will work hard to fix Magnus' messes, but she'll also work to rebalance this place."

"Then let's get in there and help cure her boyfriend, dummy. Otherwise, she doesn't have a chance." I wink at him and start up the steps to the house with my half of the dinner.

Iggy follows, bounding up to the door and pushing the Ring button with a jab. It buzzes, but the door doesn't open, nor does anyone answer. Frowning, he pushes it a couple more times, irritation flashing over his features. "Where did they go?"

I tilt my head, listening for sounds of life inside, and a noise catches my ears. "I think they're on the back porch. I hear people outside. Maybe Morgana doesn't have access to the video feed from this thing."

"It wouldn't surprise me," Iggy murmurs as we walk down the stairs and around the house on the small stone pathway. "The board was *not* happy with her appointment."

When we get to the enclosed porch, a smile spreads over my face. The tall hockey player is lying on the big patio sofa with his head in Morgana's lap. He doesn't look good, but his eyes are trained on the TV hanging on the wall as the Dean runs her fingers through his hair.

It's sweet and if I had to guess, I'd bet she wouldn't want anyone to see this side of her.

"Ding dong," I call out, hoping we won't scare them.

Morgana's eyes dart in our direction, and the bear lolls his head to us as well. "Slade, Ignatius! You're early. And you have a lot of bags."

"Yes, fair lady. We brought some of the best food in the city and in great quantities, so we have sustenance while we work." Ignatius beams as he holds up the bounty.

"Is that from Belle's?" Lucas asks in a weak tone.

Man, he is not *doing well.*

"Shrimp and grits, fried green tomatoes, spoon bread, creamed corn, hot brown sliders, green beans, black-eyed peas, mashed potatoes, fried chicken... everything you can imagine. Of course, two peanut butter pies for dessert." I wink at him, and surprisingly, the sick dude flushes a little.

"We came bearing gifts because we only have a minute amount of new information and a *lot* of new questions. May we sit?" Iggy walks over to an overstuffed armchair and places his bags on the table in front of the couch. "I have a feeling this will be a long night."

Morgana gives me a quizzical look and I shrug. "Iggy worked really hard to find a specific answer, but we ended up with unclear results."

"As if that's anything new. Welcome to my crazy life, boys," she mutters.

I know she's being sarcastic, but I'll take the invitation just the same.

L ucas is eating, which thrills me. It's slow, but the delicious treats Slade and Iggy brought perked him up a *lot*, so I can't help flashing them grateful looks as we all chow down. I have to admit this Southern cuisine is to die for and they assure me I must visit the restaurant in person with them when things settle down. Slade even invited Lucas, giving him a small smile that made his heart rate speed up under my hand.

We should definitely investigate that later.

"What's the significance of the magic originating in the greenhouse?" I ask curiously. "Since Zuzanne told you there's an organic poison and magic, it seems like that would make sense. A greenhouse would give the person access to herbs, oils, and leaves that could be used in creating poison—like belladonna or nightshade—and the ingredients for spells."

Ignatius clears his throat, looking sheepish for a moment. "That building is under the purview of Professor Kimiko Nakamura and I, uh... might have issues gaining access to it."

Arching a brow, I look at him in the way only a woman can when she *knows* a man has fucked up big time. Slade covers his mouth, trying to hide his amusement, and Lucas lets out a sigh of understanding. Since Iggy seems unwilling to expound on his own, I tap my nails on the arm of the couch for a moment before I force him. "While I'm sure she's justified in her anger towards you for whatever transgression you committed, I'm not sending an official order out until I know you've attempted to make peace on your own. We're all adults and I haven't been alive three hundred years to play secondary school games with Lucas's survival. Fix it by end of day tomorrow."

I know my eyes are glowing with irritation, and Des is moving underneath my raven locks. She needs to stay out of sight because I prefer to find out if Ignatius is only interested in me as a specimen to study or something else. Gorgon venom fetches a handy price on the black market, specifically because it can only be obtained with our explicit and conscious consent.

None of us gives it up to just anyone, and it's almost as rare as dragon scales or demon hearts.

The handsome professor pales a little as he watches me calm my inner beasts within seconds of their appearance without more than a flicker. "Your control is impressive, Morgana."

"I've had time to settle into my forms, Ignatius. We work together— mostly—and you didn't answer me."

Running a hand through his hair, he nods before looking at his hands. "I'll go talk to Kimiko. You're correct in assuming I haven't truly made amends for my idiotic behavior. I didn't mean to harm her, but I took advantage of her kindness in a way that wasn't befitting of my family's name or position. I'll let you know when it's done and if I'm successful."

"Holy shit," Slade mutters. Lucas and I look at him quizzically, and he shrugs. "I've been trying to get this asshole to apologize for defiling her greenhouse for years. You have no idea how inconvenient it is to make deals with students to obtain ingredients from there with the ban on everything 'Briarton' in effect."

My gaze narrows as I turn back to Iggy. "You really are an idiot. Stop making Slade do your dirty work when you piss people off. Grow up and handle your shit."

A sly grin comes over the magic professor's face, and he tilts his head. "Is that an order?"

"Fuck, yes, it is. You're at the top of my shit list right now and you aren't even involved in all the nonsense I have to deal with for the Society. I can't have someone who's pissed off half the campus joining me in *any* capacity; I have enough enemies to cover us all. Lock it down or I'm kicking you off the island and keeping Slade."

That will hit his pride button hard, and I did it on purpose. I am interested in Iggy—see my tragic taste in men, usually—but I won't stand for bullshit after Magnus. The mage can shoot his shot if he gets his house in order and if not, I'll consider the lovely Slade on his own. Lucas presses a kiss to the inside of my wrist, letting me know he agrees with my assessment, and I smile to myself.

My accidental mate is a hulking, dominant predator, but he has no problem with me being in charge of our bedroom guests—score.

"What the lady said, gentlemen," Lucas rumbles as he reaches for another piece of cornbread.

Batting his hand away, I lean forward and bring the plate to my lap. Carbs are good for quick energy and though his sports star physique might not thank me, I want him to keep his protein and sugar levels up until we figure out what's going on with him. My father's nutrition training prep from Swallowtail days will be immensely helpful in making sure he's eating enough for his size.

"You seem better than earlier, man. The way Iggy told the story, you were damn near death's door in Zuzanne's office," Slade says as he watches me feed the polar bear a piece of bread absently.

Iggy snorts. "Yeah, he's settling in really well."

Once he chews the bite, Lucas gives the professor a knowing smirk. "I'm feeling less like I'm going to keel over since Morgana's made me rest and take care of myself. In the office, I'd come from a three-hour team practice and once my adrenaline was used up, my body sort of gave out. Whatever this shit is, it keeps me about as weak as a baby. Ask her how long it took me to do the front steps, man."

"Luckily, I'm strong as an ox or we wouldn't have made it. Gargoyle for the win," I say with a shrug. "He's been pale all afternoon and we've taken it easy to keep him from trying to help me do shit. Since I didn't have my laptop and forgot to ask Channing to bring it, I mostly tidied up the downstairs when he fell asleep a couple of times. This entire house needs a major overhaul and I want to be ready for the team Lucas is sending to help me ditch all Magnus' crap."

"They... they made you live here and didn't clean his stuff out?" Iggy blanches, looking horrified, and Slade shudders next to him. "They didn't remove... anything?"

I frown at him and shake my head. "No, they didn't. That's why I've been bunking in the living room in a nest on the couch. Why?"

His expression is sad as he looks at me. "You're in for some very unfortunate discoveries, I fear. Magnus was not shy about describing his debauchery and his penchant for keeping trophies and prizes—from all his encounters, not just sexual conquests. There may be some particularly awful relics and shit in there tucked away like normal bric-à-brac."

MY EYES WIDEN AND AGAIN, I HAVE TO SOOTHE MY SNAKES and prevent my wings from popping out. Magnus is the *one* major trigger I struggle with and his death at my hands didn't change that. Lucas must sense my unease because he threads his fingers with mine, squeezing my hand reassuringly. I let him because I need to ground myself right now; I thought this was all junk from his travels or gifts. Never once did I consider my ex filled his house with dangerous objects and sexual trophies; it's appalling, even for him.

"What a dick," Slade says softly. "I never had to deal with him, but I've heard stories amongst the students—both grad and undergrad. I'm sorry, Morgana. No one deserves that as punishment."

I give him a sad smile and a shrug. "Par for the course since I found out, babe. I had very good reasons for what I did and though I'm not up to sharing them yet, I promise it wasn't undeserved."

"Yes, but they punished you by sending you here to clean up his admin mess at the college. Leaving this house like that was unnecessarily vengeful and extremely hazardous," Ignatius cuts in. "Whoever made that decision wasn't part of the trial—they're an in-house sympathizer. Likely, it's someone who knows exactly what pitfalls live in this dungeon."

Great. Now Lucas and I both have people trying to kill us.

"I guess that means I need someone versed in magic and cursed objects or whatever around while we clean it out?" I ask, knowing exactly what the response will be. Ignatius isn't lying, but he's also self-serving and this benefits him more than he's saying.

"Wonder where we could find one of those?" Lucas mutters as he rolls his eyes. "Be a little more obvious, dude, seriously."

Slade's eyes dance as he looks over at his friend. "It seems as if we're needed this weekend. Do we have plans that would interfere?"

"Absolutely not. Whatever is on the board can be rescheduled," Iggy replies quickly, his expression warring between serious and almost giddy.

I don't know if it's because they'd be coming to see me or the possibility of finding rare shit in the house, though.

"Fine. Tomorrow you'll fix your mess with Professor Nakamura and if it works, then you and Slade can come over Saturday to help me work through some of that garbage inside." I sigh, leaning my head back on the cushion.

My brows furrow as I consider what I have to do between then and now. Since we can't get into the greenhouse until my magical fuck-up finesses the head of the Botany department, Lucas won't be able to go to class tomorrow for certain and maybe not Friday, either. I don't want to leave him in the house of horrors alone, so I'll need to work from home.

"I should call Channing, so I have my computer and files here. Not finding a solution tonight means Lucas needs to be monitored in case this gets worse. I don't want him left alone until he's on the mend," I say as I pull my phone out of my pocket.

"Already taken care of," Slade says softly. "I had Iggy call her on the way here. She probably had to finish things before she left the office, but I'll text her and see if she's on her way."

"In fact, I did, Slade." The no-nonsense voice of my assistant startles all of us as she steps around the side of the house with my bag and a small box in tow. "Unlike *some* people, I have a great deal of appointments and responsibilities to manage for Morgana."

Chuckling at the pointed look she gave Iggy, I gesture to the open spots in my patio set. "As always, Channing, your timing is perfect.

Thank you for fielding all the office traffic for me and especially for bringing my work. How did you know I'd need all that?"

The slight ice elemental sits the box and my bag in front of the couch, then plops in one of the overstuffed chairs with a sigh. "Ignatius was kind enough to let me know Lucas wouldn't be magically cured tonight. Of course, then I required an explanation *why* a student of his stature needed to be cured and was holed up at your house, but eventually, he brought me up to speed."

That makes my face turn bright red. I'd let Channing know I wasn't coming back from my outing, but not why, because I was so confused about what happened with Lucas. Her gentle reprimand is deserved and I owe her an apology for not keeping her updated. She's proving to be a valuable asset and I need to treat her as such.

"I'm sorry, Channing. I should have told you what happened at the Science building. There was a lot of confusion and uncertainty, plus I'm not accustomed to having anyone on my side. I'll do better in the future." I give her a sheepish look, hoping to convey that I didn't purposely exclude her.

She scoots forward on her chair, heaping food onto her plate as she smiles. "I can protect you more efficiently if I have a clue what's going on. The excuses I gave today when I moved appointments around were vague, but that won't always work. Some people will require much more detail and I'd prefer enough information to keep you out of anyone's cross-hairs."

"In that case, you should probably know that Morgana and I had a small SNAFU the other night. It's going to be a thing when it comes out for sure," Lucas says as he sits up. "And by small, I mean, really fucking big, and it will be a nightmare when it gets out."

My eyes widen, and I look at him in shock. *Is he going to tell all these people we mated accidentally?*

Channing purses her lips, looking at the bulky athlete, then at me, and then back to him again. She adjusts her glasses, blinks, and finally sighs. "What, pray tell, was this small SNAFU if not you getting poisoned, Mr. Wolfberg?"

"We're mates," he says with a proud, beaming smile that overshadows the pallor of his face. His arm drops over my shoulders and I feel like a deer caught in the headlights of a Mac truck. "Nana's going to flip her wig and just imagine what a shitstorm the media will stir up. So I figured you might need time."

When he admits it out loud, Slade and Ignatius stare at him with their mouths hanging open like they're inviting birds to roost. I squeeze my eyes closed and rub a hand over my face, finally unable to compartmentalize what a circus this news is going to be when it becomes public. People can't call me anything worse than they already do, but fuck if they won't try. I'm infamous on my own and Lucas's family is feared and loved in equal measure. The online trolls will have so many versions of 'whore' queued up that it'll strain the limits of the English language.

"Mated?" Slade finally parrots. "But…"

Lucas winks at him. "Don't worry, bro. I'm learning to share. Look how good I've been so far. Totally chill while you guys hit on my girl, right?"

The horror just won't stop. I can't… Why is he still talking?!

"Lucas," Channing interrupts with a fond smile. "You're doing well, I'm sure, but perhaps you should give Morgana a few moments to absorb the bombs you dropped? She's so red faced that I'm worried she might explode."

He looks over at me as I crack open an eye and his brows shoot up. "Oh, shit, M. I'm sorry. I didn't mean to embarrass you. I just thought…"

Lifting my hand off my face, I slowly place it on his cheek. "It's okay. I'm not used to this kind of shit—mates, friends, sharing emotions, whatever. I was pretty solitary when I lived in Europe and then after the trial, I hid to keep all the nastiness away. Gargoyles typically stay within their clutch and gorgons are very solitary, so it didn't bother me. I'll get used to having you all around; I promise."

"You will?" Ignatius looks at me, his eyes asking a much more serious question than his tone implies.

The corner of my lips lifts as I shrug. "Perhaps. Though I'd prefer not to spill anymore of my secrets this evening if possible. The blood rushing to my head seems to affect my decision making."

That's the understatement of the year, for sure.

smile

This bullshit feeling like garbage is pissing me off.

I've got Morgana on board with the mating thing—which feels like a major victory given her trust issues—and I can't do a damned thing about it. My body is too weak to enjoy frisky time even though my spirit is definitely willing. In fact, my bear is growling weakly in my head, angry that he can't force me to really show our woman what mating with a bear is like.

It's no fun in my head, trust me.

Morgana looks down at me, her expression a little amused, and I wonder if she feels the battle going on inside of me. The one misbehaving snake pokes its head out of her curls, flicking its tongue at me before disappearing again, and I have my answer. Her inner beasts are frustrated as well, and the gorgon side is the more cantankerous one.

"How did this happen?" Ignatius asks, and I arch a brow at him, smirking a little. He rolls his eyes to the sky and lets out a beleaguered sigh. "I don't mean *that*. I know how *that* part works, thanks. What I'm asking is how the two of you, being from shifter families and old enough to understand how it works, mated without conscious intention."

Channing grins and raises her hand. "I know!"

We all look at her in surprise and she shrugs. "My sister is a hybrid and a fairly rare blend. Of course, she's not *really* my sister because she's much older, but I've always called her that. She's a Guardian, and she was adopted into our family generations ago and always keeps tabs on our line because they took such good care of her. I enjoy hearing about her charges because she's kind of a trouble shooter? She doesn't have permanent ones because her team are specialists. Anyway, she told me about something like this that happened recently."

Holy fuck, that was a lot of words for the diminutive ice-wielder.

I clear my throat, looking at Morgana, then back at her assistant. "Tell us how it happened, Channing. Please."

"Well, it's not as uncommon as you'd think, especially in hybrids, because their mix isn't always copacetic. Sometimes, their sides work together and sometimes not, but the magic or bloodlines that make them who they are have enough sentience to exert their wishes without the permission of the humanoid parts. My sister's friend has a charge who doesn't even *know* about supes—unemerged as an adult —and her sides have mated with several people. The supes know, of course, but she doesn't because something is keeping her from emerging fully."

Morgana blinks. "What the actual fuck, Channing. That's like... a whole romance novel worth of crap happening to one person."

"I agree," Slade says. "Growing up in my family wasn't easy because of certain things, but our younglings always knew what they needed to do so they could survive in this world. That chick has been hamstrung like a motherfucker."

"Oh, definitely. She has several mates and four Guardians trailing her at the moment because they don't know what the hell is going to happen. But my point is, when it did, my sister talked to as many retired agents and Guardians as she could to do some research. It turned out that it happens occasionally with single-sided supes, but *much* more often in hybrids than anyone realized."

"So it's my fault... again," Morgana groans as she puts her face in her hands. "How would I have known? If the Society people didn't realize it, it didn't happen with Magnus, and I never felt a single twinge with any other people I've been with... It seems like that's a damn landmine waiting to explode."

Ignatius scratches his beard, his nose wrinkled as he ponders for a moment. "This feels like information that should get distributed to all the Guardians, educators, counselors, and caladrii across the globe. Hybrids need to realize what could happen."

"I'm sure they plan on it, but until they figure out what happened in that case, they aren't likely to share. My sister said her friend had to visit the fucking Fates, Iggy. No one fucks with shit they're directly involved in, and we all know a mate bond is *not* a choice we make ourselves." Channing crosses her arms over her chest, looking determined. "I shouldn't even be sharing this because you're not under an NDA, so if it gets out, I'm toast. Keep your mouths shut."

I hold my fist out for her to bump. "I like the spunk, girl. Being around my mate is bringing out the fierce in you."

She flushes a cute pink and bumps me back, while Morgana smiles brightly. "Thanks, Lucas. I enjoy seeing my new boss smile; every time I saw her on campus before we met at the rink, she looked sad and lonely. Tonight, Morgana, you look almost happy. The Fates were right, even if you didn't expect it."

That makes *me* turn red, and I roll over to bury my face against Morgana's stomach. Of all the accolades I've received in my years being a sports star, I've never felt so fluttery in my gut when someone complimented me as I do now. I guess that's part of my bear's desire to make our mate happy and well cared for, which is a struggle when I can't sit up on my own. Mumbling against her shirt, I reply, "Stop it. I'm not well enough for my bear to be preening."

Slade laughs, and Iggy joins him. Before long, Channing and Morgana are laughing, too, which makes my goofy ass bear even happier. He's extremely glad my embarrassment is entertaining this group of people. It's fucking weird because, much like the night with Morgana, he's never given a single fuck about any group of friends or teammates I've been around.

Tonight is a fucking cornucopia of odd sensations and revelations; I can't imagine what's going to happen next.

BY THE TIME THE NIGHT IS WINDING DOWN, I'M FEELING sluggish again. It's dark, and the porch is illuminated with these hysterically cheesy electric tiki torches that are obviously Magnus' ridiculous adventurer themed decoration and the rest of the crowd is pleasantly sauced. I've refrained from drinking because of my condition, but even Channing occasionally hiccups.

The best part is, Morgana reclined against the end of the couch, letting me sprawl between her legs with my head on her stomach. Everything about this, including her fingers idly combing through my hair, is soothing to both me and my animal. I feel like crap, but there's a sheen of comfort and care over the top of that, making my blood hum with satisfaction. I don't know if I've ever felt like this and that's a sad commentary on how I grew up.

No surprise there. Nana isn't touchy feely and my parents are absent at best.

Channing sighs and looks at her watch with a rueful smile. "Time for me to turn into a pumpkin, guys. I need to be at the office by six to prepare assignments for the staff."

"We can drop you off," Slade volunteers. "I have an eight a.m. lesson and Iggy needs to catch the Professor in the morning before anyone's pissed her off."

The thought makes me smirk and Ignatius rolls his eyes at me. "You have no idea what I'm going to have to deal with. I was a dick, but she holds grudges like cursed Incan idols. I'll be lucky to come out unscathed."

"Which you deserve," Morgana reminds him with a matching smirk. "At least, according to Slade, and I feel he's a pretty fair judge of behavior, even with you."

Her declaration earns her a pout and more laughter, but our guests help us clear the garbage, then walk through the house to the front. I can feel them staring at the decor, probably communicating the same concern I had when I first stepped in here. The board used this stupid house to doubly punish Morgana, and even the others recognize it for what it is. When we reach the front, Channing looks at her boss as she holds me up.

"If Lucas hadn't arranged something, I would take care of it. This is beyond psychologically abusive and I'm making sure that assessment gets to people I know will be quite unhappy with this affront." The elemental straightens her spine and looks at the trophy room in disgust. "Goddess help us when we figure out the nightmares he has hidden in here."

I nod, having also felt the tang of some creepy shit, but I resisted mentioning it so I didn't scare Morgana. "Yeah, there's some major bad vibes in here."

"Magic," Iggy murmurs. "We'll bring a lot of cleansing supplies this weekend and get this place aired out. Anything dangerous I'll contain and we'll turn over to the archivist at the university."

Morgana looks at them all gratefully, her expression relieved. "Thank you—all of you. I'm so stubborn I would have continued to live out of a suitcase until someone forced me. It's the gargoyle in me."

That settled, they leave and we watch until their car pulls out to drive down the lane. Once they're gone, my new mate turns to me, her lips quirked in amusement.

"Are you ready to sleep or should I put a movie on to help lull us there?"

Us. That's going to take some getting used to.

"You're very... accepting of all this for someone who claims to have purposely kept herself isolated because of her nature," I reply as she helps me back to the living room. "I'm shocked you weren't more explosive when you found out hybrids have a higher chance of discovering fated mates *after* their magic mates them."

We make it to the couch and she helps me get comfortable before she joins me and responds. "I've been thrown a lot of curveballs in life. My parents never hid my adoption, but they also didn't always tell me everything. Like most parents, I suppose. They changed jobs sometimes or started additional income streams without me knowing —which was hard when it changed my status to other students because it was public knowledge. They didn't tell me before they retired and went running to their island resort. I didn't know when they meddled in my shit, either, until I was older. Plus, I've had some wacky exes, even before Magnus. I guess at some point I learned hysterics don't change whatever you're upset about. It's better to be calm and plan."

I ponder that, nodding. "I handle adversity similarly because of my chaotic childhood. It's why I was so serene when you walked into the locker room to find me with a dead body."

Morgana groans and rolls her eyes up to the ceiling. "With this poison shit, I almost lost track of that. I assume Jackson has kept the Detective from pursuing an arrest for the moment. We haven't heard from the authorities, right?"

I shake my head. "Nope. My phone doesn't have anything from them or the lawyer. Even Nana is quiet."

"Is that normal?" she squints and asks.

"At times, yes. Sometimes she goes quiet because of a big negotiation in progress or she's dealing with one of my parents' messes. She tries not to involve me in their shit, for obvious reasons."

She frowns, pulling out her phone, and leans against me as she searches for Nana's name. It comes up with nothing new, but then she searches for my parents' names.

That's when I discover why Nana is silent—she's definitely too busy.

"Fuck, they're such absolute assholes," I groan as I turn to lie down. "Why were either of them even present at some dirty rich people's party in London that got busted by every law enforcement agency in existence, I don't know. They got detained by human authorities, too."

"That's going to be sticky," Morgana murmurs. "Especially if they were... indiscreet because of... influences."

I snort. "You can say if they ran their mouths because they were high, you're right, and it wouldn't be the first time. I think if Nana wasn't who she is, the Society would have neutralized them ages ago."

Her nose wrinkles and she curls up against me, flicking the TV on. "Fucking rich people."

"Indeed," I agree, smiling to myself as I hold her.

We can argue social justice later—for now, I'm happy to let her win.

somebody's watching me

Lucas and I fell asleep on the couch watching crime shows, which made me stupidly happy. I have a weakness for human detective shit and though it's clearly never been something he was interested in, my new mate dove in with his typical enthusiasm. He decided we should watch all my favorite shows, which will be lengthy. I'm pretty serious about my addiction to mysteries, both

British, and American versions, and I've got an entire arsenal of shows to enjoy watching him experience for the first time.

When I woke up, I threw together a quick breakfast with what I had on hand and yet again, realized I have to leave campus to stock the kitchen with more than junk food and empty take-out containers. I don't want him to be alone, though, and I'm also not taking Channing away from her job cleaning house at my office. The emails she sent me confirming the staffing changes and reorganization of duties were spot on—I'd even missed some gaps in coverage in certain areas of the Dean's purview.

So once we finish eating, I turn to him, trying to assess on sight whether he's strong enough to join me on a quick trip to the superstore. His color is decent and his appetite was good, so I think he'd be okay as long as we take breaks if he gets tired. In fact, I'm pretty certain that—

"Why are you eying me like you're fitting a coffin, Morgana?"

His casual quip makes my heart jump into my throat and I smack his knee in retaliation. "Don't *say* that!"

"Okay, okay!" Lucas laughs, giving me a sheepish look. "Bad choice of words; I get it. But you *are* staring at me like I'm a bug under a microscope. What gives?"

Rolling my eyes, I sigh. "Making breakfast showed me I need to hit the store for *actual* food, especially with a hulking monster staying here. We both have big appetites and shouldn't eat takeout all week."

Blinking, he looks thoughtful, then nods. "I agree. We need more food and we should make healthier shit, so I don't fuck up my training diet. I'm always bulky and muscular because of my bear, but I need to outskate smaller dudes. I can't pack it on during the season."

"I don't want to take you out if you're not well. You look like you're doing okay now, but that seems to change on a dime. I don't want to hurt you further," I explain. "So yeah, I was kind of examining you."

His lips curve, and he reaches out to stroke his fingertips along my jaw. "I think I can handle a quick trip to Wally World, Morgana. If I get tired, I'll tell you."

"You promise?"

"I promise."

I roll to my feet, holding my hand out to him. "You'll have to prove it by making it up the stairs to the shower. We're ripe and we cannot go out in public without showering. Think you can handle it still?" My eyes dance as I wait for him.

The giant hockey player takes a deep breath and hefts himself out of my cushy couch, standing for a moment to make sure he's solid. "As long as you're willing to wash my back, I think I'll manage."

Gee, I can't imagine why he'd say that.

"Get your tight ass upstairs first and we'll see about that." Winking, I turn on my heel and head for the stairs. I want to see him make it on his own without keeling over before I even consider taking him in public. Between the two of us, infamy is our middle name, and I don't want people posting shit about us online if we cause a scene.

"If I do well, can we go get a coffee at Slade's shop afterwards?" His eyes are pleading and I snort. Lucas is hooked on sugary coffee concoctions—one thing I've learned during the time we've had to talk in the past two days.

"Fine. But I'm not helping you up the stairs!" I call behind me as I climb them and head for the main bedroom of doom.

SURPRISINGLY, MY POISONED BEAR GOT HIMSELF UP THE stairs and through the shower without toppling. We didn't fool around—much—under the hot spray, so we're out and dressing in a few minutes.

I definitely looked at every inch of him, though.

Once we're comfortable and ready to rock, I let him take the lead as we go downstairs to grab our phones and shit. Lucas looks a little better after the clean-up and though I know it won't last, it makes my chest loosen a bit. I know he's drifting in and out of his symptoms randomly and it's hard not to let that make me worry he won't recover from this shit.

Stop, Morgana. Iggy is on this.

Speaking of the errant professor, I follow Lucas out to the driveway as I text Iggy to see if he's got a hold of Professor Nakamura. He doesn't answer, so I fire off another text to Slade, hoping he's heard something. We need to get into that greenhouse and if they can't swing it, I'll have to pull rank. I really don't want to do it, especially since I'm already stepping on a *lot* of toes since I arrived. But if it means we can cure Lucas, I'll piss off every single person on this damn campus.

"Babe? You okay?"

The casual moniker makes me turn bright red, and I get flustered. "No. Yes. I mean, I'm okay, but I can't get Ignatius to answer about his little quest today. So I'm annoyed."

"Give me your keys and I'll drive," he says with a grin. "Then you can be mad at your phone all you want."

I gape at him. "Absolutely not! You're doing fine now, but you've nearly passed out several times in a matter of days. You are *not* suited for driving yet, Lucas Wolfberg. We aren't adding vehicular manslaughter to your pending charges list."

Pouting, he rolls his eyes and walks to the passenger side in a huff. "Fine, be that way."

If he does that too often, I'm going to have a bitch of a time saying 'no.'

"Get in and be good, so we can get coffee on the way home." His eyes widen and he grins, ducking into the car quickly.

As it turns out, men are just grown-up toddlers.

THE SPRAWLING MEGA-MART IS BUSY AS HELL WHEN WE arrive. I've never considered what a hardship this kind of mess would be on humans with disabilities, much less a supernatural who looks perfectly normal on the outside. Lucas grabs my hand as we walk up the crowded lane of the packed parking lot and though I know he's doing well now, I know he'll be straining by the time we finish. Luckily, we can get a cart at the front and he can mask his weariness by pushing it when it finally hits him.

"You're on cart duty," I murmur as we approach the automatic doors. "I want you to lean on something if you get tired without drawing attention. You look too damn young and hot to be falling over without someone assuming you've got a plague."

Lucas smirks at me, arching a brow. "I have a plague, remember?"

"Don't be obtuse," I growl softly. "You've been poisoned; you don't have a disease. Humans are fidgety as fuck since that big virus and if you look healthy but keel over, I'll have to call in reinforcements. Do you want to explain to your Nana why they have you locked in a hazmat area in a human hospital?"

That makes him pause, and he wrinkles his nose, but complies by grabbing a cart to push. "You win again, Dean Hardass."

I mean, I turn to stone; he's not wrong.

"Thank you. Now let's stock up on enough food to get us through two shifter appetites for a week or so, so I can have coffee and you can lie down at home." I pull out my phone, flicking through the list to remind myself of the things I'd had him put on the list while we drove.

A hand clamps on mine and I look up from my screen to find him giving me a shy smile. "Home, huh?"

My chest squeezes, but I give him an annoyed look. "No time for sappy shit. We're on borrowed time, Wolfberg."

His chuckle is deep and rumbling, but he lets go and starts walking. "Where do we go first?"

I haven't been to one of these places before. The warehouse-like store's size and the number of people are astounding. "Uh, I honestly don't know."

"Morgana, if I didn't know better, I'd think you were intimidated by a Wally World." The amusement on his face makes me blush, but he tilts his head at the spacious aisle full of displays and people. "Follow along with me on the magical journey through American big box stores."

Narrowing my eyes, I follow along as he navigates us through the towering shelves full of myriad brands of every kind of foodstuff imaginable. I'm not excited by the produce section, which makes him roll his eyes, but we tick off item by item of the non-perishables. I laugh when he shoves a massive amount of snacks, both healthy and decidedly not healthy, into the basket with zeal. Before we leave the freezer aisle, he's put tons of ice cream and other treats as well.

How does he stay so damned cut if he eats like this? Genetics suck.

"I can *feel* you brooding," he says. "I don't eat junk all the time, if that's why you look ready to murder me. But until I get this shit out of my system, I feel entitled to some bad behavior."

I whip my head around. "How did you know?"

He shrugs and gives me a smug smile. "Because I grew up around enough women who were pushed to hate their bodies to know when food is making them feel inadequate. The standards for the girls in our circles are rough—it's not surprising many of them take it out on others once they fit in. They're often hungry, under enormous pressure, and miserable."

"Yeah, refusing to eat is definitely an excuse to treat people the way I've watched rich girls in the elite groups do in the past." I can't roll my eyes hard enough at him to convey my sarcasm. It's hard for guys to understand that it's not simply being overweight that draws the venom of mean girls; it's anything that makes you different, whether it's physical, mental, or even psychological.

Lucas holds his hands up, his eyes wide as he scrambles to walk it back. "I'm not making excuses, Morgana. I know they cause a lot of damage to others. And I know it's not something that goes away when you grow up, either. My mother is a prime example of someone who got pushed in that direction and, clearly, she's never once tried to atone for the sins of her youth. Hell, she didn't even bother to do more than pop me out."

I frown, looking at him for a moment. "Your parents really abandoned you, didn't they? You aren't exaggerating."

Despite their antics in the news, I sort of believed he was just pulling the 'poor little rich kid' act to get me to feel sympathetic.

"Babe, if I see my parents outside of media coverage more than once a year, it's because one of them landed in rehab again. That's the way it's always been. I wasn't joking when I said Nana raised me."

The sadness in his brilliant blue eyes makes my heart hurt, and I step closer, wrapping my arms around his waist. Laying my head on his chest, I murmur softly, "I'm sorry, Lucas. My parents aren't perfect, but they would never abandon me. They stayed away from the trial because I asked them to, not because they believed I was wrong."

A rumble under my cheek starts up, and I close my eyes when he hugs me tightly. For a few moments. I lose focus on the busy hustling around me and just soak in the feel of someone who is connected to me on a level I've never felt before. We don't know everything about one another yet, but the zing of the mate bond lets me know it's going to be okay once we do.

"Isn't this interesting? And I'd heard you were a frigid bitch. How surprised Magnus would be—that is, if you hadn't *murdered him in cold blood.*"

confrontations & confessions

The woman in front of me looks vaguely familiar, but I can't place where I've seen her before. However, my bear doesn't like her insulting Morgana at all, and before I can stop it, a low, threatening growl echoes out of my chest. The woman simply lifts a perfectly sculpted brow at me, not moving an inch, and I let the animal flash in my eyes.

"Oh, aren't you *adorable*," she says in a syrupy sweet voice. "A bold young suitor, it seems."

Is this chick nuts? Provoking a chief-level bear of any kind isn't bright, but it's especially dumb in a human environment.

Morgana steps forward, looking at the woman curiously. It's obvious she has no idea who this is other than one of her ex's fan club. Her spine stiffens and the air of authority she exudes when she's in the Dean's office fills the surrounding space. "I'm sorry; we haven't met. You seem to know me, though, so perhaps you should introduce yourself."

Snap. Forcing her to initiate the polite exchange is a boss move in the South.

Shaking her thick sable mane, the woman tilts her chin up combatively. "He told me your manners were suspect. Now I see why."

A surge of power slides over me, and I see Des's head poke out from behind Morgana's raven waves. It surprises me—the amount of control she must have to hide that kind of raw energy from her supe sides is impressive as fuck. And she's using a form of dominant push as she glares at the rude bitch, but I didn't think either of her species were hierarchy animals.

"Since Magnus didn't feel the need to ever speak of you, I suppose you'll have to live with being inconsequential. That is... unless you were a dirty little secret, in which case I'm unconcerned with your feelings." Morgana crosses her arms over her chest, seeming larger with every word, though I know that can't be true.

My mate is a force to be reckoned with.

The nasty laugh the woman emits is grating and I watch quietly, knowing this is an alpha female battle that I have absolutely no place in. No matter how shitty she acts, my mate has to come out on top if she wants this twit to spread the rumors around that she won't put up with their childish, mean girl shit.

"I knew you were sleeping around on him, too. He swore you were too uptight and frigid, but no woman stays faithful to a man she barely sees for years. Magnus should have ditched your cheating ass and chosen me."

I snort; I can't help it. A man who cheats on one woman won't stay faithful to another. That's like lightning striking more than once in one spot—she'd have better luck buying a lottery ticket from the humans.

"Stay in your own lane, cub. No one invited the children's table to the grown up chat."

That's it.

I lift my head, holding my tired as fuck body up with the regal bearing I've been taught by my Nana since childhood. My eyes ice over with the power of my bear and I give her a cruel smile. "Wolfenbergs don't require invitations. We are the main event."

Her eyes widen as I name drop Nana and it's like her entire body wilts. "Wolfenbergs? You?"

"Such a shame the masses don't wait until they have all the information before they shoot their mouths off. It reveals breeding and, of course, that tells one everything they need to know." I smirk and place a hand on Morgana's arm, gritting my teeth as her energy zings into me. "Who are you? She asked you a question, and it's rude to ignore it."

"My name is Lailani Bergstrom," she blurts without thinking.

Hmmm. Not an influential family that I know of, though I can quiz Nana.

But Morgana's eyes narrow and she growls softly. "You reported him missing in Egypt." Her eyes rake over the woman again, this time with disgust. "The transcripts said you were an archaeological assistant. I doubt you could dig up a conch shell, much less an artifact. Of fucking course."

Hurt wafts off my mate in waves, but her face doesn't show an ounce of that emotion. Her countenance is all hard lines and anger, though it's likely directed at her ex and herself. This chick is simply an idiot who believed whatever garbage the ex-Dean was spewing and followed him like a groupie on the school's dime. Morgana seems to realize Magnus was probably doing the same on almost every trip he took and that's smacking her in the face like a brick.

"You should probably make a note about vetting future assistants and consultants for off-campus travel in all departments, babe. I'm sure Magnus had his little birds everywhere. That will save the university a pretty penny," I offer, hoping to give her an option for revenge that isn't murdering this woman.

Shaking her head, Morgana pauses, then looks back at me with much clearer eyes. "You're right, Lucas. I'll have Channing write a proposal for vetting auxiliary staff for any travel in the future—from academics to sports. I have the feeling my ex's habit of trotting his floozies around the world with him isn't unusual at State U. The rot always starts at the roots, you know."

Lailani gives us both a look that wavers between bravado and fear. She knows she's fucked up now and has no idea how to walk it back. When she continues staring, I roll my eyes and wave a hand at her. "Be gone. You'll be dealt with later. I'm sure your conduct broke a metric asston of university policies—Morgana is the Dean, after all. Open hostility and venom create a hostile work environment, you know."

When she finally stalks off in a huff, I lean on the cart. "Shit. I thought that was going to go sideways in the middle of the store, M. Is that what happens when someone really crosses your lines?"

Her laugh is bitter as she shakes her head at me. "No. That was nothing. Ask her beloved Magnus what happens when someone truly crosses one of my kind—either of them, really."

"I'll keep that in mind," I murmur as I lean in to kiss her jaw. "Since I prefer not being decapitated, I promise to not be a philandering fuck-whistle. That way, you don't twist my head off my neck. Deal?"

Morgana blinks. "You read the transcript?"

I shrug, not worried for a second. "Who hasn't? You're infamous, babe."

She sucks in a breath, pushing Des behind her hair, and looks up at me. "Let's finish this shit and go home. You're pale and I've probably created an incident. That bitch is probably tattling to someone as we speak."

"As you wish, Morgana."

I've learned that the strong women in my life are rarely wrong and Morgana is no exception. By the time we got home, I was pale and sweaty, so she hefted our bags on her back and damn near carried me to the door.

"You being this strong had to give lesser men a complex," I joke, trying to erase the worried expression from her face.

Her eyes narrow for a second, then she shrugs. "Just remember how likely it is I can kick your ass if you decide to piss me off."

She's so damned perfect for me.

We hobble into the house and she dumps me on the couch to get comfortable while she takes the groceries to the kitchen. My head is spinning and I feel worse than the first day, like that much energy being spent completely reversed any progress I'd made. I don't want to scare her, but even my bear is making noise in my head. *This is terrible and I don't know what the fuck we're going to do.* But I listen to her humming under her breath as she puts away all the food and snacks, keeping my concern to myself.

"Lucas, are you hungry? I think I'll make a pizza," she calls.

I'm not hungry at all, but I don't want to kick up her anxiety. There's nothing more she can do than the guys already are. "Maybe a little."

I hate being a liar.

My eyes close as I let the haziness take over my brain, relaxing as much as I can on the cushions. She'll take a few more minutes. I might be asleep when she finishes. Letting go of my thoughts, I vaguely hear my bear in my mind as I drift, hoping the rest will help me heal. Hibernation benefits bears and may increase my time.

Before I can slip into the deep sleep of my kind, the doorbell rings, making me bolt up in surprise. *Who the fuck is that? Channing or the guys wouldn't ring the bell.* Morgana curses and she appears, stopping to run her fingers over my brow, then heads to the front hall. I should talk to her about getting better security again, because she could have ignored the door if she didn't want to speak to the intruder.

"Good morning, Dean LeCiel. My name is Liam Spéirgheal, and this is my companion, Kaspar. We are your new neighbors."

I can almost hear the huff in my woman's voice as she answers. "It's very nice to meet you and your partner, Liam, but unfortunately, I'm unable to visit today. If you call my assistant Channing, she can—"

"You would turn away the *Prince of the Daybreak Court*?" The second voice snarls and I realize this guy isn't a 'partner'; he's a bodyguard. Fae royals never travel without one, and he sounds pissed.

"I... no offense was intended, Your Highness. I simply have school business to attend to and tight deadlines," Morgana replies smoothly. She doesn't even balk at the bodyguard's tone, which is impressive.

A soft chuckle echoes through the hallway. "Dean LeCiel, you must excuse Kaspar. He's not the most social of shifters, but he is loyal and keeps me safe. I am not here to make political hay with you. We saw you assisting a friend inside who looks very ill. I wish to offer my help —against Kaspar's wishes," he adds quickly.

At least he knows his man is a pit bull off the leash.

"Your assistance? How could you know we need help, Prince Liam?" my girl asks suspiciously.

The amusement in his tone fills the air, leaking into the room I'm in. "Because, dear Morgana, the poison he's suffering from is certainly of Fae origin. My magic can feel that of my people, even the other types. Without my help, you won't be able to heal him before it does its job."

I almost shout at his words. *No wonder Iggy can't find it; the Fae are sketchy as hell about their magic.* Morgana opens the door further and I hear fancy shoes and boots clomp inside. I can feel her mistrust, but she also won't turn away help. Our bond is lighting up like a Christmas tree as she leads them into the back room where I'm sitting.

"Lucas fell ill two days ago after practice. He ate nothing prepared out of his sight, but his water bottle was unguarded while he was on the ice. Professors Shadwell and Briarton believe it's a mix of magic and science, but that's all we know," she says as she looks at me. Her eyes darken, and I realize I must look worse than when we got home.

I tilt my head, looking at the Prince and his man. They're both extremely attractive in different ways, and I notice their eyes skating back to my woman as they speak to one another in the Fae language. Prince Liam is tall, muscled, and has curly black hair that he's got tied back in the popular man-bun style. His clothing is brightly colored, but perfectly tailored in a way that screams bespoke. It all suits him, though, and I'd wager my weekly trust allowance if he showed us his true form, it would all match like an artist drew him. His guard is dark, swarthy, and huge—if he's a shifter, it's a mythic because no normal animal is built like a fucking warehouse.

"Uh, hello? It's rude to speak in front of others in languages they don't know—at least, in their own house it is," Morgana says with a glare. "Clue me in or get lost."

Kaspar lets out a rumbling sound that gives him away immediately. That motherfucker is a storm dragon and Morgana needs to be very careful starting *now*.

"Easy, Kas. She's right; we *were* being rude." The Prince smiles and takes my girl's hand, kissing her knuckles. "Forgive me, Dean. I am so used to working things out with Kas in my native tongue that I often forget how off-putting it is for those who do not speak Fae dialects."

Morgana huffs like she wants to make a fuss as she pulls her hand back, but she nods. "So, can you fix him or what?"

Oh, we're in trouble. I felt it in the mate bond, even if she didn't.

Just like the two academics, my woman's fate is tied to these two—and she's going to *hate* that.

do you believe in magic?

From the moment I sensed the dark energy coming from down the street, Kaspar has been trying to get me to leave it alone. I demanded we investigate and when we got closer, I saw the woman helping the huge shifter up the stairs with a worried expression on her beautiful face. She didn't see us, but I knew the affliction her friend was suffering from originated in Faerie.

We can feel, smell, and taste the magic of our brethren—which was bad news for the bear.

"I need to come closer and I may need to touch him. Are you both okay with that?" I tilt my head, waiting for them both to consent before I move. "I can sense Fae magic and smell Faerie plants involved faintly from here, but I'll need a better idea before I try to undo the curse."

Kaspar looks at them both in irritation. "Which doesn't mean you can touch him without consequences. Prince Liam did *not* accept a bounty to lay this curse; he has no need for mortal money."

"Listen, you Great Value Juggernaut, I didn't accuse the Prince of anything." Morgana looks infuriated, so I have to muffle my chuckle at her nickname. "And I have no intention of touching him; I just need him to fix my fucking mate, okay?"

A feeling of regret slams into my chest at her words and I realize I was hoping I could get to know her better after this. She seems loyal, intelligent, and fiery—all things I prefer, but often don't find in the women who want to date the Prince. The bear she's sitting next to looks ready to keel over, but I'm surprised when he gives me a knowing look then a wink. *Does that mean what I think it means?*

"You can come closer, Your Highness," Lucas croaks.

That gets the Dean's attention, and she rushes over to brush his hair off of his forehead. "He's hot but also cold? It's like a fever and that's new."

Shit. I hope I haven't overplayed my hand in offering to help. There are a few nasty curses that aren't entirely removable.

"Thank you," I reply as I walk around the couch and sit down on the coffee table in front of the shifter. "I'm going to lay my hands on you in different places—nowhere uncomfortable, of course—so I can get a read on how the curse and poison are flowing in your body."

"Prince, you don't have gloves. What if it's fomite transmissible? You risk more than your own life, Liam," the bodyguard huffs. "Think, man."

"I have gloves in the kitchen. Dish gloves, but better than nothing?" Morgana says as she looks at me questioningly.

I nod at her and give Kaspar a withering stare. "That will do, Dean. Kas is being very prudent; however, I doubt touching your bear will harm anyone. I assume you haven't started feeling ill? If not, by the way your scent covers him, I believe we're safe."

That makes her face turn red before she whirls to stomp to the kitchen.

The blond athlete—there's no mistaking his build despite not knowing him—looks at me and whispers, "I won't block you, dude. She's got two other supes sniffing about, and I know how to share."

My eyes widen and he flops back onto the couch, laughing weakly. Shifters are normally so territorial and this one's animal is an apex predator. Giving me a thumbs up, especially when he expects others to join, is unusual. Kas, pretending *not* to notice the sick bear or kitchen, catches my eye. My lips quirk—this will be interesting. My guardian hasn't shown interest in a woman for a while.

"Found them!" The Dean walks back into the room, dangling a pair of hot pink and leopard print dishwashing gloves that make my retinas hurt.

Beggars can't be choosers, I suppose.

"I wouldn't have expected such... girly things of you," I say as I put them on. "More like black with spikes or something."

Her smirk makes my cock twitch. "I'm a woman of many layers, Prince Liam. Even my weapons have bling; I'm not afraid to be both pretty and deadly."

Knowing her reputation, I suppose she's not.

Kaspar snorts. "Did the blade you killed the former dean with have sparkles on it?"

The room goes quiet and I pause, not laying my hands on the bear as I wait to see if someone is going to attack over his tactless bullshit.

Morgana snorts, waving her hand dismissively. "I killed that motherfucker with my bare hands, Fin Fan Foom. Dragons think they're all powerful, but it makes them slow, lazy, and unprepared." My old friend's jaw drops, surprised she not only identified him, but admitted her guilt without a qualm. "What? The trial transcript has obviously been leaked. Who the hell cares what I say out loud now?"

I grin a little, admiring her spunk. "Quite true, Morgana. Now, let's see about removing this curse before it kills your mate."

It's her turn to look surprised, but I focus on running my hands over parts of him, feeling the darkness of the magic and intensity of the power. I sigh as I sense what they suspected is true—there is an element of magic and one of science, though without flora from my lands the science would not have worked. Once I have a basic idea of what we're dealing with, I raise my head to look at both the bear and the Dean.

"There's a mid-level *piseóg* placed by goblins, but it has traces of a botanical accelerant, so to speak. Likely someone hired a multi-race group of Fae who do hits for hire. The herbs and flora from both here and Faerie were used to weaken your body while the curse slowly killed you. It would distract most supe doctors until it was too late to stop."

"Can you reverse it?" Morgana pleads.

"I can try. I doubt their power dwarfs mine, but I'll need time to focus on unweaving the components. Do you have someone you can contact to get things to counteract the plant accelerator?"

She beams as she pulls her phone out. "Hold please." When the person answers, she rattles off my theory, then turns back to me. "Lay it on me, Prince."

"I believe cestrum or gelsemium from here. Antarachnia and Elysian Bubbleberry from Faerie. Oh, and if I'm not mistaken, a tiny brush of unicorn hair." She looks confused, and I chuckle. "It's a flower people use like... baby's breath here?"

Morgana relays the information, then sighs as she hangs up. "Iggy is on it. He'll get Slade to help him with his little mess at the greenhouse, then bring everything here. Which means, Prince, you only have about an hour before very interested supes will be dying to watch you work Fae magic. Unless you want gawkers, I'd suggest you chop chop."

Damn, this woman is amazing. I'll let her bust my balls anytime.

KASPAR WASN'T HAPPY WHEN I SENT HIM HOME FOR A FEW power boost items I don't carry on my person. He thinks this is someone else's problem and I risk calling unwanted attention to our people if I can't fix what's being done to the illustrious Wolfenberg heir.

He worries too damn much.

Once he returned, we helped Morgana get Lucas outside on her porch. Fae magic is strengthened by proximity to nature, and being in the sunshine will help—Daybreak Prince, of course. The light is our strength and I'm going to need a lot, given the time they wasted researching magics on this side of the Veil. It's a damn good thing I dropped in for a visit, or she'd have a dead shifter on her hands within a day or two.

"You know, I have a few suggestions for gardening back here—both for Fae foliage and plants from your realm. I should probably consult with your wizard so we can coordinate a strategy for this area, Morgana. I have the feeling you attract trouble," I say, as I wink playfully.

Hopefully, that calms her nerves a little. She doesn't look jittery on the outside, but I can sense her fear.

"Yeah, she's a magnet for it," Lucas mumbles weakly. "Being a Slayer isn't easy."

Kaspar snorts, arching a brow. "One dragon dead—a weak, lazy, pampered one at that—does not a Slayer equal, bear."

Morgana's gaze hardens as she stares at my grouchy guardian. "We could try for two, but I have more pressing issues at the moment. Perhaps a rain check?"

"Oh, rain checks work perfectly for me," Kas purrs with a dangerous look in his eyes. "Whenever you feel froggy, step on up. I'm not afraid of your curses."

Merciful Aed, the two of them.

"Stop!" I growl as I look between the two stubborn, overconfident supes. "We need calm and support for this magic to work. After we heal the lad, you two can snipe at one another all you like. I suspect it would be a draw regardless—which neither of you would like to admit the 'why' of. Go to separate corners for now."

"As you wish, Your Highness," the storm dragon murmurs, dipping his head.

"For fuck's sake, Kas," I mutter. He only resorts to that when he's pissed about my choices, so I know I hit the mark in his dragon pride.

The gorgeous hybrid doesn't reply. She simply moves to her mate's side and kneels by him, placing her hand on his stomach. Once she's settled, she looks up and nods. "I'm ready to assist in any way you need, Prince Liam."

Oh, the distraction of seeing her kneeling and saying my name like that.

Lucas turns his head to smirk up at me, winking before he mumbles, "Give it to me, fairy man. I'm ready."

Shaking my head, I close my eyes and start working on unweaving the threads of the Fae curse carefully. I can see all the different races who added their magic to this—goblins, brownies, Fae, fairies, pixies—it's a spiderweb of the races of my realm. Both Seelie and Unseelie cooperated for this venture, which means my father's worry about a group of multi-race assassins crossing the Veil to set up shop was correct. I don't always agree with my old man and he's more paranoid than necessary, but... his spies were correct this time. The entirety of Faerie is at risk if the Council and the Society find out about a cooperative team running around on Earth accepting hits for money.

The humans do it and the Society is aware of that little compound because it's run by one of the originals. We, however, cannot allow our citizens to wreak magical havoc on this plane.

"Kaspar, I've sensed at least seven different races' magic. This discovery must be brought to the attention of the King. His fears about the Hand of Morrigan are not unfounded," I murmur as I continue pulling at thin cords of magic. "I don't wish to return to the portal when I finish, but perhaps you could notify him in my stead."

"Hand of Morrigan?" Morgana says, her eyes narrowing. "What the hell is that? Why would they care about Lucas?"

Kaspar snorts. "You're far too intelligent to be this naïve, gorgon. Obviously, they're a group of assassins thought to be rumor. All different species from our realm, banded together to come here and try capitalism. We've been hearing whispers for years, but no one has showed proof—until now."

"A group of Fae doing dark magic for hire? The Society will lose its mind," she hisses. "Rogue shit is *not* rewarded as evidenced by me. A hit on someone as prominent as Lucas would draw their attention. Why risk it?"

The bear groans as I keep pulling on the power infecting him. "Because their first attempt was probably framing me for the murder. When it failed, they decided taking me out was easier."

Holy shit. He's probably right.

My guardian lets out a strangled grunt as he paces. "The question is: were you targeted or merely a bystander? Yes, framing you would hurt your family and the school. But also, a prominent name found misbehaving in the a sports program already in trouble would hurt Morgana. You could be an acceptable loss in their eyes."

"What do your instincts tell you, Kas?" I open one eye to look at him seriously, letting him know I want him to be baldly honest.

He shrugs and shakes his head. "This isn't enough information to determine what I think is most probable. I will need access to everything these half-assed Nancy Drews have on the situation before I can give you an accurate answer, Liam."

Morgana sighs, but finally nods. "Go into the living room. Once Iggy and Slade arrive, send one here with the plants for the Prince and inform the others to lift the magic so you can witness him working."

I smile to myself as I go back to focusing on my work.

This is not the visit I expected when we came over, but I'll be damned if I'm not enjoying myself immensely.

double, double

Convincing Kimiko that Iggy was truly repentant wasn't easy. She's not stupid; in fact, her IQ is genius level and if she were human, they'd label her some type of neurodiverse. That meant appealing to her empathy wasn't an option—she's not great with emotions and the one she's been holding was hard to overcome. With a few funding promises, I convinced her to work with us.

I think the Wolfenberg name helped, too. Their foundations control a lot of grant money.

"I still think we should have pulled rank rather than let her believe she won," Iggy grumbles as he turns the car into Morgana's driveway.

I hold up the two pouches of ingredients the Prince told Morgana we needed. "Do you honestly think we would have gotten all this without her? I don't. And making an enemy of her doesn't benefit Morgana. She *needs* more staff on her side, in case you forgot."

He rolls his eyes and gets out of the car, leaving me to hope his typical bristly arrogance doesn't end up pissing off a Fae Royal. Grabbing the bags of our stuff, I made him stop to pick up in case this takes longer than we expect; I jump out and follow him up the steps. Iggy doesn't knock. He opens the door and strides in like he owns the place. It makes me cringe a little, but I let him lead because his confidence eases my worry. Channing's call included the information that Lucas's lawyer, the great Jackson Thorne, will be here soon as well.

If we fuck this up, we're all going to be in the shit. Knowing my dad, this could start a minor war.

"Who the hell are you to walk in here unannounced?"

The growl has the timbre of a dragon—a powerful one—and I realize this must be the Prince's Guardian. Iggy snorts and crosses his arms over his chest, taking an aggressive stance. I watch as the dragon balls his fists and the swell of power in the air makes me shiver. This is going to go bad quickly if—

"What the fuck are you knuckleheads doing in here?" Morgana stomps in from the back of the house, her eyes glowing bright blue. "I told you to work with Iggy and Slade, you overgrown gecko, not threaten them!"

I smile sheepishly, rubbing the back of my neck as Morgana's eyes light on the spell pouches in my hand. "We've got what we need, though I may have made deals you'll regret later."

She shrugs. "I'll deal with the Professor when Lucas is safe and healed. Whatever you did was worth it to save my mate."

Her conviction makes my heart thud a little—will she ever feel that strongly about me? Will anyone?

"You say that *now*," Ignatius grumbles as his shoulders relax. "I'm not convinced of this Fae shit, either."

The dark, glowering dragon snorts at him, his lips curled in a sneer. "In our lands, you could be imprisoned for doubting the future king of the Daybreak Court."

"Thanks for the travel advice, but you're *here* in the human realm. Your Prince has political clout, but he's also held to *our* laws, as are you."

Ignoring their posturing, I walk over to Morgana. The strife is upsetting her; one of her snakes is hissing just shy of her ear. I know little about gorgons, but they're typically very good at keeping themselves under control. If they aren't, the rules say they have to wear eye covers. Morgana hasn't, so I know she's usually under control, and this entire situation is pushing her limits.

"Hey. Let's take this stuff back to the Prince and see what he needs Iggy to do with it. Would that make you feel less edgy?"

Her face brightens at my muted question, and she tosses a last glare at the two assholes. "Yes, it would. I'd prefer not to reconsider who I'm allowing in my circle because they can't behave like *adults*."

Iggy pales and I grin a little—hell, even the dragon snickers. I enjoy her putting everyone in their places more than I expected. Taking her hand, I let her lead me out into the garden where it appears a tall, beautiful Fae is manipulating strands of dark energy as they exit Lucas's body. His face is twisted in a grimace; that has to mean this is bad. My expression turns to concern as we come closer and I can see Lucas writhing in pain.

"Uh, are we *sure* about this?" I ask, my voice full of uncertainty.

There's so damn much at risk here, and I doubt any of them have considered it. But I was raised by a chess master who ran his gang with an iron fist and was always five moves ahead of the other factions. Looking at the larger picture is in my blood, so I have to wonder if involving the Daybreak Royal, a mobster's kid, two members of major supe families, and a convicted murderer is a smart plan. Not to mention the damn lawyer—he's also way up the food chain. This is a disaster waiting to happen.

Supes have started major wars all throughout history for much less.

"I am," the Fae turns and I realize he's dropped the more humanoid glamor most of them wear when living on this side of the Veil. It makes him even more gorgeous, and I blink for a moment.

"Stop staring at the Prince." The bark comes from his pet dragon but there's a sniff from Iggy as well.

"Don't be ridiculous, dude." Lucas lifts his head, a forced smile on his lips. "His Highness' hot factor quadruples when he lets his hair down. Even I know that."

Morgana's eyes widen, and she rushes over to scold the bear. "You don't have to be the funny man while he's doing all this shit. We can tell it hurts."

Iggy nods, dropping into a chair and scooting it closer to the table by the Daybreak Fae. "How can I help? We got all the ingredients."

"First, call me Liam, and that surly fellow is Kaspar. No need to be so formal. I'm not my father or even my opposite brethren who rule the other courts." He smiles and I swear to hell, the damn sun shines right on him like an angel painting.

"Okay, Liam. Walk me through the steps. Slade can

assist with tasks requiring additional help, while Morgana will divert the bear's attention."

"Not a child," Lucas grumbles.

"We know, growly pants. But I assume this will continue to hurt and maybe even hurt worse before it's better. They want me to keep you calm." Morgana scoots in, kneeling by his head and brushing hairs off his forehead. "The sooner we get this healing, the sooner we can move to the couch, so when Jackson gets here, you'll be clearheaded."

He rolls his eyes. "Fine, go ahead. Magic me up."

The Prince smiles briefly, then looks at me. "You'll need standard grinding and mixing supplies, then we'll have to steep it. Can you handle doing that part after the Professor does the proportions?"

I nod. "I'm well versed in casting. Living with Iggy for years has served me in that respect."

An irritated huff from the corner pulls my gaze back to the dragon. He's obviously weighing the cost of failure; he'd be bad at his job if he wasn't. He must have served in their military with the Prince as well because I can see it in his posture. None of this is protocol, and it's making him lose his grip on the power of his beast.

The electricity in the air definitely says storm dragon.

But I don't have time to mess with him, so I brush past to get the equipment Iggy will need to cut, measure, and prepare the various plants before he grinds them. I prefer to bring our mortar and pestle instead of relying on the possibility of finding one here. Once everything is gathered, I return to the patio and spread it on the table.

"Excellent." Iggy looks at Liam, waiting for instructions. Potions are his forte and he knows better than to mess with anything prior to having a recipe.

"Trim off the stalks from the cestrum. Place blossoms in mortar bottom. Then add the Antarachnia. That one can go in whole because the stems are filled with a liquid with natural anti-venom properties."

I watch as my friend carefully does as he was told, his brow furrowed in concentration. Ignatius Briarton is not one to be hurried, but I can tell he's moving as quickly as possible. I'm not sure if that's because he senses we have a clock on our efforts or because he's trying to impress the Prince. Either way, he's in his element. When the Antarachnia stems burst, a lavender liquid mixes with the crushed cestrum and after a few moments, a poof of rainbow sparkles explodes from the bowl.

"Was that supposed to happen?" Iggy looks at the Fae with a panicked expression, his shoulders sagging when the man nods.

"Don't worry, my friend. Often Fae magic produces dramatic results. This was normal, so you can pop the Elysian Bubbleberries into the mix now and start whipping it all together. It's a little like baking a cake, no?" Liam turns to wink at me and I flush.

"Not that I spend my time *baking*," Iggy grumbles as he glares at the two of us. "I'm a wizard, not a chef."

Morgana's lips quirk up and she leans in to whisper something in Lucas's ear that makes him laugh loudly. The sound eases the tension and suddenly, I don't feel as afraid. If she can joke with the dying shifter, we can all unclench a bit. It would probably help to make the vibe out here less... *angry*. I could help with that, I think.

"Liam?" I ask quietly. "Would it help if I lower the tension? I can use my powers to calm everyone down if it would assist with Lucas's healing."

His dark gaze turns to me, and he gives me a slow smile. "I think it would, Slade. It will take your friend a few minutes to get the right consistency and I'm still unweaving the curse. Making the vibe less spiky would be a gift."

"Got it covered." That said, I sing softly. It's an old tune my mom used to sing me to sleep with as a kid and I'm not sure what race it comes from. We were surrounded by so many, and my mother was the glue that held the spouses of the gang together. She attended whelpings, helped with assimilation for new members, and often played the role of head honcho of the families. Her songs could belong to any species, from sirens to demi-gods.

This one was always soothing and I can sing it without mesmerizing anyone unintentionally.

"Dude, I don't know what you're doing, but this is the best I've felt in *days*," Lucas mutters. "We should have asked you to do this much sooner. It's like the pain is being wiped away by a warm breeze."

Iggy pauses, smacking his forehead. "Damn it. I didn't think about Slade's powers. He tries not to use them so he doesn't accidentally put people under."

"Put people under?" Kaspar narrows his eyes at me. "He's a fucking siren? Since when are there male sirens? What the hell is this?"

Morgana stops his rant with a look that could kill even without her gorgon side. "Look, you cranky dick. Hybrids often have a primary and recessive side if they show more than one supe when they emerge. Because of that, they've been found to have unusual traits, rare genders, and sometimes, mixed power sets. Few gargoyles with snake hair, right? But I have it and my snakes are sentient—something rare for gorgons as well."

He blinks, staring at her for a moment. "Let me get this right. You have a transformation that can either make you a winged, tail swinging gargoyle that can turn to stone *or* you can morph into a snake woman with smart snake hair? Are you serious?"

Iggy snorts, not stopping his mixing as he answers, "She's pretty fucking special, right? If you hear hissing, you made her mad."

"Truth, bro." Lucas holds a fist out and my stodgy roommate bumps it.

What is going on here?

"What color is the paste?" Liam interjects. When Iggy confirms it's purple, he nods sharply. "Time for Slade to go steep the leftover leaves and the unicorn hair. Once it's done, we'll mix it all and it will turn into a smooth liquid. That's what our patient needs to drink."

Lucas frowns when I stop singing. I feel bad, but I've been given a task and I have to do it. "Don't worry, bud. I'll be back once this shit cooks."

"You can sing for your supper later, siren. Do as the Prince said."

Glaring at the dragon, I take the items from the pile and stalk off.

That fucker makes Iggy look humble, and I hope we don't have to deal with him ever again.

soft touch

Slade is in the kitchen working on the brew and it can't come any faster. Lucas has gotten more pale since Slade stopped singing and I'm really beginning to worry. I know the Prince swears he can help, and I want to believe him... but life hasn't been kind in the past two years. It wouldn't surprise me if the Universe handed me a sweet, sexy mate I never thought I'd have and whisked him away before I could even enjoy it. I kiss the bear's knuckles, feeling tears of frustration well up behind my eyes.

"I'm going to check on Slade. Monitor him?" I murmur to the crowd. They don't answer, but I assume they're agreeing, so I roll to my feet and head inside.

Once there, I walk past the humming siren, stirring an aromatic pot of ingredients to the living room. Putting my hands on the back of the couch, I lean down, sucking in a shaky breath. I swallow as my body trembles and tears splash on my cheeks. Lucas is too young to die, and it's not fair that some asshole with a grudge is trying to take away his future. Even if he wasn't my mate, this would be bullshit—he's talented and kind and not involved in whatever crap the poisoner is getting revenge for.

Yet someone as evil and selfish as Magnus lived for fucking centuries before he met his end.

"Morgana, are you okay?"

I whirl around in fear, not used to people seeing me in such a vulnerable state. Wiping my eyes, I wait until my vision clears and realize it's Slade. "You should be stirring. I didn't mean to distract you."

He gestures, inviting me into his embrace. "Please... let me help you."

Swallowing hard, I look at him, unsure if I can be like this in front of someone I don't know very well. "I... well. I mean, I'm just... This is really hard."

"Morgana, I won't hurt you. I get that you're probably gun shy because of him." Slade gestures around the room as the house personifies his essence. "But I'm not like that. If I'm honest, I don't think anyone at this place is, even the cranky dragon."

My brows furrow, and I step a little closer as I bite my lip. "It's not that I think you are, but I'm... I'm so damaged, Slade. Lucas and I were supposed to be a fling. I didn't mean to let him in, nor did I have a clue he might be a mate. It was so fucking fast and now he's sick..."

The smile he gives me is so gentle that I can feel it in my bones. Very slowly, he takes my hand and pulls me into his arms, wrapping me up tight. I stand there stiffly for a moment, but he hums softly, and it makes the spikes in my veins calm down. My body relaxes and I rest my head on his, closing my eyes.

"You're the tallest woman I've ever hugged," he says with a soft laugh. "I feel like a little kid in comparison."

That makes me snort and I shrug slightly. "I'm used to being bigger than most, but I will admit it's why I've always dated shifters known for their size. Men aren't usually so amused by me dwarfing them."

"Did you just say 'date'? Because even if you *are* this tall barefoot, Iggy and I won't complain. Pinky swear." I pinch his side, and he just snuggles in closer. "The dragon and Fae are tall like the bear, though. So you've got a good mix."

I wrinkle my nose and pull back, looking down at Slade in frustration. "I barely agreed to include the two of you and now you're recruiting my neighbors? How horny do you think I am, music man?"

He beams and shrugs, his beautiful eyes dancing as he looks up. "I'm very empathic and I sense auras as well. Iggy says it's a glimmer of Precog—which the siren side is known for—but I think it's because I had to learn to read people at a young age. My family has... rivals, and I had to judge things in a snap or it could be dangerous."

"Are you saying you think the Prince and his asshat guard are... meant for me... or something?" I give him a disbelieving expression. I wasn't even supposed to have one damn mate, much less a group of supes trying to vie for my attention. I'm not sure I can handle that many dudes in one space, to be honest. It doesn't take long for me to lose my temper when people are around.

"I don't know. All I know is that it doesn't feel like a coincidence. They showed up right when we needed them and had the exact knowledge we needed to save Lucas. That means something and I don't ignore signs from the Fates. They get awfully vengeful when you don't listen."

Yeah, I'm very familiar with their brand of vengeance.

"Should we go check on the brew?" I ask. I'm not ready to think about the implications of our discussion, and I definitely can't decide until Lucas is okay. "I don't want him to get worse."

"Yes. I'm sorry if I scared you, Morgana. Iggy says I'm too blunt and I should learn better social graces—which is funny once you get to know him. He's not exactly a diplomat, either." The siren gives me a crooked grin that makes my heart go pitter-patter, then steps back.

I lean down and brush my lips over his cheek. "You helped me a lot, actually. Even if your intuition scares me, you helped me quit focusing on the possibility that Lucas won't get better. I felt overwhelmed, which might frighten him. I appreciate it."

Holding his hand out, Slade flushes pink with the praise. "Stop making me blush. Praise is my thing, you know." My eyes widen and I grin a little, tucking that knowledge in my pocket for later. "We have to finish this brew and give it to the big bear before he gets worse. Come on."

He's right—for now.

I watch Slade pour the flowery mix into a big mug from the cabinet nervously. Trusting numerous new people goes against my nature, yet I must. My mother's skills never stuck with me and I definitely can't go hunting for a professional curse breaker, given Lucas's and my public profiles.

Nope. This is my only option, and it doesn't matter if I have misgivings.

"Let's go out and give this to the Prince," he says, holding his hand out again.

I take it, letting him twine our fingers together. His touch is calming as we walk over to give Liam the mug and it helps me ground myself. "What's next?"

Kaspar looms over the Fae as he mutters into the glass and I blink when sparkles zing through the surrounding air. The Prince is speaking in a language I haven't heard before—it's not High Fae, nor it is from this side of the Veil. Iggy looks fascinated as well, scooting closer to watch Liam as he chants. Everyone is hanging on the edge of their seats until a loud pop echoes through the air and the Prince grins at the glass.

"There we go. This should do it, though it might be uncomfortable," he says as he looks down at Lucas. "I'm sorry for that. You'll probably scream, but it goes away as this flushes the poison away."

The polar bear shrugs and gives him a wan smile. "Dude, I'd take some momentary pain over feeling like my life is draining from me slowly. Bottoms up."

Letting go of Slade, I walk over and drop onto the ground next to the lounge as he chugs the mixture. His face contorts, the moment he swallows it down, and he shouts as his body arches off the cushions. My hands curl into fists as Lucas thrashes around, his bellows making my ears ring. This had better make him better hastily, because I can hardly stand feeling my mate hurting—Des is hissing in my ear as if she's going to attack as it is.

"Everyone stay calm," Liam says softly. "The poison will ooze out soon and we'll need to wipe it away. Do we have paper towels?"

I nod, but I can't make myself move from Lucas's side. The grouchy dragon throws up his hands when the others stay still as well and I call to him as he heads inside, "The pantry, top shelf."

I'm pretty sure whatever he just said is 'fuck you' in that same weird language.

Liam looks over at me with a sheepish expression, rubbing his hand on his neck. "I'm sorry about Kaspar. He's very serious about his job and even more serious about protecting his friend. It makes him act like a jackass... well, most of the time."

"Jackass is putting it nicely," Iggy mutters. "That guy has a chip on his shoulder big enough to be labeled a canyon."

Lucas tries to laugh, but it comes out as a strangled moan. Scooting closer, I brush the hair off his forehead, trying to soothe him a little. "Iggy's right. He clearly doesn't like us, so I appreciate you helping my mate, despite your guard's protests."

"Oh, I don't think he dislikes you," Liam says as he looks at his watch. "If he did, he wouldn't have gone to find the towels. This is going to get gross in a minute. He'd let someone he disliked ruin their furniture and get covered in sludge."

"Covered in sludge?" I ask incredulously. "What do you mean, covered in sludge?"

His lips curve as Kaspar comes back with two rolls of paper towels and a glower. "You'll find out right about... now."

I turn back to Lucas. The aptly titled 'sludge' is now leaking from his pores, black and slimy as it runs over every inch of his frame. It's like something from a fucking horror movie or a comic book, and I have to scramble away so it doesn't touch me. Iggy and Slade back up, similarly horrified, and I take Slade's hand to get to my feet. "What the hell, Liam?"

"That's Prince—"

"Shut up, Kaspar!" I growl in irritation before I go back to his charge. "What the hell is this?"

He shrugs. "The poison, Morgana. Everything in or made by the Fae has a life force. The brew pushes it out and we need the towels to wipe it all up. Then we'll bag all the towels and burn them in your fire pit. If we don't kill it, it could escape and taint other things."

"It's like Venom!" Lucas crows, coughing as more sludge comes out of his mouth when it opens it.

Fucking men. Only a guy would be excited if his weird Fae poison was like some stupid superhero shit.

"That shit almost killed you, baby. Maybe don't be so excited?" I grumble. Kaspar smirks as he hands me a wad of towels, then moves on to Slade. "It's not really cool if it's fatal."

Iggy shrugs and takes a handful from the dragon. "I don't know. Every boy, even supes, hopes they'll get bitten by a radioactive spider. It's one of those 'become your hero' things men like."

I give him an odd look. "Ignatius Briarton, you have *magic*. Why the hell would you need to have spider powers?"

"Because it's hella badass?" Lucas gurgles around another glob of goo. "I'd prefer Wolverine, though."

Liam nods, grinning. "Gambit."

"Thor," Slade admits.

Are these idiots serious?

"Lucas, you turn into a bear. Slade, you can hypnotize people. I don't know what Liam can do, but he's the fucking Prince of the Daybreak Court. You don't *need* to be superheroes from the humans!"

Kaspar winks at me and that shocks me as much as their admissions. "They're all kids, Killer. Even the Prince is quite young for a Fae."

"Thanks for calling me Mrs. Robinson, you asshole," I mutter as I stalk away from the group. I've never felt as old as I do right now—even when I turned my first century. With a huff of irritation, I wipe some of the goo away from my 'baby' mate while I give those motherfuckers my back.

"Kas, you *never* tell a woman she's old. Your mother would beat the tar out of you for being that rude," Liam chides. "We all should help Morgana get Lucas cleaned up. We're in for a long night as he continues to recover."

Great. Hopefully, I don't murder any of these morons before the sun comes up.

wake me up

A long night was an understatement and I'm convinced the Prince knew it. The rest of the evening and throughout the night, the crew of people at Morgana's house helped me eject the nasty ass Fae poison without dying on the spot. I say without dying because I absolutely wanted to expire after the first four hours of agony. The 'Venom' wasn't cool anymore and I will definitely never *ever* joke about wanting to have a superhero backstory again.

It's been the worst twenty-four hours of my entire life, and my parents once showed up at my middle school conferences in bondage gear, high on cocaine, and holding onto hookers.

"Lucas?"

The tired voice of my new mate makes me smile despite the bone-deep ache that has settled into my body after so many spasms and contortions. "I'm awake."

"Are you going to... leak anything?" she says with a yawn. "Because I think we're out of towels and..."

My lips curve when she doesn't even open her eyes, just stretches and prepares to go find whatever I need. If anyone had told me *this* was the real Morgana Le Ciel—not the media image of a vengeful woman scorned—I wouldn't have believed them. But this woman is so much more than anyone gave her credit for, and I don't even know the entire story about her douchebag ex. She may tell me some day, but I highly doubt it's going to sway me in the opposite direction. Morgana may have killed him, but she was owed his death, and that's the only reason she did it.

I'm certain of it.

"No, I will not spew any of that shit, but thank you." I roll over carefully, avoiding all the sore spots as best I can. Brushing hair off of her face, I look down at her fondly. "I can't believe you guys all spent the past few days cleaning up after me. It wasn't a very auspicious beginning to our mating relationship."

Her laugh echoes off the walls of the living room. I remember them moving me there once the goop wasn't spilling from my pores—I think. I watch as she pulls back to stretch and once she's done, she turns back to me with a crooked smile. "Lucas, I have never once been in a relationship that wasn't absolute clown shoes and I wouldn't expect this one to be, either. We mated without intending to, and some psycho framed you, then poisoned you. Hell, none of us are sure if this is about you, my ex, or me; it *can't* be your fault, so I can't hold it against you."

A flush creeps up my neck and I have to duck my head when an intense feeling of glee fills me. I'm *happy* she's not upset with me. How very odd. "Thank you, Morgana. I promise I'm going to get this shit over LaMount cleared up so we can focus on getting to know one another."

"I'm fairly certain Jackson Thorne is going to clear it up. He'll arrive today and I'm sure Channing notified him we couldn't meet with him until today. He's probably champing at the bit to get your statement and tell us what kind of nonsense the local idiots have cooked up."

Groaning, I flop onto my back, ignoring the pain in my battered body. "Mother of Apollo, I fucking forgot about him. Do you think he'll be pissed that we've wasted his time?"

"I think when he hears what's been going on, he'll be glad he brought his entire team with him. Channing informed me via text last night that his entire team is flying in because of a case."

"Great. A group of people staring at me as we describe my weakest days, wondering how someone like me gets themselves implicated in murder and poisoned within a week's time. Just what I was hoping for when I wished *not* to die."

"Hey, he's up, guys!"

My head turns and I see Slade standing at the other end of Morgana's enormous sofa. He looks excited and, by his tone, I realize everyone is still here. "Um, hey, guys. Thank you for... all the stuff you did. I don't remember everything, but..."

"Ah, Sleeping Beauty is awake."

That asshole is still here? Damn.

Morgana gives Kaspar a stony glare as she scoots over to get off the cushions. "*Don't* start with me, dragon. I'm giving you the same warning I've given others: I'm not a morning person until I've had my coffee."

"This coffee?" Ignatius walks up with two steaming mugs of caffeine that make my mouth water. Morgana takes hers and hands me the other before she pads into the kitchen.

I hear her rummaging around and tilt my head. "You're a goddamn savior, man. I feel like I've been run through a thresher and coffee might help me get my mojo back."

"You're going to feel shitty for a few days." The Prince walks in looking rumpled. He's half dressed, unlike his bodyguard, and he looks easily as comfortable as Iggy and Slade. "The Fae poison blend they used is potent enough to linger, even after we drained the bulk of it out forcefully."

"I still can't thank you enough for coming over, Liam," Morgana says as she comes out of the kitchen empty-handed. She obviously forgot she's not stocked after the hoard eating here for a few days and found the cupboard bare. "I feel bad because I can't make everyone breakfast, but perhaps we could—"

"I already ordered food," Slade says cheerily. "I'm usually up early to take a dip in the mornings and when I got back, I couldn't find anything to fix. It's coming, but I have to leave for work at three. Will Jackson arrive before then? I'd hate to miss it."

Morgana looks at all five of us, her expression suddenly full of panic. "Miss it? You're all... staying for the meeting? Like, to help us?"

Kaspar makes a scoffing sound, but the rest of the guys nod. I reach up and offer my hand, squeezing hers gently. "It looks like we have a team, too. Seems foolish to turn down their offer."

She licks her lips, still looking like she's going to bolt any second. "Okay. You can stay for the meeting. But I'm going to go shower and get cleaned up—alone. I need... some time."

I chuckle softly, letting go of her. "Definitely not to panic, right?"

"Absolutely not," the raven-haired beauty says as she squares her shoulders. "I never panic."

We'll see about that.

By the time Morgana comes downstairs, the others have run to their homes to get cleaned up as well. She sees the empty room and breathes a sigh of relief. I'm glad to see she's still dressed down in jeans and a big comfy sweater with bare feet. I was worried she might throw her Armani armor on and any hope of getting her to talk with me about our guests would be out the window.

"Your food is in the microwave. I'm going to go up and scrub my skin raw for a few minutes, then I'll be back." I smile as I push up off the couch, wincing a bit. "Hopefully, the hot water will ease some of this ache so we can curl up on the couch until they get back."

Watching me, her eyes narrow. "What do you plan to do on the couch? It better not be marking your territory."

"As lovely as that sounds—and it does—I'm still weak for that. I want to talk about our new friends and what it means."

There's the panicked look again.

"Morgana, I know you're still healing from the trial and Magnus' bullshit. If we hadn't mated, you might even have pushed me away. I'm not stupid." I walk over to her, looking into her eyes. "But that's not what happened, and we didn't just *run into* the perfect people to help us solve my problem."

"Don't be ridiculous. This isn't a romance novel, Lucas. Random people don't come walking into your life because some driving force caused them to. It's... butterflies flapping their wings in China and shit." Her cheeks flush red and she wrinkles her nose at me. "It doesn't mean anything."

"First of all, Fate is a thing, and I know you know that. And their plans for all of us change with that butterfly flapping, which is why they weave and re-weave their tapestry. My Nana taught me all about it and she doesn't suffer fools." Sighing, I tug on the end of her girly ponytail lightly. "I'm going to go shower and you need to come to grips with the fact that there might be a bunch of Fae royalty walking the earth, but having a Prince down the street is too much of a coincidence to ignore."

"But Lucas…"

"No buts, Morgana. I almost died. I'm not kicking people out who were clearly sent to help us because you're scared. You're stronger than that; this is simply a knee-jerk reaction because I'm not dying."

She's still sputtering as I head for the stairs, dragging myself up them one by one.

I know I'm right; I can feel it in my bones.

I take much longer than I normally would to haul my ass up to the master bedroom and I glare at it as I head for her bathroom. Once we settle this shit with Jackson, this house is the next thing we're going to deal with. I want all of this scaly motherfucker's shit out of here. I don't care if it goes in a museum or a garbage can, but Morgana can't keep living in this shitty shrine to her past.

Her clothes are hanging on curtain rods and half out of suitcases and trunks. There's a pallet of blankets and pillows on the floor where she clearly attempted to sleep on the floor because she didn't want to be in the bed. With a low growl, I turn and punch the wall, leaving a dent and red marks on my knuckles. I hate that she's been treated this way and if I find out which asshole board members let this shit happen, I'm having Nana handle them. It's disgraceful even if she wasn't my mate.

I shake my head and head into the bathroom. Now, *this* feels more like Morgana. She has hair and beauty products lined up on fixtures, organized by color and type. The towels are pitch black with deep midnight patterns stitched at the hems and a long, silky robe hangs on the back of the door. The scent of lavender, dragon's blood, and jasmine hangs in the air, making my cock stand up eagerly.

Okay, maybe I'm not too tired for that.

Chuckling, I turn on the hot water, making sure it's hot and steamy before I step in. The heat makes my muscles relax a tiny smidgen and I groan happily. I've had my ass kicked all over the ice for most of my life and I've never been as sore as I am now. Whatever happened while I was getting the venom shit pulled out of me put my body through hell and I'm paying for it now.

"Focus, Wolfberg," I mutter to myself. "Make this quick and get down there before the others get back."

I don't know why I woke up with this intense drive to get Morgana on board with more mates. It's not in my nature as a guy and definitely not in my bear's nature. But something deep inside of me is screaming that those people saving me, being there to keep me alive, wasn't just happenstance. I don't know *why* I feel like this or what my instincts think is going on, but it's important. For someone who's spent the better part of his life focusing on his pro career, to the exclusion of everything else—it's a weird feeling, like I'm tied to something bigger than myself.

But I am, and this murder is just the tip of the iceberg.

Shaking my head, I use her soap and scrub the hell out of myself. The black crap is gone, but I have this icky sensation like it isn't, but I'm sure it will fade. I don't know where all these stupid thoughts about Fate and the bigger picture are coming from, but it's creeping me out.

"Next on the list after dealing with the house is finding out why I suddenly feel like a goddamn Tarot deck," I grumble. "Crystal ball shit is for the birds."

That decided, I turn off the water and get dry, then pull on the spare set of clothes Morgana bought on our trip to the super mart.

It's time for her to face the facts so that we can all work together.

getting ready

While Lucas showered, I cleaned up the rest of the mess in the living room and on the patio. Once that was disposed of, I was able to sit down and eat without feeling like something was crawling all over my skin. Despite my mother's magical leanings, I've never had skill with that end of the supernatural things, and watching the guys weave his cure was amazing to me. I owe Liam, Slade, and Iggy a great deal, though Kaspar can stick his snarky bullshit where the sun doesn't shine.

I dislike people who act as if no one matters unless they're from a certain tier of supes.

Of course, he's a dragon, which explains why he behaves like an utter tool. Outside of Magnus, I've had the displeasure of meeting a few dragons in my centuries, and every single one has been a consummate snob. Wyverns aren't as bad, but the four-legged lizards, no matter what subspecies they are, are simply douche canoes.

Raising a bite of eggs to my mouth, I grin a little. I suppose people say the same about gargoyles and gorgons. There's always been a caste system in supe society and it has multiple layers depending on power, money, pure lines, hybrids, mythicals... an entire treasure trove of variables that make navigating it impossible if you find out who you are late in life. As long as you grow up in an enclave for hybrids or true supe run locales, you're fine, especially if you attend one of the schools.

Iggy, Slade, Lucas and I have the benefit of that. I'm sure Kaspar and the Prince have lived in Faerie within the Daybreak Court until now; the Fae rarely allow their royalty to travel outside of the Veil before they're past the age of supe emergence on this side. Honestly, that's pretty much all I know about Liam's people. The Fae are secretive, tricky, and fiercely protective of the gates that separate their world from ours. They operate parallel to supe society and have a slew of complex treaties with the Society in order to stay independent. They even have reps who travel for Society meetings or large events, which is why I assume the one who was at my trial was an emissary from one of the four Courts.

"None of this helps you *now*, Morgana," I mutter to myself. "The Prince is pretty fucking important and for some reason, he's chosen to ally with you. That has to mean something."

"It definitely does," Lucas says as he walks in, drying his hair with a small towel.

I blink, my face reddening as he catches me talking to myself. "I didn't know you were so... new age. Since we mated, it feels like you're all in on the mythos stuff."

Stalking towards me with the grace of an athlete, Lucas smiles wickedly. "I'm not, usually. But it's like I've got... feelings about things. Not a voice, per se, but shit sort of comes to me and my gut says it's right."

My mother's sixth sense is uncanny.

"It doesn't worry me." I rise from my seat, taking the dishes to the dishwasher before walking over to him. "I'm used to having a person in my life who's sensitive to 'the force', so to speak. My mom is a witch, and she doesn't have the sight, but she's always been wired in."

Lucas arches his brow. "You haven't spoken of your family much. I know they supported you during the trial, but I take it you're trying to give them space? From what I know of you so far, keeping them out of the spotlight feels like your M.O."

Leaning against him, I nod. "They had good careers, with excellent reputations, and they're retired now. I don't want the press hounding them in their little slice of paradise more than they already have. So I don't stay in as close contact as I did before the mess. They don't deserve to be punished for my actions."

"Hey." The bear puts his hand under my chin, forcing me to look into his eyes. "I don't know everything about what happened—other than the news shit and what I've seen here—but you need to stop protecting everyone but yourself. You took responsibility for your actions and you were adjudicated. I don't believe you were some vengeful nut job like they've painted you to be in the media, Morgana. So give yourself a break, okay?"

I sigh, my mouth curving into a soft smile. "You're pretty good at this emotional shit, despite telling me it wasn't your thing a couple of days ago."

He shrugs, his eyes dancing merrily. "I'm a fast learner."

"Obviously."

I drag my eyes away from my new mate to see the sarcastic bodyguard smirking at us with his Prince in tow. "Hello, Your Highness. Despite your asshat friend, I'm glad to see you look a little stronger than earlier."

Liam chuckles. "My kind draws strength from various things in this world and my temporary abode is filled with things to assist me in recharging, so I don't have to slip across the Veil too often. I'm never eager to visit certain things more frequently than necessary."

"Prince," Kaspar growls, his voice holding a warning.

"Kas, don't be ridiculous. Morgana will not gossip about me when you're not watching." Liam shrugs and walks over to the cabinets, pulling out a mug to pour himself a coffee. "I think her experience with an active rumor mill and the press stalking her would prevent that."

I groan, stepping back from Lucas and nodding. "That's beyond true. I want *nothing* to do with any kind of attention from those vultures. But honestly? I wouldn't discuss your private shit, anyway. People who sit around and trash others for their amusement are vile and tedious."

"See? I'm safe to bitch about Father. No worries." Liam beams and takes a sip of his caffeine with a happy sigh.

Kaspar practically glowers at him, but he mimics the Prince's actions by rummaging for a mug. "I don't trust her and telling me to do it won't change that. You can't order me to, Liam."

Lucas's brows go up as the dragon shows more familiarity with the Prince than we've seen before. "Uh, are you guys, like, friends, too?"

"Of course, young shifter!" Liam replies with a wink. "Kaspar has been my guard since we were both children. He's just part of the very formal, very tight-assed royal family guards. They've been trained to act like they have a stick up their ass by my father's commander. On this side of Faerie, he can easily slip into our old ways. At least, when we're not in public."

"Is him calling you Liam in front of us a good thing?" I ask.

Kaspar frowns and stalks out of the kitchen, heading for the living room with his brew. The Prince chuckles and nods. "Indeed. He does not trust easily; it is his job to keep me unharmed and out of trouble. I don't make it easy on him, I fear. But if he lets his guard down, I think, perhaps, you won't dislike him so much."

"I don't give a flying fuck if she—"

"*Kaspar!*"

I snort at the Prince's stern admonishment. It's much more obvious how close they are now. "It's okay, Liam. Let's gather in the living room and wait for everyone else. I'm very curious what information Jackson has about Lucas's case and even more curious about this whole 'team' he's bringing."

"I wonder about that, too. I have met many lawyers, but few who travel with a group. It intrigues me."

Lucas takes my cup and his, refilling them before he returns. "Agreed. There were no shortage of lawyers around our family, but usually some lower minion came to deliver shit or the big gun visited. I don't recall a whole gaggle of folks descending on my parents or Nana."

Great. Is this more serious than we thought?

looking tired but clean. I notice they're dressed more casually than last time, and it makes me smile to myself. For some reason, I'm pleased that everyone but dickhead Kaspar is comfortable in my house. It makes the creatures inside me hum a bit, even the gorgon. Des isn't poking her head out—I call that a win. They join Lucas, Liam, and me on the couches, waiting to hear what the plan is.

"Okay, now that we're all here… Have you heard from Channing yet?" Iggy asks as he settles in.

"No. She promised she'd text when she arrived at the airport," I reply as I check my phone. "The planes are due any minute, so I'm sure we'll hear soon."

"That gives us an hour of mid-day airport traffic for them to fight once they're deplaned. I think we should go upstairs and start boxing shit in that bedroom. I want to get the fuckwit's crap out of this house as soon as possible."

I blink at Lucas, my face turning red. "You guys don't have to—"

"Nonsense, Morgana. What the university board did to punish you by leaving all this shit here is disgraceful," Iggy cuts in. "Magnus' hidden secrets in this unfamiliar place make it dangerous. He was not a good man, and I wouldn't put it past him to store magical items that shouldn't be accessible to most users here in a hoard. Dragons love that shit."

"True." Slade slaps his thighs and nods as he stands. "We have at least three magic users here to help identify things that need special handling. We'll work our way through this museum to his ego room by room until you have a suitable place to live."

Everyone gets up, and I follow them to the stairs. Kaspar hangs back, coming in last with a dark expression on his face. When I know no one else can see, I lift my hand and flip him off over my shoulder as we climb up to the second floor. The only response I get sounds like a cross between a huff and a chuckle, so I'll consider that a win. I don't know what I did to piss this asshole off, but I wish he'd get the hell over it.

Lucas opens the door to my spacious bedroom and every single guy flinches. I frown, looking at them curiously. "What?"

"You don't smell that?" Slade groans.

I shake my head. "Gargoyles have better hearing and vision. The snake smells exceptionally well, but only when I'm... you know. Because they do it with their tongues."

They're all silent for a moment and I think I lost them at 'tongues,' but finally Iggy sighs. "For me, I smell the magic Magnus and many, many others used in this room for fuck knows what. It's... smoky, with hints of various flowers or spice scents. I could work out what kinds of... well, I could figure out his roster if I focused."

My eyes widen in horror, and I look at the others. "And you guys can, too?"

Liam grimaces. "I can, yes."

Slade and Lucas both dip their heads, but finally, Lucas grumbles, "I can smell sex, magic, shifters, animals, and various other shit. Probably more than those two. I assume Slade and the cockwaffle can, too."

"Oh my fucking Goddess, this is humiliating." I put my face in my hands, knowing I'm scarlet with both embarrassment and fury. The telltale hiss of Des breaking free to make her anger known distracts me for a moment and I close my eyes inside the protective cover of my palms. "I'm not stupid; I know you're all being kind by not identifying all of it clearly. He had droves of people in here while I was waiting like a damn fool in Europe."

"Yes." Kaspar replies simply. "Despite having the keenest senses, I won't divulge what I know. You're trouble, but I do not need to be cruel."

Not exactly kind, either, buddy.

"That's enough making her feel like shit," Lucas growls. "Slade, go open all the windows. Iggy, go help pick up the boxes I had sent with Liam and Kaspar. Let's air out this disgusting funk and swap everything before one of us catches something."

"Lucas!" I groan, rubbing my face again. "Don't even *joke* about that. Dragon Scabies is awful; my friend Luella got it once, and I told Magnus that—oh, fuck."

"Today is the gift that keeps on giving," Kaspar mutters as he swoops down to pick up a large stack of boxes like it's nothing. "I have a feeling this won't be the last batch of unpleasant realizations. Did you buy tissues, bear?"

"I. Do. Not. Cry," I snarl through gritted teeth. Des weaves a path by my ear, hissing as the dragon passes me. She wants to sink her fangs into him, even just fractionally, to teach him a 'hard' lesson. I won't let her, although turning one of his hands or arms to stone for a couple hours would be amusing as hell.

Biting off my nose to spite my face isn't one of my signature moves.

"All females leak when they're emotional," he retorts as he drops the boxes at the end of the bed. "It's the way of nature."

"Gorgons don't," Slade offers. "I don't know about gargoyles. Iggy?"

The professor looks up, smirking a little. "Their tears are quite sought after for spell work. I wouldn't want to see you hurt, Morgana, but I would collect some for later."

"Gee, thanks. Glad my pain might help you hex some chick who pissed you off."

Iggy strides over, putting his hands on my shoulders as he looks into my eyes. "Don't take me wrong. I'd be furious about it, but I am very practical. I would gather *any* tool I thought would help me keep those I care about safe. Gargoyle tears are known for vast healing properties since they are so uncommon."

"Oh."

I fight the urge to duck my head; instead, I give him a knowing expression. "Let's get this shit done, boys. I find myself eager to have a sleeping space that isn't a fucking couch all the sudden."

"You and me both, cupcake," Iggy says with a wink, heading to help Lucas with the curtains.

Damn. Down, girl.

discoveries

Ending the call, I sigh and run my fingers through my hair. The others are still in the bedroom helping the Prince's new 'project' clean out the remnants of a foul member of my species. I don't like or trust the woman, but she doesn't seem like someone who deserves the filth I scented when I walked in there. I know the Society put her through hell for taking her vengeance, but I think if they figured out what we did within five seconds of being in place, they might have let her go with a slap on the wrist.

Magnus was a depraved, perverted motherfucker who obviously didn't give a single fuck about the woman he asked to marry him.

I stepped out briefly to take a call from one of the commanders at the Palace. We check in frequently when situations evolve and though I often leave out major details about the Prince's life for all of our sanity, they also keep me apprised of what's going on in the Daybreak Court while we're on this side of the Veil—especially when the information is as juicy as what Lorcan just shared with me.

A group of supes from a small town an hour from here entered our lands a few days ago, claiming to be on a vacation. That isn't anything new, but they were accompanied by an unemerged supe, several alumnae of this college, and the son of a senator from this state. The Prince's family did what they always do... send in the other princes and the king to feel out the honored guests. Lorcan said one of the tailors messed with a pair of be-spelled glasses she was wearing and that's when I lost my temper.

A scandal with the Society would cause Liam to be called home and he would have that mischievous shit's head.

I told Lorcan to find Fiannula and deal with the designer, then have the head of the royal guard call me. We need to figure out exactly how much trouble this idiot may have caused by skirting around the rules of the treaties. He said their party left for the Harvest Court this morning, so it's possible I can contact one of the folks there to salvage things. I'm not sure *how*, of course, because we don't even know if her little trick worked.

"Sweet Aed, help me untangle this before a dumbass tailor causes a fucking *war* with those tight assed supes," I mutter as I head back into the former dragon's den of smut.

"What's going on, Kas? You look stressed," Liam says as he cocks his head at me.

Shaking my head back in response, I lift a chest that stinks to high hell and back. "This thing needs to *go*, and I advise the professor to follow me downstairs to figure out what he kept inside of it."

Morgana looks at me in horror as I heft the enormous thing up and turn towards the door. "That's... person... sized."

Fuck yes, it is, and it goddamn smells like it, too.

I could say that and send her running for the bathroom to cry, but I shrug. "Might be. There's magic, though, so I need the prof."

Liam catches my hesitation and grins. That motherfucker knows I chose not to be a dick to the woman, and he thinks it means I'm softening. I'm not, but as I said before, I don't *have* to be needlessly cruel. I am often hesitant to get involved in such a volatile situation. Adding in the shenanigans of our relatives in Faerie means I'd prefer not to draw the scrutiny of anyone the Society has their eyes on.

"I'm coming, Kaspar," Ignatius says as he stands and dusts off his pants. He was digging underneath the vast bed before we move it, making certain it wouldn't uncover anything untoward.

I doubt we're going to hide much from a woman as smart as Morgana, especially since we're ridding the house of shit belonging to someone as depraved as Magnus. But that's not my job to work out— the rest of these assholes can handle telling her what all the shit we find means. I'm good at lifting and carrying the heaviest shit out, not comforting some aggrieved ex-fiancé.

The bespectacled academic follows me out the door quietly, and until we get to the steps, he doesn't say a word.

"That chest is trouble, right?"

My answer is a snort. "You could say that."

"This was used for... punishment, you think?" The professor eyes the box with a curled lip and I nod.

"Likely. Whether it was sexual or plain control or both.... who knows? Sounds like the owner of this place deserved his death. It's a coin toss. But look," I murmur. Stooping, I flick open the small panels at the bottom of the head and foot of the chest to reveal the caged over mesh. "This is the breathing ventilation—at least, when he allowed it."

Ignatius shudders and I have to hold back a chuckle. I always forget the supes closer to human—casters and the like—don't have the same animal instincts as the rest of the supernaturals. Their senses aren't as heightened, which is why he didn't notice the smell, and their penchant for the dark rarely leaves the lighter shades of gray.

"This is barbaric, even for him," he says with a sigh. "Why are you whispering?"

I snort. "I'm simply speaking in low tones, Professor. While the lady of this museum of the grotesque may not have super scenting unless her snakes come out, gargoyles *and* gorgons are known for excellent hearing. I do not believe she needs to hear this conversation."

He gives me a begrudging look of respect, nodding. "Okay, so how do you know about this shit? Is the Prince...?"

"Fuck, no," I grin as I feel along the seams of the lid to find where the catch is hidden. "Daybreak loves to promote the shiny, happy Fae persona of the Seelie, but there's a ton of darkness there. If you've been with the court for a few centuries, you see more of this shit than you ever want to. However, Liam embodies what people *perceive* Daybreak to be. I'm not saying he has no kinks, but he's not into the pitch black side."

The professor lets out a breath slowly. "Good. Morgana likes to be in charge, but she also likes to be challenged. I believe her desire to be in control stems from whatever small portion of his evil Magnus showed her. The more we discover, the happier I find myself that she killed him before he had her legally under his thumb."

I don't know what to say about that—the dean doesn't seem like a woman I'd enjoy seeing crushed, though.

"He would have destroyed her, eventually. They all do; Liam has a brother who enjoys breaking his toys." Pressing my lips together, I realize I've said more than I should and turn back to the chest. We need to get it open to see if it simply needs to be cleansed—physically and magically—before disposal or if we have a *much* bigger problem on our hands.

"Don't worry, man. I won't tell her you have an iota of compassion. You can keep pretending you're the one made of stone." Ignatius laughs to himself, then scratches his chin. "Want me to bust it open yet?"

"Not yet. If you hit it just right, all our evidence gets destroyed."

He frowns and tilts his head. "What evidence?"

Merciful Crone, fucking casters can be dim with politics.

"I have worked security for the royals for centuries, Ignatius. Since the Prince is taking a vested interest in Morgana, I have to strategize how to get her out of whatever the fuck mess she and the hockey player are in. Thus, as we clean up, gathering evidence of her ex's depravity might give us leverage with your Society. It could get them to back off her punishments and possibly remove the target from her back. *That* is in my best interest because I won't have to take a metaphorical bullet for the Prince if he's caught in the crossfire somehow."

He blinks, pondering that for a moment, then grins. "Okay. I'm on board. We get this damn thing open, photograph the proof, then we'll get rid of it. That about it?"

I nod, continuing to slide my fingertips around the edges as I circle the nasty wood and iron prison. "Hopefully sooner rather than later. Luckily for us, I'm not allergic to the iron in the damn thing like Liam would be."

As soon as the words leave my mouth, it hits me and by the horrified look on Ignatius' face, he gets it, too. This is a prison specifically made to weaken types of Fae—it's constructed with far more metal than necessary for its design. I crack my neck, pushing the fury of my dragon back as I think about smaller beings from the other side of the Veil.

"If he wasn't dead, I'd kill the son of a bitch myself," I mutter. Suddenly, I have a lot more respect for the woman in the house. Obviously, this fuckwit dragon was well versed in magic—perhaps even a hybrid—and she took him out all by herself. The hunter in me has to appreciate the skill it had to have taken to locate, plan, and execute an operation of that difficulty by herself.

"Get this thing open or I'm blowing it up," the professor growls in agreement.

Done with being careful, I allow my dragon to press against my skin just enough to bring forth my claws. Slipping them under the lid, I give it a hard yank, wood splinters and I have to turn my face away for a moment, but as soon as I lift the lid, the stench gets worse. A sigh of relief escapes unbidden when I realize there isn't an actual dead being in the trunk; it's simply been used for captivity without ever being cleaned once.

At least, I'm assuming that from the smell.

"Jesus fuck, what an evil asshole," Ignatius says as he chokes on the unignorable rot coming from the wooden cage. "This is pure filth. He could have had anyone under his thumb scrub it, but he chose not to."

"Another method of control," I say as I bend to examine the inside. I'm holding my breath now, but dragons excel at that shit, so we're good. "I don't think this was just a sex toy; I think he used it to teach people lessons. It probably had enchantments on it when he was alive that kept various beings from using powers to escape. This is how he scared the entire fucking campus during his reign. This and likely other just as sinister shit."

"Do we tell her? It might ease her conscience." The professor is snapping pictures of the disgusting prison with his phone, pausing occasionally to turn away and get fresh air.

"Not yet. I'll let Liam know. We need to check with all the courts to see if there are missing ex-pats or visa students they're searching for. A supe using this has no qualms about killing or letting go of the broken survivors."

I have to be careful not to raise red flags with my queries, though.

The visitors flitting about Faerie with a spell broken by one of our court make this tricky. If we draw too much attention to our court from the Society, they'll delve deeper into *our* treatment of guests and then... Neither Liam nor I wish to be called home for good. We enjoy the Veil's delights and come and go as we please. Plus, Liam is slated to be the newest diplomat from our Court when he graduates, which saves him from some half-assed political marriage bullshit. His parents will allow him latitude to find someone who might be more advantageous here rather than a waif from Midnight or something.

This asshole dragon is fucking shit up even from the grave and if I have to help Morgana stop him, I'll happily sign on to the Magic School Bus for a bit.

rude awakening

When Iggy and Kaspar return from stowing the weird trunk in the shed outside, I try to figure out why they both look like someone died. Neither seems eager to give it up, so I go back to helping Lucas pull down the curtains. He's not as strong as me, especially when recovering, but he's good at staying close, so I feel less exposed by this nightmare.

A room full of men I barely know are finding out just how cuckolded and naïve I was when Magnus was alive—I fucking hate it.

"I know you're mad they won't say what they did out there, but consider it might be because you don't *want* to know," Slade says as he walks over to take the pile of stinky linens to put in a garbage bag.

Blinking at him, I open my mouth, then close it. He probably can't help reading me—powerful sirens can have trouble controlling their gifts—and I know he's only trying to help. I'm unused to people looking out for me, especially men, so I'm overreacting. I give him a small shrug, tilting my head. "That's probably true, but I'm so used to taking care of myself. It makes me feel powerless to be in the dark."

Lucas wraps his arms around me, rubbing his cheek on my shoulder blade from behind. I'm much taller than him on this stool and it's kind of cute. "Morgana, you don't need to know every disgusting thing that person did to control your life. No one in this room believes anyone but you is running this show."

Kaspar snorts and shakes his head, but Iggy, Slade, and Liam just grin at me. My lips curve and I allow myself to lean into Lucas for support. "Thanks, babe."

Ugh. How clichéd am I? I have to figure out a name better than that or I'll feel lame.

Iggy whips the comforter and pillowcases off, handing them to Slade before he does the sheets. "Take this shit. Thank hell she can't smell it. Wolfberg, how fast can you get shit here if we find a mattress for her online?"

The bear moves back, and his smug grin makes my stomach flutter. "Try me, spell sucker."

"Sweet baby Polyphemus, the two of you are going to drive me insane. Especially with *that* one..." Slade points to Kaspar, "... pulling his BS as well. Work together so we don't make Morgana even more stressed out, please?"

Tucking my chin, I grin at him. He and Liam are peacemakers—I need that for sure. There's too much dick waving in this room. "Slade is right. It would definitely help if we could *try* not to attack each other. Snark is okay; I don't mind that, but just... don't be assholes."

"*Macushla*[1]," Liam says and Kaspar's scowl deepens. "We will all behave to the best of our abilities. Right, gentleman?"

Slade nods, then Lucas, and finally, Iggy throws up his hands. "Fine. fine. I'll try not to bait the shifter."

"I agree to nothing and he can't make me," Kaspar grunts. "You know better, Liam."

The Prince rolls his eyes, muttering something in Gaelic under his breath before waving at the dragon. "He says that, but he won't be truly awful since I asked. Don't worry."

"Now that we cleared that up, I'm going downstairs to grab a tablet," Slade says as he holds the full garbage up. "I'll take this to the curb. Once we're back, we'll measure the room and let Lucas work his magic to arrange for the new bed."

"Fuck yeah. We're going *huge*. This room is half the upper floor—it's plenty big enough for something we can spread out in." His eyes twinkle with merriment, and I feel the color drain from my face.

"Um... *we?*"

He nods, raking his hand through his golden waves. "Yeah. You, me... whoever gets invited. Whatever."

Holy shit. Holy shit. Holy shit.

"That... remains to be... decided," I mutter as I turn back to the section of the room I'm working in. I can't deal with their flirting *and* this bullshit in Magnus' room. It's too much. Not to mention, Jackson arrives later today and I have *no idea* what he's going to say about Lucas's case.

Liam laughs softly, then walks over to spin me around. "Don't hide. You have a buffet of men clamoring for your attention, *macushla*. A prince, a wizard, a musician, a sport star, and a grumpy ass war hero—who could ask for more?"

I swallow hard, looking around as panic uncurls in my gut. "That's what I'm afraid of. This kind of shit *never* works out for me—not even with one person. How can I expect any different when it's five?"

"Those other people weren't us," the Prince says with a smirk. "Now stop worrying and let's get this done so you're not living in that monster's filth."

Hallelujah to that.

By the time Lucas and Liam work their rich guy magic, it's late afternoon and we've had two deliveries of stuff for the bedroom. The room is now filled with a bed so enormous I have no idea how they got the mattress in and it's decorated to the nines in a calming slate gray and black motif. I showed Liam furniture when he asked and I don't know how the actual hell he got it here, but the wrought iron bed frame and shining dark Gothic furniture arrived within hours. There's not a damn trace of my ex anywhere in this space and I finally feel like I have a place to escape.

I'd cry if I could show that kind of vulnerability in front of them.

Instead, I'm sitting in the living room eating the pizza Slade ordered while we wait for our guests on pins and needles. Channing messaged that Jackson's plane taxied in while we were finishing up, so we decided to relax until they arrive. Lucas has my feet in his lap and I'm leaning against Iggy's shoulder while some mystery show plays in the background.

"You know, you're awful calm about all of this, Wolfberg," Kaspar says as he eyes him. The dragon is seated far from me in the room, causing eye rolling from all of us.

Lucas grins. "Well, I've got the fucking Shark coming to do my defense and Nana behind me... plus, Morgana believes me. And I'm not dying of some whack Fae poison anymore. I'm feeling #blessed, man."

"Ugh, *don't* be that guy," I mutter. "Only douchebags *say* hashtag something out loud."

Slade snorts, then covers his mouth. "Sorry, dude, she's right."

"Fine," my new mate pouts. "But I feel lucky as hell and you guys are all part of that. It all has to get better from here, right?"

Liam arches a brow and shrugs. "Perhaps. It depends on what this lawyer says about the evidence they collected. I assume traveling here means it's not good. Good news could be given in a phone call, yes?"

I suck in a breath as I realize he's right. "Damn. He's right."

"Don't worry, M. I didn't kill the asshole, so whatever they have is circumstantial. There's no way they can make this shit stick. LaMount was a major asswad; he had enemies on and off the ice. Anyone could have done it." Lucas sighs as he squeezes my foot. "Hell, we don't know what he was into, but all the players in the league thought he was dirty somehow."

"Dirty how?" Kaspar nails him with a serious look. "That sounds important."

"Fixing games. Trying to end careers. Gambling, maybe. Rumors about girls. Nothing I can prove, just whispers," the bear says with a shrug.

This is stuff we have to tell Jackson; his team can look into it.

"That's definitely shit the Shark needs to know, man. He's got people coming with him. I assume it's helping him build your defense. They'll dig into crevices that fucker didn't know he had. When he was alive, I mean." Iggy scratches the back of his neck, looking sheepish. "I have some experience with PIs because of my family."

I arch a brow at him. "You do, huh?"

"The Briartons are often the object of vendettas. It happens when you're high ranking magical folks. Supe PIs were always sniffing around as I grew up." His expression turns darkly smug as he takes a drink, then continues. "Now that I'm of age, I handle that shit on my own. As a kid, they had to teach me what to do, though."

Those are stories I can't decide if I want to hear or not.

"You realize everyone here has... baggage, right?" Lucas asks me. His eyes meet mine and he licks his lips. "I'm not snow white; I was a dick in high school. Not evil or anything, but not... great. Kind of a bully, actually."

Slade coughs, looking down as he mumbles, "I grew up in a mafia family on the coast. I've seen things. I've done things I wish I could undo."

I blink, my eyes widening as I look at the remaining two guys. "And you?"

Kaspar rolls his eyes. "Don't be dense. I'm not part of this, but I've been in wars and protected Fae royals from childhood. My soul is black as soot—which should tell you what I'll do if you do anything to harm my friend."

"Merciful Aed, Kaspar. You make yourself sound like you're as bad as her ex. You aren't, but if I'm honest, I'm not clean, either." Liam gives me a rueful expression. "I'm a Fae royal and everything that comes with that. I've spent most of my life bullying the bullies. And I've always done what it takes to mete out justice when I think it's deserved."

I'm being courted by a room full of villains. What. The. Fuck.

"So you're telling me none of you care what I did to Magnus—or why —because you're all a bunch of rich jackasses?" I give them all an amused look as I try to digest that information.

"That's about right," Lucas says with a grin. "No one's perfect. At least we know you can handle yourself when the cameras descend."

"C-Cameras?" I choke.

Being in the spotlight was the worst part of my fucking trial.

"Morgana," Slade says softly. "You realize that being part of the investigation will bring the press. If they figure out about you and Lucas... he's related to the Wolfenbergs *and* accused of murder. Add our pedigrees to the mix and... there's likely to be a lot of attention."

For a moment, I feel like I'm going to vomit, and Lucas runs his hands up my legs soothingly. "I-I didn't think about that. I'm not a fan of the press after... you know. But... I won't run away when Lucas needs me, either."

His grin spreads across his face, and he darts forward, grabbing my face in his hands. "That's my girl. Give 'em hell, Slither."

I recoil a bit, my face flushing at the nickname. "Stop."

"Nope," he says as he beams. "My mate is the biggest badass on this damn campus and whoever is framing me is going to find out what happens when they fuck around. I can't wait."

The dragon guard eyes me for a moment, tilting his head. "Do you have control of your hybrid sides? You can't turn anyone to stone or go on a flying rampage if you get angry."

Des pops out of my ponytail, hissing at him in indignation. I chuckle and let her threaten him; I know she won't call the others out if I don't give permission. "I do, thank you very much. I'm not fresh off the fucking truck. You *know* how old my species both live."

He grunts, and Liam tilts his head as he smirks. "I think you, me, and Kaspar are the oldest in the room. The others are mere babies, Morgana."

My eyes narrow. "Watch it, Your Highness. It's rude to ask a lady's age."

"I don't have to ask," Kaspar says as he leans back in his chair. "I already know."

Well, fuck you, too, charcoal breath.

------

1. Darling

knock knock

The group waiting for the Shark is one of the most interesting I've ever been in. Morgana is enchanting, and the hungry looks all the men are giving her make me want to rise to the challenge. Funnily enough, I'm usually the biggest asshole in the room —as Slade *loves* to point out—but that honor is taken by the churlish dragon sitting in the corner. I know he's here to protect the Prince, but I'm confused why he's staying this close if he wants no part in our... possible dating situation.

Perhaps the scaly one doth protest too much?

My lips curve up as I study him, pretending not to pay attention to the lively conversation going on. I'm fairly certain my second assumption is the correct one and I'm going to enjoy seeing him brought to his knees. A loud buzz sounds out, pulling my focus from Kaspar as Morgana's eyes widen and she stops talking. That's her phone and this must be Channing, letting her know the lawyer has finally arrived.

"Morgana," she says as she picks it up and answers. "Yes, Channing. I understand. He's brought the entire team? Oh, goodness. Well, we could—you set up one of the houses? Yes, of course, I approve. Keeping them close is—Okay. We'll see you soon. Good job."

Arching a brow, I wait for her to relay what she learned. I'm not surprised Channing is thriving under someone like her. She's allowing our old friend to take control and show her capabilities for the first time in years. Channing Oswald is *very* good at what she does and her previous bosses didn't give her a moment to blossom. Magnus' administration was so controlling that only the strongest staff could rise above his corrupt bullshit.

"What's going on?" Slade asks quietly.

Morgana sighs. "Jackson's plane has landed. Well, both, really. He has an entire team coming—I don't know most of them, but since they'll be here for a while, Channing arranged for them to stay in one of the houses on Chancellor Row. It will make it much simpler for them to strategize and have access to everything they need."

"They'll be staying on this street?" Liam says with an amused look. "That's a lot of access, Morgana. Are you certain about having that much scrutiny near your home?"

Good question, Your Highness.

"I don't mind. I have nothing to hide, Liam. My trial exposed damn near everything about my life before I got here and I'm not hiding mating with Lucas. Sure, we're not making it public, but I won't deny it if anyone asks." She leans into the big bear and he rumbles happily.

"What about... the rest of us?" I ask, tilting my head. "Will that affect anything?"

She shrugs. "Who knows? You're all right; the press has skewered me to bone already. What difference does it make if they find out I'm in a poly dating situation? At least I'll be honest about it rather than being a cheating asshole, like my ex."

Kaspar snorts. "Small comfort, but not less true. I doubt the Prince's family will care much. It's much more common in the Veil, of course."

"Nana will understand when I tell her what happened," Lucas says confidently. "She's always hoped I'd find a fated mate. She thinks people turn out like my parents when they marry non-mates to settle."

Well, at least two of the families won't kick up a fuss.

"Iggy and I will have issues. Not because it's you, per se. It will be because both of our families have expectations about our futures. Mine may be mistaken about what they expect, but they'll be... vocal." Slade flushes and ducks his head.

I chuckle at his euphemism. "He's right. His criminal ties will make their opinions known, but we've been managing that for years. My family will be obnoxious and behave typically for rich old money supes."

"I appreciate the heads up, guys, but what does this have to do with Jackson and his team coming?" Morgana frowns, tilting her head. "I doubt they're going to publicize our lives."

"No, but they'll dig into *everyone* in Lucas's life to ensure they have every crumb of information the prosecutors could bring up if this goes to trial. If they didn't, they'd be shitty ass lawyers." Kaspar makes an annoyed expression, then continues. "We'll all be fodder for their research *and* the mud-slinging of the other side if Jackson cannot snuff this out quickly."

"Do we think he'll be able to nip it in the bud?" she whispers.

"If anyone can, it would be the Shark. But... sometimes, once the ball is rolling, it's impossible to stop the momentum," Liam replies. "If he can't prevent Lucas from being charged, that's when the storm will begin."

And that's when we're all going to need to band together... even the irksome lizard.

THE KNOCK AT THE DOOR MAKES MORGANA JUMP, DESPITE knowing it was coming. Kaspar stands, glaring before he heads for the door. I will not argue with his obvious need to vet the people coming before they join the party. He's clearly competent and we've already dealt with one dead body and one poisoned heir.

Channing's voice carries into the living area as she practically growls, "We're here for a meeting with my boss, you giant dickhead. Move out of the way before I move you myself!"

Fat chance of that. Channing barely weighs a hundred pounds soaking wet and Kaspar is built like a brick shit house.

"Should I go..."

Morgana tilts her head, the errant snake twitching by her shoulder. "No. Perhaps we'll let them find common ground."

My rebuttal is cut off by a chorus of loud, dark snarls coming from the other room. I'm surprised to see Morgana's eyes flicker for a second—just long enough to look serpentine and absolutely delighted before she leans back into Lucas calmly. "Okay, what the hell?"

Channing marches into the room followed by two hulking supes, one dark and one light, a golden boy, a nerd, and the tallest leprechaun I've ever seen. The dragon is right behind them, looking angry as hell and ready to bite someone's head off. "Morgana, your doorman needs a course in appropriate guest reception."

"Does he now?" our girl replies, her voice filled with humor. "Prince Liam, take note of Kaspar's deficiencies for later."

"I do fucking *not!*" the bodyguard roars at my diminutive friend.

Surprisingly, Channing doesn't cower when the enormous lizard gets in her face. Instead, she puts her hand on her hip and juts her chin out. "You definitely do, jack ass. Back off—and try a mint. Yikes."

The golden boy bursts out laughing, holding his fist out to her. "Sweet cheeks has *bite*. I fucking love it."

The Prince stands, preventing Kaspar from venting his rage further. "Perhaps we should do some introductions? I'm Prince Liam of the Daybreak Court. Kaspar is my well-intentioned, but rough-edged friend and guard. That's Ignatius Briarton, Slade, and of course, Lucas is sitting with Morgana. We appreciate you coming."

The outsiders look at one another for a minute, then Captain Good-looking shrugs. "I'm the bear's lawyer; of course we came. I'm not sure why the rest of you are here, but I enjoy a party. This cute little geek is Eli, the mischievous looking one is Foley, blondie is Rainier, and the sour faced one is Kendrick. I brought everyone because your delightful assistant told me my client was poisoned. It changes everything."

"Why?" I ask. "What about the attack changes your stance on the court case?"

The mop-headed nerd pushes up his glasses. "Because we feel it was an attempt to prevent anyone from finding out who really killed LaMount. If Lucas died under suspicion, people would believe the story that he killed Pierre because of a rivalry and then got killed for revenge. It ties the whole thing up in a bow. Murder is never that simple."

Lucas frowns, and Morgana squeezes his hand. "You think Lucas is being framed to cover up something else?"

"I do," Rainer cuts in. "We need your truth, Dean, to understand how and why. Inform us about the undisclosed aspects of the trial. Don't insult my intelligence by protesting it; I know better."

What the hell is he talking about?

Our girl's head drops and I can feel the tension radiating from her across the room. "I... I can't."

"They told you it was spell-locked, right?"

Again, I look at the enormous blond guy skeptically. "Who the fuck are you, man?"

Jackson rolls his eyes, walking over to drop into a chair. His pet nerd drops onto his lap and he sighs. "Look. My team is... let's say, a bit morally gray. Rainier worked for various agencies ranging from human to supe to other over the years. His species is rare and very useful in many situations. Exceptions have been made because he's so valuable. If he says he knows something, he knows. So spill it."

"It's spell-locked, yes."

Morgana's answer shocks the hell out of me. That sort of confinement was outlawed centuries ago. What the fuck else did they do to this woman in return for not killing her? "Is that all?"

Slade squints at her and then shakes his head. "No. I *knew* I sensed something when we first met. There's more."

"Geo tag," the dark man says. He and Kaspar have been glaring at one another since they got in the room and I'm pretty sure they're deciding whether or not to kill each other.

Morgana doesn't lift her head as she whispers, "Yes."

"*Unacceptable!*" Lucas roars as he sits up straighter. "They have you spell locked to keep you from telling people the truth *and* geo-tagged to track you? What the fuck are they doing? I'm calling Nana."

"Wait." Eli shakes his head as he looks at us seriously. "Your grand-mother might know already, Lucas. She's not part of the tribunal, but the eldest, most powerful members are usually aware of judgements. Their control over Morgana is something that can be dealt with later. We just need to trick the lock long enough for her to help us connect the dots. Removing it is an 'another day' item."

"How in the hell do we do that?" I ask curiously. "I've never heard of a way to beat those. What about you, Liam?"

The Prince shakes his head. "I've not heard of one, either. They're indestructible."

Fucking perfect.

"That's our first order of business then," Jackson muses. "K, this is one of yours. I know you'll be skulking around campus on your own, but... contacts."

The man nods, not taking his eyes off his new nemesis. "Understood."

I arch a brow, looking at the newcomers critically. "You really think you can solve an unremovable spell created so long ago no one remembers who first uttered its words?"

Channing blinks. "My sister and her cadre have been working for the Fates."

Jackson's head turns slowly until he's looking at my old friend. "Your sister... is a Guardian?"

"Yep. She's somewhere secret in Europe, doing some task for the crones with her Guardian mates. I don't know what, because she can't tell me." She flushes pink, pushing up her glasses nervously. "Why?"

"Because your sister is working with the best friend of my other favorite client." He laughs and shakes his head, looking at the guy on his lap. "I'll be beer battered cod at the fish fry. Jojo's BFF is shacked up with this adorable woman's sister. How incestuous—I love it."

Slade coughs. "Uh, that's not exactly what incestuous means..."

Eli rolls his eyes. "Of course not. He's being... Jackson. Ignore his odd phrasing. He simply means it's a very, very small world in the South.

In fact, it's sort of like all roads lead to Whistler's Hollow at this point."

"And the roads are just *filled* with delightfully rebellious women," Jackson says with a grin. "I'm just happy to be in the middle of it all."

Good thing someone is.

working for the weekend

The shame I felt when I had to admit that I not only have spells preventing me from discussing the 'extra' tasks I've been given and the tracker is enormous. I'm little more than an animal on some human TV show, watched for the amusement and benefit it provides my captors. No one's ever questioned me about *why* the Council decided, only what I was required to do as punishment. I don't know if that's because the magic in my lock prevented interviewers and nosey Nellies from wondering, or if people are genuinely afraid to appear to question their authority. Either way, I didn't break the enchantments since the others guessed, so I'm not suffering any ill-effects... yet.

Who knows if that will change?

"I don't understand what the Society thinks Magnus was up to that would warrant this kind of barbaric measures," Channing says. "Even if someone *is* framing Lucas, what do they gain from it?"

"I don't know. Frankly, I also don't know how many other people they may have 'special' spells attached to. The picture could be much wider than we've considered." Jackson shrugs as he leans into Eli.

The hacker pushes his glasses up, tilting his head as he looks at Jackson curiously. "You think there's something global they're watching? Perhaps a threat that runs deeper than two murders?"

I frown, trying to remember the things the tribunal said in the trial. I know they had obscuring enchantments in place and my memory of the event has been carefully curated. They told me so when they cast my current shackles. But people don't always consider erasing things they don't realize someone else heard or saw. I might recover something important. "If so, my memories may hold a clue. The head magistrate had their weavers do shit to it, but it's possible I have details lurking they didn't know I picked up."

The blond hottie grins broadly. "That sounds like a job for Foley, if I've ever heard one. You could probably let the baby mobster help, though. Maybe the Prince."

"Excuse me?" Iggy grumbles. "I'm well versed in—"

Kendrick snorts, and Ranier fist bumps him before shaking his head. "Not in this kind of magic. They wouldn't have used someone from the Earthbound magical vein. Only fairytale, Fae, or mythicals, so it would be harder to find the right skills to undo it. Mages and witches are a dime a dozen, Professor."

He looks offended, but it's Slade who nods. "That seems sensible. My parents never use the human magic sects for their real dirty work. Magical mojo from you guys is pretty common—sorry, Iggy."

The mage damn near pouts, making Kaspar and Lucas laugh. My bear gives Ignatius a pointed look as he shifts a little. "Calm down, man. Note they're not asking us shifters to do shit that isn't kicking someone's ass. We're not useful unless it's our fists and you don't see me complaining."

Kaspar arches a brow. "Speak for yourself, rich kid. Dragons are mythicals and have magic of their own; it's simply counterproductive in this instance."

Oh, fuck. We're back to dick measuring, and now there're ten guys.

"Gentleman, I don't think picking at one another will help us short or long term," Channing interrupts. I smile at her, proud to see her blossoming since she's gotten to spread her wings. "If Jackson has an assignment for Kendrick, perhaps we should divvy up the rest of the work? Morgana and Lucas will have to return to their duties tomorrow, as will everyone else."

"Stupid classes," Lucas mutters in annoyance. I blink at him and he shrugs. "They're a means to an end, M. I have to take and pass them to continue being eligible. My goal has always been pro sports after college."

Liam clears his throat. "I'm in a similar boat, unfortunately. Taking things here keeps me away from my father and court. I'm earning this master's to hopefully outlast the bloody tyrant."

"I want to pursue my major, but doing it at school keeps me from my family business as well," Slade says with a shrug.

Iggy sighs and rakes his hand through his hair. "Teaching prevents my father from demanding I lead the regional covens and shit."

"Holy shit," Eli whispers. "You're all ducking family obligations? Jackson ducked this shit for over a decade until his dad fucked off. I'm in actual *hiding* from my clan in Europe. Rainier joined his first paramilitary group to get away from his pride and Foley doesn't know who his family is. Kendrick doesn't tell anyone shit, but I assume he's got issues, too."

My nose wrinkles as I stare at them. "Am I the only one in this room with parents who don't suck?"

Channing snorts. "Affirmative, Morgana. You'll find quite a few hybrids, agents, inductees, and people involved with the Society have less than desirable roots. They find a home within the bonds with other powerful supes they never had growing up. I believe the statistics for hybrids who are left in the enclaves joining is about ninety-two percent."

"Sounds about right," Rainier murmurs. "And there's a fuck ton of lost ones out there being watched by those Guardians secretly for late in life emergence. I know a witch who's been watching a woman since elementary school that didn't show her first signs of supe behavior until college. She lost track of her for a bit and has recently located the missing charge, only to find she's exhibiting both magic *and* shifting. It's a bit of a mess."

Something about that makes me sit up. I recognize the tale; there was a discussion. "I think that triggered a memory. When I was waiting for the trial in holding, there was a woman who came to speak to them urgently. She'd found someone important, and they had to postpone for a few minutes while she shared the news. It was good news, I think. Something about a panther."

The blond merc whips his head around, looking at Jackson for a moment. They have some sort of dude eyebrow conversation before the lawyer smiles. "I have some idea of what that involves, but we don't need to worry about it *now*. Some problems can stay on other supes' plates until it's necessary to examine them."

I don't like the sound of that at all.

AFTER A FEW HOURS OF DEBATE AND A DINNER DELIVERY, we finally hammer out what everyone handles. I'd hoped it would be simpler, but honestly, with that many dicks in the room, I'm surprised no actual fights broke out as alphas wrangled for control. Both Channing and I had to intercede several times, much to the amusement of the more passive men present.

Jackson will start by visiting the precinct, district attorney, and any reasonably local officials to get a feel for their taste for prosecuting such a high-profile supe. It sounded reasonable, and since Channing's assignment was to liaise between our group and his team, I knew she'd make sure he looped us in frequently. Eli and Kendrick had the digital and physical research angles—background, interviews, and snooping on everyone involved in the case. Iggy, Slade, and Liam are going to work on the spell shit, including figuring out what might have been used to cover the tracks of the actual murderer at the rink. Lucas and I have to go back to normal routine, keeping our lips sealed about everything as we pretend life is normal. Kaspar and Rainer will work contacts in the private security and intelligence communities—both supe and human.

It's a goddamn lot and once more, I have the thought that I'd kill my asshole ex-fiancé again if I could. Being told he might have been involved in some broad global conspiracy and fucking this place up so badly that I'll be digging through financials until I'm ready to die is more ambitious than I would have pegged him for.

Of course, I wouldn't have pegged him, period, because he always had to be in charge.

Snorting, I press my lips together at the image, and suddenly, everyone is looking at me. Clearing my throat, I smile. "Sorry, something funny popped into my head. Continue, Eli."

The hacker winks at me as if he knows where my thoughts went, and I narrow my gaze. I know Jackson said he's a techno mage/incubi hybrid, but I don't know if he has the mind reading shit. He might just be good at 'vibe' sensation—the Cubi are fucking amazing at that.

"I plan on infiltrating the local and state law enforcement databases, plus I'm going to have another go at some of the local Councils. If I find a vulnerability in a small network, I can piggyback it all the way home to the main servers. That might give me the location of the farm and then Rainier can scout it. Once we do that, Kendrick will try to get to whatever they have magically air-gapped—which will be the double secret probation shit we're looking for in terms of bigger picture."

Kaspar nods, seeming to understand the jargon fairly well. "You think everything they've done that is being kept quiet for safety, diplomatic, business, or intelligence reasons will not be connected to the web. That makes sense, and it is fairly standard protocol even for the royal family in Faerie."

I frown at him. "I'd think everything in Faerie is kept in like books or scrolls. But I've never been, honestly."

Liam grins, tilting his head. "Come now, *Saaladir*. We're modern creatures, despite staying steeped in our heritage. We have plenty of tech—much of it more advanced than the humans like the Council. Perhaps when we settle this nonsense, we will all travel to my homelands for a weekend. My family is difficult, but we'll pay our respects and then go wandering."

My eyes sparkle as I glance at my companions. "Would you guys go?"

"Fuck, yeah, I would," Lucas beams. "I've never been, either. Passports to Faerie are fucking hard to get approved."

"I've been," Iggy says with a smirk. "But I spent the entire time working. It was an undergrad research project on magical variances between species. I want to go when I'm not obligated to stay in a small hut."

Slade gives me a shy smile. "I'm also new, but I want to be included."

Jackson snorts at us, shaking his head. "What the hell *is* it with that place lately? My other client has been there for the better part of a month and I promise you, she's pissy as hell about it. The royals are *all* dicks and there's some weird shit going on behind the scenes that's causing all sorts of shit for her."

Kaspar and Liam exchange a look and the 'Hand of Morrigan' name flashes in my head. *Is that possibly the root of Jackson's friend's issues?* I want to tell him, but the Prince catches my eyes and subtly shakes his head. Whatever that is must not be something getting shared outside of his people, even if it would help visitors. I frown, but I nod imperceptibly so he knows I understand.

"Well, I'm sure if the Prince is with us, we'll be safe," I chirp, hoping to change the subject.

"Doubtful," Jackson mumbles, and Eli elbows him. "Fine, fine. I'm sure you'll be okay. But no one is realm-hopping until we deal with this LaMount shit. Cross-realm phone calls are fucking pricey and I've had to pay for enough of them to speak with Jojo."

"Dude, you're The Shark. You own seven private jets and enough property to stay in the supe hierarchy. A phone call is what you're worried about?" Slade gives him a confused look.

Jackson shrugs, flashing pearly white teeth. "Waste not, want not, little maestro. I'm all about making every dollar count. Plus, I hate doing expenses with that snooty goblin who does the financials and taxes."

A lawyer being a tight-fisted spendthrift? Say it ain't so.

fuck the police

"**I**'m feeling much better," I mumble around a mouthful of bagel. "Seriously. Don't worry about it. Practice and my two classes will be fine."

Morgana sips her coffee, already perfectly coiffed and outfitted in one of her sexy, badass suits. "I didn't say anything."

"You didn't have to. I can feel you watching me like a damn predator." Wiping my mouth, I wink at her. The big meeting yesterday laid out all our plans and I could also feel the relief spread through her once we had things settled. My new mate enjoys having specific directions and a structure to follow, though she prefers to come up with it herself.

The family thing will be a learning experience for her.

Her cheeks flush and she flicks her gaze back to her iPad in annoyance. "Fine. I am *slightly* concerned. If there are any issues, please let either me or Channing know, okay? I have bad thoughts about anyone giving you shit about the couple of days' absence. It's very odd."

Covering my chuckle, I pretend to scratch my jaw as she scrolls through the schedule her icy assistant sent her. "Yes, ma'am."

"Don't be a shit," Morgana murmurs as her brows furrow. Something has her attention now, and she doesn't like it one bit.

"What's got your tail in a knot?" I ask as I gather the breakfast stuff and put it in the dishwasher. "You look pissed suddenly."

Sighing heavily, she looks up at me and her expression softens in a way that makes my chest tighten. "Nothing to do with you. I have meetings with several departments that I believe will be contentious. I'm sure Channing tried to space them out, but it was only a matter of time until a bunch of Magnus' minions wriggled their way onto my calendar. They're all afraid I'll cut their budgets—and some of them should be."

I grin, loving the evil gleam in her eyes. "Show them who's boss, babe."

"Oh, I will." She pauses, then glances back at me. "Not because they're his old friends or whatever... because the allocations for funding in this place were decided by someone who was more interested in getting his dick wet than actually running the school."

Pressing my lips together, I wink. "Why not both?"

The look on her face is fucking priceless—I can't wait to hear what she did tonight.

THE COACH KEPT HIS MOUTH SHUT ABOUT THE MISSED practices, and I'm not sure whether that's because someone in Morgana's circle handled it or if the Shark used his resources. Either way, he didn't take it out on me and, surprisingly, the other players weren't gunning for me. Practice went smoothly, especially because I dumped my water bottle out at the end to ensure no one caught me unawares again. I don't know if I'll ever feel safe leaving my shit in an open space again.

Holy shit, this is what women feel like in bars.

That hits me like a Mack truck and though I've never been that kind of douchebag, I feel the need to apologize to every chick I've ever met for it. It's an anxious, sinking sensation in your stomach as you dart your eyes everywhere to watch for malicious intentions. What a load of centaur shit for them to have to deal with everywhere they go. I'm having a conversation with Nana about supporting more survivor charitable groups the second she calls. If I'm this big and this antsy, women as petite as Channing probably hide tasers in their damn bras, for fuck's sake.

"Men suck," I mutter under my breath as I stalk across campus to my Modern History class. Obviously, I know I'm one, but this revelation is really fucking unsettling and I'm feeling like shit on behalf of my whole damn gender. "But maybe I can help."

"Who the fuck are you talking to, Wolfenberg?"

My eyes narrow as the loud voice of one of my teammates catches up with me. Brock Slater is *the* stereotypical jock bro, and I'm definitely not in the mood for him to pitch the winter sports frat again. He's a sophomore, and I'd lay a fat Benjy that he gets points or some fucking reward for recruiting. "Myself, Slater. What do you want?"

"Bro, it's not what I want; it's what I can *do* for you," he says. His dark hair is messy from the helmet, and he looks like he stepped out of a Land's End catalog. His hand lands on my shoulder and I have to struggle not to shake it off. "*Tau O* is a *perfect* fit for you, man. We're all Society-bound men who have the right credentials. The opportunities are endless."

I am in no mood to be hard sold a frat quietly referred to as the 'assault bros.'

"Look, dude. I know I'd be a huge get for you and whatever system they have to push you into recruiting would reward you. But I'm not interested in *any* frat. I've got enough on my plate. Besides, wouldn't this whole 'murder' thing make your efforts worthless?"

Brock snorts, then throws his head back and laughs. "Hell, no. Tau men frequently have to defend their honor from haters and slutty bitches. We won't judge you, man. I mean, that asshole was French, wasn't he? Serves his cheese eating ass right."

I have to stop walking to process the many, many things wrong with that little diatribe. There's so much to unpack that I can't even move while I'm trying to work out how in the hell anyone is supposed to respond to such blatant.... everything. Misogyny, xenophobia, psychopathy...I mean, Brock Slater hit the fucking trifecta of crazy in three damn sentences.

When my internal outrage is calm enough, I shake my head at the Sasquatch shifter. "Still gonna be a 'no,' man. As... interesting... as that sounds, I'm not available for partying and pledging. Between practice, meeting with my legal team, and school, I'm booked up."

I do my best to smile at him, then turn on my heel to head towards the Beauregard Humanties building. Honestly, I want to put some distance between me and the mythical. I knew he was from the land of dueling banjos, but that was next level bullshit. The difference between his 'offer' and the thoughts I was having before it makes me even more adamant about convincing Nana to reallocate some shit. I don't even fucking care if my name's on it; I just want it done.

And I'm definitely telling Morgana about that goddamn frat.

My history teacher is a tedious, very monotone sloth shifter that is making me want to shoot myself in the eye. He's been covering what led to the time the humans call the Civil War era for forty minutes. It obviously *was* not the cause they think—or at least, not exactly the cause they think. Nothing in our history is spot-on how the other biggest species on the planet describes it. Supes of all kinds have been working together to mask the magical world from them since time immemorial.

They definitely acted like super fuckwits during that time, but there was also a mass shifter enslavement as well because magic users are dicks. It spanned a lot more than just the US and the Society had its hands full quelling the kidnapping of shifter and mythicals. They were too damn busy saving our people to deal with the humans—who, of course, fucked everything up spectacularly.

Most kids learn this stuff in middle school, so I don't know why Peabody is going over it with a fine-tooth comb.

"You will find out that my class is based on reconfirming the knowledge you should have been given in your lower form classes, then adding the mature context of adulthood to the situations we discuss."

My brows furrow as I listen to him drone on. All I'm hearing is that this bastard is going to re-iterate the same shit we learned before. That's a monumental waste of money and time—and this class is required. *Just fucking peachy.* Not skipping or falling asleep will be a challenge.

"Do you have a question, Mr. Wolfenberg?"

I blink, looking up to find the sloth glaring at me—I think, it's hard to tell if he's glaring or squinting. "Uh, no, Professor. All good up here."

His expression is sour and I sink further into my chair. I don't know if I made a face or if he's more perceptive than he looks. Neither is a good prospect, so I need to get my shit together. The last thing I need right now is to draw negative attention to my academic performance. Coach might not have chewed me over the practices, but eligibility is no joke. Not to mention the issues it would cause Morgana if I end up on a list of athletes not pulling their weight.

My phone buzzes in my pocket and I pull it out, keeping it under sight line to make sure I don't cause another disturbance.

Morgana: Everything okay so far?

Papa Bear: Right as rain. Modern History is a joke. Check on the prof.

Morgana: You think he's one of Magnus'?

Papa Bear: If he's not, he's stayed under the radar in reviews. This idiot is teaching shit we learned in high school and it doesn't feel like a review. It feels like the lesson plan for the year.

Morgana: At a college level?

Papa Bear: Yep. In a required course, no less. Just sayin'.

Morgana: What is that ridiculous name you have in my phone, Lucas?

Papa Bear: Gotta go, babe. Check on this guy. See you for dinner.

She doesn't respond, but I feel her amusement in our bond. The more distance I get from that toxic shit, the more I can sense her inside me. I haven't mentioned it because she might flip her wig, and we have plenty of other shit to deal with. But I wonder if she's noticed it, too, or if she's so focused on the next task that she's missed it.

Maybe it's why she texted me out of the blue?

Good thought; I'll ask Professor Shadwell the next time we see her. She'll definitely have some tips about what we should expect—at least from the bear perspective. Morgana might only get the gargoyle from her dad and fuck if I know who knows a damn gorgon. Maybe Iggy or the Prince can handle that research.

It occurs to me that for the first time in my life, I don't give a rat's ass about the other men orbiting my girl. I mean, I wasn't ever serious about anyone in school, but I still gave a shit if other assholes got in their space. My bear's always been possessive, but he's okay with the men who crashed into our world in the past few days.

Okay, that's only sort of true. He hates that dragon motherfucker, and I agree with him.

Honestly, that's because I feel he's going to hurt Morgana before he wises up. I don't think Iggy or Slade would like that, and the Prince is a hard read. He's friends with the dick, but he seems to have an old world gallantry about him. Maybe he'd slap the idiot, too. Staring at my notebook, I doodle a few thoughts, smirking to myself as I consider what kind of fun we could get up with so many supes in one room.

"Mr. Wolfenberg!"

My eyes fly up, looking to the angry voice at the front of the class guiltily. That's when I see it's not the lazy sloth professor, but that dingy detective—Kowalski—standing with his hands in his pockets, looking very smug. I don't take my eyes off him as I send one word in a text to Morgana: nine-one-one. Carefully slipping my phone back in my pocket, I give the asshole a bright grin. "Detective Kaiser Roll! How nice to see you! I'm a little busy getting an education at the moment, but if you'd like to set something up with my lawyer..."

"Not this time, rich boy." He looks over his shoulder and two officers in uniform come in, heading up the stairs of the lecture hall like freaking secret police. "This time you're coming to my house when I say so."

I'd love to kick these dudes' asses, but this is not the time.

Standing, I look around as if I don't have a care in the world. "Well, if you insist..."

"I do." Kowalski smiles and I shudder as the crumbs clinging to his bushy beard practically tremble with his glee. "Because you, Lucas Wolfenberg, are under arrest."

Shit. Nobody expects the Spanish Inquisition—not even The Shark, it seems.

fury

The door bursts open on my meeting with the coaches of the swim team, and I have to keep myself from reacting when Channing bustles in like she's on a mission. She doesn't acknowledge the two angry looking shifters; no, my assistant heads straight for me. When she approaches, I lean down a bit for her to whisper in my ear and this time, I can't keep the emotions off of my face.

How goddamn dare *that asshole set foot on my campus without speaking to me? I don't care if he works for the fucking* Kremlin.

Straightening, I look at the dolphin and shark in front of me with an irritable expression. "Gentleman, lady... we will have to reschedule. I have urgent business to attend to that cannot be put off."

"Of course she does," the bulky hammerhead hybrid grunts as he gives me a filthy look. "No respect at this place anymore for their money makers."

Oh, today is not *the day, and I am* not *the one, buster.*

My wings pop free and my size grows as the gargoyle and gorgon inside of me unleash their fury at our mate being taken without permission. This isn't the right arena, but fuck if I have a choice. I've never mated with anyone before and no one's told me how to get them under control when they're threatened. Des hisses as she pokes out from under my hair, doing her snake dance as I work to get a grip. "Marinus, I suggest you choose your next words wisely, because I'm going to give you a chance to retract that offensive shit."

His companion sinks lower in her seat and he scoffs. "Fucking prey shifters are useless."

"That remark violates HR Policy 467.2.3 regarding species-ism and derogatory language used towards co-workers," Channing pipes up. "Since there are three witnesses to the infraction, you are being put on notice immediately. Dean LeCiel will sign the form for the file after she handles the emergency. Keep in mind, three infractions that violate hostile work environment policies are grounds for termination with revocation of any existing staff benefits, such as housing, tuition for children, and sponsorship for any events in the competition arena. You will not be reimbursed for any costs incurred after your employment is severed."

I blink as a slow, evil smile creeps over my features. "Is that what you'd like, Marinus? Would you like to continue racking up infractions until you give me the perfect reason to let you go and ruin your career? I can and I will, especially since I've ignored the many unacceptable remarks you made during this meeting."

"As if this... *woman*... has the guts to back you up when I sue those fancy pants off you," he scoffs. "Your little pet there just said it requires witnesses."

"All meetings in the Dean's office are recorded for everyone's protection now," Channing says. "It was a demand made by the board after they learned of previous misdeeds committed under the auspice of 'school business.' Morgana had to sign a waiver to allow it to begin any time the door opens."

She's not wrong, and I wasn't thrilled with having to do it, either. Once again, my ex's bullshit caused me to get punished, and it chafed like a pair of burlap underwear. But I did it to satisfy the overlords that sent me here and keep the peace. In the Society's headquarters, all I wanted was to flee and vanish from the media's attention. I'm lucky I didn't sign away anything worse than what I did—my state of mind wasn't conducive to defending my rights.

"That's true," I finally add. "So your behavior has been fully recorded and sent to the cloud within the servers to the Society. I highly doubt I'll get much push back if I choose to speed up your exit from this university. The way Magnus ran this place was a disgrace and we will no longer allow our employees, students, or alumnae to behave as they have been when representing State U. The thin ice we're on with the eligibility committee forced our hands, but I'm in charge of getting it done."

Marinus shoots to his feet, pulls off his ID, and throws it at my desk. His face is bright red with anger and I have no doubt my ex would have coddled him. The shifter is a former supe Olympian and one of the most famous coaches in the US. However, this display of temper isn't even the worst of his behavior and I know the donors are tired of his name being all over the media. There will be backlash for letting him quit, but I'll find someone easily as good and less volatile to help our students if it kills me.

"I'm done here. Trust me, when you lose me, you will be, too." He spins on his heel, stomping out with his threat hanging in the air, and I can't help myself.

I burst out laughing. My incredulity at the fragile male ego must be shared because once I really get going, Channing and Sylvan join me. The dolphin hybrid relaxes for the first time since she entered the room as she giggles in the high pitch tone of her kind and I have to wipe tears off of my face. Once I finally get under control, I clear my throat to speak. "Sylvan, I'm sorry about this. I truly nee*d* to go handle something. Please allow Channing to rebook your meeting about the women's team later in the week?"

Her smile is broad as she catches her breath. "For the first time in years, I'm actually looking forward to that. Now that Marinus is gone, my girls won't have to worry about a lot of things and for that, I appreciate you, Dean LeCiel. Do what you must, and I look forward to Channing's call."

Sighing in relief as she gives me another smile then heads out, I turn back to the elemental next to me when the door shuts. "I'm going to kill that fucking detective. He'll wish he'd been born without balls when I get through running them through a grinder."

She grins. "Before you ask, yes, Jackson and his team are on their way."

Sometimes, my judgment of people is so very on par—it makes mistakes like Magnus even more infuriating.

"Let's go, then."

THERE'S A FUCKING *GAGGLE* OF PRESS AT THE FRONT OF the station when we arrive, and that does nothing to soothe the anger coursing through my veins. This is a staged scene—someone made certain to drop the news that Lucas was arrested during class. I sit in the back seat, scrolling through my phone until I find Eli's text thread.

Morgana: I want to know if the leak to the press originated from the State U Wi-Fi by the time we leave this building. If it did, I want to know the first post's exact location and device ASAP.

Eli: Understood. Jackie's not happy, either.

His gift for understatement is noted as I flick the chat away and look up at Channing in the driver's seat. "I want to know who let that dick on campus without informing me. Once you find out, their ass will be in my office at nine a.m. tomorrow morning. I don't care if I have to hire an entirely new goddamn security staff because of this; everyone on campus will know what crossing me gets them."

Channing grins broadly. "Hell, yes. I hoped we might clean house in that lazy ass den of assholes. You'll agree when I tell you the horror stories I've been privy to over the years."

"We'll deal with the immediate problem first, then you can brief me on the troubles with our security staff one by one." I look out the window, reaching up to coax Des into hiding, so she's not obvious in any press shots as we walk in. "You can't win a war of a thousand cuts without getting blood on the ground and I'm going to smear it all over theat damn campus."

My assistant grins again, hopping out to come to my side and open my door. I step out, my expression concealed by the dark glasses covering my eyes. Cameras and phones click as I hurry up the stairs to the door. Channing stands at the ready as I turn to look at the metaphorical vultures watching us hungrily.

"State U is deeply concerned by the aggressive tactics of the law enforcement in this community. Like any private entity, our grounds are not open to Draconian seizures of students without informing the university of their presence or intentions. We will take our concerns to both the Mayor, the Council, and the Society. Even magical law enforcement has limitations and today, they have exceeded what is allowable by the law. Thank you."

A dull roar of questions echoes behind me as I enter the building. Channing follows me and within minutes of entering, we're greeted by Rainier and Foley. They nod at my assistant and she ducks her head as she wiggles her fingers.

Huh. Interesting.

"The nerve of that son of a bitch," Foley mutters. "Jackson's going to have his badge before the end of this. They concealed the fucking arrest warrant because Eli's spiders should have caught it before the ink was dry."

Rainier grunts. "Pushed it through with a crooked judge—they only have his presence in the locker room, which is circumstantial. There's not a shred of physical evidence that ties him to the murder. People will suffer when the boss gets done with them."

My lips stretch into an evil smile as I listen. That sounds perfect, if you ask me. I want the people who went around me to invade *my* territory without *my* consent to learn a serious lesson about who they're fucking with. If they don't, I'll never be able to keep the college a safe haven. Gargoyles crave the creation of safe spaces in their midst and I won't be able to control my rage if I cannot protect my home.

"Good," I reply as we head down the hall. "Channing has contacted the board, and I dropped a bomb in the press before we came inside. That should give us cover when we leave. "

"Do you think we'll be able to bring Lucas home tonight?" Channing looks worried as she pushes her glasses up.

Foley gives her a charming grin. "Don't worry, lass. Our boss never loses and this won't be the streak breaker."

My eyes narrow when she flushes again, but I don't have time to give it more thought.

"He doesn't have an option. If he fails my mate, I will tear him to pieces myself and deal with the fallout later. We all know I've done it before." That stops all of them in their tracks and I pull off my sunglasses, shrugging. "What else can they do to me? Knock me off? With my mate facing a death sentence for murder, it wouldn't be a punishment."

"Hardcore," Foley mutters as he rubs the back of neck. "You're a hell of a woman, Morgana."

Rainier jerks his chin at me as if showing his approval as well, and I cock my head at them. "Now that we've established I'm a badass, let's go see what's happening with Jackson and Lucas."

"Right. Follow me," Rainier says, turning on his heel and heading to an enormous door at the end of the hallway. He waves a card at a reader and we're able to go through it, leaving me to wonder how he got clearance to wander through the station.

The Irishman winks at me, bobbing his brows when he sees my confusion. "Rain is fucking connected. There's very little he can't finagle with this kind of shit."

"Good to know," I murmur. "I'm sure it will be useful in the future."

"When we break your boyfriend out of a supe prison?"

I laugh as the adorable hacker comes towards us. He's carrying a bunch of devices and I assume he's hard at work figuring out everything we need to help Lucas. "Yes, I suppose it would be very helpful if he had contacts in the prison system, then."

"Rain has contacts *everywhere*," Eli says. "Jax doesn't keep team members who aren't at the top of their fields. The best hacker like me, the most connected ex-military, the trickiest motherfucker and—"

"The scariest asshole alive?" Foley cuts in.

As if he's been summoned, Kendrick appears out of the shadows, glaring at us with his arms crossed over his broad chest.

"Maybe not the scariest, but damn, he's quiet," I say with a laugh.

Hopefully, they're not all blowing smoke up my skirt; Lucas's future depends on it.

help

"I don't think it's a good idea to be so involved in the politics on this side," Kaspar says with a grimace. He's doing arm curls on the couch, muscles bulging with the effort of the heavy weight he's using. "Just because the woman intrigues you…"

I roll my eyes. The first female that's caught my eye in over a decade and he's pissed that she's not what he imagined. Sometimes, I want to grab my friend and shake him. I *know* he likes her as well, but he's too damned stubborn to admit it. The damage from his past still haunts him despite my total rejection of the Harvest Court lady who broke his heart.

Kaspar knows I did *nothing* to encourage her—in fact, I actively tried to discourage her crush at every turn. But his shame from not being enough *and* failing to protect me from a Fae who turned out to be extremely dangerous is a burden he hasn't dropped over the past fifty years.

I don't know if he ever will, but I think Morgana has a good chance of helping us both heal.

"She's the one, Kas. I feel it in my magic... in my bones. You just have to tru—" The buzzing of my phone on the counter interrupts my measured approach to getting him to stop being such a dick.

"Answer it. You will not change my mind."

I walk over to the island and pick up my phone with a sigh of annoyance. The name on the screen makes my brows raise, and I swipe it open quickly. "Good morning, Professor."

Ignatius' voice is tense as he relays the news of Lucas's arrest and the subsequent dash to the police station. I hear Slade banging about in the background—or I assume it's the siren—and it makes me wonder what they're up to. Once he sends me the pin for the station and I confirm it, he tells me to let Morgana and Channing know they'll be along shortly. He hangs up, leaving me to ponder the clues I believe I gathered while he spoke.

"What did the mage want?" Kaspar grumbles as he puts his weight away. "Some errand for us? Doesn't he realize you're—"

"Morgana's at the police station. Lucas was arrested this morning with no warning." My friend blinks, understanding the vast amount of corruption that likely took place to produce a secret warrant, enter campus without the Dean knowing, and show up to arrest a rich, elite supe sports star in public. "He said Jackson's team is there, but

Morgana will probably need even more pull to cancel out whatever levers the people behind this pulled."

His eyes flash with his dragon and I feel the air in the room electrify enough to make the hair on my arms stand up. He might demur about the lovely Dean, but this reaction tells me more than he wants me to know. "Did he send the big supe to investigate security?"

That means it would be his first move, and Kas is a consummate strategist. "No. They're all busy working things at the station. Perhaps you could drop me there to lend my considerable influence to their cause and then double back to do your own thing with the campus security idiots?"

His toothy grin tells me everything I need to know. My old friend will terrify them until they give up the person or persons who allowed the detective to enter campus without being cleared through administration. Kas simply does not fail... ever... no matter what he thinks about his ex. "If you can catch a ride back with the others, your command is my pleasure, Liam."

"Thank you," I murmur as I sit the phone down. "Let's get ourselves presentable, then we'll head to the cop shop." He snorts and I shrug. "If I'm coming as the Prince and you as my guard, we can't show up in grimy sweats without shirts, Kaspar."

"You're the Prince even if you're wearing a goddamn trash bag. I don't know why you worry so much about appearances." His rejoinder is common, and I chuckle while we make our way upstairs. "It's appeasing your father, and we both know *that's* a losing bet."

"Yes, yes." I pause at his door, giving him a rueful look. "I'm well aware of how much I disappoint him, just like you know that your own father is more loyal to the King than his family."

"Low blow, Li. Low blow." He winks and ducks into his room, shutting the door behind him with a click.

Kaspar is my closest confidant and oldest friend—something Angeline could have destroyed if we hadn't been as bonded as we are. Instead of ripping us apart, it drew us even closer and made him tighten our circle to almost nothing until I started classes on this side of the Veil. I still believe he convinced his father and, by proxy, mine, to allow it because it would keep us away from the intrigue and betrayals that happen so often at court.

But that doesn't matter now because I believe I may have found the center of our bond.

"And she comes with other powerful, non-objectionable mates who would compliment us," I murmur to myself in satisfaction. Heading into my room, I smile as I make quick work of pulling out a pair of slacks and an oxford. I want to project the image I know will sway local yokels, but not be so formal it's questioned.

My mother always taught me clothes can make the man and define the world around him—something Kas has never believed. Regardless, he'll toe the line and outfit himself similarly because even if he doesn't subscribe to our theories, he'll support me without question. Once I'm clothed, I go into the bathroom and fix the traditional braids and hair people would expect, then freshen up. The last thing I need to do is the most irritating because I avoid adorning myself with the required elements of my heritage here—but the Prince won't make an impression without the everyday imprint of his crown.

Fucking Earth dwellers and their silly ideas of Fae royalty.

With a sigh, I go back into my room and pull the ancient bejeweled chain that forms a loosely shaped crown over my forehead from its home in the safe. I have much more formal ones stored in more secure places, but this will work for today's excursion. Kaspar walks in as I'm fiddling with the clasp in the back and rolls his eyes, pushing my hands away to help.

"You wear your inheritance so little that you're hopeless with it, Prince."

I snort as he futzes with it, making sure it's settled correctly with my hair curling around it and the braids draped just right. "That's because I hate it and you know it. Are you ready to go?"

He grins. "I'm ready to ditch you and do some dirty work."

Good enough for me.

WHEN WE ARRIVE AT THE POLICE STATION, THERE'S A MOB of reporters in front. Kaspar growls in annoyance, steering around them to take us away from the gaggle. I can flex my muscles inside, but if I want to avoid a call from the King, I shouldn't be seen in the tabloid photos as I walk in. Once we find a back entrance, he has to negotiate with a low-level cop who must be tasked with keeping reporters away. Once the green rookie saw my crown, he moved so fast he might as well have left tracks behind.

"Even the supe cops in this world are idiots. He had zero proof you didn't buy some replica online—I would refuse to leave you here if I wasn't aware The Shark's team is inside. His people seemed reasonably competent, so I'll indulge you, Li."

I roll my eyes. He could refuse all he wanted, but if I truly wanted to elude him, my magic would trump him every time. I simply prefer not to use it for frivolous shit like giving him the middle finger for being over-protective. "I appreciate your largesse, old friend."

The car comes to a stop, and he gets out, checking the area before he opens my door. Though I believe it unnecessary, he flanks me as we walk up a set of short stairs and ring the buzzer on the door. It opens slowly, and another young officer squints at us.

"You the Fae Prince?"

Charming.

"I am Prince Liam, yes."

He sighs heavily, nodding as he holds an arm out. "This way. Your friends are in interrogation or watching it. I'm supposed to bring you there."

My smile is friendly, but the tone I used is full of authority. "That doesn't work for me. You may take me directly to your Chief and once we speak, then I will allow you to escort me to our group."

Kaspar snorts as the kid babbles about his duty, then finally cuts in, "I am leaving the heir to the Daybreak Court, Prince Liam Spéirgheal, in your care, Officer. Every thing you do will be reported to King Spéirgheal, do you understand?"

The poor guy's face turns white as a sheet, and he gulps. "Yes, sir. Right. I'll take you to the Chief right away, Your Highness."

Giving Kas an irritated look, I wave him off. Now this kid will be clammed up as hell and everyone in the building will play along with the 'royal asshole coming through' schtick. I was hoping to leave that until it was completely necessary, but now that's not an option. Playing the role of my father's son chafes and I hate it... but I'll do it for Morgana and the young bear.

"Your station is very small for a bigger city," I comment casually. It's a backhanded slight and I know the cop feels it when his shoulders scrunch a bit, then he forces them down. "I expected a much more robust investigative team for such a high brow case. Perhaps I should contact my friends in Sibbies to take over..."

"Those guys will fall all over themselves to accommodate a famous kid, right?" His voice is full of resentment and I can almost feel the bitterness in the air. Competition like this explains why the solve rate for most murders is as low as it is—even supernatural agencies refuse to work together. "Justice shouldn't have a price tag."

I blink, my lips curling at his admirable yet naïve, take on the situa-tion. "You may be surprised to find I agree, Officer. However, I also know my friend is innocent and the current case against him is so thin you can see through it. Justice should also not be lazy and full of false confidence."

That shuts him up for a moment, and I wonder if this kid realizes some of his superiors aren't as dedicated to the same ideals as he is. If the shitty detective is unpopular for sloughing off his work onto others or taking shortcuts, this will be easier to finagle. I look around, studying the people we pass carefully to see if they're malleable or steadfast in their belief in what's happening in this place.

Detective Moron seems to have a fair number of people who expect him to get his ass handed to him—and they're looking forward to it.

"I can work with that," I murmur to myself as we approach a long, wood paneled hallway that leads to a much nicer section of the building. This is obviously where the muckitty-mucks keep their offices, far above the rank and file, who sit in dreary cube farms with stale air. The change says a lot about the people I'm likely to meet in this big room behind the double doors with shining brass handles at the end of the hall.

"I'm sorry, Your Highness. Did you say something?" the kid asks as we stop in front of the ornate entrance.

"No, Officer. Don't worry; you didn't miss a thing."

But that detective better hope he didn't, either, because I feel it won't be hard to get the brass behind this door to sell him right up the river.

under pressure

T he detective has Lucas and Jackson in an interrogation room that's reminiscent of one from a TV procedural. He's definitely feeding off this situation; it's probably the most important case he's had in his entire career. His glee has created a far more adversarial atmosphere than is needed, especially because he hasn't processed my mate yet. In fact, he took them straight to the box without passing 'Go,' and I wonder if the arrest was all for show.

If so, Jackson Thorne is going to eat him alive and spit out the gristle.

I don't know the guy that well other than reputation, but his behavior so far has only increased my confidence in his abilities. He's a smug, self-assured motherfucker because he has the skills and influence to back it up. Lucas is in good hands despite his obvious discomfort at being prodded by the pastrami-eating fool in there.

"You were found with the victim. What other conclusions are we supposed to draw, Wolfenberg?"

The blond hockey player shrugs, his expression guileless as he shoots back, "I don't know. Isn't investigation *your* job? I can't do it for you, man."

Jackson holds up a fist, bumping it with Lucas before turning back to the lumpy detective. "My client isn't here to help you find your ass with both hands and a map, Detective. He's here to answer questions, though the method of retrieving him from his classes is a matter for the courts now. Since you haven't filed the arrest paperwork you used to force him to come here without benefit of counsel, my team is suing for false imprisonment, Miranda violations, and oh-so-many other charges once I have time to find every single piece of case law I can use to tear this precinct and you to tiny little pieces."

"Huh. Good luck with that in this town," Kowalski retorts as he leans over a chair to sneer at the handsome lawyer. "You'll find that kind of shit doesn't fly here."

I watch as Thorne's smile widens and the flash of teeth reminds me why he's called The Shark, despite it not being his shifter form. "I appreciate the heads up. We'll apply for a change of venue as well. I have the *perfect* one in mind. Morgana, dear, if you're out there, can you note I need to call my college buddy?"

Grinning a little, I tuck that note in my head for later. I'm glad Jackson realized I wouldn't be able to stay away from the observation area while Lucas was being grilled. Ranier nods at my questioning look and I raise my hand to knock on the glass once in response. Lucas perks up a little, sitting up straighter in his seat now that he realizes

I'm here. We get a glare from a frumpy-looking woman that I assume is their ADA, but since she hasn't spoken to Rainier or me once, that's only a guess.

Channing pulls out her phone, her fingers moving over it furiously. "I'll add it to his documents, Morgana."

"Thank you, lovely," Eli says from his spot in the corner. He's hunkered down on the floor with a full complement of tech surrounding him. I'm amazed he even heard us with the weird headphones he's got in his ears, but now's not the time to question the hacker's quirks. "Jackie will be grateful. He would have asked one of us if he hadn't specifically wanted the handsome bear to know our Dean is here watching."

He would have, huh?

I shoot a look at my assistant and she flushes a bit, pushing her glasses up as she clears her throat. "I assume Jackson isn't overextending you with extra work, then, Channing?"

"Oh, no! No, his team is very conscientious. I'm simply helping facilitate some administrative things so Eli can focus on his..." she looks at the mousy woman and then continues, "... his much needed research duties for the case."

Rainier snorts and it occurs to me that somewhere between the locked door and this room, Foley and Kendrick have disappeared. I'm not sure if that's a good or bad thing, but it's certainly worth noting. Jackson's team gives me the sense that they operate right in the gray areas of the law—something that would shock me, except lawyers are the most crooked motherfuckers on the planet and defense attorneys are the worst and Jackson sits on a throne of bodies in his field. It's unlikely he got there by being a rule follower.

"Your friend can do all the 'research' he likes. Lucas Wolfenberg is going to be arrested for killing his rival hockey player; his money can't get him out of this."

Turning to face the woman, I step closer, towering over her as I meet her gaze. "You have nothing but circumstantial evidence. Your arrest warrant was obtained under false pretenses and you're acting in bad faith. I don't know which of your higher-ups approved this mess, but Jackson is going to have every single one of your jobs. You don't scare us."

"I wouldn't think I'd scare a convicted killer, Dean LeCiel." She gives me a dark smirk and I see beneath the veneer of her frumpy facade. "You killed Magnus and essentially got away scot-free. I don't know why you're so adamant about this student, but I will enjoy humiliating you in the press and the courtroom for your past sins."

Just fucking peachy—another Magnus acolyte. Was he fucking this entire goddamn city?

I probably know the answer to that and if I hadn't already severed his goddamn head, I'd do it again in a heartbeat. Everywhere I go, I fucking run into more of his conquests and they are determined to make my life a living hell, as if it's my fault he was a crooked, cheating, malignant narcissist who cuckolded me with every damn person in the city. Women like this infuriate me—always have—and my punishment for refusing to put up with his shit is being attacked constantly.

The door to the observation room opens before I can respond, and I'm surprised to see Prince Liam enter with a *jittery* looking woman in an expensive suit. His eyes are full of mischief as they join us, and I wonder what he's been doing while we watched Kowalski grill Lucas. I don't see Kaspar, which I can't decide if I'm relieved by, so this was a solo mission.

One that required a crown? Holy shit.

"Morgana, this is Chief Ponylakitu. She's in charge of the precinct, and we've had an extremely satisfactory chat." Liam grins and winks at me. "Chief, this is State U's new dean, Morgana LeCiel."

Extending my hand for the obviously cowardly official, I grasp her palm hard. "You've been backing the wrong horse, Chief. I don't know why you and this ADA are standing behind Kowalski, but I assure you, associating with him is a mistake. He's only going to take you down with him when he finally steps too far over the line."

"Hmmm. You think so?" the chief says as she watches the detective continue to antagonize Jackson. Our lawyer has the grumpy idiot outmatched without turning a hair in his perfect 'do, but the big lug keeps hammering at them. "People often underestimate the power of those who will get dirty for their aims."

Liam rolls his eyes, imploring a divine force to strike the woman down. "Chief, as we discussed before, you may have a small, rabid support system in this area, but they cannot save you from what's coming when your detective plays this out. He won't care if it ruins your career or lands you at odds with your superiors or officers."

"That won't happen," the beady-eyed ADA interjects. "Even the Prince can't prevent what's coming. We have evidence you don't know about."

My gaze narrows on them, and I see Eli look at me with a fierce expression. He'll dig through everything and find out what she's talking about, but he needs me to help. *I can do that*. Putting on my most condescending smile, I look at the attorney as if she's very dim. "Listen, Miss.... whatever your name is. I don't think you understand what kind of pull we actually have. You'd do well to lay your cards on the table in there with Mr. Thorne."

"Valencia." The woman glares at me as she holds out a business card. "Assistant District Attorney Veronica Valencia, bureau chief of the Homicide division."

Eli snickers from his spot in the corner, and I hear keys clacking as he gets to work. I needed her name so he could run checks on her, just as he was probably doing on the Chief from the moment she walked in the room. If Jackson is telling the truth about his skills, we'll have work-ups on these new players by evening. That will allow us to figure out why in the hell they're going up against someone as powerful as Lucas's Nana and what backup they have.

They're too confident not to have back-up and I'm beginning to believe this is bigger than one hockey player's murder.

I can't let her know she gave me exactly what I wanted, so I nod. "I'd love to say it's a pleasure to meet you, Miss Valencia, but under these circumstances... I feel we are destined to be at odds if you have aligned yourself with this madness. Surely someone with your experience recognizes the precarious position the police are putting you in? Their vendetta is motivated by something other than evidence—what, I'm not sure—but Jackson's team will find it and expose them."

"The detective and the Chief have provided enough circumstantial evidence to convince a judge, Miss LeCiel. I would be *very* careful accusing so many respected members of our community of bad intentions. This city is a diverse place with lots of powerful special interest groups who believe in making certain the wealthy one percent face justice."

Rainier coughs to cover his laughter, and I arch a brow at the Prince. He doesn't look bothered in the slightest by her little jab. I guess when you're the heir to a throne, you get used to random people acting like they're the supernatural Che Guevara around you. I might agree that the wealthy should pay their dues and be held accountable, but I definitely don't think Liam is the person to aim at. From what little I've heard since we met, it's his father who's the issue. Valencia can go after that dick all she wants, but I'm not about to allow her to be disrespectful to the man who came to help my mate.

"Veranda," I begin, purposefully butchering her name. "I'm not sure what cause you and your friends think you're supporting, but Liam isn't the enemy. Lucas didn't kill LaMount—he would have been crazy as fuck to sit there and wait to be found if he did."

Her glares sharpens when I mis-remember her name and she snarls, "Perhaps he wanted to be caught? People in his family are known for their love of publicity—even if it's bad."

Is this chick out of her mind? No one uses murder as an attention-getting tactic.

"Miss Valencia, I believe you've mistaken the young bear for a psychotic mastermind," Liam interrupts. "While that may be a trope in a crime show on TV, it's simply not the case in this situation. You're all overstepping your authority and the Chief promised she would help temper your overzealous assumptions. Has that changed, Chief Ponylakitu?"

"I... well, you see Prince... I'm..."

Rolling my eyes, I walk forward and knock on the glass again. It's time for Jackson to quit playing with his food. This is going nowhere and I can't imagine how chaotic it will be once Iggy and Slade arrive. They, too, have connections they'll press for Lucas and this station will be overwhelmed with rich dudes trying to influence a group of nutters who are being puppeteer'd by someone probably not even in this state. The whole damn thing is a farce and we need more information before we come at them any further.

Jackson smirks as he hears the sound from my side of the glass, sitting up in his chair. "Unfortunately for you, Detective, that was your curtain call. Now either charge my client or cut him loose. We're done playing with you."

Everyone in the room is silent as we watch the detective stare for a moment before he finally growls, "Fine. But don't leave town."

As if that was part of our plans during the school year.... what a douchebag.

control

I ggy and I have some sway over things if we bring our family names into the mix, but as we speed toward the police station, I'm not sure exactly what we can do if Jackson and the Prince haven't succeeded. I suppose if we were looking to go on the lam, I could use my song and he could use cloaking magic. I highly doubt Morgana would approve running from her problems, though.

After all, she stood in front of everyone and flat admitted to killing Magnus Corona, infamous scholar, and Dean of SU.

"What if we can't help Lucas?" I ask Iggy as he weaves through traffic like a madman. He wanted to open a gateway—something frowned upon unless in desperate emergencies—but I reminded him the station would be shielded.

My roomie looks worried and tired, two things he's usually good at masking. "That's not an option, Slade. We signed onto this like everyone else and if we have to the bend the rules, so be it."

I arch a brow as I consider what the morally ambiguous Briarton heir would call 'bending the rules.' He's not known for being a straight arrow as it is. "What rules? And how would we bend them?"

"Don't be ridiculous, Slade. Just because you choose to be on the narrow while you study doesn't mean your old bad boy persona isn't dying to get out." He gives me a wicked grin that makes my gut clench.

As usual, Iggy is spot-on in his assessment of me.

Whipping the car into the lot as if we're in a racing movie, he hops out and makes an impatient sound when I don't follow suit. Squinting, I look around for the source of disquiet prickling over my skin. I don't like how this place feels, nor do I like how the energy if affecting my siren side. "Iggy, there's something *very* off about this place. Do you feel it?"

The mage closes his eyes, murmuring under his breath as he holds his hands in the air. I feel the magical shockwave hit as he sends it out in concentric circles to find what's bothering me. His eyes pop open and he turns to me with a serious expression. "You're right. There's powerful magic here—a lot in varying types. It's as if different magic wielders have touched the space somehow."

I nod as I rub my arms with my hands. "Ones with bad intentions. It's vibrating in the moisture in the air. I can hear the tiny hum of disturbance in the atmosphere."

Walking around the car, he shuts my door before turning to place his hands over mine. "*Tuere quod meus est. Serva malum ab animo. Proles Hecate praecipiunt.*[1]"

Sniffing at him, I frown. "I hate when you use Latin. My Latin sucks, Iggy. You know the aquatics prefer Greek."

His hands squeeze mine and he chuckles. "Well, I prefer the strongest spell possible and you know witches, wizards, mages, and such are more powerful when we use Latin. I don't know why, given the history of our powers, but it's simply the way it is."

I step back, inhaling slowly before I nod. "Fine. Do you need to protect Morgana or anyone else? Maybe the Prince acted without words?"

Iggy shrugs as we head for the front of the station. "I don't know. I'll be able to sense if they've been taken care of, as will you. I assume Jackson has his team permanently warded by something like a brand or tattoo. This would be the most efficient for their work."

"That's kind of cool," I murmur. "Like very badass super spy shit. We should do that."

He opens the door, arching a brow at me with amusement in his eyes. "Are you going to be the one to ask Morgana to get branded? If so, let me know ahead so I can bring popcorn."

As we enter, I notice people are determined not to look at us as we head toward the back. The text from Channing gave us their location, but I thought someone would meet us when we arrived. Apparently,. they're far too busy to pause and the rest of this building has stayed the fuck away.

Probably not the worst outcome; Iggy's not very compliant when questioned by people he thinks are beneath him.

I finally spot Foley at the very back edge of the big squad room and he jerks his head to the door behind him. We pick up the pace, reaching the bored-looking redhead as he's swiping a card that cannot belong to him.

"Aye, lads. We're about done. The granite lass and my boss gave them a good what-for and now we're waiting for the paperwork to be cleared, so we're certain nothing lingers in the system."

"Did they actually arrest him?" I ask worriedly. That kind of shit is hard as hell to erase, and I don't think we have time for that kind of distraction.

Jackson's man shakes his head. "No. Boss is gonna have a helluva lawsuit prepped by next week; you can put your savings on that. Nothing about today was kosher and we can't figure out how anyone was roped into it."

Iggy blinks, then clears his throat. "We may have answers—vague ones, but at least it's a lead."

"You just got here, Magic Man. How could you possibly know what's going on?" Foley says as he rolls his eyes. "You lot are too full of your-self down here."

Ignoring the weird 'down here' comment, I gesture around us. "From the second we got out of the car, I could feel magic in the air. My gifts are in water and the vibrations hum at different frequencies on the moisture in the air. He sent a pulse out with his magic and agreed that this place is polluted with magic from various magic-wielding supes."

"So?"

My roommate huffs at the disdain, shaking his head. "Dense is a poor look, McNamara. It's not a leap to extrapolate that the outrageous behavior of the people involved in Lucas's faux arrest might be under spells or compelled. Since the signatures here are all over the place, I believe whoever is framing him must have access to a *lot* of different species in their little... ring."

Foley hums for a moment, his expression thoughtful and then finally nods. "Alright. You're not as dumb as I suggested and you might have a point. If that's the case, my team is well protected. But what about your people?"

"It depends on whether the players were infected here, one by one, or in some other way. If it was here, I placed a shield on Slade. I, of course, have my own. We hoped the Prince might have handled the others." Iggy walks to the door Foley has his hand on and gestures for him to open it. "But we should verify that quickly."

"Compulsion and control spells are extremely verboten and carry harsh punishments," I murmur as we make our way to our friends. "Whoever this is, they aren't scared of anything."

That's what makes them so dangerous.

Foley mentioned that the small conference room is better than the interrogation viewing room the others endured. Lucas is cuffed, but he's so big and muscled that I'd be surprised if he couldn't break out of those without breaking a sweat. With a furious look, Jackson fills out forms while everyone else sits at the far end of the table.

Prince Liam has his fingers steepled in front of his face, his eyes on the cops at the door. He smiles briefly when he sees Iggy and me, leaning back in a more relaxed position. "Welcome to the nuthouse, gentlemen."

"Fucking right," Rainier snorts as he continues texting on his phone. Eli is working on multiple devices next to him, but he lifts a hand to give us a thumbs-up. "These people are dead—legally, of course— when Jax gets through with them. I cannot believe this bullshit."

I tilt my head as I look around. The only missing people are Kaspar and Kendrick; I dread asking where those fuckers went. "Foley said they're releasing you?"

"Yeah, dude. Jackson scared the fuck out of them and once he's done, we can go." Lucas sighs heavily, looking tired. "We're going back to the lair. The grumpy silent dudes got sent to... I don't know.... beat answers out of people."

Morgana smiles at me, gesturing to a chair nearby. "Come sit with us. I'm glad you came."

"Wild horses, pet," Iggy says as he joins us. His gaze falls on the Fae before he leans in to whisper, "Your Highness, did you....?" He waves his hand through the air.

Liam chuckles and nods. "The moment I arrived. I knew the shifters could not sense it. Morgana and Lucas are safe. Of course, Jackson's people assured me they have other ways of subverting those problems."

Channing ducks her head as she mumbles, "I'm not sure what you all mean. Is there a danger I don't know about?"

"And what the hell did you do to Lucas and me?" Morgana follows up. "I wasn't informed of any problem."

Shit. Iggy blew their cover.

"Rain, take Channing and deal with her security, please?" Jackson mutters as he works on the papers. "I can't believe she was left out. You can do it without K, right?"

"Why are *you* taking her?" my old friend huffs. "The Prince or I can do the requisite..."

"No." Eli cuts him off, finally looking up from his screens. "Rain will do it. She's also working with us on this project and we need to be confident in the method."

"I'm the *Prince of the Daybreak Kingdom*," Liam says incredulously. "How can you possibly think you'd be more capable than I at this procedure?"

The tall mercenary pushes off the wall with a smug smirk. "Because the method we use is different and will accomplish what we need while you will cast a simple, temporary charm. I won't hurt the woman." He turns to Channing, who now looks like she wishes she could sink into the floor. "You know that, right, Specs?"

I arch a brow at the nickname, watching her reaction to the dangerous man now walking toward her. There's something going on with the girl Iggy and I have known for years. I've never seen her quite this flustered, despite typically being reserved. "Chan, are you okay with Jackson's guy helping or do you want the Prince to help?"

She frowns at me, clearly unhappy I brought the spat to her feet. "Well... I...." Sucking in a breath, she huffs it out again as she straightens. "I believe if they require extra protocols for me to assist them with Lucas's case, then I will have to submit to whatever it is, eventually. So, Rainier can do it right the first time and we can stop focusing on me. I'm not the one in trouble."

Morgana smiles a little as she looks at her friend. "Mmm. That is very logical, Channing. I can't argue with that."

Then why does she look like she's ferreting something out?

Rainier holds his hand out to our friend. "Let's go. Jackson will be done with the forms soon, and we'll all be on our way. I want to finish this before you fly back to your nest."

"It's settled then." Liam also looks suspicious as he watches Channing leave with the guy, but his focus returns to Morgana and Lucas quickly. "Lass, for the record, I couldn't mention what I did with all the other ears in the room. Please know it was necessary, and I'll fill you in when we get back to your place."

"Mmm. You most certainly will, Prince. Not a fan of being kept in the dark, especially after my ex made me look foolish for years."

Ouch. I guess that's fair, but Liam just took a direct hit.

"Babe, don't be mad. He probably protected us and that's always good, right?" Lucas speaks up again. The tension in his frame is obvious, and I bet he's struggling with his animal. I doubt the bear enjoyed being shackled, and he's being very calm and controlled. "This has been a shit day and I think we all want to go home to talk about all this in private."

"That we can agree on," Foley pipes up. "This is why I hate coming to backwater burgs for jobs. They don't follow rules, they make shit up, and instead of being normal rich fucks, they use dangerous methods to hide their corruption. It's unpredictable, which I like, but it puts my people in danger, which I don't."

"I don't think you could have put it any more succinctly," I tell the fidgety redhead. "And it's why this won't be nearly as simple as you probably assumed. Small towns and even small cities are full of history and backroom bargains."

Morgana snorts as she shakes her head. "That makes everything three times as hard. Our focus is being disrupted by a multitude of individuals with various motives."

And god help us if anyone else throws their hat in the ring—I might even have to contact my father.

---

1. Protect what is mine. Keep the evil from invading his mind. The Children of Hecate command it.

let's get it on

The ride home is quiet until we're outside of the city limits. Only then does Lucas turn in his seat to look at Liam curiously.

"I know Jax told me you went to bat for me. That was cool, man."

I smile to myself at the relative simplicity of how men communicate big things. Catching Liam nodding in the rearview, I move my focus back to the road as I speak. "It's weird that this amped up so quickly. The people pulling the strings must have very specific timelines in mind to force the police to take such drastic measures without proper support."

"But what are they aiming to achieve is the real question," Liam says. "Obviously, screwing with Lucas fucks with the hockey program. It distracts you, and possibly Fräu Wolfberg. But none of those things seems worthy of such an elaborate scheme."

Lucas frowns as he slouches in his seat. "Unless there's shit we don't know about. Fuck if I know what Nana is voting on or involved in with the Society or her Council. M is reviewing financials for every department at the college. Maybe there's something hidden in that? Wouldn't surprise me."

My brow furrows. "Or maybe both can be true? My placement here allows someone with nefarious intentions toward the Council to discredit findings based on my past. If I discover some Ponzi bullshit or goddess knows what else, they'll say I'm compromised. You being on trial would allow them to do the same for your grandmother."

"Bad PR." Liam sighs and I wait for him to continue. "That's certainly a Fae tactic used in many coups over the years. The kingdoms and courts are easily breached for the major reasons anyone does shit: patriotism, money, or love. We're all susceptible to the base enticements at some level."

"Patriotism?" I snort and shake my head. "I don't know if that's a real thing anymore, especially in supe communities."

Liam scoffs in response. His hands land on the seat backs as he leans in. "You're taking a narrow view of it, lass. Whether it's loyalty to kingdom, court, pack, Council, or even a specific sect, all our people can be motivated by wanting to take care of their brethren. If they're bent certain ways, they also want to negatively affect those they consider lesser as well."

"Maybe you *are* paying attention in those grad classes," I say with a grin. "That's very politically strategic thinking."

"It's sneaky as fuck," Lucas says as he crosses his arms over his chest. "I'm just not... underhanded like that. It's good I've got Thorne's team and you guys to handle that. I guess I didn't get the snake oil gene from Nana or my idiot parents."

"Ah, but that makes you a rare shifter, Lucas. Someone who speaks plainly and is honest in their interactions without fail is not something you come across often, especially in the circles you grew up in. Perhaps it is why you were targeted? Your profile suggested you wouldn't flee the scene to avoid being accused."

By Hera's shiny girdle, he's probably right.

"I think you're right, Li. Lucas makes a good fall guy because he's *not* a shady asshole. He won't run or outright buy his freedom from suspicion. They can count on this being a giant, ridiculous circus for as long as their pawns play ball." Fury wells in my chest because I have so many things I have to do for my sentence and now I have actual things I *want* to do personally.

Like spend time with my mate and these men who seem determined to worm their way into my life.

"Being a good dude is actually working against me...The internet would lose its *mind*," the polar bears says with a chuckle. "I mean... that's never true, right?"

"Rarely."

The Prince laughs and I feel the tension in the car ease as we enjoy a moment of levity. "Kaspar is out doing what he does best. I believe Jackson said Kendrick is doing the same. They should yield some clues, at the very least. I assume the centuries of experience ferreting information will give them the best chance for success."

Squinting at the mirror, I grumble, "Didn't give them manners, though."

"Truth. What is it with super dark, dangerous 'K' dudes and grumpy ass attitudes? I feel like it's a thing," Lucas says as he taps his fingers on his leg. "Not that I have a clue what the creepy dude on #TeamShark is. At least we know Kaspar is a storm dragon who'll fry our asses if we piss him off. I can't imagine what 'Tall, Dark, and Malevolent' can do."

I pause briefly and shake my head. "He's not a dragon. I can smell that. My senses aren't as good as yours, Lucas, but my snakes know what that tastes like."

"Gross," my mate mutters. "Not your snakes, obviously, because I think it's hot. I hate that it makes me think of old crusty dragon balls before you stabbed him to death. My bear dislikes that imagery *a lot*."

Liam clears his throat. "My magic isn't overly fond of it, either. If I'm being honest, I'd prefer to know he was out there so we could deal with him in a much more painful fashion than you did."

I feel my face heat and it makes my gut clench in fear. Lucas is my mate, but the other men are... questions marks at the moment. I don't trust how eagerly my mind and body respond to their possessive shit. It was hard enough to accept that Lucas and I were bonded *forever* after what I thought would be a one-night stand. Now the rest of them have stormed in and refuse to leave.

It's a bit much for someone with as many trust issues as I have.

"Well, unfortunately for you, I ran the motherfucker through so many times I severed things. So it's not possible." I shrug, trying to shake off the uneasy feeling that they don't understand how much my gorgon enjoyed taking her vengeance.

A low growl echoes in the car as I turn onto the road that leads to campus and I arch a brow at the bear next to me. He sniffs, looking unrepentant. "You're hot when you're vicious, too. The Prince agrees... I can smell it."

I choke on my reply, putting all my energy into not wrecking as I head down the main drag toward Chancellor's Row. "That's... good information to have?"

"I'd say so, considering the teacher and the fish are headed back to class and everyone else has fucked off to do their tasks. It means the three of us have the house to ourselves."

My eyes widen as I look at my mate, then back at the smug-looking Fae royal.

Are they suggesting what I think they are?

The running monologue in my head is loud enough that I feel like the men in my car should have been able to hear it as I navigated back to my house. I'm no wilting petal, nor am I inexperienced in group activities, but somehow, this has me on edge.

He's a Prince, for fucks's sake, and Lucas will inherit a bajillion dollars someday.

Not that I'm impressed by celebrities or royalty—in fact, my disdain for Magnus' family tree in the dragon clan is part of why his death was such a scandal. Their family is deeply connected to some muckitty-muck dragons throughout Europe and so his murder was a much bigger deal than a normal, everyday supe. His uncle wanted me put to death by dragon fire, and made sure everyone in the courtroom knew it.

But... I'm an adopted kid with teachers for parents and before my ex, a pretty unremarkable life in terms of stardom. We were pretty solidly middle class, and that wasn't a big deal to me. I didn't yearn to be a famous pop star or some shiny CEO; I just wanted to work in academia. I enjoyed school and the atmosphere, so it was a natural fit.

Meeting Magnus at a charity event changed the trajectory of my life forever.

I pull into the driveway, turning the SUV's engine off and removing the keys. My body is on auto-pilot as I try to figure out how to come to terms with the situation I'm walking into. It's not like I'm going to drop to my knees and mimic that movie from the 90s with cries about not being worthy. However, I am still concerned about how I'm going to be received by all these crazy rich people families and their minions. It's making me nervous about their proposal and I don't like it.

"Morgana," Lucas says as he approaches me carefully.

Blinking, I look up at his handsome face in surprise. I didn't realize he'd come around to my side of the car. "Mmm?"

His hand brushes a lock of hair off of my face as he smiles. "Get out of your head. I don't know what you're stewing on, but if it's about the Prince and I... You have nothing to worry about."

"As if," I scoff, slamming my car door shut. "I'm not worried about the two of you. You're not the first two men to proposition me—not even the first to do it in a car."

There. Now I feel less exposed.

"Good to know, *Salaadir*. But you're not wrong to wonder how this will be different." Liam tilts his head, holding his hand out to me. I move towards him without thinking about it, and he grins. "There are many differences—both subtle and less so—between species, as well as ones that vary when you encounter a royal or an alpha."

I take his hand and my temperature spikes by a thousand degrees as his hand squeezes mine. "I didn't know that."

"Especially when you are likely one yourself," Lucas says as he joins us. "Because you, my slithery mate, are likely descended from alpha blood. That's probably why our first time was so... explosive."

"Who told you that?" I ask as they escort me up the steps to the front door.

His lips curve, and he winks. "I'll never tell."

We'll see about that, my gargoyle growls in my head.

The guys stop, blinking at me. Lucas grins broadly as he lifts my free hand to his lips. "I *felt* that. One of your sides just surged throughout the bond like a steamroller. It made my bear want to wrestle for dominance. What was it?"

"The gargoyle," I murmur as I punch in the code at the door. "She didn't like when you said you wouldn't tell me."

Liam lets go of my hand, moving his to my lower back as he ushers me inside. "Now we know which side is the most in charge, Morgana. Your gorgon might be a defender, but the gargoyle is dominant. And she wants you to be as well."

I give him a look that says 'duh,' and he shrugs. Rubbing the back of my neck, I turn to Lucas. "He doesn't have an alpha inside of him. Will it always anger your bear?"

"Hell if I know. He doesn't hate the idea of fighting for control, though, so perhaps we just have to encourage them to play nice and take turns."

The scent of flowers fills the air and I turn to see Liam growing vines out of thin air, letting them curl as they grow toward the ceiling. "I can help with that. There are lots of ways magic can enhance things, Morgana. Have you been with a magic user before?"

"Not Fae," I admit, as I watch the flowers in awe. "Twin demi-gods for a short time, but they... were a bit too flighty for my taste. And a small vampire coven... all before Magnus, obviously. But no one with the kind of magic you have."

Liam winks as he whispers, "The magic both your professor *and* I have. Not to mention what variations the siren and Kaspar possess."

I snort. "Kaspar will *never* be a concern. He's made that very clear."

"Yet he's out sleuthing for clues."

Shaking my head, I lean back into Lucas with a sigh. "Because you asked him to, and it's his duty."

"Not this. It has nothing to do—officially—with court business for the moment. This he could refuse if he so chose." Liam grins as he steps forward, pressing me between the polar bear and his own muscles. "But he didn't even protest much. You should think about that."

"But not now," Lucas says as he tilts my head to one side. His lips brush over my neck and I shudder. "Because right now, we have plans."

Oh. Well, I can't ruin their plans, now can I?

intrigue

This campus is chock full of supes who are completely clueless. I have no idea how these idiots even function. Most of the students I've encountered barely realize the leadership here has changed unless they're athletes. The sporty looking people echo sentiments I assume are coming from their well-to-do parents or bullheaded coaches. Nothing they offer tells me a damn thing about who might try to frame the bear, nor why any of them are even considered qualified to attend a university.

The gargoyle's ex may have played games with admission standards for the college players as well as fucked up the finances.

Of course, most supes aren't quite as... cerebral as the Fae, so my impression may be skewed. Living at Court for as long as I have makes you expect a very shrewd populace. No one in that realm may progress through their education without passing extremely rigorous examinations. Even the teens in the court families act as if they're much older than their age. It's a constant game of multi-dimensional chess in Faerie, even in the more pastoral areas outside of the major cities.

I have noticed that the more expensively outfitted the students are, the more helpful their misguided rumors are. These kids are tapped into whisper networks because of their wealth, and despite not knowing their ass from their elbow, they have tidbits I file away for later. One group of girls seemed to believe Morgana *ate* Magnus, which... is fairly impossible based on anatomy, but they murmured a lot of details they'd gleaned from their parents about the woman.

Who knows if any of it is true, but I'll vet the info later.

I'm glad Liam sent me on recon; my talents lie in feats other than diplomacy and I'm more useful to him doing this. There are plenty of muscled supes in the lawyer's group, and I doubt anyone will have to flex for the golden hockey god in the middle of the police station. Hopefully, they're more competent than the version of law enforcement at the school. Between the students and staff I've chatted up, I've uncovered a great deal of troubling news about that group of morons. They are ill-trained and equipped, many are fiercely loyal to the dragon, and they lord authority over the less fortunate students in ways that need severe punishment.

"I wouldn't trust these clowns to patrol a dog park, much less keep high profile students and staff safe. No wonder the royals sent me along with Li," I mutter to myself as I head for the coffeeshop where the siren works. "I'd feel safer in the middle of a fucking riot than I do here."

As I approach, I chide myself for staying at the house when everything went down. After Lucas healed, I should have left to vet the men's living and working spaces. Any of those places could be infiltrated by the poisoner, the murderer, or an infinite amount of dangerous folks. My desire to see how the events unfolded is baffling, and it may have put everyone in jeopardy.

I won't make that mistake twice.

Stepping into the small cafe, I look around suspiciously. This place is packed with potential food and drink to slip something in, not to mention all the accoutrements like sweeteners and syrups. I'll never be able to inventory it all without help from Liam. He'll have to visit to do a reveal and we might even need the mage to help parse all the data. It's a security nightmare.

"Welcome! What can I get you?"

My gaze whips to the earnest looking twenty-something behind the counter. She looks perfectly respectable, but so do most assassins at court. Appearances are far too easy to mask when someone is determined. "I haven't been here before. What's the most popular?"

Whatever it is, that's the first fucking thing I'll have tested.

"We have a fabulous oatmeal cookie frappe that students love. Or maybe a fruity tea? We can do bubble tea and boba now."

I blink, looking at her in confusion. *What the fuck? Is that coffee?* Waving my hand, I shake my head. "I fear that's too adventurous for me. How about a double espresso black?"

The face the worker makes is comical, and I huff in amusement. Liam probably would have let her build some monstrosity, and had a fun chat about what he liked or didn't like with the girl. Out of necessity and training, he's much more sociable than I. But I refuse to pretend some mountain of sugar and whipped cream is coffee. Despite her disappointment, the girl gets to work on the drink, tilting her head at the display case.

"We have fresh pastries and breads. Are you in the mood for a nibble?"

Fuck no. I have no idea what the hell is in this shit.

"Perhaps I'll take a few things home for my... roommate. I don't think he's been here, either, and he has a bit of a sweet tooth. Give me one of everything." I give her what I believe to be a charming grin, but it doesn't seem to help her disquiet.

"Um, okay. I'll put that together once I'm done with the coffee."

Nodding, I wander through the small shop, noting the magical signature on a shelf by the wall. Something here was placed to spy on people and I'll eat my hat if it doesn't belong to the professor. I've watched him looking at his 'old friend' and their scents tell a vastly different story than their mouths. He's a controlling little shit; the problem with the plant teacher was due to his indiscretion. However, I didn't hear a word about the siren's activities.

Non-mythical shifters are fucking weird about sex and I have zero problem saying it.

"I'm sorry," I say as I turn back to the girl. "I didn't get your name. I'm Kaspar and I am the guard for Prince Liam."

Her jaw drops hard enough to be funny, but I don't laugh. When she recovers, the petite blond clears her throat. "Oh, my. I... My name is Lyndsay Krysten Harold. Pardon me for not being able to properly address you."

I frown. There is no 'proper way' to address the Prince's second—at least, not on this side of the Veil. *Does she think she should curtsey? How odd.* Instead of laughing, I give her another smile. "Don't worry, Miss Harold. I'm a worker bee like you. In fact, I'm here scouting about so I can report back to His Highness about various rumors on campus he's worried about. Might you have information I can relay? I hate to impose, but..."

The sentence hangs and I can see her practically salivate at the chance to gossip. Swallowing my distaste at the sycophantic need to suck up to someone who seems important, I sit down at the table closest to her counter and wait. I feel that this girl gathers nuggets of spurious accusations via eavesdropping and snuggling up to anyone who seems to have a smidgen of power while she works. I'd bet I'm not the first person to pump this well, nor will I be the last. She's looking at me with such sparkling enthusiasm that I'd peg her as a major source of the rumor mill on this damn campus.

Slade needs to know that, so I'll mark that discovery down as well.

"Sit with me and let's chat. The Prince will be very grateful."

"Bye, Kaspar!"

The bookish looking girl waves happily as I exit the shop with my bags of food. Prior to participation, a thorough examination is required, but the samples aren't my greatest acquisition from this journey.

Lyndsay not only gave up unsubstantiated gossip she'd heard at this job, but she also spilled information from her other job in the admissions office, despite an NDA.

"The complete lack of morals some of these supes have," I mutter as I stride across campus. "Legally speaking, she's toast if we report her, but she's also given me a great deal of slander to go along with the private information from the office. She'll be lucky if she's able to find a position anywhere after graduation. I can't imagine the wealthy families around here not abandoning her to her own devices when they find out what she's shared."

My lips curve up as I think about Morgana or her twitchy assistant firing the girl for her breach, then the ripple effect that will spread across campus and in the private sector. I'd feel bad about her prospects for a future, but when you are so desperate for attention that you behave like this girl, you're all but begging someone to put a stop to it. When they do, crying foul is simply idiotic. If you make your reputation poor, that's how you'll be viewed.

There's just no substitute for loyalty—not even willingness to get your hands dirty.

Pulling my phone out, I hit the speed dial and frown when my friend doesn't answer. That almost never happens. Liam has answered in the middle of a lecture before, so I know he doesn't give a fuck who or what he interrupts. I don't sense danger or trouble through our bond, so he's not in a precarious position. I growl softly, hitting the button again as I stalk to the far end of campus to head for the secluded street both the Prince and Morgana are housed on.

"If he's left his damn phone in the car or at that station, I'll kill him," I grumble to myself. "I know he's caught up in this mess up to his damn neck, but leaving me on read when I'm out doing his blood-hound shit is ridiculous."

Very few people in the world are able to give the Prince of the Daybreak Court the same hell I do, but Liam and I have been paired for longer than this country has been around. Our families have an even longer history, so my comfort level with the heir to the kingdom is born of years of trust and companionship. He supported me when I was at my worst and never once asked for his father to replace me. I might have deserved it, but as I said, loyalty is a richer currency than almost any other.

Which is why I worry about his newest obsession so much—if Liam's mate is a hybrid living on this side of the Veil, what consequences will that have?

His father is a major asshole, and he needs to step down to allow Liam to rule. The Court and the kingdom need a ruler who isn't a tyrannical old fart. But falling for someone who not only has a life entirely outside of the Veil and comes with a gaggle of others from various walks of supernatural life is a tough sell for his subjects. They don't mind the poly aspect—only the non-Fae part. It will be a big deal and I think he's underestimating how difficult people will make his life.

"I wish I had a better view of this fucking situation so I could provide him with more than my gut instinct. He doesn't trust me with the gargoyle because of my past, but... I just don't know." I turn onto the street, driving slowly so I can study the other houses in the row. They were all empty when we moved in, but there appears to have been some new residents added to the beginning of Chancellor's Row.

Great... more people to check out.

It suddenly occurs to me that the lawyer's team has a hacker. Perhaps if we mention new players on the board, he'll do the mind numbing basic checking via the internet and I can follow-up afterward. That would allow me to focus on the current targets I have lined up for tomorrow. Now that I've identified a leak in Morgana's admissions department, I need to go after the other ones. Picking them off one by one will narrow the list considerably.

My brows furrow when I see the car in the driveway. I didn't think they'd be back this quickly. When I left the Prince, it seemed like he would spend most of the day at the station. Shaking my head, I ease our specially detailed SUV into our own driveway and hop out. I doubt Liam even came to our place if he returned home with them. No, he's probably not answering his cell because he's busy chatting strategy or some shit with Morgana and her bear.

Interrupting before the others arrive will give me time to explain what I've found without a crowd.

Satisfied with my decision, I hop out and head down the street to the Dean's house. We'll figure out how to plug her coffeehouse mouse leak, then plot which departments I should focus on first.

Liam will be pleased as fuck.

hot to go

The pair of supes advance on me as we get further into my house, and I smirk. "Boys, I'm not sure if you know this, but you're not my first group rodeo. And I'm not exactly docile."

Lucas chuckles softly as he looks over at the prince. "Did you think Morgana was going to be a compliant submissive, Your Highness?"

That earns him a responding laugh as the Fae pulls his shirt over his head in that stupidly hot dude way. "Not at all, *mathan òg*. In fact, I rather hoped she'd take charge. I prefer learning what my woman likes from her own lips."

If that's true...

Darting forward, I yank Liam closer by his waistband, kissing him hard and fast. A thrumming zings through my veins when we touch and I groan when my ursine mate moves to press against my back. The Prince lets me control our kiss, twining his tongue with mine while Lucas wraps his arms around me. I lean into his hard cock, rubbing my ass against him while I brush my tongue against the small points of Liam's Fae fangs. Most people don't realize the royals have much more pronounced canines than other fair folk, but I've had enough interaction with them in the past to know.

When he finally breaks away, the magic in his eyes is so bright I can feel it on my skin. "*Salaadir*, you are playing a dangerous game."

"Am I?" I grin at him playfully as Lucas runs his large hands up and down my torso. He cups my breasts, and I moan when he tweaks my nipples. "Perhaps I enjoy games as much as you, but I only play them in private."

"That would be a pleasant surprise, indeed," he murmurs as he watches me writhe into the bear's hands. "We should move this upstairs. I fear there are far too many pieces of clothing in our way."

Winking, I turn in my mate's arms, waiting for him to heft me up. My legs wrap around his waist and I have to hold my breath as he starts up the stairs. I'm not a small woman and trusting that he can not only hold me up, but carry me up this incline is a big leap. But Lucas handles it without breaking a sweat and I hear Liam rumbling behind us.

"Your bear has one of hell of an ass, *Salaadir*. He's flexing muscles most people only dream about."

Lucas stiffens for a moment, then suddenly relaxes as he looks down at me. "Don't be jealous, Princey-poo. Maybe our girl will share."

I'm sorry.... what?

My voice is soft as I look up at the hot hockey player gripping me close. "You don't have to do anything you're not comfortable with, baby. A group dynamic doesn't require you to experiment."

His grin is brilliant but a little shy as he flushes. "Maybe I've been curious before, but the environment I'm in wasn't conducive to admitting it. It might be awkward at first, but... if I trust anyone to make sure I'm comfortable, it would be you, Morgana."

"You know I can hear you both, right?"

Lucas chuckles and looks over his broad shoulder. "Then you should be very gentle with me because our girl will not."

I pinch his arm, grinning as he kicks the door open wide so we can enter. "You're an adorable brute, Lucas Wolfberg."

"I am, but I'm *your* adorable brute. Now get naked, woman."

Liam closes the door behind us, stalking over to the bed to watch me pull my clothes off slowly. His hungry gaze makes the gorgon inside of me slither in delight and Desi pops out from under my hair to hiss excitedly. "She's poisonous, yes?"

"Not to her mates," Lucas says as he pulls his shirt off to reveal the small snake bites at the tops of his biceps. "It's trippy and a bit like an aphrodisiac."

My face turns bright red as the Fae looks even more like he's going to devour me. "Lucas! I don't tell *everyone* that. People would hunt us down like they do Cubi and vamps."

"Not true if it's only mates who don't get poisoned, lass." Liam undoes his pants, dropping them to reveal a gorgeous, muscled body simply glowing with tattoos from head to toe, "It's like these. Most women will never see the markings of a royal like this."

Licking my lips as my eyes roam over every inch of him, I croak, "Why?" The mattress dips when Lucas's naked body presses to my side and I shiver in pleasure. His heat and the hard jut of his dick make my thighs clench in anticipation. "What's the big secret?"

"Fae Royals can *only* share magic like this with their mates. If the tattoos are visible on us, they will also appear on our mate or mates. Obviously, my magic knows this isn't simply a fun little afternoon delight." He pauses, tilting his head at me with a worried expression. "Is that okay?"

I'm about to answer when a throat clears. My blonde bear gives me a sheepish expression as he murmurs, "I think the better question —'cause she's obviously going to say 'yes'—is whether it's cool that *I* can see them, Prince."

Holy shit waffles.

I'm shocked when Liam's eyes widen with delight. His lips curve up as he darts forward without a word and yanks Lucas into a deeply sexy kiss. I press my thighs together with a groan of pleasure, knowing I'm so goddamn screwed. They're a study in light and dark in terms of personality and appearance, but the savagery of the kiss is making my whole body hot. Despite his inexperience, Lucas is handling this awakening like slipping on a perfectly tailored coat.

"Mother of stone and magic," I mutter as they finally break apart. "That was so completely hot and totally unexpected today. I need someone to touch me before I implode."

The shy look my mate gives the other man makes my chest tighten, but his mouth drops to my shoulder to suckle at the healing bear bite soothingly. It ramps up the flood of wetness leaking from me and I arch up against the Prince. When he starts on the other side, working his way down my chest in tandem with Lucas, I whimper low.

These men will be the death of me, I fucking swear to Medusa's girdle.

Liam continues making his way down to my stomach, nibbling each of my ribs before tracing his tongue around my belly button. His hum of appreciation vibrates over my skin when Lucas's dick jumps on my thigh. I bury my fingers in his hair with one hand, then tug my mate up to kiss him thoroughly. The small groan that escapes in my mouth makes me smile against his lips when the Fae's hand snakes over my body to stroke him while he suckles on my skin.

"Does that feel good, big guy?" I breathe against his mouth. His eyes flutter and he nods before swooping in to kiss me again. The amount of lust in the room makes me want to tie them both down and tease them until they beg, but that's for another time. Letting Liam discover us together while Lucas experiences his first time with a male is so fucking hot that I can't describe it. I've never been part of someone's first anything before and watching is addictive.

"Yessss..." he says with a sharp exhale.

His hips jerk against mine and I'm about to reply when the warmth of the Prince's mouth hits my pussy. It destroys my focus as he spreads me open and dives in, licking me from front to back before heading for my clit like he's on a mission. Lucas grunts in pleasure, inhaling again before he buries his face against my mark. I feel sharper teeth grip it and I know he's being worked just as thoroughly as I am.

"The smell of you two together is intoxicating," Liam murmurs against my soaked cunt. "I could do this all fucking day, you know. *Mathan òg*, I'm going to taste you now. Be prepared."

Lucas doesn't respond, but the moan that echoes from his chest makes me squirm. Skilled fingers replace the mouth he's using on my mate, and I ride them, pushing against the thumb positioned just so to make me shiver in delight.

"Odin's fucking balls, Liam.... that's...."

I grin, leaning in to nip Lucas's ear while Desi strikes his shoulder. He shivers hard against me and I let the intensity of this moment coast over me. Our Prince may be in the driver's seat, but every bit of this encounter is about pleasing me and I know it. "Baby, he wants us to come for him. He needs it so we can fuck until this pretty new bed breaks with the ferocity of your bear."

A finger slips out of the wet heat between my legs, teasing my ass, and I arch into it, gasping as it enters me. The teeth on my mark dig in deeper and a small whimper escapes my mate before he answers in a gravelly voice, "I'm so close, M. And I want it. I want the... three of us... to... holy fuck, that's..."

When Liam doesn't answer, I know his mouth is occupied with my big guy's big dick, so I drop my head and do something he hasn't experienced yet. I close my eyes and let out the other side of my supernatural powers until my skin turns to smooth, cool stone. My tail whips around to cup his balls as Liam licks and sucks him, teasing just enough to make him shudder. Rocking my hips harder and faster on the Prince's hand, I bite with all four elongated fangs as the wave of orgasm crashes into me.

As stars explode in front of my eyes, I feel the air heat and a breeze coasts over me. The scent of flowers and sunshine fills the room and by the time I open my eyes, I'm shocked to see my bedroom turned into a veritable meadow of blooms, vines, and Faerie flora. A buzzing sound precedes the soft brush of a pair of beautiful bat wings that drape over Lucas and me until we finally come down.

Letting go of him with a soft 'pop,' I watch as Liam slithers back up to us with a very satisfied look on his face. "That was so delicious that I couldn't stop the visual effects. Are you ready for more, *mo chàirdean gràdhach*? Because I cannot wait much longer to allow my full essence to release."

What the actual fuck does that mean?

I don't get the chance to ask, though, because Lucas grabs his face and kisses him hungrily. His response is good enough for me because my chest aches again. "Yes, Liam. Please, now."

"Where?" he says with a slow, possessive grin that makes me gush again. "Would you like to have us both while you... show our bear what else you can do? Or...."

"Both of you inside of me this time," I rasp as he immediately slicks his cock with my juices. "Lucas, get the lube for him, darling."

He obeys without pause, handing the small bottle from the night-stand to the prince before settling against me. "I've done nothing like this before, but it's…"

"It feels perfectly natural? It is, *mathan òg*[1]. I can feel it with every bit of my magic and all my connection to the Earth." Liam flips me to my side, lifting my thigh to rest on Lucas's so he can line up and sink in. Once he does, I can barely breathe until I feel the Fae's cock at my ass. "See how she's aching for us? It was meant to be."

Everything feels so fucking amazing that I can't even panic about his 'forever' talk.

When his dick pushes into me until I'm completely full with both of them, I moan low and dark. Desi hisses and then a chorus of hisses respond to her. I know it means the entirety of my powers will release soon, which normally I don't allow. But with them…. I won't have an option. The things I withheld from Magnus will come out, and hope-fully, the Prince is correct. If we're all supposed to be together, it won't make them run.

"Lucas, you start and I'll follow." Liam growls softly against my ear, and I remember what I'm going to do. My tail darts between us to gather as much slick as possible before heading towards Lucas. "Mor-gana, my fated, relax. You're so tense and I know why…. let go for us."

I don't know if he truly gets what that means, but as they rock in tandem and the shocks of pleasure flow through me, I do as he asked. I close my eyes and savor every shiver, groan, and snarl as we move together. The tip of my tail slips into my adorable bear to give him the first taste of what he'll eventually feel and he damn near crushes me in his grip, but I don't back away. Tendrils of magic zip around us, and every inch of me focuses on chasing the enormous climax barreling closer. When it's almost too much, the glow of my heart heats my chest and I know the crest is going to hit.

"Bite…. now…." I gasp as my head falls back to expose where they need to be. My claws dig into Lucas's hips, my tail pushes in deeper, and all the snakes make their move when teeth touch my skin again.

In a blinding flash of power and magic, it feels like my entire world explodes and I scream into the aether, clutching the two men who seem to have captured my soul without even trying.

Despite the consequences, my glow grows until it melds with Liam's and my eyes flutter closed.

I don't care what the cost is; this was meant to be.

---

1. Young bear

headstrong

As we pull up to Morgana's house, a pulse of magic nearly causes me to hit the large SUV parking in front of us. I hit the brakes, blinking and sucking in a deep breath. Slade looks at me in concern, but I just wave my hand. There's nothing he can do to help; I absorb more than I should when people use their powers around me and I don't have time to shield. It's one of the reasons I make such a good professor—I can keep the folks who don't have precision control from killing their classmates accidentally.

It's also why my father fucking hates me; I'm more powerful than him by leaps and bounds.

"Will that stick with you?" my friend murmurs as he studies me.

Shaking my head, I let out another breath as the energy flows over me. "Unsure, but damn, that was a big one. I don't know what the fuck they're getting up to inside, but we should go see."

Before I can maneuver the car into the other spot, that damn grumpy dragon bursts out of the SUV and bounds into the house like his ass is on fire. Slade looks at me and groans. "That's not good. He's way too much of a hothead."

"It's going to be complicated until he gets that flaming head out of his ass, for sure," I agree. "Let's go help our girl and the others before Captain Asshat makes them pissy."

The car slides into the spot next to his armored monstrosity and we both hop out, hurrying to the porch where the door is hanging open. It's obvious Kaspar has damn near taken it off the hinges and I mutter a spell to patch the damage so we can close it.

"Man, he really needs a damn chill pill," Slade says softly. "It didn't even feel like anyone was in danger. Why go totally psycho?"

Because he's a crazy ass dragon and they're all *like this.*

Huffing in irritation, I turn to the steps as loud voices echo off the walls. "Fuck. He's already screwing it all up."

We take the steps two at a time, arriving at Morgana's bedroom door just as she delivers a stinging blow.

"You're jealous that he wants to be with someone other than *you,* you scaly shithead."

Well, that wasn't subtle.

"Guys, come on. We talked about this already." I peek in the room to see Lucas sprawled on the bed like the golden god of sports he is, looking totally unruffled by the intrusion.

The Prince looks more frustrated, standing with his arms crossed over an impressive chest. He's wearing sweatpants I assume are borrowed from the bear, and his usually neat hair is a mess. It's obvious what went on from the scent alone, but when my eyes hit Morgana, they almost bug out. She's got a sheet wrapped around her in a messy tumble, looking like an ingenue in a French film.

"I'm not jealous of your silly tryst," Kaspar says with a snort. "I am concerned because I felt the magic from the street and…"

"It was mating magic?" Liam says with a smirk. "That it was, my friend."

Damn, that crafty royal shit—riding back with them definitely gave him the edge.

Scales ripple over the bodyguard, and he looks as if he's truly struggling not to shift. Once they fade, he gives the Prince a dark glare. "Your father will know. This is a disaster."

Morgana finally moves, stepping into the middle of the fray with her eyes flashing. "I'm not used to people discussing things that impact me as if I'm not present. I don't care who the fuck you work for, dragon. You wouldn't be the first one I've slayed, nor am I worried about the punishment."

"Wait, wait," Slade says as he sneaks past me. "This is all getting out of control. Morgana's choice in mates or mating is hers and the recipient's. Well, and maybe Lucas, too. But… that doesn't mean there are no consequences for free will. I think Kaspar is failing to communicate that this decision may have some we are not aware of."

"That was pretty good, dude." I grin at Slade, and he ducks his head, looking oddly pleased at the praise. I never can figure out his reactions and it's gotten worse since Morgana came along. "But he's right. The dragon is fucking this up epically, but I assume he's worried about the evil Fae Daddy smiting someone. That about it, dickface?"

Kaspar huffs smoke rings and I watch him closely. I'll need a water enchantment and possibly Slade's help if he unleashes dragon fire. That stuff is hard as hell to put out and resistant to normal water. "The siren is correct. Liam has been promised to many women as a possible betrothal by the King; who knows what political alliances this will disintegrate? Not to mention, mating with Fae will leave obvious marks, unlike the simple bites of the bear. There are mating tattoos that will eventually show and likely follow to the bear."

"That's kind of cool," Morgana mutters and I grin at her. She has no idea, but she will.

Lucas frowns, thinking about it for a moment, then shrugs. "I like ink and Li's hot. I'm good with it."

"Odin's rusty codpiece, you're all dense," the dragon grumbles. "Do you realize that if both you and Morgana show up around town with Fae markings—particularly royal ones—anyone who knows what they mean will not only realize you're connected to the Prince but also to one another? Fuck, it's like explaining shit to a troll."

Ouch. Trolls are pretty thick as a species.

"Maybe it will require a glamor to cover them?" I offer. Morgana gives me a grateful look, and I shrug. "I'm quite skilled at them, you know."

"Fae mating marks can't be covered with other magic. It is our inability to lie—you can't cover up that you belong to someone else because it might trick them about your status," Liam says softly.

Slade tilts his head. "So Fae can't cheat on their mates?"

"Uh, yes, they can," Kaspar grunts. "They just can't lie about it."

Interesting. I'm not sure I'd survive in Faerie—deception was ground into my bones from the time I could talk.

"That's why you're yelling? Some tattoos? Seems like an overreaction," the bear says as he stretches again. "But what do I know? I'm a murder suspect."

"I'm an actual murderer," Morgana adds with an impish grin. "Guess it can't be that scandalous for me."

"Not even when you're the Dean?" the dragon asks with a cocked brow.

"Especially not then given our previous Dean, moron," I shoot back as I walk into the room to find a place to sit on the window seat.

How is this guy an actual bodyguard when he's this dumb?

Lucas smothers a guffaw, grinning. "Good one, Prof."

Even the Prince cracks a smile as he walks over to stand behind our girl. "Kaspar, I'm well aware of all the implications. We'll have to deal with them one by one, as they come up. My father is fairly distracted by all his mistresses and the Hand at the moment. We both know he's not exactly tuned into the goings on of his children, even on a boring day. The mercenaries and preventing war should keep him busy enough."

"And your mother?" The dragon gives his friend a pointed look, and that drains the color from his face.

"Uh... well..."

As quickly as she allowed him close, Morgana gives Liam a big shove. "You idiot. Your *mother* is going to get involved? I'll kill you myself."

Slade clears his throat, his expression thoughtful. "Does everyone in this room have living parents?"

I heave a sigh, nodding. "I do and it will not be a treat to have either interested in my life."

"Second that," my roommate says as he turns to the others. "Morgana's folks are in Greece, right? Retired?"

"Yes, but I'd like to keep them out of anything for as long as possible because the trial was really hard on them," she murmurs softly. "They didn't deserve all that flack just for raising a hybrid they adopted."

Lucas leaps up from the bed, glaring as he walks over to take her hands. "Babe, my parents gave birth to me and they could give a fuck less what I do. I wouldn't torture anyone with their presence for all the money in the Wolfenberg vaults. But Nana is going to want to meet you, eventually."

Our girl looks like she's going to throw herself out the window, so I take pity on her. "I think the Prince said this dick's dad is alive at least. So that rounds us all out. At least now we have an idea how many assholes we'll have to fend off."

Kaspar clenches his fists, shaking his head. "You don't need to worry about me. I returned because you have other worries."

"What the hell does that mean?" Morgana tosses her raven hair over her shoulder, then blinks and looks down at herself. Her lack of clothing has finally sunk in. She frowns and stomps towards her closet. Yanking the door open, she steps inside and closes it before calling, "Just speak loud enough for me to hear, jackass."

Liam chuckles, his eyes dancing with fondness at her jibe, and I feel a pang of jealousy hit me in the chest. The bear holds his fist out and they bump knuckles, a clear camaraderie formed now that they've experienced their mate together.

Fuck. I want that, and I've never wanted that before in my life.

"You have a gushing leak in your admissions department. The amount of information and libelous gossip she provided me with very little prompting suggests to me that you need to put the entire staff in your building in with a truth taster."

Slade blanches, looking disturbed. "Are you sure that a good..."

"Yes." The dragon didn't even give him time to finish, and I assume he found more than one yapping girl from the admin pool.

Morgana pops her head out of the closet, frowning. "Where the fuck am I going to find a goddamn unicorn shifter? They're as rare as dragons who aren't giant assholes."

We all look at one another and burst out laughing as Kaspar fumes and she ducks back into her space to finish dressing. I'll admit, I don't know where to find one outside of the Society, and I doubt anyone else does. They really are sought after and have to keep themselves hidden so people don't kidnap them for personal gain.

"I know where one is," Slade says softly. "But you will not like it."

I blink in surprise, then realize it must have something to do with his gangster relatives at home. "Slade, you don't have to…"

"If we need one, I do," he says with a sigh. "My parents have one who is indentured to their… organization. You probably don't want to know much more than that because the story is fucking awful. I wish I didn't know it, but the dude really fucked up. So if we visit my family, we could request… a favor."

Oh, hell no.

"No way," Morgana says as she comes out of her closet dressed in comfy clothes. "First, Lucas isn't supposed to leave the state. Second, I can't just hop a plane to the coast—I'm tied down, too." She points to where her wing would be and I cringe. That shit is barbaric. "Third, why in the hell would your criminal parents agree to it? I'm no one and I'm sure as fuck not ending up indentured to them like this poor unicorn."

"All excellent points," Liam says. "Not to mention, going into some gang's territory is quite dangerous. Supe empires are tricky with visiting heads of state."

"It wouldn't matter if… uh…" Slade fumbles for a second and I finally get what he means.

This would cost him big time—even if the outcome was positive in the short term.

"You're suggesting she mate with you, which will give Lucas and Liam free rein to join you. They know me, and Kaspar would be required to accompany his royal. We'd all be able to go in with no special permission and your parents would be hard pressed to deny their heir's new mate."

What they don't know is that finding his mate will have consequences easily as dire as the dragon was reminding the Fae prince about. Slade will have to present her at one of the Appalachin meetings of the heads of the criminal and mafia empires, then show her off at parties.

During breaks, he may need to assume family responsibilities. It would end his dream of being completely free of them for good.

"I don't know, Slade. Finding out the truth from the staff will not clear Lucas, nor will it fix all my problems," Morgana says slowly.

The sound of a throat clearing makes us all look, and Kaspar shrugs. "Actually, it might. If someone in Magnus' old band set Lucas up to smear you or even be involved in the poisoning, the likelihood of those bobbleheads all gossiping together is high. You might even figure out what the endgame is besides getting you in trouble. This can't all be about his crusty dick; that's insane."

He's got us there.

cold hearted snake

I know that Slade and Kaspar are right about interrogating the staff at university, but I'm having trouble figuring out how I'm supposed to do something so permanent unless it feels right. Mating with Slade doesn't feel wrong in theory, but until we're intimate, I won't know for sure. I've been attracted to him from the second I saw him, but I've certainly been hot for people who were not my fated in the past.

His soft eyes meet mine and I see the flush creeping up his neck as he looks at me. I feel this gentle, sweet siren has been told he's not enough his entire life. After my experience with Magnus, I know *exactly* how that can damage a person. Reaching out, I take his hand, lacing his fingers with mine.

"I'm willing to test the theory if you are, Slade. But..." I swallow hard, my emotions welling up inside as I drop my gaze to our joined fingers. "...please don't feel as though you have to do this now—or at all—to help Lucas and me. Clearing him is important, but not at the expense of anyone else's happiness, especially if they had... other things in mind for their future."

Ignatius snorts, crossing his arms over his chest. He wants to say something, but I guarantee it's not about the thing I've sensed when the adorable grad student looks at his long time 'roommate.' The mage is definitely oblivious as hell to *that* situation and I will not be the one who spills the beans unless it becomes my purview as a mate. If that happens, it's open season on serving him a steaming pile of truth about stringing someone I care about along.

Slade squeezes my hand, his beautiful aquamarine eyes sincere as he looks at me. "Don't be nervous that you're going to hurt me with rejection; it's not possible."

I didn't know sirens were fucking mind readers, too.

"He's not reading your mind," Iggy says with a grin. "He knows because you can hear him sing without being influenced. It's something only a mate or someone with a powerful enchantment can accomplish."

A thought hits me and I snort, covering my mouth as the hilarity of the situation hits me. *Oh, this is funny.* Licking my lips, I fight the urge to tell the stuffy idiot what I just realized—he thinks there's nothing between him and Slade because he cast an enchantment when they became roommates and has never lifted it. It's why he's never even considered the thing I can plainly see, despite not knowing them for very long.

"What's so funny, babe?" Lucas asks, his head tilted curiously.

I get myself under control, shaking my head at him. "Nothing. I never imagined doing something like this while I was sentenced here. The Fates adore amusing themselves, I guess."

It's a lie, but I'll tell him my theory later.

Liam leans in, his hand reaching out to touch where my hand is tangled with the siren's. "You know that the bear and I are behind you, no matter what you decide, *Salaadir.*"

"Fuck, yeah, we are," Lucas grins as he sprawls in place. "After time with you and the Prince, I'm so fucking on board it's ridiculous. Fuck anyone who has something to say about it, too."

He knows I'm worried about what's going to happen when people find out. I've already got a reputation as a killer because of my trial, and this sort of thing will fly around the microcosm that is State U like wildfire. Two students and a prince are salacious as hell, even if they are fated mates. I'll be fielding a lot of intrusive questions and hateful rhetoric once it gets out.

"*I'm* not okay with any of this," Kaspar mutters grumpily. "But it seems like the most prudent course of action."

My jaw tightens and I glare at the asshole dragon as if I could crisp him with my mind. "Yes, I'm aware you're 'anti-Morgana' and you'd rather dip your dick in acid than touch me."

Every guy in the room winces, and I roll my eyes. Men are so fucking weird about their genitals. A threat to pull out their intestines with my claws or inject my snakes' venom into their eyeballs would be *much* more painful, but mention hurting their cock and they shrivel like an overcooked hotdog. It's bizarre as hell.

But useful.

Des pops out from under my hair when I think about venom and I sigh. "Look at what you did, fuckhead. You made my troublemaker choose violence."

Kaspar snorts. "It's not my fault you're centuries old and can't control your shifts, hybrid."

The way he says the word makes me bristle and before I know it, *all* my snakes are loose and I no longer have raven tresses—I'm all gorgon. My eyes itch as they fade to golden and elongate to slits, then a low hiss pushes its way out of my mouth. His ridiculous bias against me has no basis other than what the press reported, and I *know* he knows that shit wasn't true. Kaspar is being mean simply to hurt me, and I'm putting a stop to it now.

"Youuuuuu..." I snarl as I point a clawed finger at him, scales shooting up my arm as I stand. "You will ceasssse to treat me like garbage. I have done nothing to earn your ire, ssssstorm dragon, and if you cannot be civil, you will be ssssssstone inssssstead."

My eyes are not on his—yet—because I'd prefer not to follow through on my threat. It would hurt Liam and put me on the radar for the fucking Daybreak Court's assassins, so for the moment, it's more of a promise. But if I lift my gaze, he will definitely harden and it won't just be in his goddamn tight-ass pants.

"Morgana..." Lucas says softly. I feel when he approaches as my forked tongue flicks in the air, but I don't move. "As hot as this is—and *believe me*, scaly snake Morgana is fucking hot as hell—you know you can't turn the dickhead to stone. Not now, anyway."

Joke's on you, mate. I can and I will if he doesn't cut this bullshit out.

"For fuck's sake," Kaspar huffs. "All I said is that you can't control your shifts. Why are you losing your shit?"

My slitted eyes blink and it hits me that he really *doesn't* know why I'm pissed. If that's true, then perhaps he didn't mean his words the way they sounded. He's a goddamn fool, but he might not be a damn species-ist dickhole. I draw in a slow, calming breath and do my best to push back the gorgon. It takes a minute, but I get her under control enough to respond.

"I'm going to give you the benefit of the doubt *again*, though it pains me to keep making exceptions for your stupid ass assumptions." The dragon glares at me, and I stare him down. "I'm angry because your words and inflection conveyed a dislike for hybrids, which is detestable. If you didn't mean to sound that way, you need to think harder about the words and tone you use when speaking to people. I'm also frustrated as *fuck* that you cannot simply give me a goddamn break. You can hate me all you want, but maybe keep it to yourself? It's cruel and totally unnecessary to keep prodding at me."

Kaspar blinks at me, his eyes wide as he takes in my rant. The other guys look pissed when they hear how I feel, and it's beyond obvious that he's in the minority with #TeamMorganaSucks. The dragon runs a hand through hair, his aura agitated as he huffs a smoke ring, then looks at me. "I did not intend to imply that. Hybrids are doubly gifted supes, not lesser beings."

No mention of your asshole behavior to me, huh?

I open my mouth, but he holds up his hand. The dragon swallows hard, and I see the smallest hint of vulnerability on his face. "I have a reason for being churlish, though it's not an excuse. Not because of anything you did, but my reason is valid. I will, however, try very hard not to berate you as much. I didn't think you cared enough for it to be harmful."

"Dude, are you fucking serious?" Lucas moves from behind me, his icy eyes flashing at the elder supe. "You are way too fucking old to be this dense. Who cares if she likes you or not? Either way, you don't have a free pass to be an insulting asshole in her house—a house you know we're trying to rid of the offensive, abusive dipshit who treated her like a damn Kleenex until she took her due. Don't act like you're ignorant of the effect you have when you spout bullshit because no one is buying it."

Slade looks up at him, his pretty face pinched as he sneers. "Even if you have the emotional range of a sponge, you know saying nasty shit to people is hurtful. Try again, and apologize less like you're making an excuse."

The dragon spins on his heel, pacing back and forth manically for a moment before he speaks again. "You don't understand. None of you get it. Only he does."

We turn to look at the Prince and he sighs softly. "I understand, old friend, but you have allowed your past injury to infect you more than I knew. I thought when you agreed to stay here with us you might thaw, but it seems like you're only getting worse. Do you want to go home and assign another guard to me? I would dislike it, but if it would spare you…"

No, no. I do not want to be the cause of that.

"No!" I say, grabbing Liam's hand in panic. "Don't punish him. I… I can learn to live with it. I have before, and I can't bear thinking I've caused a rift between you and your oldest friend and protector."

Kaspar turns back to us, his face a mask of shock as he squints at me. "You would let me continue to hurt you if it allowed Li to be happy and safe?"

"Duh?" I reply in confusion. "It's not like Magnus was warm and cuddly. I've lived with worse than some mean barbs. I'll get used to it—"

This time it's Liam who stands. "You will *not*. I refuse to allow you to take back the appropriate boundary you set. I am certain the bear and I agree we cannot see our mate in pain because my supposed *friend* cannot deal with his own issues."

His words get Kaspar's attention and the expression on the dragon's face changes again. He scratches his head, looking frustrated before he growls, "I need some fucking space."

Without waiting for a response, he storms out of the room, and the door slams shut in his wake. I don't hear his car start, so I assume he's walking back to their place until a loud boom outside corrects me. Within seconds, a pelting rain hits the roof of the house and lightning cracks across the sky outside the window.

"Well, shit," Liam mutters as he walks over to look at the sudden storm. "All we can do is wait."

I wrinkle my nose, feeling Des finally slide back into my hair. "What do you mean?"

The Fae gives me a rueful smile as he turns back to us. "Kaspar only shifts in this realm when he is so overcome by emotions that he fears he will do something rash that will harm others... or himself. I'm not sure which option caused this outburst."

"He might... hurt himself?" I whisper, feeling ill as I voice the words.

That is not what I wanted.

"Kaspar holds a great deal of pain he has not dealt with healthily. It comes from our past and though I have done everything I can to help him, he is not ready to let go of it yet. I won't let him hurt you because of that. Making that clear has him very conflicted, so yes, he will probably punish himself."

"I don't want that."

Liam sighs and shakes his head ruefully. "I don't want that, either. I never have. If anyone is responsible for his pain, it's the person who caused it. But he can't confront them, nor can he blame me, so he takes the responsibility himself. I have endeavored for many centuries to get him various forms of help to process that heartstring wound. As a dragon, it will only get worse the longer he lets it consume him."

Guilt floods me again, and I drop my head to my hands. I shouldn't feel empathy for someone who has been bullying me, but I do. This kind of thinking lead me to allow Magnus the grasping, gaslighting control he had over me. I can't go down this path again. We have too much to do for me to dedicate my spoons to helping a dragon who is purposefully nursing an old wound.

Whatever Kaspar needs, he won't get it from me unless he apologizes— period.

just like fire

Morgana is struggling with the dragon's flight, and it's as obvious as a flashing sign over her head. Liam insisted we needed to give the guy space, which Iggy and Slade didn't argue. I, however, have a bit of experience with emotions being so big you might explode. If it wasn't for my Nana, I would have a lot more issues than I do now. When my anger and self-destructive bent appeared in middle school, she made certain I got the help I needed.

It's harder than it looks to have strung-out, fame seeking fuckwads for parents, even if you are rich.

"M, you can't take his shit on your shoulders," I murmur as we lounge on the couch. I'm working on make-up work from my missed class, and she's powering through the shit Channing dropped off. "Kaspar's problems predate your involvement."

"I know that," she replies absently as she marks up papers in a folder labeled 'Discretionary Flags.' Once she's done, she meets my gaze, her eyes tired. "I just don't enjoy thinking about him off self-harming or getting in trouble because I triggered something."

I snort. "He triggered you first. I bet he's not moping about hurting you."

"He might be," Liam says and we both turn to give the Prince a smile. He'd gone home to grab things he wanted near while we hunkered down to work. "Kaspar often realizes what an ass he's being, but can't quite stop himself."

"Sounds like a 'him' problem," I mutter as I flip the page of my Econ textbook. "Morgana can't be responsible for his stupid shit."

"She's not."

Well, hell, the gang's all here.

Slade and Iggy stroll in with their own bags, settling on the adjacent furniture as the professor makes his statement. The siren shrugs, his smile rueful. "Iggy's awfully blunt, as you know."

"When he wants to be," Morgana snarks, and I arch a brow at her. She just winks and goes back to whatever budget nonsense she's working on.

"That brief exchange felt very... cozy." Liam hops over the back of the other couch with his bag and flops onto it in a very un-royal manner. "Are we all getting along better because we're mad at my friend?"

"Maybe," I chuckle as I continue reading the chapter I need to finish. "Strife does bring people together."

Morgana looks up from her paper and my dick twitches as she gives me a stern look over her glasses. "Lucas, focus. You said you have a quiz to make up tomorrow."

Liam grins broadly, kicking his feet up. "Ooooh, that was a 'Mommy' tone if I've ever heard one. You're in trouble, bro."

I laugh as I duck my head and bury myself in the heavy book again. As if I'm touching that shit and getting on the bad list. The Prince is way too full of himself. "I have nothing to say, buddy. I'm studying."

Slade pulls out his books and Iggy fans out a pile of tests he's going over, signaling that all of us need to get to work. The room is muted except for a few stretches and sighs, but I enjoy the feeling of them around me. I spent most of my childhood with nannies and various staff unless Nana was in residence—something that was less common as I got older. My parents were *never* around, so this little group is making me feel something I haven't before outside of sports—that I belong.

We all stay like that for a bit—that is, until Morgana's phone rings. She picks it up, frowning as she listens to the other person on the line. I watch as the telltale sign of her irritation, the single snake, curls around her jaw. The sound of me clearing my throat gets the other guys to pay attention and by the time our woman hangs up, we're all on edge.

"What's going on?" I ask.

Morgana taps her fingertips against her lips, thinking for a second before she answers. "I... that was Channing. She said we should grab a car and head for the back fields of the equestrian program. The campus security division has received a bunch of calls of a disturbance, but before they responded, they checked in with her."

I arch a brow. "Since when does she have that power?"

"Since some asshole detectives were let onto campus to drag you away in public," Morgana says absently. "They can call me if they cannot reach her, but I don't want those idiots trampling all over student or staff rights because they're poorly trained monkeys in uniforms."

"I assume you're going to fix that," Iggy says wryly. "I won't fight you on it, by the way. Even if it hits the budget lines, we need better safety measures here. They almost tasered some elemental students doing homework in the woods last spring."

What?

"Why would…" I blink. "Did the idiot hire *humans* to be guards at a supe college?"

"No, but he might as well have," Slade pipes up. "The moron put *wolves* in charge. We all know how stupid that is."

I pinch the bridge of my nose, unable to believe this place didn't fall apart at the seams years ago. "Everyone knows they're smart and great at tracking, but their rigid pack shit prevents them from deciding without—"

"Input from the alpha. Yes, I believe that was the purpose," Iggy says ruefully as he sets aside his work. "And since Magnus likely ignored them, the calls were made by a shifter with the designation who wasn't concerned what might happen to students of species not valued by wolves."

"Anyone who's not a wolf?" Morgana snorts. "Yeah, that sounds like Magnus."

"Well, if security is being alerted and we still haven't heard from Kas…" Liam frowns and the rest of us move when we realize what he's thinking.

The fucking dragon is out there spooking the goddamn horses and Zeus knows what else.

"Looks like we're headed for the horse paddocks," I say as I slip my shoes back on. "Make sure you're wearing colors the fool can see. You know how dragons flame first and ask questions later."

"Not red," Liam says as we break to grab jackets and shit. "His dragon is not a fan."

I wonder why the hell that is?

WHEN I TURN ONTO THE BACK ROADS OF THE UNIVERSITY, I feel the hairs on the back of my neck stand up. My bear senses trouble, and it's not just a fucking dragon having a temper tantrum. There's something bad going down nearby and we're headed right for it. I growl softly and the sound is echoed by my mate next to me.

"Do you feel that?" the Prince asks.

I nod, and before I can plan a response, he and the mage mutter in foreign languages. One is Latin, that I'm sure of, but the other is... Gaelic, maybe? Regardless, a bright light forms on either side of the backseat, then it spread over the car until they meld together. As a shifter, I rarely get this close to magic users, and it makes me a little antsy until Morgana grabs my free hand.

"They're warding the car, babe. It's for our protection, not to trap you."

"How did you know I was—"

Her lips curve up. "My mother was a witch, remember? My dad had her practice casting on me, so I wouldn't lose my shit if she had to protect us at some point."

Slade frowns. "That's weird. Weren't they both professors at Swallowtail?"

"Yep," Morgana says as she shifts to look out the windows. "My entire life was teachers until Magnus fucked up and I had to go on trial. Why?"

"Seems odd that your parents would practice that kind of thing with a child," Iggy says. "For a major family like mine, or maybe a gang leader's son like Slade or a prince…"

"I don't know *why* they did it. They said it was important, so I did what they asked. It wasn't much different from all the other shit my dad had me learn. Mom's magic stuff never took when she tried to teach me, but that's because I'm not magical."

The guys in the back are right—I was a huge target as a major shifter heir and no one taught me how to deal with magical protections. Something feels wrong, but no time to investigate. The back fields are approaching quickly and the feeling of bad juju is intensifying as we head toward it.

"Be careful, Lucas. I don't like this… heavy presence." Liam catches my eyes in the mirror and I nod, going back to focusing on the road.

We drive for another mile when the sky in front of us lights up like an explosion and I almost slam on the brakes. Morgana's hand tightens on mine and I look down to see it's turned to stone. She's going to shift soon and we definitely have to get the fuck out of this car. Hitting the gas, I speed toward the glowing skyline as if our life depends on it—and maybe someone's does.

When we get close enough to see the wings of an enormous dragon fighting yet *another* enormous dragon surrounded by electricity, I skid to a stop. Liam curses under his breath as we all hop out of the car. My bear pushes at my skin and I know I'm going to need him, so I drop to my knees and let the shift come. A loud roar fills the air as my hands turn into enormous paws and the white coat covers me from head to toe.

Colors explode in front of me as the change is completed and I have to stop for a moment to see what the hell is happening. To my right, a fucking enormous gargoyle with bright blue eyes, wings, and onyx skin is digging into the ground as if it's going to take off. On the left, I watch in awe as the Prince drops all pretense of a glamor, transforming into a seven foot tall light show with vines and flowers trailing all over his limbs up to the crown that seems to emit sunshine that makes his huge wings glitter with golden highlights. Iggy and Slade are behind him, sparkling with their own magic as they look to our girl.

This is utter chaos.

"I will take the air. Prince, take the ground with the shifters. Ignatius, watch my back as I fly."

Before I can respond, Morgana pushes off and flies toward the battling mythicals like she's on a mission. I struggle with speaking—even as an Alpha shifter—in full bear form, so I pop into the Prince's mind as we walk toward the fight.

~ What's the plan? ~

"We find out what the fuck is going on and where the hell a fire drake came from. To my knowledge, there are none registered in the area."

Of course, he and Kaspar checked the registry for other mythicals when they moved in. Those species have the hardest time not getting into territory battles when they live in proximity. I nod my big ass head, then move faster toward the two reptiles and the shadow of our mate cutting across the sky ahead.

"We will need to subdue it if it's just a rogue," the Fae says as he glances at Slade. The siren winks at him and I huff in relief.

I'll fight anything to protect Morgana, but a dragon is a bit much for me.

Unfortunately, once we're close enough to see what's going on, that plan goes out the window. Not only is there a furious firedrake dodging the electrical strikes from the Prince's pissed off storm dragon, there's an entire crew of fuckers on the ground trying to bring Kaspar down. Even as a bear, my eyes widen as I note there are various types of Fae, shifters, magic users, and even a goddamn pack of wolves.

"What the *fuck* is going on?" Iggy yells as the magic users turn their attention to him. A bolt of sizzling dark magic flies past his ear and he snarls, shooting the short witch right in the gut with a ball of energy that knocks her flat.

I can't answer, but it doesn't matter because the wolves and a group of fucking misfit cat shifters get my scent. If I could grin, I would. Wolves are bigger than people think; so are tigers and lions. But even more impressive than that are my paws are over an inch and half wide —large enough to span almost two dinner plates—and when I smack a bitch, they go down. The first two wolves that come for me get knocked aside like bowling pins as I move towards a gallop. Those fuckers can run faster than me, but once I get going, it's like being hit by a fucking tank.

Hopefully, I can distract these dipshits while Morgana and the Prince handle the fucking dragons—if not, this is going to go south very quickly.

night on bald mountain

Swooping through the air, I keep my eyes peeled for the guys on the ground. The damn dragon is dangerously out of control, and I can't tell if this is going to swing our way. Kaspar is powerful—even more than I thought—but with our focus split between his opponent and the other fuckers down there, we can't combine our strengths to help him.

"Look, dude, I get you hate me, but why the fuck did you get in a scrap with a *fire drake*?" I yell as I pass the storm dragon's auricle to dive around the next wave of fire.

~He says this isn't his fault. ~

I blink when Liam speaks in my head, but the information is helpful. If Kaspar didn't pick this fight, that makes the people on the ground part of an attack force rather than misguided friends. Assuming they were was a gamble, but I was hoping we hadn't walked into a giant battle on the State U campus.

So much for that.

~I know it looks bad, but he says he came here to burn off his anger and the drake showed up with his friends soon after. That means they followed Kaspar. ~

I have little time to react to the Prince's words before another stream of fire nearly crisps me for my distraction. "Goddamn it, this fucker is determined."

A puff of steam comes out of Kaspar's enormous nose, cloaking my path as I work to get behind the fiery lizard. It's obviously not the first dragon I've fought, so I know what to do to weaken it; I just need the opportunity. If I can get out of his line of vision, I can get close enough to use one of the snakes. Des would love to poison the reptile who thinks it can attack my people without consequence.

The next loud roar catches my attention and I look down to see Lucas in bear form, absolutely wrecking his way through the shifters. Pride wells in my chest; he's fierce as hell, despite his pampered teddy bear appearance. Magic blasts shoot through the air as I weave my way around the huge mythical, so I know Iggy is doing what I asked.

But where is Slade?

Suddenly, a soulful song fills the night sky and my eyes widen when it echoes off the rolling hills of the back pasture. It's loud enough to fill the atmosphere and press into my skin, but it doesn't affect me. I lick my lips, momentarily distracted by more proof that Slade is my mate.

The only people who are not affected by sirens' songs are their mates or those with enchanted objects to prevent the spell of their music from invading their brains.

The fire drake slows a bit, but doesn't stop. That confirms the theory that it was sent after us even more than Kaspar's words. It had to have some sort of spell to keep the damn song from completely freezing it —the shifters on the ground are paralyzed now and the guys are focusing on the magic users. The slowdown helps, allowing me to move behind the dragon's head. Grinning, I work my way around it while dodging the various stray shots the mages get off until I'm able to glide up the drake's back and land on its neck.

My entire body tingles as I dig my gargoyle claws into the armored scales for purchase. Both my hands and feet are holding tight while my wings are in position for maximum aerodynamics as the monster flings his body around mid-air. I have to do this or Kaspar will resort to a much bigger response that will possibly damage the entire fucking campus. He hasn't called tornadoes or violent storms yet, but I know it's coming.

"Des, you all have to help me. I don't want to lose these men. For the first time in a long time, I'm almost happy," I mutter. I know it seems crazy to talk to my snakes, but they understand me, especially Des. My claws dig in deeper, and I close my eyes as the gorgon side bursts free of the shackles I typically keep it locked into.

The stone on my body shimmers with scales that cover it, and my eyes ache as the yellow and blue mix together. My dual natures don't always get along and when I allow them out simultaneously, it hurts as they fight for control. This time, however, they seem to be more in sync, because the burning fades and my hair stops whipping in the air when it shifts to all onyx colored snakes. I growl low, bending to put my face against the hot as hell hide of the drake and wing a prayer to the goddess into the universe.

"Morgana, don't!"

The voice is panicked as it calls out to me, but I ignore it. I know the Prince is worried I could get burned to a cinder as I hold on to the heated scales, but he simply doesn't know enough about my species. Gargoyles from different clutches are made of varied stones, and while my skin looks like it's made of onyx—it's not. It would take enormous heat, even for a dragon to even affect me that way. I've never met another of my kind, even a hybrid, whose outer armor is made of the same stone as mine. If people knew, they'd come for me, so both me and my parents have kept it a secret my entire life.

Magnus' betrayal had to do with my secret and it's why he had to die for his sins—not that I've told anyone that, even the Society at trial.

Gritting my fangs, I continue pressing against the dragon as my snakes tear at the scales to find a weak spot. They should get to one soon, and when they do, the poison they inject will put a stop to this fucking battle. I'll let go and the damn thing will fall from the sky like a piano in a cartoon. I just need a little more...

"Morgana!"

Oh, no.

My eyes pop open and I stare blankly at Liam as he flutters close on his elaborate butterfly wings colored like the sky at the break of dawn. "No, Li, get out of here. You don't have enough armor to—" The dragon senses my fear and bucks, trying to throw me off while I talk to the Prince as he darts around carefully. "Go back to help the others; I have this."

At least, I think I do.

"Holy shit, Lady M," he says as he looks at me. "Lucas is going to be *pissed* he didn't get to see you like this. You're like a Greek myth come to life."

"Flattery will get you nowhere, butterfly boy," I grunt as I dig into the dragon harder as it bucks more. "I have to concentrate. Go help Kaspar get his shit under control if you need to be here."

Liam looks unsure, but the frustration in my voice must convince him I mean it. He flutters off to go whisper to his own dragon.

Once he's out of the way, I breathe a sigh of relief and concentrate again. I have to get under this damn hide so Des can infect the damn lizard. The only way this battle ends is if we take the biggest weapon out, and we won't be able to keep it here in the back fields much longer. My claws dig harder and I let out a cry of anger, as it still doesn't expose any skin to help.

Time is running out, and my options are limited. The only remaining option has *never* worked for me, but perhaps with my new friends, it could be different.

~I'm going to connect with your magic. ~

My mother insisted the gorgon part of me was pre-disposed to magic through the mythos of their creation, but none of her magic training *ever* took. Liam is a lot more powerful than a witch, especially as a Fae Prince. If I can borrow even a slice of his power, I should be able to rip one of these damn things off and do the deed.

~Everything I have is yours, mate. ~ Liam replies.

That response wigs me out a little, but I shake it off as I rack my brain for the right words to do this. I need to access his magic and channel it through my hands and my snakes. I don't speak Gaelic, so hopefully, Latin will do. "*Mater cronum, da mihi aditum ad tuum filium.*[1]"

A spark flits through me and I almost let go in shock, but luckily, I keep my purchase. I swallow hard and recite the next line. "*Me vires mutuas ut feram hanc malam vincam. Defessa ab his qui nos nocent.*[2]"

Des hisses loudly and my limbs shake as magic flows through me. I'm old—much older than Iggy, Lucas, or Slade—and the amount of power I have is immense. But this... this is on a different level entirely. I have no clue if this is *all* of Liam's magic or a fraction, but it's intimidating as fuck. Shaking my head to clear it, I throw my head back and let out a mighty gargoyle roar before tearing into the dragon's back like it's made of paper. Scales go flying, revealing the tender skin I needed access to.

Now, we're even, you fiery asshat.

As soon as the flesh is exposed, my snakes go for it, sinking their fangs in and making the monster scream in pain. The effects are almost instantaneous—I feel them under me as the poison works its way into the mythical's bloodstream. When the scales below me harden into stone, I grin like a maniac and command my girls to release. I have to get off this stupid thing before it drops from the sky like the rock it's becoming.

"Take cover!" I yell to the Prince and his electrified bodyguard. "Tell Lucas and the others to clear the field. He's going down."

I feel the shock run through my new mate, but I don't have time to be smug. Instead, I let go of the slowly petrifying lizard and push off into the air. My wings catch a draft from the wind Kaspar is funneling through the field and I head towards the ground where we'd parked in a controlled dive. This damn beast is going to make a dragon-sized hole that will take forever to fucking fill, and the damage will cost a fortune.

There goes my damn budget.

By the time my feet hit the ground, I realize how ridiculous it is to worry about my Society assignment when it's obvious that not only is someone framing one of my wealthiest students, but now a team of assassins attacked another wealthy student's bodyguard. Either this is a war on rich supes, or there's something very specific connecting them—like me.

"Son of a bitch," I pant as I bend over and brace my hands on my knees. I hear the thumping of people running toward me and look up to make sure it's my guys. The giant polar bear is followed by glowing men and a winged Fae Prince. I drop my head again as I try to make the world stop spinning. "Give me a minute."

I feel their gazes on me as I let my system come down from channeling that much unfamiliar power, including pushing the gorgon back into her cage. It's hard to control the bloodlust when she's fully out, and I don't want to hurt anyone by mistake. Soft footsteps approach and I'm surprised when a hand lies on my back between my wings to gently rub.

"You're okay, Morgana. We're okay. Even Kaspar is—" Before Slade can finish, the fire drake crashes to the ground with a mighty shake of the earth. I lose my balance, falling to my knees on the grass as everything around us vibrates with the impact. "Holy shit."

I grimace as I look at the mess, rubbing a hand over my face. "We have to call for Guardians. They need to question everyone still breathing, including this dick who just made my week infinitely harder."

All eyes whip to me, but it's Iggy who finally asks, "The dragon is... alive?"

Sighing, I give them a tiny smile. "Yeah. Encased in stone, but not dead. Gorgon justice sucks pretty hard."

Now they wonder what someone could do to warrant me killing them instead of enduring this—great.

---

1. Mother of crones, grant me access to your son.
2. Loan me your strength so I might defeat this evil beast. Protect our clutch from those who would harm us.

secrets

O nce Lucas shifted back, we decided he should call his Nana to get Guardians on-site. To my surprise, she only asked brief questions while he was on the phone with her, but he assured us she'll want the complete story later. Morgana grumbled at him to put his damn clothes on, and I nodded at Kaspar to let him know he could shift back and do the same. Our girl was already back to normal, not wanting anyone to show up and see her in anything but her human form.

There's merit to people knowing what she can do, but not now.

"Li, that thing was *not* registered. I checked every registered and Council supe within the agreed radius when we arrived."

Pinching the bridge of my nose, I sigh. "America has more unregistered supes and hybrids than any other country because of their... inclination to buck authority. You couldn't have known there were creatures hiding amongst the shadows, Kas."

"It's my job," he grunts.

"You kinda suck at it." Morgana's smirk doesn't help the scowl on his face, and I put my hand on her arm. "What? He does. Fire drakes leave trails of destruction wherever they go; it's why they're more tightly supervised than most dragons. Outside of storm dragons like dumbass here and Mind wyverns—they make up the top three dragon dicks who can't be trusted to hold their wads."

It would be easier if she wasn't on the nose with her statements; Magnus must have shared that tidbit.

"Listen, you overgrow bat—"

Lucas's eyes flash and he puts his hand on the dragon's chest. "Stop. This isn't helping us figure out how all this shit ties together and what the fuck we're going to tell the Guardians when they arrive."

The professor and Slade look at one another, then Morgana before chiming in, "As little as possible."

I chuckle and nod my agreement. "Yes, that seems prudent. The only connecting factor between Lucas and me is our wealth and status, *or...* our connection to Morgana. That concerns me; while I have a guard specifically because rebels like the Hand of Morrigan are always looking to cause chaos, Lucas does not. They avoided direct confrontation with him, which must hold significance."

"But *why*?" The gargoyle almost wails that question and we all look at one another. "Magnus had followers, sure, but this is so much bigger than their petty squabbles. They might have access to a fire drake, but for fuck's sake, a murder cover-up that's fooling the cops? No way."

That seems far-fetched for a group of deluded women and men worshipping a dead guy.

"If you're right, then we need to trace this back farther than just Lucas and me. Ignatius, you may need to do some work in the school's link to the shifter archives. Kaspar will visit our home and see what he can scrounge up in the Daybreak Court's archives regarding the Morrigan and ties to rebel groups here. And we definitely have to go through with Slade's plan—no question now."

The guys—except for Kaspar—all agree, but they look at our mate, waiting for her to weigh in on the topic. Morgana leans back against the car, her head tilted up to the stars. I know her mother was a witch, so perhaps she places some stock in the alignment of their places. She's quiet for a minute or two while she thinks, and when she finally speaks, her voice is soft and husky. "I'm worried I'll get you all killed. If these people are after me for some unknown reason, continuing on this path will only put more people in danger."

Lucas snorts and walks over, lifting her off the car so she has to wrap her legs around his waist. He's strong as an ox, which I think Morgana likes more than she admits. She's not tiny, but the bear picks her up like it's nothing. "Babe, the only person who hasn't said they're here for the chaos is the dickwaffle dragon. The Prince's influence compels him to comply, rendering it inconsequential. Stop disbelieving what we're telling you. When you do that, the Headless Fuckhead wins."

Her eyes go wide and it's like he just unlocked something in her brain. The rosy lips I adore form a perfect 'O' and her body goes completely still in his embrace. "Y-You're right. Magnus wins if I can't ever—Oh, fuck me."

The siren grins a little, looking adorably endearing as he walks over and presses against her back. "That's right. If you can't let go of his emotional abuse and move on with your life, you're stuck living in the past as he dictated. And yeah, he definitely wins because you're letting a dead man run your life."

"Plus, I'd absolutely love to take you up on that offer, and I can't when you're gloomy," the bear says with an eyebrow bob.

Even Kaspar laughs at that, and my chest warms a little. I know he'll get there, but I have to keep him from burning the bridge irrevocably before he does. "Okay, so what are we telling the Guardians?"

Morgana shrugs as the two men sandwich her, then snaps her fingers. "Oh! We took a romantic walk in the fields. Like, swoony style."

I arch a brow. "You want that in Council reports?"

"Fuck no," she mumbles as she deflates. "They need nothing else to bug me about. This shit is going to make my budget even more disastrous."

The professor clears his throat and waves his hand in the air. "Perhaps we tell them the 'almost' truth? We say Kaspar was out flying—which he's allowed to do—and encountered the drake. He contacted me for help and since you're the Dean, I invited you along."

Morgana thinks about it for a moment. "Naturally Slade would come with you since he's your roommate and Dickface McScalyAss would reach out to the Prince. How do we explain Lucas?"

"You'll have to hop out of his grasp, but you can say you were meeting with him about the legal case," I whisper. "Our visit to the police station earlier may have been reported to the Society."

"Okay. That's what we're going with, as well as we have no fucking clue why these assholes are here."

Thank fuck, we agree.

I can feel the approach of other supes, so I nod. "Time to put on innocent faces. They're almost here."

"Well, what the bloody feck is this shit?"

Pixie... mixed with something. Interesting.

The crew behind her is just as fascinating as the purple-haired woman standing with her hands on her hips as she glares at the stone dragon. There's a rainbow-haired woman who gives off a familiar vibe to Morgana, an enormous dude who is definitely some kind of dragon, and finally, a lithe amused looking fellow who reeks of the sea. I've seen a few Guardian 'fixer teams' in my lifetime, but this one is so oddly close to our own makeup that it makes me shiver.

"This is the fire drake and its companions that Fraü Wolfberg reported," I reply smoothly. With the others struggling, my ingrained diplomacy takes charge. "I am Prince Liam Spéirgheal, first heir to The Daybreak Court, keeper of the Veil. Who, may I ask, are you?"

"Oh, shit," the aquatic guy says as he gives the pixie a reproving look. "Please excuse my companion's enthusiasm, Your Highness. Saoirse wasn't raised in your lands, only here. I am Zasha Fydor Petrov, and this is my school."

"Your school?" the shifter snorts and shakes his head, his beard vibrating as he laughs. "More like my clutch, minnow. Allow me to introduce myself, Prince Liam. I am Tharin Drakos of the ice wyverns."

Kaspar's eyes widen, and he gives me a slight frown. I don't know what quarrel the ice wyverns have with the storm dragons, but it must be over dishonesty. Otherwise he wouldn't have weighed in so publicly. I smile politely, turning to the ladies. "They overpowered you, I'm afraid. Rubbish manners for such noble mythical shifters."

The pixie lets out a peal of laughter and I see the hint I needed—she's also a veela. "Naw, don't be worried, Your Highness. My best friend

Jolene always says men are never more in the way than when they're not even needed in the equation. Zasha and Tharin love to throw their weight around, but Julia and I are the brains out of the outfit."

Morgana walks over, holding her hand out with a grin. "Your friend sounds delightful and quite wise. I am Morgana LeCiel, Dean of State U. The Prince introduced himself, but going clockwise, this is Professor Ignatius Briarton, Slade, Lucas Wolfberg, and the jackass over there is Liam's bodyguard. You can call him jackass, too, or I guess Kaspar."

I have to hide my chuckles behind my hand, coughing as the Guardians all laugh at her bluntness. Once it dies down, I tilt my head. "You know all of us, but I didn't catch your names, ladies. At least, not all of them."

"Julia Ricci, actual commander of this unit, and this is my slithermate, Saoirse O' Flanagan. We're fairly informal, which is why everyone is claiming they're in charge when that's not the case."

Nodding, I jerk my chin at the mess nearby. "Kaspar came out to stretch his wings, which I'm sure Tharin can relate to. He was attacked by the fire drake—which we had no idea was living in this area—and the other species on the ground joined it. We had to subdue it before it wreaked havoc on the entire college."

Saoirse walks over to the stone beast, kicking it gently. "Yep, the woman is one of yours, J. This is living stone."

Julia whips her head around to squint at Morgana, and my hackles raise. "Holy fuck, you're *that* Morgana."

Our girl stiffens, immediately frosting over as she looks at the Guardians. "I am not out of my radius without warning. There's nothing to report. I didn't start this shit, either. I only contained it."

The wyvern walks away from the group with the water shifter, leaving us with the two women. Now that they know who my mate is, I find myself on edge whether they're going to believe us. But the flashy pixie gives her a brilliant grin and slow claps. "You are a hero, lady. Even my charge—the bestie I mentioned—thinks so. Socking it to a cheating crooked lizard is fucking epic. And you may not know it, but many people think you got the wrong end of the dildo with that trial."

Iggy snickers at her words, then Lucas, and before long, only Julia and Morgana are left assessing one another seriously. I suppose it's because their kind is rare and they're trying to figure each other out, but we can't stand here all evening while they play 'who has the thicker snakes.' Kaspar is still standing there glaring and not talking, so I sigh and take over again.

No wonder Saaladir and my old friend hate one another so much—they could be twins.

"Fae aren't much bothered by multiple species of our kind in small areas, but I know various dragons and gorgons are. To get this moving so everyone gets to sleep tonight, we should dispense with the bluster."

All the women look at me and I almost shrink back—that wall of ice is chilly as fuck.

"The Prince is right, of course," Morgana says when she recovers. "What do you need to know?"

"You said this drake wasn't expected. Did you check the registry?" Julia asks in a no-nonsense tone. "It's not a formality in the States."

Kaspar snorts. "No shit. We've been here a long time, just not at this location. I checked both the Society's and the dark net sites. No drake mentioned."

Saoirse bounces on her toes. "That means this is *ours*, Ju-Ju. We get to pry out of these dumbasses why they're here and how they hid this big asshole. I can't wait."

"How will you do that when he's encased in stone?" Slade asks curiously. "The others you can wake up because I subdued them with my song."

Tharin stomps over, his gigantic frame looking like he's a character in a fantasy TV show despite his normal dress. "We have many resources at our disposal, young siren."

"So are we done?" Morgana asks as she looks around. "I have no problem with leaving this mess to you for the moment. I'm tired and I will have a fucking nightmare in logistical issues with repairing the damage done tonight."

Julia and Saoirse exchange a quick glance, then nod simultaneously. The gorgon is the one who speaks, though, and I'm inclined to believe she truly is the leader. "You may go. Seer has your names in her memory banks, so we'll know who to look for if we have more questions."

Thank fuck.

One by one, we turn to get in the SUV when Zasha's voice rings out. "Just a quick Q from me, eh? *Why* do you think you were attacked by a multi-species group with such firepower?"

I smile innocently, putting on my most regal face as I shrug. "Your guess is as good as mine, Petrov. But I am a Prince and people seek to unseat rulers all the time. For all I know, my father did something disagreeable within the Veil I am not privy to."

It's likely, and my constant worry, but he doesn't need to know.

That said, we pile into the car and I relax for the first time since we arrived at this field.

Now all we have to do is avoid another catastrophe like this and we'll be fine.

the plan

The trip back to my house is quiet. We're cramped and most of the guys are banged up. It took a few minutes of wheedling, but I finally consented to sitting on Lucas's lap in the back while the damn dragon took the wheel with the Prince up front. Iggy and Slade are scrunched into the back with us, but they seem fine with it. I'm exhausted from blasting the damn fire drake with everything I had to encase it in stone—usually, my targets are *much* smaller than that. It ate up a great deal of magic I'll have to regenerate, so I'm not sure I have it in me to argue this bullshit tonight.

Not to mention discuss the stupid Guardians and what we're going to do about the rest of our fucked up shit.

Kaspar pulls into my driveway, and suddenly, the vibe in the air is *very* heavy. I open our door, needing to get out of the stifling atmosphere before it makes me angry again. I'm owed an apology—a sincere one —and a promise that fucker won't treat me like garbage again to soothe his own trauma. I survived one broken dragon taking his shit out on me and I'm not letting this one get the chance to do the same.

When the others stay in the car, I frown. I don't know what they're doing, but I need to lay the fuck down and eat something before I crash. Tonight's activities were damn draining. They don't move, and I shrug. If they want to have a dude meeting in the car, I'm not standing around like a fool while they chat. I wiggle my fingers at Lucas, then trudge up to the porch to let myself in. Physical keys are a pain in my ass and I make a mental note that I hope sticks in my brain to ask Iggy and Liam about transitioning us to something less object based.

Not everything has fucking pockets, and it's hard enough to keep track of my damn phone.

Striding into the house, I flick on the lights only to shriek at the top of my lungs. The two guys sitting on my living room sofa smirk at me and I put my hand to my chest to quell the thumping of my heart. "Poseidon's salty ass crack, Jackson. You scared the stone off me."

It's not hard to hear the thundering herd of men approaching at my strangled yell of fear, so I wait until they pour into the room in various stages of defense mode. Eli laughs from his spot next to our lawyer, and I have to stop myself from shouting again when Channing appears in the doorway to the kitchen with a tea tray.

"What the hell is going on in here?" Lucas growls. He looks tired, but he's got big ass bear paws, so he was definitely mid-shift when he realized who our uninvited guests were. "Fuck, man, it's not the night for surprises."

Iggy lowers hands covered in glowing magic and Slade's aura goes back to normal as they see their friend. Unfortunately for everyone, the last two to join the pissed off party are Liam and Kaspar, both of whom are much deeper into fight mode. Kaspar has scales and glowing eyes while the Prince is damn near shedding sparkles everywhere as his magic fills the room.

"Guys, guys, guys," I say in a tired voice. "Calm down. It's okay. We're not in danger."

Liam huffs, turning off the light show so easily even Jackson looks impressed. "By the stones on the henge, I almost cast first and asked questions afterward. Are you three *insane?*"

"I'm sorry. Jax got the message that shit went down here and we regrouped to drop in immediately. Rick, Ken, and Foley are headed here as soon as they wrap up the leads they're following right now."

Slade rushes over to help Channing with the tray, despite being filthy and covered in the mess of our battle. I laugh softly, finding his innate chivalry adorable but crazy in our current state. Looking pointedly at Jackson, I clear my throat loudly. "Okay, people. With an invasion foretold, some of us *must* get cleaned up. Entertain yourselves until we get back."

Lucas beams as he takes my hand, especially when I don't fight him. "That's right, suckers. We fought a fucking dragon and we're covered in sweat and *winner.*"

Artemis, save me from competitive dudes.

"Yes, well, it's a good thing we brought things this afternoon," Iggy says as he runs his hands through his hurricane-blown hair. "And better that there are three showers."

"I'm going to our place," Kaspar says. As soon as he turns to leave, I make a face at his back because I'm completely over his bullshit. "And don't think I didn't feel that, Morgana."

What?!

"He's got your number, *Saaladir*," Liam says softly. "He'll get there."

"Whatever," I mutter. "Lucas, let's go. Li, you can come with us, and Slade and Iggy can have the guest room showers."

"Ooooh, developments," Jackson calls as we trudge towards the stairs. "I'm excited now."

"He's the weirdest lawyer on the planet." Lucas isn't wrong, so I don't correct him. Jackson Thorne is fucking odd, but he's the best, so we have to put up with his eccentricities.

Liam chuckles behind me, his voice husky as he replies. "At least he's on our side."

"I'd shudder to think of what he'd be like as opposition," Iggy agrees. "Channing told me that hacker is so insanely skilled that he has contacts in governments and the criminal world. He's working on tracking some other hacker who's gone missing as a side project."

I frown, not liking the split focus, but if Jackson thinks he can handle it, I suppose it's okay. "Interesting."

Slade and Iggy wave as they peel off towards the guest rooms, and I look at Li and Lucas. "No funny business. I'm tired, sore, and so hungry I might consume the next person who pisses me off."

"*Au revoir*, Kaspar, we hardly knew ye," Lucas cracks and we both look at him for a second before we burst out laughing.

Damn. I needed that.

Iggy and Slade are already tucked into spots in the living room when the three of us amble downstairs. I kept the guys from misbehaving—barely—but getting all the grime out of our hair and off our bodies wasn't easy. Turns out running through horse pastures and having fiery ash everywhere is something that goes south pretty quickly. I'll remember that for next time, though I hope to shit there's *not* a next time.

"Had trouble with your hair, eh?"

I grin at Eli's question. The kid is pretty perceptive, even if his lover is smirking like a douche canoe. "Fight remnants were deeply embedded. It was insane."

"A few of us have longer hair. I'll shoot Channie a text she can share with our artisan witch's info. Not price friendly, but the woman works miracles with removal spells. A bunch of her clients are Guardians, so you know I'm not yanking your chains."

My brow arches as I take in the nickname. I'd forgotten I wanted to check in with my assistant about her loan to the legal team. I need to remember that for later. "Thanks. I'd prefer we *don't* need it, but seeing as we're caught in some ridiculous mystery plot..."

"Speaking of Guardians," Kaspar says as he slinks in from the front. "A small group of them appeared when we called for help. Is the Society sending strike teams out again? It's been centuries since that was necessary."

Jackson pauses, his face contorting as thoughts churn in his mind. "Not like it was then, but yes, teams of experienced Guardian agents and assassins are being sent out to deal with the disruptions globally. Currently, there are more unexplained issues than ever before."

"Why?" I ask. "Why are there so many disruptions?"

"No one knows," Eli whispers dramatically. "It's an enormous scandal. More unemerged folk are gaining powers at later in life points... everywhere from eighteen to forties. Those can be handled by current

Guardians and occasionally some extra support, but it also appears that nefarious groups are... working together."

"Like the gangs or mafias?" The quiet siren asks, though I know it must pain him to do so.

"No, well... not entirely." Jackson sighs and shrugs. "Groups that are already on watchlists for being a threat to keeping our shit under wraps. The Prince knows The Hand of Morrigan, but whispers say there are demons forming alliances, witches, aquatic rebels... hell, even humans are having troubles according to my sources in the HQ."

"What the fuck does that mean?" Lucas frowns. "Like, why the hell would anyone give a shit about me, other than I'm well known."

"Your grandmother, cub," Liam replies as he snaps his fingers. "But why are they focusing on Morgana as well?"

Channing looks up from her teacup, tilting her head. "Tell them, Jax."

"Oh, fine, sweet cheeks. But you owe me a rescue if she comes for my hide." The lion shifter grins and leans forward over Eli's lap. "I'm sharing this with you, but it's strictly need-to-know information. But since it's close to home... maybe it's related."

I lean back against Lucas, listening intently. "Spit it out."

"My old friend lives an hour from here in the Hollow. It's a small town that feeds kids to here like a fucking hamster wheel. There's been an awful lot of turmoil going on since she moved home. I can't go into why she came back, but she and her little harem of hotties have been digging into a lot of shit from the past. Disaster keeps plaguing them—on more than one continent and realm—and her best friend is a Guardian in one of those groups."

My eyes narrow. "Doesn't happen to be an Irish chick with a rainbow haired girl and two sexy shifters, does it?"

"Hey, that's the Guardians, yeah. How'd you know?" Jackson says excitedly. "Saoirse has been Jo-Jo's Guardian since she left the country years ago."

"Those are the people who just met us by the stone dragon." Iggy rubs his temples. "Perhaps the events there and here are related."

"And maybe some others," Eli mumbles. Jackson gives him a dirty look and he shrugs. "Look, I'm part of a lot of collectives and my job is hunting information. I know more than most and you can't ask me to keep it all secret, J."

Liam holds up his hand, waiting for everyone to get quiet. "I, too, have heard disturbing reports of The Hand wreaking havoc in Faerie. I'm going to assume your friend has traveled there recently by the way you included 'realm' in your statement."

"She just got back from a tour of your lovely lands, in fact. A mess ensued, partly influenced by her unemerged status."

"You took someone *unemerged* into Faerie?" Kaspar looks like he's going to keel over in shock. "How did anyone think that would go well?"

Jackson shrugs. "Jo-Jo's a stubborn Southern woman, and some dream lady told her to go. It was a risk, but other than some very dangerous confrontations, all's well."

The dragon and the Prince share a glance, implying inquiries only outsiders can answer. Instead of pressing them, I look at Jackson seriously. "Can Lucas leave the state? We're planning a trip to see Slade's family. It's research, but I don't want some dickface yanking us off of a plane."

"Well, why didn't you say so, Morgana Rosanna Danna? I have plenty of planes you can borrow." The lion shifter looks delighted, and Eli sighs heavily. "Eli will have to check the schedules for me so we make sure I don't get a nasty-gram from dear old dad, but I'm sure we can help. As for the Yogi over there, I'll clear it with the DA. He's not been formally charged, so we should be able to notify them."

"What do you think you're going to find out there?" Channing asks quietly.

I shrug. "We don't know. He's going to talk with his father, which I guess includes the mating thing."

When all three of them look at me like I've grown another head, I realize what I've done.

I just admitted out loud what our plans are and now the biggest gossips around know.

california girls

"**G**ood job," I mutter as I move closer. "Now this motor mouth will tell all his friends about our trip like he just did with theirs."

Morgana rolls her eyes at me, and I wonder if she tires of doing so. "Jackson will not spill the beans to randos. He wouldn't have told us about this Jo-Jo's trip if we weren't trustworthy."

I snort, shaking my head. "This self-absorbed idiot thinks everyone is trustworthy if they pay him."

Lucas glares at me, and I return the dirty look. His money doesn't scare me; the Court has more money than the Wolfberg's stored in their shoe closets. "Kaspar, you're the fucking worst, man. Just keep your paranoid crap to yourself. Maybe it helps you protect the Prince to be so jaded, but the rest of us would like to believe we have a snowball's chance, okay?"

"If you want to blow sunshine up your own ass, have fun." I cross my arms over my chest, my eyes meeting Li's. "But he's my responsibility and my duty, so I'm not going to back down because you're all dick drunk."

"Delicious," Jackson whispers, and Eli elbows him in the ribs. "What? It *is*."

"Morgana and her men are still finding their ground," Channing cuts in as she narrows her eyes at the leonine lawyer. "Don't be rude, Jax. You understand there can be waves when mixed groups come together like this."

What does that mean, I wonder?

Regardless, I can't let these people distract me. My fury earlier put me far from my Prince if the dragon had attacked closer to campus; I just got lucky when I ran into it. "If Thorne will allow us to borrow his plane, it will help keep us off the radar with the Court, a slew of over-involved relatives, and perhaps the Society... except for one thing."

Her eyes widen, and she smacks her forehead, finally realizing the flaw in their ointment. "My tracking spells. I'm not supposed to leave State U without proper clearance. It will take ages to get through that red tape."

"No, it won't." The polar bear smirks as he nuzzles his nose against Morgana's hair. "Nana will take care of it. And yes, grumpy lizard, she can be trusted. That woman has more secrets locked in her head than the fucking tombs of the pharaohs combined."

I arch a brow at him. "And she doesn't have a security team on her only grandson twenty-four hours a day?"

"I was trained after the first three kidnappings when I was a kid." He shrugs as if it's nothing, and I blink. The children of the Fae royals have guardians, cadres of guards, and magic to keep would-be assailants at bay. Lucas sighs and looks at us seriously. "I don't look like it, but I can withstand a fuck ton without even trying. Nana made sure no one would try to use me ever again."

Maybe I've misjudged the little shit; the look on his face is more serious than ever before.

"Fair enough," Iggy says. "Jackson and Eli will go do their research and plane booking shit. Lucas will get Morgana a furlough. What else do we need before we head off to the land of sun, surf, and shifter mafias?"

Slade looks uncomfortable, but he finally sighs. "I need to reach out to old friends and gauge the atmosphere. Hopefully, they can let me know what kind of *mood* my father and his minions are in. It will help us plan for contingencies."

"What contingencies?" I ask. "Magical? Physical? Emotional? Give me something to work with, kid."

"*Don't,*" the mage says as he shifts slightly to block the siren. "Slade's family treats him like crap, so yeah, we need to see if the old man is in one of his bouts of fury about his eldest son refusing to be a mobster. Also, yes, we should worry about magical and physical responses to our arrival. Bringing unknowns to their territory without calling first will piss the giant fucking tuna off."

Morgana frowns, biting her lower lip for a moment before she speaks. "What is your father, Slade? Not a siren, right? Males are extremely rare. They come from recessive genes passed on the mother's side."

Look who's a goddamn geneticist now.

As if she can hear me, the gargoyle whips her head around to give me a withering look. "I'm a unique hybrid, and that's hard when you're young, especially if you're adopted. I did a lot of research, so stuff it, briquette breath."

The siren chuckles and nods at her. "You're correct, Morgana. We are rare and that is how the trait passes. My mother is half kraken, half unknown magic user—and yes, we've tried to identify it, but there's some weird spell blocking her past. We assume the siren is from her, but no one can prove it."

The Prince squints at him curiously. "Not to be rude, but is it possible your dad...?"

"Oh, very much so, but my next oldest brother, Tracer, is full kraken. Beck and Duke are hammerhead shifters like Axel, I'm a siren, and my triplet sisters are all the most likely to be extramarital indiscretions because they're all hybrids." He pauses for a moment, as if thinking about it hurts him and I file his support for his mother away for later. "Coral is part siren, part mermaid; Isla is part kraken and part shark; and Roxy is part mermaid, part selkie. That shit puzzles everyone, but it's what it is."

That's a fucking nightmare of possibilities, especially if he's not mentioning whether they have magic.

"Great," Morgana says with a grumble. "I've always been awesome with aquatic folks—not."

Slade's eyes widen and I almost laugh. "Well, I mean... I'm not like... I know gorgons don't..."

"Fuck, kid, calm down," I grunt. "She knows you're okay."

That's my good deed for the week, for goddamned sure.

"You know, I'm pretty certain he's going to come around, peaches," Jackson says to the lounging gargoyle. "Just give him time. Dragons are the most stubborn supes I've ever met. They're worse than demigods or demons, for sure."

Blowing a soft breath of steam in his direction, I bare my teeth. "We also have no problem fricasseeing nosy kitty cats who annoy us."

"You'd have a hard time flying everyone to California on your back," Eli says with a small grin. "Not impossible for a storm dragon of the size I calculated, but not very fun."

"Guys." The small woman Morgana is fond of leans forward to address everyone. "As fun as this thrust and parry is, don't you think we should all get to work? It's getting late and if Morgana and the guys are going to the West Coast in a few days, there's a mountain of work to be done. She's missed so much with Lucas's trouble and now the dragon, and if she doesn't put face time in at the office, I'll have trouble keeping them in line while you're gone."

"She's right. I need to get my shit together, go into the office and kick some ass before we leave." Morgana looks at each of us, her eyes dark. "Kaspar, work on security and stay out of my face. Jax and Eli will get our transportation. Iggy and Slade will deal with the welcoming party, and Lucas will get me a reprieve."

"What about me, *Saaladir*?" Liam asks quietly. "What can I do to help?"

I'd prefer he simply go to his classes and *not* draw extra attention to himself, but he won't listen to me. "Li…"

Morgana smiles, her expression grateful as she interrupts me. "Just do your classes and then come stay with Lucas and me. Being close will be enough."

Gag.

"That I can do, as well as order some things for our trip." She protests and my Prince shakes his head. "Nope. No one gets to complain. If my connections aren't of help for this mission, then I'll make use of one of my other redeeming qualities—filthy rich git."

"You're not Tony Stark," I grumble as I roll my eyes. "Don't be ridiculous, Liam."

"Hush, Grumpy Dragon," he replies. "I'm going to enjoy spoiling people; no one ever lets me. It's exciting."

I watch as he lets out a zing of magic; the sparkles traveling out to each of our new circle and spiraling around them for a few seconds before coming back to the Fae. It's a parlor trick, but it makes everyone 'ooh' and 'ahh' as he beams. They don't realize he just used magic to take all of their measurements for whatever insane spending spree he's going to go on.

"There we go. Now everyone can focus on our roles and jobs without worrying about packing anything except personal and magical items." Liam looks proud of himself, and Morgana rises to her feet, crossing to the Prince quickly.

Her hand comes out to cup his face, and she smiles softly. "Thank you, mate. I appreciate you taking care of everyone, even if we didn't admit we needed it."

"Okay, that's our cue, sweet cheeks." Eli stands at Jackson's urging and Channing joins them. "We're heading out, and we'll drop Miss Channing off on our way to meet the others. They should have met with the Guardians who cleaned up your enemies—something that will help us trace their friends down—and we've got a long night of hacking to do."

The look on his face says that's not all he's planning, but I have zero intention of pointing out Morgana's friend being that close to her counsel.

The gargoyle stands, walking to the door with her friends, and I look at my Prince.

"Liam, this trip is…"

"Dangerous? Indeed, old friend."

Huffing, I walk over to him, feeling dread in my bones that I can't explain. "Yes, but not just that. It seems… superfluous. Can't we use other sources closer to the school? Why get mixed up with mobsters and criminals?"

Ignatius smirks at me. "Because if a bunch of supe baddies are pairing up all over, don't you think major criminals would get offers to join in? Even if they wouldn't—like Slade's father—riches would tempt them, too. Axel trusts no one, and he knows non-aquatic supes can't really take away his territory, outside of deities. He doesn't have a good motive to join, but others might."

I ponder that for a moment. "Like The Hand. The royals' strength prevents them from establishing a foothold in Faerie. But someone combining power with them might offer to help. And that offer could be replicated to displaced supes in all the realms: Faerie, Earth, Hell, the Gardens, and Mounts…"

"Exactly." My head turns to see Morgana standing with a smug look on her face. She shrugs as she pads back into the living room. "You've been too caught up in suspecting me. Whatever strategy skill Liam keeps you around for has been pushed aside to be snippy with me. I'm glad you're back in the game."

Running my hands through my hair, I look up at the ceiling, not wanting to admit she's right. "Okay. Fine. I'll back off of you and try to focus on this fucked up chess board. But if you…"

"Yes, yes. If I step a toe out of line, you'll zap my ass with lightning," she says as she waves her hand. "I get it, man."

I can't help it. I crack a smile this time. *She really is indefatigable.*

"You got it, toots."

That makes her grin a little as she herds the others from their seats. "Let's go get everyone set up in their rooms. I won't be able to sleep if I think I have another dragon roaming this place unchecked."

If only she knew…

leaving on a jet plane

B iding our time as Jackson, Lucas, and the others arrange this damn trip has been absolute torture. Channing and I slogged through the budget of some of the smaller departments—depressing as that was—and made a lot of notes on how criminally under-funded their programs were. We brought in a few professors, students, and even alumnae to give us firsthand dirt on what their lives were like under Magnus' regime.

The Society wanted me to clear up the corruption here, but I don't think they expected me to take it this seriously.

That doesn't matter to me in the slightest—if I'm going to put this entire campus through the ringer, I'm going to ensure *all* the students are given a fair shot at education for what they pay. The days of allocating eighty percent of the budget to the Dean's pets and sports team are over. It will make waves, but Channing and I are making sure we have the evidence to back up our moves. The graduation rates and post-university career success stories will bear out some of them, but testimony will make it even more compelling.

"Morgana, I agree with your efforts, but this is going to make the target on your back worse," my assistant says with a sigh. "People at State U have been accepting the way it is for a long time. Getting them to shift will be difficult."

I chuckle and shake my head. "Honestly, Chan? I don't mind if everyone is up in arms. We're going to find backers when they hear how completely fucked this shit is. Donations earmarked for specific programs, scholarships, and events have been funneled through the correct accounts, only to be moved to unapproved ones as soon as board meetings are over. No one was auditing this shit and we're lucky it's been kept secret this long."

She grimaces as she looks at the papers in her hands. "That's true. Most of the financial chicanery happening under Magnus broke laws in both worlds, and that draws attention supes don't need. The Society will have to do a lot of PR spinning once this becomes public record."

"Exactly." I toss my set of printouts onto the table, sighing as I lean back in my chair. "We're going to be untangling this for years. Magnus had a small flotilla of assholes working hard to hide all his bullshit. I don't know if they were skilled humans or if he also had magic users go over it with distraction enchantments. There's just no way a question was never raised about any of it unless he was double-dipping on his security."

The ice-wielder pushes her glasses up, tilting her head as she studies me. "Your ex was very good at keeping his circle tight and full of worshippers and grifters who benefited from keeping his secrets. We'll be working on this for quite a while. Does that bother you?"

"Fuck, I don't know. It would have been a couple of weeks ago. I wanted to do this time and get the hell out, you know?" I grin a little and shrug. "Now I'm attached to people and trying to solve some big Nancy Drew 'Mystery at the Supernatural University,' so I guess I'm less eager to run away."

Channing laughs softly, her eyes dancing. "I can't say I blame you for that. Sexy men and searching for clues is way more interesting than hiding yourself on some tropical island until the bad press goes away."

I'll be damned; how did she know?

"You're very observant, Channing. I knew there was a reason I hired you."

A knock interrupts our humor, and my new friend leaps up to go to the door. She waits for me to nod before opening it, then smiles when she sees Lucas leaning against the doorjamb. "Dean LeCiel, there's a student here to see you."

Her voice is full of suggestion, and I feel my face redden as the muscled bear lopes into the room with a smirk. Lucas winks at her as she scurries into the outer office, shutting the heavy oak behind her quickly. His eyes rove over the table full of accounting paperwork and he clicks his tongue. "Damn, Morgana. This looks like my nightmares come to life."

I snort. "That makes two of us, baby. Numbers have never been my thing, but prisoners do *not* get to choose the punishment for their crimes, no matter how justified they were."

"Pity. I would have lobbied to be head shoe shiner at the palace before this shit." He walks over to me, putting his hands on my shoulders and massaging them firmly.

"Shit, that's nice," I sigh as my eyes close. "And yeah, I could have survived a lot to avoid this, but it brought me here to you guys, sooooo.... I'm not complaining."

I can feel his eyes on me and imagine how broadly he's grinning. Lucas is starving for praise and love, even if his grandmother was good to him, and he lights up like a Christmas tree when I give it without being asked. His parents are stupid, selfish assholes and so was every dumbfuck who used him for his family name before now.

Damn, that almost sounds like I'm...nope.

Shaking my head to clear it, I open my eyes and look up at him with a grin. "To what do I owe this unscheduled visit, mate?"

"Nana got the old farts to agree. She just texted me during my last class, so I headed here to tell you in person." His smug grin tickles me; I know he didn't actually do more than ask his rich relative to fix something, but he's so adorably proud of himself.

"Good job, baby. I'm glad my GPS won't go off and send Guardians winging their way to Bay City to arrest me for leaving my invisible cage."

"That's bullshit, anyway," he grumbles. "As long as you do your shit and serve out your time, grounding you in one place is fucking stupid and spiteful. I asked Nana to figure out just who requested that extra bit of security so we can check into them."

And again, he surprises me with his strategy. No wonder he's a Captain.

"I doubt she'll be able to find out someone's hidden motives, but... thank you," I murmur up at him. "You're really making it hard to focus on doing shit when you're not around."

His chest puffs up, and he preens a bit—which was my goal. I didn't think I'd ever find anyone who made me feel safe or like I want to take the risk of sharing myself with them again until this brash young bear stomped into my house, but I'm not stupid enough to reject it. Between him and the Prince, I fell asleep every night this week in a cocoon of warm, sated comfort like I've never experienced before.

"Want to walk across campus with me for a coffee? I think the pretty boy is working."

My smile widens, and I pull away so I can scoot out from the table. "Why didn't you lead with that? I'd love to visit Slade. He and Iggy have been so busy getting their stuff covered for the trip and dealing with 'secret' sources to scout his dad. I haven't seen nearly enough of them."

Lucas nods, holding his hand out. "It's afternoon, anyway, and I'd be surprised as fuck if you've eaten since breakfast. And before you say it, *no*, coffee does *not* count, even if you filled it with a bunch of fluffy shit."

Damn. He's got me there.

"Stop being impressively observant and chivalrous. You're making me look bad," I grumble as we walk to the door. When we exit, Channing winks at me and I sigh when I realize she's heard every word.

"I'll set your phone and email to 'out for lunch,' Morgana. I don't want people chasing you while you eat." My bear gives Channing a double thumbs-up, and she flushes brightly. "Make sure she's back before her meeting at two, Lucas."

"Got it Chan-o-rama!" he calls and I chuckle.

I don't know how he charms damn near everyone around us, but he does. Polar bears aren't known for being friendly, nor are spoiled rich guys, but Lucas Wolfberg is an exception to almost every rule. I think that's why he burst through my defense so easily; he's simply not what he seems from the outside. His actual personality is fucking adorable and infinitely endearing, with a broad capacity for fun and adventure.

I haven't been around anyone with that kind of joie de vivre in an extremely long time.

"Okay, Lady M. So you usually have a large vanilla cappuccino with whip, sweetener, and some fluffy shit. But *today*, I want you to try something new. We're flying to a place neither of us has been to meet criminals we don't know tomorrow... so adventure is on the docket."

I blink at him. "Were you reading my mind, you nosey parker?"

He laughs and shakes his head as we leave the admin building to head across the quad. "Nope. But I'm all about experiencing new shit. It's been an awfully good week for that, yeah?"

Flashes of him and the Prince together and with me assault my brain and I nod. "Uh... yeah. Yeah, it has."

"Bad girl," he coos playfully. "Not in public. You're going to draw supes with good noses if you don't clean up that dirty mind. But yeah, you caught my drift."

I shake my head again and suck in a deep breath, then let it out slowly. "Okay. So the theme of today and by extension, the trip... is try new shit?"

"Fuck, yeah, it is!" Lucas pumps his fist in the air and I laugh. "I mean, why not? If people are trying to frame me, kill you, and who knows what the others have going on... why *wouldn't* we enjoy ourselves every minute?"

When you put it like that...

"Okay. I'm in." He grins and I look at him seriously. "Who else is involved? Have you asked Li or the others to play along?"

"Nope," he says with a pop. "But I'm going to. Liam will *definitely* accept 'cause he's very adaptable. Slade might—which is why we're going there now to get our caffeine and protein on. Iggy? I'm not sure about him, but if we convince Slade, we can get him in, I think. The dragon will be harder."

"Uh, I highly doubt Kaspar will play along with *anything*, especially if I'm in," I reply wryly. "He's got a giant hard-on for being a jerk to me and nothing else."

"Mmmm, I don't know about that," my bear says as we get closer to the coffeehouse. "You're giving him too much leeway with his shit, and that's what he enjoys."

I frown as I grab Lucas's arm and look at him. "Are you trying to tell me he gets off on pissing me off?"

His finger taps my nose as he grins. "Bingo, Lady M. You get the stuffed animal and a free spin of the wheel."

"How about I just join your delusional yet sexy ass for lunch instead?" He chuckles at my grumpy reply but follows me as I stride toward the shop in irritation.

"You can deny it all you want," he sing-songs, "but I promise you, the dude is just edging himself. He'll give in, eventually."

Shooting him a dirty look, I yank open the door to the beanery and beam at the siren behind the counter. "Afternoon, Slade. What's the story, morning glory?"

Lucas wasn't wrong in calling him a pretty boy, and the flush that crawls up his neck is even more enticing. "Hey, guys. What are you doing here in the middle of the day?"

"Nana got Lady M cleared to fly, so we're having lunch to celebrate. Also, she doesn't eat if people don't remind her."

Slade frowns. "That's not good for either of her energy sucking sides."

"Oi," I say as I slap my palm on the counter. "*She* is right here and has been alive fifty times longer than either of you. I'm aware of my bad habits, boys."

They both look sheepish, and finally Slade murmurs, "The usual, then?"

I shake my head. "Nope. I promised Lucas adventure, and that's what we're doing. Tell me all the weird, special shit you're doing."

Even old gargoyles can learn new tricks, after all.

Contrary to the concerned frown I gave her, I'm really quite pleased Lucas brought Morgana in. Iggy and I spent the past few days in talks with people from my previous home, and I think we'll be able to slide in without too much turmoil. Finding out Lucas made good on the promise to allow Morgana to travel without restrictions lifts an enormous weight off my chest. If he hadn't been able to make good, Iggy had lots of not-so-savory ideas on how to fiddle with her tracker that I was certain would lead to problems.

Problems being a euphemism for scary trials for breaking Society edicts, of course.

I look at the woman in front of me, waiting with an expectant expression and grin. "Today's special drink is a Cold Rose Coffee. It's arabica coffee with skim milk, rose syrup, chocolate syrup, and whipped cream, lightly garnished with rose petals and pink rock salt. I think you'll enjoy the light, summery yet indulgent taste."

Morgana blinks at me as if I've lost my mind, and it's hard not to laugh. "Shit. Okay, give us both one, coffee maestro. I didn't expect such a departure from normal, but... hit me with your weird-ass food special next, I guess."

The hockey player grins at me. "Please let it be something that stretches her boundaries. I'm loving this."

"I made Vegan BBQ Pulled Jackfruit sandwiches fresh this morning. I made the BBQ sauce to complement the fresh jackfruit, simmered it, then top it with a veggie slaw with vegan mayo on slider buns. It's complimentary for the summery coffee, and definitely mimics a pork or chicken BBQ sandwich." My lips quirk when Morgana gives me a dirty look once she figures out this is totally meat and cheeseless.

"Lucas, you are so dead," she grumbles. "Fine, give me the fluffy ass, no protein sandwich. But I'd better have an enormous amount of *non-sexy time* meat for dinner to make up for this. I'll never be able to survive on Slade's hippie dippy shit, you know."

Both Lucas and I snicker as I head to the back to prepare the sandwiches. I'm aware both she and the athlete can't eat as lightly as my sea-faring body, but seeing her look of horror was definitely worth it. If we're together as often as I think we will be, we can all work together to make meals that give everyone the nutrients they need. I ponder for a moment, then pull out my phone, making a note to email Professor Shadwell for resources to use. She'd definitely know where I should look to plan for such disparate supes.

"Slade, those things look tiny on the menu! We need like ten of them," Lucas calls from the front. "Don't make that face, Lady M. I'm suffering, too."

Classic.

I make their load of sliders quickly, forgoing any fancy plating as I head back into the coffee shop. To my surprise, the Prince is now sitting at a bistro table he and the dragon pulled up next to Morgana and Lucas. He smiles, waving as I put the plate on the counter and move to get their coffees fixed.

"Afternoon, Slade. I see you have our family well in hand," Liam says with a smirk.

"Vegan, Li. Can you imagine? I'm a *carnivore*; what did I get myself into?" she mutters as she pouts adorably. "The things I do for this stupidly handsome boy, I swear."

Lucas literally preens as they both look at him and I grin. I've never been in a family quite so openly affectionate—mine is more about who's in favor at the moment—and it makes my heart flutter a little to think I'm part of this one. Even Morgana's grumpiness is tinged with fondness, and I can feel the warmth in her emotions from here.

"He is quite lovely, you're right." The Prince elbows his companion when he snorts, then turns to me. "I will wait until you're done with their order, Slade. Don't fret."

How did he know that? Fuck, this guy is powerful.

I hadn't even thought that in my head yet, but the Prince knew I was a little stressed over ignoring him to finish Morgana's drink. "Thanks. I like to make sure everyone's taken care of and I get a little anxious when I feel I'm not achieving it."

Morgana looks over at me as I work, watching closely as I sprinkle the last fancy bits on the coffee. "You know, you really take this seriously.

Are you planning to open a coffeehouse when you finish, or is it just something you enjoy?"

Blinking for a moment, I ponder her question. I've never considered that. Of course I want to do something with music when I finish my studies, but I love working with customers and pairing the food and drinks and the music for the atmosphere here. Maybe I would like to have my own place, especially if I could have musicians in playing live, including myself. "I... No one's ever asked me that. I'm not sure."

That gets a crafty grin from the Prince, who arches a brow at the bear. They do a 'bro' eyebrow thing before Liam nods and looks at me. "I think it's a good idea and we'll absolutely back you if you want to explore it, eventually. Lucas and I certainly can get you off the ground, and I'm certain Morgana can help you develop a business plan."

"Hell, yeah, I can. Iggy can make sure it's warded and safe, and Grumpy McFirePants could set up security. It would be a successful family project once we're not ducking conspiracies and murder raps."

Holy shit. They're serious.

"I..." Licking my lips, I focus on the plates and glasses, stacking the tray to bring over to the table. Once I bring it to them, I gather enough courage to look at them. "Thank you. I don't know if it's what I want—though the idea seems really appealing—but knowing you'd all support me if I wanted to do it is..."

Morgana reaches out to take the tray, setting it on the table before she grabs my hand. "I believe in you, even if it's been a short time, and if we're all going to be a family, that's what families do."

Not the one I grew up in and they have no idea how significant this is for me.

The lunch rush breezes by as my new family sits in the corner and makes plans for the trip. They probably think I'm not paying attention as I help people, but I've noticed *a lot* about them all as they work. The Prince is very strategic, and he approaches things like he's storming the gates while his scaly guard likes to point out the holes or gaps left afterward. Lucas injects humor when people bicker, but he also sees different issues—probably from his experience on the ice. Morgana takes everyone's input, reorganizes it, and then figures out how to execute their ideas without leaving anyone out.

It's kind of perfect, and I'm enjoying watching them all.

When the clock hits three, the door blows open to reveal Ignatius wearing a very smug expression. "Greetings, all. I'm surprised to find the entire brain trust here. Don't we all have... things?"

Kaspar rolls his eyes, scoffing at my roommate. "Of course we did. Liam and I finished up our required projects and his classes, then came here to find the others having lunch."

"That's true. Lucas came to take me to lunch, but I had Channing reschedule some of my meetings so I could work from here while we discussed the trip planning." She winks at me playfully. "It's not like my ex spent even half his time in that damn office, so I think remote work in the coffeehouse is acceptable."

"Who the hell is going to question it?" Iggy winks at her playfully, then strolls over to the counter where I've got his usual coffee waiting. "Thanks, man."

"Speaking of having jobs, why are you here?" I reply as I squint at him. "Don't you have one more class today?"

He puffs up, looking smug as he joins the others at the table. "I've gotten all the coverage Slade and I need to go on this little adventure. My part is taken care of, and since you all seem to have missed the group text Jackson sent, I also come bearing news about departure."

Everyone pulls their phones out like lightning and he snorts as they all check them at once. I give him a wry look. "Way to bury the lede, Iggy."

"I thought you all knew Thorne said he had the plane ready at the airport for us to leave in the morning." He shrugs and sips his drink with a sigh of pleasure. "How could I know they were all ignoring tech to work up plans on Morgana's laptop?"

Morgana looks up, her eyes closing as she groans. "Tomorrow? That means everyone has to go home and pack, plus we have to do it all tonight. No wonder you canceled your last class."

My brow furrows. "I won't have coverage until five. Iggy, please return to our place and assemble everything while I complete my tasks here."

The Prince nods, looking over at Kaspar. "We will need to visit our house to get prepared. Can you arrange for a larger SUV to transport us to the airport in the morning?"

"I can. I'll contact home to make certain they received the information about this as well. I haven't heard from my father yet, which is odd." He shakes his head and rises to his feet. "I know it's not late yet, Liam, but we should go to the house and begin preparations. Many things need to be within reach on this journey."

"He's right, honestly. I'll probably have to swing by my place to get things I haven't brought to your place, Lady M. I definitely don't have a suitcase, nor anything suitable for a formal occasion."

The gargoyle swivels her head to pin him with her stare. "Formal wear?"

I grin and shrug. "If you don't have suitable stuff unpacked, we can hit the designer row in Bay City, Morgana. I may not draw a crowd here, but I'll certainly be able to get us into the fancy places at home. That town is wired like an embassy with the members of the Families."

"Great. Just fucking great," she mutters. "I have a bad feeling about how irritated I'm going to be the entire time we're there."

Kaspar smirks at her. "Welcome to the club."

Her gaze is sharp enough to cut down a lesser supe without a word. "You... had better remember the discussion we had before you took off in a pout and we had to come save your scaly ass. We're jumping into a shark tank and I swear to Aphrodite's thong, if you humiliate me in front of all those people... you'll regret it."

"Now, now," Iggy says as he holds his hands up. "We all agreed to behave. As long as there's people outside of our family around, there is *no division*. Capiche?"

Morgana nods, but she eyes the dragon warily until he gives in. When he finally does, she blows out a long breath. "Ensure everyone brings necessary items for self-protection. Even if everything goes well with Slade's family, I don't know what other problems we'll run into."

I think about that for a moment and nod. "She's right. Bay City is full of criminals, mobsters, glamazons, sports stars, and everything else you'd expect from a big city on the coast. There will be other threats, especially if we get pulled into any events my family is attending. We need to stay on our toes and trust no one but each other."

"That doesn't sound good," Lucas says with a frown. "Is it really that dangerous?"

"It's an immense city, secretly run by supe factions, including the Society, gangs, and rich people. Of course it's that bad." I chuckle as I run my hand through my hair. "The humans don't have the slightest clue who's really in charge, but the push and pull of the good versus the morally gray is pretty hardcore. You'll see."

"On that cheerful note, it's time for everyone but surfer boy here to head out." Kaspar eyes each of us as he waits for the Prince. "We'll meet at Morgana's for dinner at seven p.m. Bring everything you need and get yourself ready."

They all stand, and Morgana comes over to lean over the counter and gives me a hug. "It will be okay, Slade. No one is going to let your family tie you down or harm you."

I don't know that she realizes just how hard it will be to keep that promise...

FIND OUT WHAT HAPPENS IN BAY CITY IN THE BONUS SCENE here.

Preorder Book Two in Secrets of State U here.

reviews, print, and merchandise

If you have enjoyed this story, please review it.
It helps other readers find my work,
which helps me as an indie author.

Thank you!

Reviews are appreciated on the following platforms

TikTok
Instagram
Facebook
Bookbub
StoryGraph
Threads
Goodreads
Amazon

To purchase print copies or merchandise, go to The Worlds of Cassandra Featherstone

get a secret bonus scene!

For a secret bonus scene that follows this book, *click the link below, sign up for my newsletter, and get your freebie.*

Get your bonus scene here!

stalk cassandra featherstone in the dark corners of the web

JOIN MY FACEBOOK GROUP AND FOLLOW ME EVERYWHERE!

WANT MORE?

SIGN UP FOR MY BI-WEEKLY MANIFESTO FOR A FREE SERIES SAMPLER:

Join my Ream as a FREE follower or exclusive subscriber to get access to cover reveals, WIPs, Serial Stories, and personal chats from me!

CASSANDRA FEATHERSTONE

sneak peek: bloodthirsty

QUEEN BEE

They dim the lights in the club, and the spots click on as the curtain slides open.

It's a full house tonight in the little burlesque club off the Rue Pierre Montaine.

Chez Arc En Ciel is not well known compared to the *Moulin Rouge* or *Le Lido*, but the wealthy from both sides of the Seine gather here for shows four nights a week. If you pass the various layers of security checks to even be permitted to book a reservation, you also have to be able to afford the two thousand Euro per guest cover charge. If you don't eat or drink anything, that's all it will cost; however, that would get you blacklisted.

Intro music pumps through the speakers and I stand on my mark in the opening position. My cane is resting on the wooden boards of the stage by my front foot as I pretend to lean on it. Roars of applause echo through the room as our troupe of dancers catch the lights, sequins sparkling like diamonds when the stage lights rise. We're dressed in pinstriped black pant suits and fedoras to match the big band style opening to the song. As soon as the horn-filled intro finishes, the dance begins.

I follow the routine with precision, snapping and popping my hips to the beat as we spread out across the stage. You wouldn't know by the fake smile on my face that I'm scanning the crowd. Two fan kicks later, I've rotated past the proscenium, and I think I've found my mark. Twirling, I stop in the place I need to be for the bridge, singing along as if my life depends on it. It might, to be honest, because I need to sell my cover tonight, so no one notices me.

The Guillotine moves in the shadows, but tonight, she's in the spotlight.

My ass shakes as I dance my way through the song, swinging the prop cane I'd replaced with one of my design. You wouldn't know by looking at it, but it's not the painted balsa the other dancers have for a very specific reason. I need it to complete the mission that forced me to spend two months in Paris working my way into this job at *Chez Arc En Ciel*. If I can't strike tonight, the surveillance, counterintelligence, and time spent building this cover are wasted because my mark is leaving for Asia tomorrow.

Tonight, the Cobra dies for his sins.

The break of the song slows the music and the dancers pour into the crowd to wiggle around the rich assholes. It's choreographed, but it's also to advertise each girl for private dances in the lounges upstairs. We're not strippers—not that there's a damned thing wrong with a woman using her body to support herself—but we do bare more skin in the closed rooms. The *laissez-faire* attitude of the owners means as long as we kick them thirty percent of the fees for those dances, they don't care what any of the girls do in the rooms. I'd find it sleazy, but the girls who work here are highly skilled performers who choose to make thousands of dollars a night rather than peanuts in some ballet troupe or chorus line.

By the time I've flirted my way to the VIP tables, the Cobra is staring intently at all of us. Spotlights pin each one of us on the floor at the bass hits, and I swivel my hips as my free hand slides down to the secret spot on my jacket. In unison, we tear the jackets off to reveal rhinestone studded bras with straps crisscrossing our waists like shibari ropes. A lift of the fedora and pop of my hip, along with the beat, draws the fierce-looking brawler's eyes directly to me. I pout prettily and stalk towards his table with the swagger of a tiny dicked asshole that owns a monster truck.

His thin lips pull back over the famed curving fangs he had implanted. Dark, glittering eyes follow every move I make as I approach, and I pretend to whip my hair from side to side as I check for his guards. They're here somewhere, but I need them to be far away so I can beat my escape before they notice. When I get within inches, I tap his leg with my cane and spin around to shake my ass in his face. The grunt of approval makes me want to heave, but I turn, holding onto the prop with both hands. My feet click on the floor in a soft shoe step as I make 'fuck me' eyes at the dirty bastard. He leans back, his pants tented as he gestures towards his lap.

Fucking gross.

I don't care about his weapons trade or what happens when people get the shit he moves. I have no clue why I have to take him out. The reason they have sentenced him to death isn't part of my contract, and I'm nothing if not a dispassionate observer of the darkest parts of human desires. Twelve years at *l'Academie* ensured I care very little about anything that isn't directly related to my ability to complete my jobs.

Sighing, I dance closer and drop onto his rather unimpressive erection and wiggle. There's plenty of cloth between us to prevent him from doing anything I'd make a scene over, so I focus on the task at hand. I slip the cane behind his head, resting the wood against his neck as I tug him forward. The move reads as playfully bringing his face to my breasts, but at the last second, I click the release built into the custom weapon. One end slides open to reveal the razor sharp garotte and before he can say a word, I yank it through.

Faint gurgling is the only noise besides the end of the song, and I carefully slide the sides of the cane together. Climbing off the nasty fucker, I put my hands on his cheeks so I can pretend to flirt with him while I arrange the head so it looks as if he's leaning back in the booth. It needs to look realistic to allow me to return to the stage with the others. When I have it settled, I back away from the booth, blowing fake kisses as I walk backwards through the crowd. I almost collide with a dark-haired guy with his collar pulled high as I head for the stage, and I roll my eyes. Whatever celeb that is trying to keep their face away from the paps is doing a shitty job of it.

The entire troupe takes a few bows and shuffles off of stage left to the wings. I exhale a sigh of relief when the next group enters on the opposite side. I haven't heard shouting yet, so I don't think the Cobra's men realize he's down. Now I take this emetic pill, have a vomiting episode, and I'll get sent home.

That's when Arabella Montaigne, the burlesque dancer, will cease to exist, and Remy Arsine Benoit will re-emerge.

I smile to myself as I chew on the tablet that will have me retching my guts out in a few moments. This is a more complex extermination than I usually prefer, and I can't leave my normal calling card behind. The Cobra's head had to remain in the booth rather than get delivered to his home in a basket.

Such a shame, that. I quite enjoy the reactions my little gifts engender when they're discovered.

Walking into the dressing room, I carefully strip my costume off, putting all the pieces in my bag. Every item in the locker room that belongs to gets placed in the duffel carefully as I wait for the effects to hit me. It won't do to leave loose ends, even if my prints have never touched a single surface in this place. My gut roils and I turn, facing one of the other dancers as the vomit finally comes. Gracelia screams like she's being skinned when I hurl on her and it's everything I can do *not* to smirk through the chunks.

"*C'est la merde!*" she shouts, running for the showers as if she's on fire.

It takes less than a minute for the owner to send me home for the night. I walk out the back door of the building with everything just as the sirens scream.

Perfect timing, as always.

I jump into the first cab I can hail, directing him to the *Hôtel de Crillon*. Their suites are the ritziest in Paris, and it's my go-to hideout when I'm here. I used to only stay in the Bernstein Suite, but some rich fuckwad purchased it six months ago. If I could track them down and beat the hell out of them, I would, but I booked my schedule until late 2025. Assassins with my skill set and accuracy are getting harder to find. They forced the old guard into retirement because they refuse to adapt to the digital age. Too many cameras, crime labs, and hackers running about to do everything Cold War style.

The future of murder for hire is millennial, people. We're old enough to be stable, but young enough to be agile with new technology. Plus, most of them are broke AF from crooked ass student loans.

It's not an issue I have, but I've been in the business since I hit double digits. You don't survive *l'Academie des Invisibles* if you haven't killed someone before the end of primary school. It's unheard of.

I was eight the first time I used the weapon that would become my signature.

Shivering, I tap on the window of the cab and bitch the driver out. He's taking a longer route than necessary to raise my fare, and I'll have his guts for garters if he doesn't knock it the fuck off. A string of curses in French erupt from him when I voice the accusation, and I slam my palm on the window with enough force to crack the plexiglass barrier. He almost drives into another car, but when he regains control, he makes the requested adjustments to our route.

We arrived at the front entrance after a few more arguments and a traffic jam around the *Champs*. I throw the euros at him in disgust, memorizing the medallion number for later. He's not worth my time, but I have quite a few contacts who might be interested in blackmailing a cabbie in town. Getaway cars are cliche in the crime world now. Most ne'er-do-wells like myself find greater comfort in anonymous taxis or ride-share accounts hacked through the deep web accessed on burner phones. If your ride doesn't know you're a villain, there's no one to flip if law enforcement comes looking.

I never look the same for any job—ever.

I will not use Arabella Montaigne as a cover in the future, and once I move to the location of my next job, I'll ensure that she meets with a terrible fate. It's a lot more work to slowly kill off my alters once I've used them, but it's also why I've never even come close to being caught. The dancer with long wavy red hair, freckles, and big green eyes will never grace the streets of Paris again after I hop a plane. She will, however, get a minor story in the paper and an obituary when I decide how she tragically dies.

The Guillotine will rise from her ashes and be reborn.

JUST A GIRL

Delores

Sighing, I look around my bedroom at the posters and decorations covering my walls. My obsession with pop music, musical theater, and high school rom-coms sickens my parents. They would prefer me to be into heavy metal and horror movies like the other kids my age.

Being the only child in a family as prominent as mine is difficult when you don't fit the mold. My parents—like their parents and all my friends' parents—are apex predators. Preds rule our world, and the division between us and prey is so severe that we regulate them to a completely different echelon of society. Prey shifters are weak and beneath our lofty abilities. The ruling class of elite predator families stretches back generations, and they've evolved into a bunch of assholes who only care about succession and greed.

My animal has not manifested yet, but it will soon enough. Luckily for me, none of my friends have manifested their inner animals, either. I'm part of the in-crowd at school, and my boyfriend, Todd, is the most popular guy in my class. While he and I aren't officially engaged yet, we've talked about it enough that I know it's only a matter of time before he puts a ring on my finger. I should be on top of the world, but I can't help but feel like my life just doesn't fit me the way it's supposed to.

Every teenager wishes their life was different, but I dream of becoming an entirely different person. Not inside, mind, because I'm pretty comfortable with who I am. I don't want to be part of this legacy, this society, or even this family. They are all focused on competing to be the richest, the deadliest, or the most powerful, and I want no part of it.

I walked over to my closet and pulled out the outfit that I had chosen for my tour of Apex Academy. My mother hired her personal designers to create a custom school uniform for today and expects me to present the 'appropriate' image of the sole heir to a Council seat.

I hate having to pretend to be like them because I'm nothing like them.

Regardless, I pull on the short, pink pleated skirt, three quarter length sleeve blouse, knee socks, and Mary Janes that comprise the uniform for my exclusive private high school. Since I'm using a 'college visit' day to tour the Academy, I'm expected to represent Shifter Secondary as well.

Shifter Secondary is the most exclusive high school for unmanifested shifter teens on the East Coast. Unfortunately for me, it was not my parents' first choice for my education. They hoped I'd follow in their footsteps by choosing to force my animal to emerge early. If I had done that, I could have attended *Apex Academy Lower School*.

I didn't have the stomach to use my body in that manner at fourteen.

Their heirs followed my lead, which made my mother and father furious and their hoity-toity council colleagues angry. My closest friends, the Heathers, also refused to force their animals to emerge, as did Todd and his friends. That was the first time the adults in our circle decided I was a bad influence. After that, I had to toe the line at every turn, ensuring that I followed all the strict rules and regulations that govern the heirs to council seats.

Everywhere I went, I had to dress in a manner befitting the next Drew to sit at the table. They forced me to take dance lessons, piano lessons, diction lessons, and other more humiliating tutorials to prepare for the day that I became a true predator. In our society, teenagers have no say in how we prepare for our animals to emerge.

Your parents make all the decisions, choose your friends, choose your mates, and decide every detail of your life down to what you eat every single day. At least, that's how it is in my family, because my mother is from the old world.

She came over from Slovenia when she was incredibly young and met my father on the society fundraiser circuit. Her idea of preparing her daughter for the future involves lessons in makeup, clothing, jewelry, and on how to keep your mate satisfied. Lucille is completely uncon-cerned about whether I end up happy, only that I attend to my council seat and my husband's *needs*.

Once I get dressed, I grab my vintage Vuitton bag and peek at the mirror for a last check before I head downstairs. I tuck my perfectly highlighted blonde tresses behind my ears, and the smokey eye and winged liner are on point with this year's fashion trends. I apply a quick swipe of cherry red lip gloss and open my mouth, inspecting my teeth to make sure they are pearly white. Even though once I develop threatening incisors or sharp fangs, something will inevitably cover them in blood, my parents want my smile to look like a toothpaste commercial.

It's all such utter bullshit.

I take a deep breath and turn on my heel, heading for the door. I can already hear my parents yelling in a Scotch and vodka induced rage in the drawing room. It's only eleven thirty in the morning, for Hera's sake.

Lucille and Bruno don't fuck around with cocktail hour. They are nicely sauced by ten a.m. every day, without exception. I can't remember a time when my parents didn't get drunk off their asses at an event or party, much less in our 'home'. They liquor up and fight until they part for the day, and then start again once they arrive home from their daily commitments.

I brace for the barrage of criticism my mother will subject me to when I cross the threshold. Closing my eyes, I whisper words of encouragement to myself via lyrics to some of my favorite songs, desperately trying to hype myself up before she can tear me down.

"Delores! I hear you breathing at the top of the stairs, darling. Come down this instant and let your father and I inspect your presentation."

My mother's purr *sounds* friendly, but believe me, it's not. I roll my eyes as I make my way down the stairs, knowing my mother won't hesitate to send one of the staff if I don't acquiesce to her command. Most of their staff would gleefully jizz themselves with being chosen to drag me downstairs for inspection.

At this time of day, the only servant in the drawing room will be Matilda—my ex-nanny turned personal assistant—and that request would test her loyalties. As the only person in my household who has my back, I don't want to put her in that position, so I answer. "Yes, Lucille. I'm on my way."

I'm not allowed to refer to her as 'mother' because it makes her feel old. 'Lucille' is always what I've called the woman who supposedly gave birth to me. I'd be tempted to disbelieve we shared any DNA at all if it weren't for our similar bone structure. She's about as nurturing as a rattlesnake, and if it weren't for Matilda, I might have died as a child. If the kitchen staff whispers are accurate, I have to accept that my mother neglected to feed me much of the time.

"You coddle her far too much, Lucille," my father growls. "As the heir to our family seat, Delores will come without being instructed to do so. We will not tolerate her insolence after her animal emerges. She will behave as I command or suffer the consequences."

The last of Bruno's rant echoes off the marble walls of the foyer as I step onto the hideously expensive, endangered teak floor. Schooling my features into the mask of indifference I wear whenever I have to deal with them, I enter their den of drunken fights with my spine steeled for an emotional assault.

"I apologize for my tardiness, Father. I only wished to perfect the image I will present during my tour of Apex Academy. I realize it is imperative I impress the Headmistress and her staff."

The humanoid features of his face shift seamlessly, and the hungry crocodile inside of him gives me a toothy smirk. "You will impress them, daughter, or so help me... I'll send you to Bloodstone Isle."

My stomach drops like a stone as I barely suppress a shiver.

Bloodstone Isle is a reformatory school. It's surrounded by spells and enchantments to prevent students from escaping—a feat that has only happened once in its one thousand years of existence. The most feared cat group in the shifter world—the Khan ambush—runs the school, and they're rumored to consume errant students when the Council allows it.

It's the threat both rich and poor shifter parents used to keep their children in line. Wealthy parents like mine use it as a method of controlling any heirs that refuse to conform to the rigid structure of our society. Predators don't value the lives of those who are weak, and they label heirs who refuse to take their rightful place at the top of the food chain weak. Everyone knows Bloodstone is full of criminals, miscreants, and psychos, and even they don't seem to survive.

Bloodstone is a death sentence—pure and simple.

"Y-yes, Father. I understand," I croak out. As if the pressure of touring my new school isn't enough, now I worry the Dean will relay something to my parents that gets me shipped off to Death Island.

"Bruno, darling, if you scare her, she'll frown. That causes wrinkles. Delores, chin up and smile for us."

Swallowing the lump in my throat, I flash my mother my brightest smile. Her blood-red lips curve, and her leopard fangs burst free as she all but purrs. "I will not have you sullying the family name, Delores. It's bad enough that your education gave you ideas about your value beyond breeding stock. You will take the seat on the Council when it is time, but the husband we select will control the business—as nature intended. Do you hear me?"

My eyes narrow briefly, and for what is possibly the millionth time this week alone, I nod at my mother to appease her temper. "Yes, Lucille."

"Excellent!" The leopard fades as she claps her hands. "Matilda!"

The tiny woman steps up, her eyes wide behind her glasses. She's a pred, but the smaller size of hawk shifters puts her in the servant class. I believe she genuinely lives in fear of one or both of my parents deciding to eat her. "Yes, madam?"

"Fetch Bruiser. He will accompany Delores to the academy for her tour. Tell him to take the Escalade—it won't do for her to arrive in a tiny car—it will draw attention to her extra weight. We must make an impression."

Matilda nods, and I feel the fear radiating from her, and I don't blame her. Bruiser is one of my parents' bodyguards and our frequent chauffeur. He's a Komodo dragon shifter and the house staff are terrified of him. It's hard not to be, given that he prefers to play with his food, then eat it after it's dead. The kitchen crew believes he 'handled' the gardener that looked too long at my mother when I was ten. He disappeared without a trace.

Once Matilda scurries away, I watch my parents drink and bicker about their plans for the day. Bruno is going golfing with a congressman, and Lucille is going to the spa. We all know that both outings will include stops at the homes of their current pieces of ass for a quickie, but no one talks about it. The appearance of the loving couple has to be maintained, although neither of them has slept in the same room since I was a baby.

They don't give a damn about fidelity; I learned that at an early age. Children often discover things they shouldn't because of adults discount their ability to understand the conversations happening around them.

I stopped keeping track of who they're boning long ago, because I'd need an assistant to keep the affairs straight.

While my parents' marriage is a sham, I remind myself that my boyfriend, Todd, isn't like them. Yes, his parents only own half the live entertainment industry, but my father allows me to see Todd. The other parents will force the Heathers to accept an arranged betrothal, and I'm grateful I'm lucky enough to have found the perfect match on my own as my high school sweetheart.

"Delores, Bruiser is ready to escort you to Apex. He's pulling the car around now," the hawk shifter says softly.

Snapping out of my reverie, I smile at the trembling woman. Bruiser must have scared the living hell out of her. For no other reason than it amused him, I'm sure. He's as much a brute as his name implies, and I don't look forward to riding alone to the academy with him.

Something about that shifter gives me the creeps...

sneak peek: veiled flame

LOSER

Kat

The little blue icon on my app has been glaring at me all day, but I'm too damn nervous to open it. Everyone at Woodlawn High has been buzzing all day with their notifications and the squeals of joy and moans of despair were too much for me to take. My anxiety is through the roof—this is the moment I've been waiting for since middle school, but I can't seem to force myself to bite the billet and check.

Maybe it's because I don't have the support system most of my classmates have?

That's probably true, given I've always been a loner and I don't fit into any specific 'caste' here. It's hard to make friends when you get shuffled from foster home to foster home over the years. I've rarely stayed anywhere long enough to make a friend, much less a group of them.

I'm not delinquent or anything—the families I've been placed with just return me like a pair of pants that doesn't fit after a year or so. The caseworkers click their tongues sympathetically and hunt down a new placement, but I've never been given a reason *why* people don't want me around. One lady said I must be born under a bad sign and hell if I knew what that meant other than I'm not good enough to keep around.

It would be different, almost understandable, if I misbehaved or got bad grades. But I don't—I'm always in the top five percent of my class and I do everything I'm asked. I don't even lord my smarts over the other kids or adults. Being presentable and unassuming was something I adapted long ago to improve my probability of staying in a home long term.

Unfortunately, it never worked and though I should be a shoo-in for scholarships and acceptances galore, I can't bring myself to be rejected yet again.

So I wait for the last bell of the day, slinging my bag over my shoulder and trudging home to the latest in my temporary housing. I can't even contemplate looking at the possible heartache waiting for me in the college application system WHS insisted we use. The fear is too great and despite knowing I'll be on my own for good at the end of this year, I'm unable to risk the pain.

I hate being this way.

My court mandated therapist says it's some sort of attachment disorder that's common in foster kids, but I think that's bullshit. The problem isn't *me* not forming attachments; it's asshole adults not forming one to me. Being left at a safe haven in a fucking basket as a baby wasn't because *I* did anything wrong—again, fucking adults couldn't handle their commitments.

As usual, I arrive home to an empty house. There are two other kids who live here—Bryce and Blake—but they're at football practice. Of course, the Jamesons *love* them; they get to strut around at games because their strays are the stars of the team. I'm not mistreated, but I'm definitely an afterthought. Both of my 'parents' are still at work, so I drop my bag on the couch and head for the kitchen to get a snack.

Don't get me wrong. I *could* have been placed in far worse homes than any of the seven I've been in since elementary school. None of the ex-fosters starved, beat, molested, or abused me. They were all decent folks with jobs and houses that weren't hellholes, but they never liked me.

I have no idea why. I tried to be everything they wanted.

But when the end of each school year came, I was handed in like a textbook and off I went to some group home until the next contestant stepped up. It baffled everyone, not just me, but that's what happened every single time.

Sighing, I pull some fruit out of the fridge and grab a soda. I have homework to do and if I want to have time to work on my stories, I'll need to get it done before the house is full of people at dinner time. Bryce and Blake will have gotten messages about their applications, too, and I'd bet my pinkie toe those idiots got into some big sports school. Brett and Allison will be oozing happiness for them and I don't know if I'll be able to keep food down if I have to admit my failure when they ask.

Being eighteen sucks ass.

After I grab my books and tablet, I head down to the den. I have to give my current parents credit; they set up a very nice workspace for us to study in the converted basement. By the time they took me in, the Jamesons created a cozy room down here where the three of us could relax and do our work for school without being interrupted. It might have been more for the boys than me, but I appreciated it all the same. Desks, a couch, big chairs, and bookshelves fill the space, making it almost seem like our mini-library. They even put a small fridge for drinks and snacks in case we had to be up late to cram.

It's my favorite place in the entire house and I spend most of my time here.

I sink into the huge armchair, putting my drink and snack on the side table. It only takes a few minutes to arrange myself in the soft cushions and I pause to tug my headphones out of my pocket. Music always soothes my jagged edges and I need it to stay focused on the bullshit AP Calculus I need to keep my average up in. My course load is heavy, but I applied to tough colleges. I wouldn't have a chance to get in, especially on a scholarship, if I wasn't taking equally challenging classes in comparison to all the prep school kids.

As always, the sounds of Vivaldi carry me away as I scrawl equations on my screen and before long, thoughts of the blue notification completely fade away.

"Kat!"

The shouts barely register as I continue working on the problem set, gnawing on my lower lip in concentration.

"Jesus fuck, where is she? I could eat a hippo!"

"Kat!"

Thumping followed by what could pass for a stampede of elephants jerks me out of my math filled trance when Bryce and Blake come down the stairs. They smell as bad as the aforementioned pachyderm's cage, so they must have rushed home right after practice. The blond twins glare at me as if I'm the offending element despite being sweaty and covered in dirt and grass stains.

This doesn't bode well.

Usually, they're tired and hungry after practices so I'm used to cranky ass boys, but tonight, there's a light to their faces. That had to mean they've gotten their letters and dinner will be a gush fest in honor of their perfection. I'm going to need all of my strength to fake smile and nod as Brett and Allison fawn over them.

I don't begrudge them their success—not really. They work hard and play even harder on the field. It's not their fault they're the American dream teens and I'm the nerdy basement troll no one wants. But it's awfully hard living in the shadow of their bright light, especially when I'm no less intelligent or talented.

"I'm finishing the AP Calc, guys. What do you want?"

They roll their eyes at me before Blake scoffs. "It's not due until Monday. You're so hyper."

Duh. I take anxiety meds, douchebag; of course I'm 'hyper.'

"I can only be who I am, Blake." That earns me a snort from Bryce and I know it's because he thinks that's the problem. "Is dinner ready?"

"Almost. Get upstairs and set the table so we can shower—Brett's orders." Blake grins smugly.

The two of them seem to always arrange it so chores get passed to me for some half-assed reason and this is no exception. Sighing, I put my stuff aside, fully intending to hide down here after the dinner mess is cleaned up. Likely by me, but like I said, I could definitely live in worse foster homes so I let it go. Doing some chores isn't worth risking the group home for the last few months of my high school career.

They take off running up the stairs and I wait for them to disappear before I follow suit. My phone is tucked in my pocket and I feel like it's a stone of shame I have to bear. I know once the adults make over the twins' success, they will remember me, and I'll be forced to find out what disappointment lies in wait for me. The dread weighs on me, but I head into the sunny kitchen and pick up the pre-prepared pile of plates, silverware, and napkins on the counter.

Allison looks up from the stove and gives me a half-smile, nodding as I take the dishes into the dining room. Like I said, no one is mean or horrid, they just seem...obligated. After a while, it makes it hard to waste time trying to be bright and sunny. Being reserved makes it a hell of a lot easier not to feel rebuffed when they don't pay attention to you regardless.

"Make sure you include champagne glasses for your dad and I!" she calls from the other room.

The twins definitely got acceptance somewhere big. Brett must have gotten the bubbly on the way home.

Once I set the table, I return to help Allison bring out the roast and sides. I'm a little amazed at her efficiency when it comes to getting the housework done while working full time, but I suppose it's something people with real parents get taught as they grow up. My home life has been so fractured that I haven't learned how to cook more than very basic shit from YouTube videos. That may be a problem after graduation, but I've never felt comfortable enough to ask Allison if she'd teach me. I'm sure she would try, but it doesn't feel right.

"How was school, Kat?"

I look over my shoulder, seeing Brett in the entry to the dining room. He's already changed from work and smiling, but I see the distraction in his eyes. He's waiting for the boys to come down. "It was fine. I've got a Calc test at the end of the week. I'll be studying a lot to get ready."

"Good, good. No matter what happens with applications, keeping your grades up will ensure no one pulls any offers," he says.

Those words aren't for me. They are for the two wet haired boys who just appeared behind him.

"Kat's too much of a geek to ever let her grades slip, Dad," Blake says as he pushes past his brother and drops into his usual chair at the table. "Grab me a Powerade since you're in the kitchen, mouse!"

Both Brett and Bryce stare at me and I turn around, heading to the fridge despite the fact that I was *not* closer than the other twin. Out of habit, I take two of the drinks and a soda for myself. I've been here long enough to know Bryce will send me back to get him one as well. It would feel like typical sibling stuff, but for some reason, I just *know* they do it to fuck with me. I have no idea why I feel that way, but trusting my gut has been the one thing that helped me get through all the upheaval in my life over the years. It's a good gauge for knowing when I'll get booted or if people are being earnest in their reactions.

The therapist says that's some sort of trauma induced early trigger warning shit, by the way.

After I hand out the drinks, I sit down on my side of the table and we wait for Allison to come out. Brett is at his seat at the far end of the table and the twins are punching each other as they look at something on their phones. I know where this is all going but I drop my gaze to the table, swallowing the coppery taste of fear as it courses through my body.

I'm going to be exposed and there's nothing I can do to stop it.

Read the first three episodes free on Kindle Vella: https://www.amazon.com/kindle-vella/story/B0BSTMB1X3

about cassandra featherstone

Cassandra Featherstone has channeled her lifelong passion for writing into a flourishing career, a journey that started when she first grasped a pencil as a gifted child with ADHD.

Her debut novel, born during the solitude of COVID lockdown in March 2020, draws on a tapestry of personal encounters and insights that resonate deeply with her readers.

An international bestseller, Cassandra has topped Amazon charts in categories such as LGBT Anthologies, LGBTQ+ Mystery, and Bisexual Romance, among others. Her works navigate the complexities of bullying, PTSD, body dysmorphia, mental health struggles, personal reinvention, and the empowerment of claiming one's own space. Importantly, Cassandra offers a thoughtful and respectful portrayal of LGBTQIA+ relationships, subtly reflecting her own connection with the community through her narratives.

Her literary repertoire spans sci-fi fantasy, urban fantasy, paranormal, and comedic genres in academy whychoose settings, with a strong commitment to portraying consensual, safe, and accurately depicted BDSM and kink lifestyles. Her books are an invitation to explore transformative stories that are both inclusive and engaging.

Often affectionately called 'The Muppet' for her wacky theater kid personality, she resides in the Midwest with her tech-savvy husband, their creatively inclined college student, a literary-minded dog, and four scheming cats.

READ MORE AT CASSANDRA'S WEBSITE OR HER FACEBOOK PAGE. SIGN UP FOR EXCLUSIVE CONTENT AND UPDATES HERE.

FIND HER ON ANY OF THE SOCIAL MEDIA BELOW AS SHE *LOVES* TO CHAT AND *NEVER* SLEEPS!

THE MISFIT PROTECTION PROGRAM SERIES

Road to the Hollow

Return to the Hollow

Home to the Hollow

Rejected in the Hollow

Revealed in the Hollow

Healing in the Hollow

Revenge in the Hollow

AUDIO OF THE MISFIT PROTECTION PROGRAM SERIES

Road to the Hollow

APEX ACADEMY CAPERS

Come Out and Prey

Let Us Prey

In Prey We Trust

Oh Holy Spite (3.5 novella)

Eat. Prey. Love.

Prey It Ain't So (4.5 novel)

Prey It By Ear

AUDIO OF THE APEX ACADEMY CAPERS SERIES

Come Out & Prey

Let Us Prey

In Prey We Trust

TRANSLATIONS OF THE APEX ACADEMY CAPERS SERIES

Come Out & Prey (German)

Let Us Prey (German)

In Prey Trust (German)

DISCORDIA UNIVERSITY

Veiled Flame (Book One)

Quiet Burn (Book Two)

Zero Spark (Book Three)

AUDIO OF THE DISCORDIA UNIVERSITY SERIES

Veiled Flame (Book One)

Quiet Burn (Book Two)

SECRETS OF STATE U

Blood on the Ice (Book One)

Suspicions on the Stage (Book Two)

TBA TITLE (BOOK THREE)

FAETAL ATTRACTION

Hell on Wheels (Book One)

Jammer in the Box (Book Two)

F.E.A.R. ACADEMY

Failed State (Book One)

Trigger Protocol (Book Two)

VILLAINS & VIXENS

Bloodthirsty (Book One)

Ruthless (Book Two)

Wicked (Book Three)

AUDIO OF THE VILLAINS & VIXENS SERIES

Bloodthirsty

Ruthless

TRIANGLES & TRIBULATIONS

Hoist the Flag (PQ)

Yo-Ho Holes (Book One)

**CHILDREN OF THE MOON-
WITH SERENITY RAYNE**

New Moon Rising (Book One)

Waxing Crescent (Book Two)

Waxing Gibbous (Book Three)

Samhain Secrets (Novella 3.5)

Full Moon (Book Four)

Waning Gibbous (Book Five)

Waning Crescent (Book Six)

RISE OF THE RESISTANCE

Ream Exclusive Prequels

Hooked on a Feline (Book One)

Peacock Me Like A Hurricane

Love The Way You Lion (Book Three)

TBA Title (Book Four)

REAM SERIALS

Secrets of State U

Discordia University

Denizens of the Dark

Faetal Attraction

Agents of the Ouroboros

Rise of the Resistance

F.E.A.R. Academy

ANTHOLOGIES

Unwritten

Shifters Unleashed

Jingle My Balls

Love is in the Air

Silent Night

Snowed In

All Hallows Eve

www.ingramcontent.com/pod-product-compliance
Lightning Source LLC
Chambersburg PA
CBHW070827020826
48982CB00015B/775